T0348381

This Terrible True Thing

This Terrible True Thing

a visual novel

Jenny Laden

BLACK STONE PUBLISHING

Printed in the United States of America

First edition: 2023
ISBN 979-8-200-89567-0
Young Adult Fiction / Coming of Age

Version 1

Blackstone Publishing
31 Mistletoe Rd.
Ashland, OR 97520

www.BlackstonePublishing.com

For Richard and Isadora,
who would have loved each other to no end.

This, here, is a good moment to squeeze into a bottle.
Preserved. Intact.
Safe and sound for when the air gets cold and the sun hides.
Breeze fanning the afternoon sun, gently convincing the
flies to leave us be.
The beach obeys the laws of gravity nicely, all horizontal.
Grounded.
The ocean heaves. Sighs.
Again
Over
Again
Tiny creatures upended every minute.
Endless motion.
Endless disruptions.
Again
Over
Peaceful from a distance. All the chaos turned to foam.
Dad sleeps in the sun with his hands folded on his chest,
a tanning vampire. My feet dig into the sand, my hat
shading my eyes.
This new blank book invites me to start again. To look at
the world, to figure it out.
Ideas to organize.
Lists to remember.
Secrets to keep safe, to keep me safe.

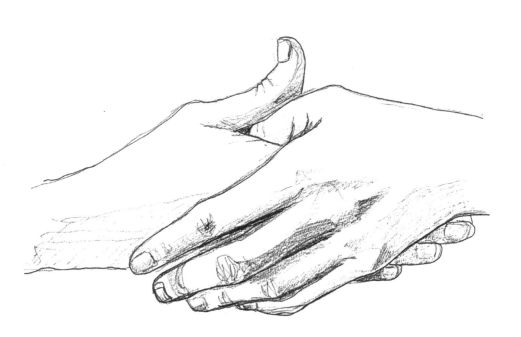

1

"Here Comes the Rain Again"

"Don't even think about it," Dad says. But I'm already pushing the cassette tape into the car stereo.

"Arthur liked my music," I say, hoping to send him on a guilt trip, as the drumbeat starts.

"Oh please, Arthur adored everything about you. The very definition of unconditional love. Isn't that a gay uncle's job?" He starts motioning his hand toward the eject button, signaling me to make it stop.

I eject my summer mixtape labeled Sunshine & Lollipops. Amy and I made it at the end of junior year to keep us connected all summer.

I sigh, hoping to jolt my dad into sympathy.

"Fine," Dad relents. "For Arthur. But not that one. Let's listen to that lady with the orange hair."

"Yes!" I quickly find the Eurythmics tape and shove it into the player before he changes his mind. Annie Lennox wears her hair in a buzz cut dyed bright orange like an Easter egg, and she sings about love and obsession and rain. The strings and the synthesizer start as I stare out the window. The music sounds like rain itself. I sing along low and steady. Dad smiles.

I dig into my big green army bag to triple-check I have my new sketchbook. I read over yesterday's entry, the first in the book, at the beach. My legs got burned from that dose of sunshine, but I don't mind. Summer is ending. That means school, homework, and college applications are coming. One more godforsaken year of the Baxter School, New Jersey's snottiest boarding school.

Sometimes I cannot wait to get older, like I want to fast-forward to the next chapter of my biography already. One where I'm surrounded by people who make great art, or write great books, or just do anything great. I know I'm lucky to go to a good school, but the old, musty, traditional thing is aging fast for me.

I look out the window as we pass diners and fish tackle shops and all the New England things I associate with stories my parents have told me about how they met in college, and then Dad meeting Arthur just afterward. We switch from one highway to another heading toward Providence, Rhode Island. Knowing Arthur went to college there, I wonder if he stopped at that gas station or passed through this toll booth. When he was a senior in high school, did he worry that he wouldn't get into RISD like I do?

"Danielle, look in my briefcase for a yellow folder. I can't remember what time the tour starts," Dad says, turning the music way down to a nearly imperceptible volume. Leave it to Dad to bring his briefcase to beach vacation.

Inside the brown leather bag, I find a set of multicolored file folders. A yellow one labeled Danielle Colleges has a few other college brochures that I have repeatedly refused to read. Our tour starts at eleven fifteen. It's my second visit. Last spring my mom drove me up here from Philly. She'd started asking over and over where I was interested in applying to college. I only had one answer: Rhode Island School of Design, RISD. I told her and Dad that if it was good enough for Arthur, it would be good enough for me. I thought that would seal the deal on their approval. But I was wrong. Like many parents, they think if they ask me the same question enough times, I might change my mind. But I didn't even want to visit anywhere else. Mom and Dad think I'm squandering my opportunities. They try to veil their worry about my wanting to

EURYTHMICS

be an artist (a.k.a throwing my future down the toilet) by saying that I need options. But I think they ought to be impressed with my decisiveness. It's like when I was a little kid and they'd offer an apple or an orange, when I knew I really just wanted a cookie.

When Arthur was alive, he always stood up for me, and I think my parents actually listened to him. Of course, his art hangs in museums around the world, so he had clout. Clout I lack.

We arrive in Providence, after two hours of Bach and Ella Fitzgerald. (The Eurythmics only lasted through Side A.)

"I guess it's move-in week, huh?" Dad says as we sit in traffic behind station wagons unloading boxes and duffel bags, reminding me of move-in day at my boarding school. But all these artsy students with combat boots and piercings and half-shaved heads are nothing like the kids at Baxter. These kids probably also left places they didn't belong and found each other. As we near the visitor parking area, I see a giant red banner: Welcome Class of 1995! I'll graduate college in '96, but first I have one more year of high school.

Inside, Dad collects more brochures before our eleven fifteen tour with Lindsay, who has green hair and a nose ring. When she tells our group that she's majoring in photography and minoring in performance art, I sneak a quick glimpse at Dad's face. The slight raise of his right eyebrow speaks volumes. "Dad, please," I whisper as we walk past the RISD Museum of Art.

"What?" he says, knowing damn well what he did, smiling slightly, and I laugh.

This is an art school. I can smell it. And it smells nothing like Baxter, which has the odor of old stuffy upholstery and long-standing tradition. There's actually room to breathe here, to make things, to fail marvelously and try again. The students here clearly live and breathe their art; it's in their clothes and their walk and how they talk to each other in this late summer light. A big clunky punk-rock confidence, a combination of nihilism and community. The plaza outside one building is covered with sawdust. Years of spills and splatters dried and layered. Like leaves in a forest becoming the floor. This mess feels like home to me. This mess smells like living, breathing possibility.

Walking backward, Lindsay leads us past an outdoor bulletin board layered with posters for exhibition openings, singing groups, improv classes, a band looking for a bass player, clown workshops, welding assistants, roommates needed, locations for condom distribution, and announcements of the Gay-Straight Alliance student meetings. A guy wearing a black T-shirt with a pink triangle and the words ACT UP underneath whizzes past us on a skateboard. Entering one of the studio buildings, the sour smell of turpentine hits me in a rush, and a goth girl with messy jet-black hair similar to mine looks at me the way you look at someone with the same winter coat. She's wearing a T-shirt that says The Cure, and she nearly smiles as she passes. But she doesn't because she's cool. I'm cringing that I even made eye contact. Her black hair looks shinier than mine. I knew I should have left my hair dye in longer.

Down the hall, someone is playing Siouxsie and the Banshees, and my body wants nothing more than to stay here forever. To weave myself into this fabric, to become part of this system. Lindsay takes questions from other parents about class sizes and curriculum requirements as we walk the halls. I peer into room after room of easels, tables with caked paint, rooms full of potter's wheels, shelves of materials, and platforms for models to sit. Did Arthur paint in this building? If I believed in ghosts, would he be lurking here?

Our tour finally arrives back at the main building on Waterman Street. Lindsay is wrapping things up. I raise my hand, tentatively. She looks at me and says, "Yes? You have a question?"

"Yeah," I say, worried my voice sounds too eager. "What are the application deadlines?"

"Oh, sure. For early decision, it's November 15, and for regular admission, it's January 15."

Ok! It's August 24. That's over two and a half months. No problem. I feel Dad watching me calculate all of this as Lindsay thanks us all for coming. We walk away from the group, but I don't want to leave yet. My feet slow their steps. Can't I just, like, phone in senior year? Or take a GED test? Dad sees me slowing down and reads my mind in that way only he can. "No, Danielle," he says with a laugh, wrapping his long arm around me. "You cannot stay here. We need to get home to Philadelphia, go to Arthur's unveiling, pack your bags, and get you back to high school, from which you need to graduate."

"Your realism is a bummer, Dad."

Dad puts a big smile on his face and says, "Senior year! It's gonna be so fun!" in his best cheerleader voice.

"Yeah, yeah. You just want your den back."

He blows me a raspberry and points to the car. Visiting RISD is actually a helpful transition back to school after a ten-day beach vacation in Cape Cod. But it kills me that it'll be a whole year until I can live here.

The long drive south to Philadelphia passes quickly. New England's oysters and quaint white churches transition to pharmaceutical company headquarters and chain restaurants. Dad tires of his music and lets me play the Eurythmics, Side B.

"Right by Your Side." Arthur loved this song. He used to make me dance with him whenever it came on. At my Bat Mitzvah he led a line dance all around the room when it came on. Dad is bobbing his head to the music. I've seriously waited for this moment my entire life: Dad enjoying pop music. He's got his tastes, but I admit his mind has been more open these past few years. I know I complain, but it's good to have parents who are willing to at least listen to music written after 1950.

I flip the tape back to Side A. Dad allows it.

Through the car window I read, Trenton Makes. The World Takes. The giant sign over the Delaware River always reminds me of Shel Silverstein's book, *The Giving Tree*. Arthur used to say the Giving Tree was a "monstrosity of martyrdom." But I loved how he read it to me when I was little, his voice getting round and warm when he read the tree's lines, giving endless commentary about the boy's lack of compassion toward the tree. He'd read the boy's lines like a whiny, sniveling anti-environmentalist brat and make me laugh and laugh.

How has it been a year since he's been gone?

I take out my sketchbook to draw but all I want to do is talk to him.

You made the world better, Arthur. And you keep on being gone.
How has it been a year?
Nearly every day I remember something you told me,
it comes back, over and again.
Still gone. Still.
You believed in me when I didn't believe in myself.
You'd know how to handle all this doubt.
I don't know if I'm good enough to get in, but I don't want
anyone else to know that.
Tomorrow we unveil your gravestone.
You'd have liked the drama, but I'd rather have you here.

Back in Philly, on the sofa bed in Dad's den, which becomes my room when I'm here. I imagine myself, one day, living in some giant loft, making paintings as light pours through the huge windows.

I dial Amy's house from Dad's phone, imagining myself beside an exposed brick wall, curtain flapping by an enormous open window. Drawings tacked to the wall, paintbrushes everywhere, my fingers stained with colors, my overalls caked with paint.

"Hello?" Hearing Amy's mom's voice brings me back to reality.

"Hi, Mrs. Myers. It's Danielle. Is Amy home?" I say, making sure I put a coaster under my water glass, not wanting to stain Dad's oak desk. This is not my loft. I almost laugh at the thought of ever having coasters. I open my new sketchbook and start drawing Amy from memory.

I hear Amy walking the long phone cord into her room and shutting the door. "So, how was it?" She asks, knowing I've been obsessed with visiting RISD for weeks now.

"Perfect. Our tour guide had a nose piercing and green hair, and the entire campus smells like turpentine," I sigh.

"Ew. But, well, I'm happy for you. I got my application packet today from Berkeley."

"Already? Wow, that's fast."

"Yeah, they don't mess around."

I imagine Amy at Berkeley: jogging every morning, drinking beet juice, studying political science, and turning into a vegetarian. She's going to love it.

"So, tomorrow's the thing? The uncovering?" She remembered. She loved Arthur too.

"Yes, the unveiling," I say.

"Sorry I can't come with you. My mom is making me go see my grandparents and run a million errands. Are you OK? I mean are you nervous?"

"No, I'm not speaking. It'll be fine. I'm not worried."

"Call me after, if you need. I'll be here, folding things. What's your timing for Monday?"

"Well, you know my dad. We'll be ridiculously early," I say. Amy is the one person who relishes my father's punctuality.

"Ugh, Danielle, you're so lucky," she groans. "My mom is going to take forever to finish packing the car with multiple pauses to yell at my sister. And we'll get there sometime around midnight."

"But Amy, River Hall, top floor!" I remind her of our extreme good luck with senior housing lottery that got us our first choice of rooms.

"Aw yeah. That big room. Yes! And dude, senior year! It's going to be magical."

I groan, just like she knew I would.

This is my hiding place.
Like this world is one big game of hide-and-seek, and this
is my secret spot.
I can let down the wall that faces outward.
Why is Baxter so exhausting?
The wall I build, the secrets I keep, the hiding I do week
after week.
Amy doesn't get it, really.
She loves me, sure, but,
when you're not hiding, you don't know how heavy it is.

2
"Blackbird"

After a shower, I search for my dark gray dress and find it at the bottom of the closet. Shit. I put it on but it's got some serious creases. Maybe Dad won't notice.

I walk out to get some coffee and feel him looking at me.

"No," he says, barely looking up from his newspaper.

"No to the coffee?" I ask, pouring milk in already.

"Danielle. The dress. Go change or I'll iron it if you have nothing else."

"Well, if you don't mind," I say, smiling and heading back into the den to change into my robe. My dad has tried to teach me to iron, but the fact is he does a way better job. I'd probably burn holes. I offer to scramble eggs, and he takes me up on it.

After breakfast, my dress pressed, I get my short black hair in some semblance of order and find what Dad calls "suitable footwear," which means black flats and not combat boots. Then we climb back in the car for the unveiling.

Cemeteries always feel so far away. For some reason, the Jewish cemeteries around Philadelphia always seem to take hours to reach.

"Dad, did we do this when Grandma died?"

Both of my dad's parents were gorgeous. Fancy gorgeous, like in old movies. My grandfather wore cuff links and neckties all the time, and my grandmother had her dresses made by a professional tailor. They died, five weeks apart from each other when I was eleven, just a few months after Dad came out of the closet.

I'm not sure how they took it. I mean, we all had dinners together after that, and no one seemed upset, so I guess they accepted it. My memories are all before and after Dad came out. Dad came out of the closet like a zombie awakening from a long slumber, bumbling his way out the door. A lot of moments from that preteen time are blurry now, but one has stayed crisp.

Back then, we saw Dad twice a week: Wednesday nights and Sunday afternoons. It had only been six weeks since Dad moved out, but our weekly routine was already feeling normal. Divorce is like a drastic haircut: At first, it's so shockingly different, that you question who you are. What is life even? Then a few weeks later, it's just what it is. That Wednesday Jake was home for his fall break from his sophomore year at Baxter, and we went to Silvio's, the best Italian outside of the Italian Market, Dad always said.

Jake ordered mussels and ate nearly all the bread. He talked forever about some girl named Gigi and how she was in Baxter's production of *Death of a Salesman*, which sounded like the most boring play ever to me. I twirled my plain spaghetti on my fork and wondered if I would be as annoyingly self-absorbed as Jake when I turned fifteen. I thought about how much more fun it was to be alone with Dad. Jake had gone back to school just after our parents told us they were getting divorced, so for the past three months, until that night, it had only been me and Dad. We'd had Wednesdays and Sundays together, and now Jake was here, taking up our space.

When the server took the plates away, Dad took a sip from his water glass and took a long breath in, like he was about to start singing. Jake and I took the hint that Dad needed our attention and waited.

"Kids," he said quietly, "there's something I need to talk to you about."

My chest felt suddenly tight. Like the night they told us about the divorce. But that already happened. What else could he possibly need to tell us?

"First off, let me just tell you how much I love you. I'm so proud of how you are both growing up and how well you've handled things between me and your mom. I know it hasn't been the easiest transition, but I am just really impressed that you both are handling this all with such grace and understanding." He said this like he'd memorized it. Maybe he did.

"Now, here's the thing. Your mom and I decided to break up after I shared something with her that made our marriage impossible. Sometimes, people realize things about themselves when they're already grown-up. Things that are maybe not easy to admit. Sometimes it takes that long to figure yourself out." He was looking down at the table, almost like he needed to convince himself of what he was saying.

Jake looked at me with an expression that said, *Has Dad gone crazy?*

Dad kept his monologue going, ". . . and sometimes people see themselves clearly and cannot pretend anymore. You can't pretend to be something you're not, and you can't lie to the world about who you are. Sooner or later, enough is enough. You must be real. You must be yourself."

What was he talking about? He really did sound like he was in a corny musical and about to sing a ballad about life's great long highway or something. I started to smile but did my best to hide it with my hand.

Jake saw me and his eyes twinkled. I knew we were both about to crack up. We'd been known to do this at the worst times, and we'd learned to avoid each other's eyes or we'd burst. Somehow the more serious the situation, the funnier it felt. I knew we were both thinking that Dad sounded nuts.

Then there was silence. Dad was holding his water glass in both hands. Not moving, not speaking. He looked somewhere between sad and embarrassed. My smile vanished.

"Dad?" I asked, "Are you, um, OK?"

He looked at me like I'd woken him from a nap. Then he turned to Jake.

"Oh, guys, yes. Yes, I'm OK." He held out his hands to reach for each of us. "I need to tell you, and it's scary but necessary. I need to tell you that I'm gay."

Even now, I don't know what the right response to this would have been. But then, at eleven, I only vaguely knew what being gay was. The world of adult sexuality is not something most eleven-year-olds think about. But in that split second, I thought of Arthur. Somewhere deep down I guess I always knew that gay was what Arthur was, without ever being told.

Dad continued, "This doesn't change how much I love you or that I'm your dad. I'm not a different person. I am not becoming a different person. I'm simply being honest about who I actually am. That's all. It doesn't mean I'm going to run down Spruce Street in a red taffeta dress. But I need to be honest and live as openly as I can as a gay man."

Even with this rehearsed speech, there was something in his voice I had never heard before. Fear, maybe. Worry, for sure. His hands shook a little as he reached for his glass. I thought, He's afraid we aren't going to love him anymore. I took his hand back in mine and saw he had a tear falling down his cheek. I put my other hand on his.

"It's OK, Dad. I love you. Even if you do want to wear a dress. It doesn't matter to me," I said quietly, already knowing to keep it between us.

I looked over at Jake for backup. He said, "Me too." We weren't laughing. But Dad grew a small smile.

"I know this is all a lot for you guys, so please tell me if you have questions or want to talk about this more. It is a lot to adjust to. I've only had this conversation so far with your mom and Arthur. So please, ask me anything. The most important thing is that I love you both and don't ever want to hurt you in any way."

Even then, I knew that it wouldn't hurt me. I did not know yet how mean the world could be toward gay people, but it was clear that Dad wasn't doing anything to hurt us.

My dad had always followed the rules. He did what he thought he should: went to college, then law school, found a smart and beautiful wife, and had kids. I think people in his generation didn't see a lot of forks in the road that allowed them to do all of those things *and* be out of the closet. And keeping the secret worked for him. Until it didn't.

After that night, everything in my life was sliced into two parts: Dad's and Mom's. Friends, time, holidays, vacations. All split in half. And one half—Dad's half—was defined by his being gay. This was fine when we were with his friends, but anywhere else, I learned fast that it was best not to talk about it.

And even though my dad came out, I don't always know how or when to be so honest. I learned quickly that much of the world is awful to gay people and, as it turns out, their kids. I didn't want to tell people because I didn't really want to know how they'd respond. I was hiding myself from other people's hatred. I still do my best to keep this truth secret when it feels scary, to be honest.

Amy knows all about my dad, and I told Brian last year before we broke up. He wasn't cruel about it, just confused, responding with a contorted face as though I told him my father was a space dinosaur. I wonder if Dad sees it the way I do. Does it feel like before and after that big moment? Does he divide the world up into places he hides and places he's honest? Still now?

Dad's voice brings me back into the moment, in the car, driving to the cemetery to Arthur's unveiling. "Your grandmother and grandfather both had unveilings, but it was a long time ago. I think you were twelve, maybe." We take two more left turns, and suddenly, we drive through huge iron gates.

"But what's it for? I mean, why go back to the cemetery?"

"It's a Jewish tradition to visit the grave one year after burial," Dad explains. "It's part of how Jews remember their loved ones and mark the period of mourning. A year after burial, we ask God to grant the departed peace and rest, as a final step in the grieving process, and they unveil the headstone. Hence the name."

Arthur died from a stroke last year. It was sudden. He wasn't even sick. I couldn't say goodbye. I've missed him almost every day since then. And now, even more as I start this RISD application process. I keep imagining how much easier it would be if he were still here. I've learned this year that you don't grieve people all at once. It comes in waves, unexpected and sharp. Then there are moments when you're smiling, knowing they'd want you to be happy, and it doesn't feel wrong. It's a seesaw.

"OK, which way?" I hear Dad mutter to himself. I have unfortunately inherited his terrible sense of direction, so I don't even try to offer suggestions.

Arthur and Dad met in the 1960s at a drugstore. Dad turned around and saw Arthur. He immediately thought *That looks like someone I would know*, and then Arthur said "Benjamin Silver! As I live and breathe!" They'd gone to summer camp together when they were kids. Arthur had a good memory for faces, I guess. After that, they became best friends.

Arthur was out of the closet when he met Dad. Sort of. He was open about being gay when he could be, but careful not to reveal it when it might be costly. I guess I always knew on some level that Arthur was different, but I don't remember the moment I knew he was gay. It wasn't like it was announced to me. It just was always there. Like how someone has curly hair or is a good singer. Kids don't always see that stuff when they're little. At least I didn't.

Dad, on the other hand, took great pains to stay in the closet. After that night at Silvio's, he would sometimes find ways to give us history lessons about gay people, but usually away from other people or at home. He told us how it was nearly impossible before the 1970s to be openly gay. It was illegal in many states for gay people to keep custody of their own children, several states had laws criminalizing gay sex, and it was—and still is in 1991—perfectly legal to fire someone for being gay. So, people hid it however they could. I did wonder if he was trying to get off the hook, somehow. Maybe he felt guilty for deceiving us for so long. He didn't want to break up our family and have us hate him.

But I never felt angry with him for being gay. I get angry at homophobia but not my dad. I never took his secret-keeping personally. It was his moving out and living apart from us that hurt. And all that hurt Mom too, which was hard. Although they were very different, my parents shared a lot and the break was sudden and complete.

Dad always said he and Arthur were like two sides of a coin. Arthur was the extrovert, Dad the introvert. Arthur wore flowery shirts, bleached his hair, pierced his ear, loved to dance, and listened to music from this century. Arthur had boyfriends, threw fabulous parties, and traveled all over the world. He lived in places where other gay people lived like New York's West Village and San Francisco, before moving to Philadelphia in the late 1970s. His house on a little side street near Washington Square had velvet couches and textured wallpaper and he had a teeny fluffy dog named Mildred Pierce, a Joan Crawford character.

Dad, on the other hand, is the quiet guy in the background who hates having his picture taken. He's awkward, tall and unathletic, anti-social, and rarely comfortable in his own skin. He does not experiment with fashion. He wears Docksides boat shoes, khakis, and maroon polo shirts. He isn't loud or campy, though he loves this in others. I've barely ever heard him even mention sex. He told me once he went to a night-club and "tried pot." All it did was make him sleepy, he said.

Dad taught me about opera, Shakespeare, and world history. My mom taught me about friendship, responsibility, and joy. Arthur taught me about fashion, music, and, of course, art. Arthur was my third parent who I could say anything to and never get in trouble.

After driving a long stretch of winding road, we see a collection of cars in the cemetery. Dad parks, and I see a small tent and people gathering. Dad's friends Robert and Susie are waiting for us. Robert wears a black T-shirt with a pink triangle on it, just like the kid at RISD, and a black blazer and jeans. When I first met Robert a few years ago, Dad told me that he was a professional activist. When I asked Robert what that was, he just said, "Honey, I'm a professional pain in the ass." Susie, wearing some awesome chunky female goddess necklace and big black bracelets, is a hospital therapist. She's short, British, and sometimes seems cranky, but I've learned that's just her way. Dad calls her Kitten, which must be some inside joke. She says hello, gives me a stiff, small hug, then goes to talk to some other friends. Robert, Dad, and I start walking to the grave site together. Dad is walking ahead of us, limping slightly on the rough terrain.

"So, kid, how was the RISD tour?" Robert asks me as he unfolds his sunglasses and puts them on. Robert has the jawline of a movie star.

"Let's just say, she's smitten," Dad says, turning around to answer.

I just sigh, looking off in the distance, remembering the smell of turpentine.

"Yeah, I see that," says Robert. "And what's coming up this year at the Baxter School for precious, privileged children?"

"Senior year. The usual, I guess. Oh, there's an art history class I'm psyched for. Super cool teacher. Plus, advanced painting. And physics, English and precalculus."

"What, no proms or weird senior pranks planned?" Robert pokes at me.

I roll my eyes. "Oh God, please," I mumble.

"You are too cool for school, aren't you?" Robert jokes. Robert has the best way of laughing at people while making them feel respected. I don't know how he does it.

I see Dad looking at me. He thinks I never tell him anything and only slip out intel when other people ask me about my life. Robert smiles and loops his arm through mine as we walk. "Tell me more about this awesome art history class. Why's it so special?"

"I don't know. Ms. Davis is cool, I guess. She grew up all over the world, and she just has this, like, bigger view of the world than most of the people there. I had her sophomore year for world history and loved her. She's the very first Black female teacher ever at Baxter."

Dad nods. "Yes, Ms. Davis; she went to Oxford, I remember." Dad visited that year for Parents' Day, and I remember him raving about her for weeks after. They really bonded.

"Aside from Ms. Davis, it sounds a little like you're over Baxter?" asks Robert.

"Yeah. It's like the only part of the world most of Baxter knows is the five-block radius of their parents' mansions and that campus. Or a resort in the Swiss Alps."

"So, what's the class on?"

"It's modern art history, so we'll start at the end of the 1800s and go 'til now, I guess." I didn't actually read the description, but I'm not about to tell Dad that.

"So, will you be covering how art intersects with historic moments like world wars or political movements?" Dad asks. I know where this is going. Dad's a lawyer. He lives to expose the weaknesses in my arguments.

"I don't know, Dad, it's an art history course. I don't know how much war is involved." I immediately regret how bratty I sound, but he's annoying me.

"Oh, it's involved. Trust me," says Robert. "Wars are constant, and they always affect culture and the economy, which affect art. It's inescapable. War is like the mortar between the bricks." Robert rarely avoids an opportunity to talk about history and politics.

"Well, there you go," I say, hoping this satisfies Dad, though I sort of wish I'd said it myself.

"All right, so aside from RISD, got any other irons in the fire, just in case? Someplace that's a sure thing?" Robert asks.

I steal a quick look at Dad.

"Oh, hey. There's a thought!" Dad practically shrieks. There it is. I was hoping to hold onto a dreamy, calm Beach Dad today, but I should know by now, Beach Dad stayed in Cape Cod. Dad wearing a bathing suit on the beach a few days ago is way more mellow than Dad wearing a gray suit in a cemetery today.

I'm silent. I can't have this conversation again. I try hard not to roll my eyes.

I turn to Robert. "I'm applying early, so I just need to write an essay and submit a portfolio of artwork, like a project that holds together. Oh, and I have to get recommendation letters from two people."

"Danielle, you have to figure that out. Adults need enough time to work these requests into their schedules," Dad says, using his lecturing voice, assuming I'm an irresponsible mess.

"Ugh! Benjamin, give her a break, for Christ's sake!" Robert vocalizes exactly what I'm thinking. I know he's sort of kidding, though.

I close my eyes to pause and go back to speaking to Robert. "I already asked my art teacher, Mrs. Funk, last spring, and Arthur had promised to write one." We stop walking as we are near a large group, gathered around a small black tent by the grave site. Dad turns to me and his face softens, he says nothing. "I'm hoping Ms. Davis will write the second one for me; since I had her in tenth grade, she sort of knows me."

My eyes are stinging from the sun. It starts to sink in that we are visiting Arthur's grave and that he is in the ground when he should be in the sunshine, standing with us, helping me win this argument. Discussing all this art school stuff without him is lonely and hard. I find a spot under a little shade while Dad and Robert go speak with some of their other friends.

Fifty people stand near Arthur's headstone just up the hill from a creek, under enormous trees with golden leaves. It is way too pretty a day to mourn. A breeze whooshes through the trees. He'd have wanted it like this: Beauty everywhere. Unrelenting and impossible to miss.

A wave of perfume rushes past me, like a ghost floating into my face, a soapy sweet scent inside my nose. The source is behind me. I glance back at a beautiful Black woman nearly seven feet in heels, with a flowing gray coat, long black wavy hair, and dangling earrings shimmering in the sun. I don't want to stare so I turn back to face forward.

"Danielle?" I hear a deep, smooth voice say.

I turn back around. "Yes," I say carefully, not sure how she knows me. She tilts her head, smiles, and opens her arms, walking over to me.

"I'm Waverly," she says, nodding and smiling, like I ought to recognize her, which I don't. But she knows me somehow, and so I smile in return.

"Hi?" I say. She puts one hand on my arm and with the other, we shake hands, and I realize hers are the large hands of a man and looking at her neck I see an Adam's apple and realize that she is a man, or had been a man, once, I think. My art teacher once told us to always note the Adam's apple when we are drawing men or women. A small but essential detail. Regardless, this woman smells so good and seems truly thrilled to see me.

"Arthur told me all about you, Danielle. His protégé. He said you looked like a punk rock Liza Minnelli, so I knew it was you right away."

Waverly

My hair stands out on sunny days. Arthur used to call me "Liza with a Z."

I laugh and say, "Yes, that's me. It's so nice to meet you, Waverly. So, how did you know Arthur?"

"I do his— Well, I did his taxes," she says, nodding, reassuring me it was true. "Walter Green, Certified Public Accountant," she whispers, tilting her head and pulling down her giant sunglasses so she can look into my eyes. "But, you know, we were dear friends!"

"Cool." I don't know what to say to an accountant. Or to a person with two different names.

"I didn't mean to intrude, but I just wanted to say hello. Unfortunately, I was unable to attend the funeral last year, so you and I haven't had the chance to meet. You must know that Arthur loooooved you so. Talked about his little Dani all the time. And I know sometimes when grown-ups die it's hard on young people, and sometimes we don't tell you kids how important you are. But you were so important to Arthur, sweet baby girl. Really. I don't know if it helps, but you ought to know that."

I stand there, quiet for a moment. Her words soothe something deep and sad inside me. I've felt like this for so long, kept it mostly to myself. Her words hit me like water getting to the deep roots. "Thank you," I say. I guess I needed to hear that. My eyes start tearing up.

"Oh, honey, I know." She pulls a Kleenex out of her purse and hands it to me. She puts her other arm around me as more people gather around the grave site. I close my eyes and suddenly feel just tired. I forget where we are. I forget that I hardly know this person. I forget everything except Arthur. And how absent he is now. Waverly is very good at giving hugs.

She begins to hum gently, like she's soothing a baby. The vibrations radiate through my head as I lean on her chest. "Oh, baby girl, he's right here with you." She pulls away from the hug and points to my heart. I sniff and smile. "And he's living right inside here." She points to her own. She looks down for a moment, reflecting. The sparkles on her eyelids twinkle in the sunlight. "So much loss we've gone through with this godforsaken disease."

Disease? Arthur died of a stroke. That's what Dad told me. What is she talking about?

I offer her my tissue, which is still dry, my sudden tears now absorbed by her coat. But she isn't crying. She shakes her head and says with a low man voice, "Honey, if I cried for every funeral I've been to these past years, I'd be dead from dehydration. You know what I'm saying? I believe we must celebrate life. Arthur wouldn't want a bunch of sad, saggy queens crying over him, would he?"

I shake my head no.

"No, sweet Danielle. No. We celebrate the preciousness of life, the courage of our sisters and brothers to live in the light of their truth and revel in the profound, delicious, shameless glory of LOVE." With this last bit, Waverly raises her arms, like she just finished a song.

She smiles and gives me a kiss on the cheek, her stubble cascading across my skin and the smell of cigarettes and bubble gum lingering on her breath.

"I honestly quake with fear at the loss of this generation. I mean who in God's name is going to make the world gorgeous?" She glances at me. "Well aside from you, of course, brilliant girl. This goddamned virus is taking us all down. Like dominos."

"Virus?" I ask.

She looks at me with surprise. "HIV, honey, AIDS. You do know what that is, right?"

"Yeah, I do," Of course, I know what AIDS is. But Arthur didn't have AIDS. Why does Waverly think Arthur had AIDS?

"Yes. Arthur went quicker than most. Merciful, I guess, but still a tragedy. And now they're getting so close with all those drugs . . . But still we drop like flies. Such a terrible thing." She stares off into the distance.

Wait, what? Arthur didn't have AIDS. Did he? Am I losing my mind?

"Um, I'm sorry, Waverly, but Arthur died of a stroke. He wasn't sick. I don't think he had AIDS," I tell Waverly, thinking maybe she's confusing Arthur with someone else.

"Oh, it was AIDS. It's always AIDS now, honey," she says just as a hush falls over the crowd. The rabbi gets to the podium and begins to talk, but I'm not really absorbing it. Remembrance. Blessings. Something about a covenant with God.

Could that really be true?

My head feels light. Not dizzy but spinning.

He knew. Dad must have known this whole time. And he never told me.

A guy with tiny wire-rim glasses and a plaid suit plays the guitar and sings "Blackbird" by the Beatles. Arthur's favorite song. It suddenly sounds different now. Less a lullaby and more like a secret message. All this time.

One by one, people stand in front of the group to speak about Arthur. His paintings. His shows. His success. His elegance. His charm. His achievements. My chest continues to pound. One by one, they reflect as I half-listen in a strange silent panic. I know this doesn't make Arthur any less dead, but why wouldn't anyone tell me this? Was it a secret?

My chest keeps burning.

And now it's Dad's turn.

He speaks about Arthur's endless wit and wisdom. ". . . He somehow knew the secrets of the human mind and heart. That's what made him such a good artist—such a successful one for sure—and such a good friend. I can't say we never argued, but ultimately, friends aren't only there to make you happy, they're also there to help you learn, grow, and become more of yourself."

How could Dad not tell me the truth? It's been a whole entire year! Every word makes me want to throw things. How could no one tell me? No one but Waverly, the truth-telling, sparkly eyed, strongly scented accountant.

It's always AIDS now.

I'm trying to recall every conversation I had with Arthur before he died. Our last visit to the museum to see the Vermeer show last summer. We went for a café au lait and they'd run out of milk, so I had my first espresso and got a headache. I try now to scan every moment to see if he ever seemed different, or sick, or worried, or anything. Did I miss something? It wasn't in his obituary, which I taped into my sketchbook last year. No one at the funeral last year said the word *AIDS*. And no one is saying it today. Do all these people here at the unveiling know?

Arthur was never shy about who he was. Why would he keep this a secret?

Eventually, I walk back to the car and wait for Dad to come and unlock it.

After we both get in, I immediately open the window.

"Robert and Susie are going to meet us at the reception," he says. "It's not too far away." He notices me staring ahead. "You OK?" he asks. I turn and glare at him.

"You told me he had a stroke," I say calmly.

"What?" he says, cleaning his sunglasses with a handkerchief.

"Did Arthur have AIDS?" I say, barely making noise with my throat.

His eyes take this in, but he stays still, remaining calm.

"Who told you that?" is all he asks. He doesn't deny it.

"Waverly, his accountant. Who I've never met before in my life. Waverly told me Arthur had AIDS. Is that true?" Dad takes a deep breath and lets it out slowly. Maybe stalling for time. I wait. It's his turn.

Finally, I hear him take a big inhale. "Yes, Danielle. Not many people knew. I didn't know that Waverly knew, actually, but maybe it's gotten around. Yes. Arthur did have AIDS. But also, his death was unexpected, and he did have a stroke, but yes, he had the HIV virus which made his immune system very weak."

"How long did you know?"

"A few months before he died. I think he thought that he'd beat it somehow. He didn't want people to know. But I guess Waverly doesn't know that."

"Did he actually tell you to keep it from me?" I cannot believe he wouldn't want me to know the truth.

Dad pauses a moment, not sure what to say, then decides, "He asked me, specifically. 'Don't ever tell Dani. She'll only worry, and she doesn't need that.' He thought you should focus on school and art. He knew you wanted more than anything to get into RISD and he didn't want to interrupt your life like that. He asked me, and he was dying, and I had to say yes to him. It all went downhill fast. I didn't have enough time to change his mind."

I try to picture a world where this secrecy is kindness. Did Arthur really think that or was he embarrassed? AIDS isn't usually met with understanding or calm. It makes people frightened.

"Was he afraid I'd be scared of him?" I ask, trying, really trying, to understand this all.

"No, Danielle," Dad stops. "At least, I don't think so." He looks out the window.

I try to remember how his body looked before he died. Was there something I didn't notice? Dad had known some people who'd died, people from his gay support group, friends of his new friends. But no one I knew well. Not like Arthur.

I'd seen people on the news with cheekbones jutting out with big dark purple spots everywhere, in wheelchairs or hooked up to an IV in a hospital bed. I'd heard stories about AZT, the new drug for AIDS.

But Arthur never looked like those guys on the news. Was he right to keep it a secret? Was he worried I'd stop loving him? Would I have? Would I have been afraid to see him or touch him if I'd known?

"I don't get it. Why would he keep it from me?"

"He was resolute and didn't want to be talked out of it," Dad said. "My guess is he felt ashamed. He knew you looked up to him. He didn't want to disappoint you."

It never before occurred to me that Arthur could be ashamed of anything. He'd always been so confident. How is it I never saw this other side of him, one of shame? "But if he knew he was going to die, why not be honest with me?"

"He didn't know that he'd die so quickly, honey. It was like dominos. That was unexpected. Honestly." Dad speaks calmly, but I hear an edge in his voice, growing nervous.

"But AIDS is a 'death sentence.' Isn't it? Did he not think he'd die?"

"People make unsound choices when they're scared," Dad continues. "Arthur had his reasons. And, quite frankly, it was his choice to tell you or not. I'm sorry you found out from Waverly, but I was just trying to respect Arthur's wishes. I didn't mean to deceive you, Danielle."

"It's not fair."

"What isn't fair?"

"He left me here. Didn't even say goodbye, and you didn't tell me the truth."

Silence that fills the car, seeps out through my window, is cold and hard. "What about Mom and Jake? Did they know?"

He just takes a deep breath and whispers, "Yeah. They knew."

"Wow, so you were all in on it, huh? Seriously?" I cannot even believe this.

"We didn't know what else to do," he says quietly.

"What a shame that Waverly had to open her big glossy mouth, I guess."

As I sit in this rocky anger, another thought enters my mind, rolling over me in icy, nauseating dread.

"Dad?" I whisper.

He doesn't hear me.

"Dad?" I say a little louder.

Silently staring at the road in front of him, he takes a deep breath and whispers, "Yes?"

"You'd tell me, right? If you had it? The virus? You'd tell me?"

He takes another deep breath and looks ahead, not at me. "Of course, Bunny."

I exhale. Of course, he would.

He starts the car and immediately turns off the stereo, and we drive to the reception in silence.

Don't let him get it.
He's going to get it.
Don't let him get it.
Who do I even say this to?
How can I even ask?
He's careful, right?
He's OK, right?
If Arthur got it, then . . .
No. Just don't.
Stop.
He's fine. We're fine.
It's fine.

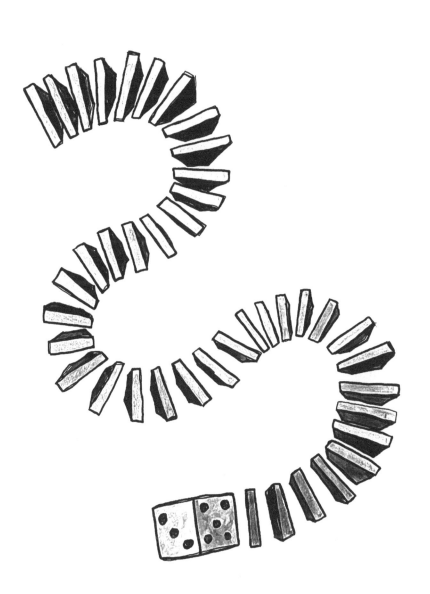

3
"Heart Of Glass"

Philadelphia in late August is like the last five minutes of a test. You want to make sure you did all you could, but it's sweaty and nerve-wracking. Mom is visiting from California to see me and Jake before school starts, and that means sitting through a long, multicourse meal with an assortment of her friends.

We're inside a French bistro on Thirteenth Street, and it's hot. There's one fan in here and the humidity is peaking. My butt sticks to the chair, and I'm so thirsty. I ate too many Doritos this afternoon while I was packing. My end-of-summer ritual is getting all the junk food I can before Baxter feeds me apples and granola bars until Christmas. Dad says if snacking were a competitive sport, I'd go to the Olympics. There is exactly one waitress here and apparently zero glasses of water. Mom is talking to her friends about her neighbors in San Francisco and their French bulldog, which she is describing in detail. Jake stares into space, so I need to keep smiling and look like I'm listening. I could drink a fish tank of water right now. God, the world is on my nerves today.

Not only do I have to apply to RISD without Arthur, but every

time I think about him, what used to be this soft warm comfort is all deceit and lies. What else don't my parents and Jake want me to know? Do they all think I'm some crazed fragile mess? Am I?

Before the divorce, Mom and I used to have fun. We'd play Monopoly and make quilts. Even though she is a tenured professor of journalism, deep down she always loved crafts. We'd go look at quilts in Amish Country and try to replicate them. Her understanding of a sewing machine was mind-boggling. I've never been patient, but she taught me persistence, and even now when I'm making some painstakingly detailed drawing, I remember making those quilts, stitch by stitch.

But after Dad left, Mom was more brittle and less available. She went back to working full time, so we had less time to make things together. I spent more time with Arthur or my friends, and more time at Dad's tiny apartment, but I also felt ever-present guilt that I should be with Mom.

After visiting Jake one weekend at his boarding school in New Jersey, I decided I wanted to be there too. In my mind, Jake and his friends were like grown-ups, living on their own without parents nagging them. I asked my parents if I could go there too for high school. I think they were surprised since I was the kid who hated camp and always felt homesick at school trips or slumber parties when I was younger. But with their divorce and everything else happening, I guess it seemed like a good idea for everyone.

Mom's friends here at the bistro are chatting about a ballet performance they saw last week and the new Meryl Streep movie coming soon. I'm finding it impossible to enter this conversation, so I just sit quietly and listen, wishing I was anywhere else. An air-conditioned museum would be nice. Or sleeping. Or painting and listening to loud music. I have Blondie's "Heart of Glass" stuck in my head.

Mom turns to Jake and says, "So Jakey, what wonderful things are awaiting you back at Harvard? What are you taking this year?"

"Well, you know that I'm completing a double major in political science and economics, so I'll be focusing on postindustrial manufacturing as a global construct and its impact on developing countries." I have no idea what Jake is talking about most of the time. I look around the table and, like me, no one knows what to say to that.

Mom stares at him a little too long before smiling and saying, "Wow, that's fantastic. You should speak with my old college professor, Dr. Rothstein. He's an expert in colonialism and agriculture." Mom always knows someone tangentially connected to pretty much any conversation had by any human. It's really a superpower. Jake mumbles, "Sure." Jake used to like jokes, and he used to blow bubbles into his soda, and he used to laugh deeply. Jake has this great laugh, actually. Like a happy foghorn. But now he's sort of perpetually irritated, and he talks to everyone like they're idiots he can barely bring himself to tolerate.

Then it's my turn. I know what's coming. "And Danielle," Mom starts, looking around the table, making sure everyone is still listening to her, "is going into her senior year at Baxter!"

"Oh, in your brother's footsteps! Are you top of your class as well?" asks Linda, who I have never met before. Oh, Linda, what a terrific question.

I smile. "Nope. I am not. That would be Erica Kelly. She's way smarter than really anyone on earth. Even Jake. I think she got a PhD over the spring break last year."

Jake perks up, watching me, shaking his head and sighing at my sarcasm. My big brother barely hides that he thinks I am a ridiculous waste of time and resources. Mom's lips tighten into a little ball to keep from reprimanding me in front of everyone.

"All right, doll, for real now, where are you applying?" Mom's friend Ruth asks me. She's a tiny Jewish lady with a scratchy voice and a large bosom. I love Ruth. I'm not mad at Ruth, but here we go again.

"I am applying to the Rhode Island School of Design." I let that land.

"Oh. RISD is very prestigious and hard to get into. What about a safety, doll?" she follows up, sucking on the lemon she fished out of her iced tea with her fingers.

"Saving on postage and living dangerously, Ruth," I say.

Ruth puts the lemon back in her iced tea, digs some calamari into red sauce, and laughs. "OK, well, good luck, doll. I expect to see your paintings at the museum in a few years, huh?"

I laugh back. I glance over at Mom who is not laughing. I think I should be able to manage my own college application process, like I manage my life at boarding school. I mean, why does she want to be involved? It's my life.

After dinner, we decide to get ice cream. Jake walks next to me and quietly asks, "Dani, are you seriously not applying anywhere else?"

"Oh God, not you too. No! I'm going to RISD. End of interrogation. Thank you."

"Yeah, but it's not entirely up to you if you get in. You do understand that, right?"

"Gee, Jake, thanks for the vote of confidence. Much appreciated. Don't worry, I'm not going to come squat in your dorm at Harvard if I don't get in. I won't be your problem. Promise." He rolls his eyes, as we walk into the ice cream shop.

Don't they even hear themselves? I mean, would it kill them to be supportive?

After her friends leave, Jake and I walk Mom back to her hotel. I am still stewing, even after ice cream. Hot and angry.

"So Arthur's unveiling was a barrel of laughs. Missed you guys," I say, wanting them to know how annoyed I feel.

"Oh, honey, that's right. I'm so sorry I couldn't be there. How was it?" Mom puts her arm around me.

"Well, I was lucky enough to meet a very tall, sparkly person named Waverly who told me that Arthur died from AIDS, which is apparently not news to you, but it was news to me."

Her face morphs from concern to a painful grimace.

"Oh, honey." She lunges forward to try to hug me. I pull away. I look over at Jake who is staring at the sidewalk.

"Yeah. Dad explained it all to me. I know everything."

"Please understand, Danielle. It's what he wanted." Mom starts to defend herself.

"Oh, I understand that you all kept the truth from me. I understand you think I'm a child," I say plainly, letting the words settle onto them like sawdust.

"No, honey, that's not true. I think Arthur wanted to protect you. He loved you more than anything." Mom slides her arm through mine, trying to connect.

Jake silently wills himself out of the conversation.

"Yeah, well, anyway, forget it. I don't care." I'm lying to myself now and wanting to get out of this moment. Nothing they say will bring him back or change things. "I'm done. I can never win. You guys never listen to me."

"All right, Dani, enough," Mom says curtly, as she pulls her arm away. "Which is it? Child or grown-up? It's time to choose. You can be pissed as hell that Arthur died, but you have to respect his choices. And being an adult is understanding that sometimes things don't go how you want them to. Sometimes people make decisions you don't like. But you have to try to be compassionate and understanding and take yourself out of the picture. It was Arthur's truth to reveal or keep hidden. Not ours, and not yours. So, if you want us to treat you like a grown-up, then act like one."

I stand still, stunned, silent. I cannot argue with that.

"And seriously, Dani, you need a safety school," Jake chimes in.

I am not saying one more word. They don't get it. I'm going to RISD. I finally open my mouth, but only to end this conversation, "I need to go pack. Dad's driving me to Baxter first thing tomorrow."

"And that means 'first thing,' I know." She tries to joke, but I'm just a stone. She hugs me anyway. "Consider some other schools, Danielle. You might want options by springtime. A lot can happen between now and when you graduate next May."

We hug goodbye. Mom whispers, "I love you. Just think about it."

Why isn't anyone rooting for me? Arthur would. He'd do it beautifully. He'd call them all a bunch of turkeys.

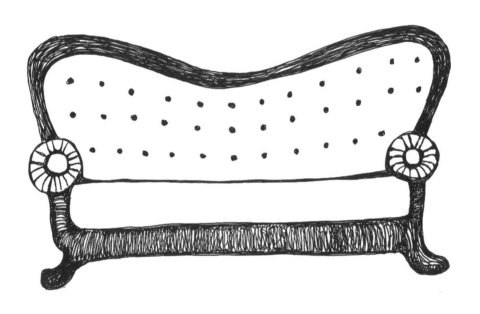

I thought you'd still be here now.
Still here to witness my small triumphs
And see me through the big dark caves.
To sit with me and talk through all these things I don't understand.
But you and your virus were hiding from me.
Did it hurt to die? Were you scared?
I wish I could have held your hand.
When we sat together on your couch, and I stroked the pink velvet back and forth,
were you scared? Or ashamed?
How I wish I could have one more hour with you there.
Tomorrow, I return to the nightmare of closed minds and stone archways.
Counting the days, the minutes, until I can leave and never look back.

"Danielle Florence Silver, we were supposed to leave eight minutes ago." Dad's voice is calm and low. He's standing in the doorway of the bathroom with his hands on his temples, like he is trying to keep his brain inside his skull. Oh, right. But I forgot to pack my bathroom stuff. I walk into what I know is his nightmare: bottles everywhere, opened shampoo, a half-packed makeup bag, and a sock hanging on the shower rod for some reason.

"Wow, Benjamin Edward Silver, it looks like a bomb went off in here!" I squeeze past him to start picking up all the dirty cotton balls, underwear, sunscreen, toothbrush, face wash, and the sock. Dad closes his eyes and shakes his head.

"This is why God made boarding school," he mutters as he walks away.

"I can hear you, you know," I say as I start throwing things into plastic bags. I have my systems. Toiletries in a white plastic bag. Art supplies in a black one. Apparently, I did not inherit my dad's organization genes.

"Please have your suitcases by the door in the next five minutes so I don't lose my mind." It's nice how Dad uses the word *suitcases* because honestly, he can't bring himself to admit I am packing my belongings in garbage bags and an army duffel.

4

"Smells Like Teen Spirit"

I've been in the gym for all of three minutes, but the smell of Polo Sport deodorant is already making my eyes tear up. I'm pretty sure that Derek, Baxter's resident ogre and linebacker on the football team, bathes in the stuff. He and his sidekick, Don, walk toward me in coordinated football jerseys, somehow pushing a cloud of putrid scent in their path. Their matching baggy jeans look like balloons. Derek passes by, too close, as usual. "Lezzo," he whispers near my face and then winks. Some things never change. And by *things*, I mean assholes.

I want a seat at the very top of the bleachers for this special first assembly. Amy waves to me from the front row. She's sitting with her field hockey team and keeps beckoning me to sit with them. I love that girl but I am not sitting with the jocks. We discussed this earlier today, but maybe she forgot. After we moved our stuff out of storage a couple days ago and put up the posters in our dorm room, Amy all but vanished into the black hole of sporty people. I support her decisions, though. Later we will gossip about fashion choices and who's dating who. For now, we place ourselves in our designated social circles. By senior year, it's good to know where you stand . . . or sit. At the top of the bleachers, I nestle into the back corner

seat, perched high to view the vista of the back-to-school assembly. The other artists aren't here yet, but they'll file in. Late and sullen, to be sure.

I take out my blue spiral notebook, destined eventually for physics, but empty enough to suffice for a sketchbook today. Assemblies are where I do some of my best work, frankly. Especially these sporty ones. I barely listen to whatever the coach person is saying. Football or field hockey? Something about a homecoming dance. A new gym? Who cares?

Looking into the crowd, I see a lot of trying too hard. Plaid is certainly on the rise, and the gravity-defying hairdo where girls mousse their bangs to shoot straight up and somehow also have a scrunchie bun happening remains a trend that won't die. The student population at Baxter has to collectively use a hundred gallons of hair mousse each week. I'm surprised they don't have it next to the hand soap in all the bathrooms.

Finally, the art gang shows up and takes their place along the back row. They are experts in avoiding both eye contact and participation. Daria cut her hair into a bob and bleached it in stripes, and Kyle has done some impressive safety-pin accessorizing work on his cardigan. I nod to them and roll my eyes in solidarity.

Daria leans over and whispers to me, "Did you hear Mr. Thorne isn't coming back? They're not replacing him either. It's seriously fucked, man."

"What? Did they fire him?" I'm shocked. Mr. Thorne has been here forever. He taught sculpture at Baxter for at least twenty years. He was also skilled at being an oddball that everyone loved.

Kyle leans past Daria to join in, "Budget layoffs, I heard. What with all these new expenses." He waves his hand to indicate the gym, the teams, the coaches on display. "They can't keep employing creative types, I guess."

"Wait, so, Funk is the only art teacher now?"

"Yup, tiny Mrs. Funkelberg is the last one standing." Kyle's disdain for Baxter grows daily. Last year, we lost Ms. Dudley, who taught woodworking and ceramics. We still have the potter's wheels, but no one actually teaches with them now. Mr. Thorne would cover it once a semester, but now that's gone too.

"It can't just be money, can it?" I ask. "I mean, look around. This place is dripping with funds."

"It's not the amount of money, sweet innocent Danielle. It's where it comes from and where it goes," explains Daria. "As long as little Buffy and Muffy can play field hockey and polo or whatever the fuck they play on those perfectly seeded, custom manicured lawns, and then go inside and bounce balls around in a shiny new gym, then hey, the school's keeping its customers happy. Thorne's sculpture classroom is under construction already. To be a new office for the Phys Ed department, we can't even use it."

"Isn't there someone we should talk to?" I ask, not accepting what they're saying.

"Listen, Dani, you can talk all you want, but nobody's listening," Daria says, resolved to her stance of disdain. "Especially to us." She takes a nail file out of her bag and starts filing down her black fingernails.

"Don't worry, there are only 179 more days of school, and then, 'Sayonara, assholes,'" Kyle says, blowing his bangs out of his face.

I draw in my notebook as I half listen to speeches about the Baxter way, traditions, expectations, winning, and other nonsense.

Athletes belting out the school song echoes through the gym and I want to implode from the cringe factor.

When it finally ends, I slip out a side door of the gym to go to the mail room to get my box. Dad said he'd sent it overnight express. Every fall I start the semester waiting for the mail. The mail room supervisor, Lloyd, knows me by now. He knows I'll arrive just after school starts to look for the box of forgotten gems my father always sends me. Lloyd is serious, and some might say, he has one mood, a bad one. His gray hair thins more each year, but his disinterest never fades. He is not charmed by me. I even brought him a box of chocolates last year. He just said, "Thanks," and put them in his bag. He didn't even notice they were dark chocolate.

You know that bag that you pack that has all the important stuff in it? The bag that has your black-and-white Doc Martens, your entire CD collection and Discman, your sketchbook, and those very expensive Sennelier oil pastels that you got for Hanukkah? That's the bag I left at home, sitting by my bedroom door with a Post-it stuck right to it, literally saying Don't Forget! Dad insists this always happens, but this year was supposed to be different because I had the Post-it!

I now know that a Post-it is only useful if you read it.

Baxter's mail room is the stuff of dreams and nightmares. In the physical sense, it's a room in the back of the first floor of Old Main, past the bathrooms and lost and found, with tiny doors of shoebox sized mailboxes lining the walls. Each tiny door has an even tinier lock into which you have to insert a tiny key, which you have to keep somewhere safe or you never, ever get your mail because Lloyd, mail room overlord and king, does not like to replace these itty-bitty keys. Inside, you find mail and occasionally the bright pink slip which means you got a package. Surprise! We boarding school kids have a lot of independence, but we don't get to buy junk food after school and are forbidden from crossing the nearest highway for a box of doughnuts whenever we want, so care packages are the next best thing. Or, they could be, hence the optimism/dread divide. Sometimes a kid gets a package full of homemade chocolate chip cookies, or games, or comic books, and other times they get boring textbooks, Band-Aids, or toothpaste.

The mail room is a big part of our lives. It's our lifeline to the rest of the world. Sometimes I check my mailbox two or three times a day if I'm expecting something, or just wanting any sort of knowledge of the world beyond Baxter. Or I come here to buy stamps, hoping for additional doses of mail to arrive.

But Lloyd seems to have gone on break.

I guess if I worked in a boarding school mail room during the first week when pretty much no one was expecting to receive anything, I'd sneak out back for a midmorning cigarette too. In his sad tiny office, pink package slips litter the desk. Piles of unsorted mail lay in bins. Aside from a Batman comic sticking out of his messenger bag, there's not an ounce of personality here. While I wait I check my mailbox. When I twist the handle, the little metal door practically explodes. Letters from Mom's trip to Paris last month, art supply catalogs from Pearl Paint, announcements from New York art galleries, and the fall exhibitions magazine from the Philadelphia Museum of Art. I always forget that the mail doesn't stop when we leave school for the summer. But there, nestled in between all that mail, is a magic pink package ticket. "Yes!" I mime throwing my hat in the air like I'm freaking Mary Tyler Moore on Nick at Nite. Of course, this sends my backpack flying. No, Danielle, you're not gonna make it after all. Not today, at least.

I turn around to find that my backpack has vomited its contents all over the floor, when suddenly there is this boy, a stranger, holding out my emergency tampon like he's offering me a pen. I grab it from him so fast it's like it was never there at all.

He's a vision. He looks like Keanu Reeves, but cuter. Unimaginably cuter. Like Keanu's baby brother. He's wearing a white oversized Wham! T-shirt and has a very clean black backpack on his wide shoulders. His hair is way shinier than mine, and it's wavy and dark brown. Is it shimmering? His eyes are like warm pools of chocolate syrup with lashes for days, and then holy hell, his lips. So plump and big and round, I sort of want to take a nap on them. Snap out of it, Danielle!

He's still holding out his now tampon-free hand like he's some sort of mannequin while the rest of my junk lays at his feet. "Here, uh, let me help you," he says.

He bends down and picks up my mail while I shove everything else back into my bag.

"Well, Danielle Silver," he says, reading my name on the pink form, "looks like your package has arrived."

My lips can't talk because his adorable face is making me crazy. He just looks at me, waiting. "What?" I finally shout, like he is across the street.

"Here." He hands me the pile of envelopes and catalogs and postcards. "Package, right? The pink thing, isn't that for packages? I'm new here."

"It is," Lloyd grumbles as he walks back into his little booth, the scent of a cigarette still clinging to his faded chinos. "Here you go, again, Danielle." He pulls down a large cardboard box from a shelf. Lloyd is also unfortunately aware of my annual bag displacement and return. Dad's swirly handwriting on the label is visible from here. "Slip," Lloyd demands with more authority than necessary.

I pass my pink slip through the slot and he unlocks the package pass-through and slides my box out. I breathe a sigh of relief and notice the gorgeous guy is still standing next to me, tilting his head like a puppy in wonder.

"Whaddya get?" Baby Keanu asks.

"Uh, just some stuff I left at home," I say, ignoring Lloyd's judgy face. I'm already tearing off the box's tape. When I open the cardboard flaps, there it is, sitting on top, all pretty like a cherry on a sundae.

"Thank God," I mutter under my breath, but Keanu hears me.

"Is that a journal?" he asks.

"Well, yeah, a journal-sketchbook."

"You're an artist?" he asks like he just discovered a dinosaur bone in an archaeological dig.

"Well, I'm— Yeah, sort of. That's a terribly subjective title, really, not to mention pretentious but I'm, well . . . let's say I'm in training?" Oh God, ew. Training?

"Can I see it? I mean, I won't open it; it just looks so cool."

I hand it to him. The mossy green leather has a texture more like cloth, with a thin strap that goes around it like a wrap dress, and ties back on itself. It's thick enough to last me all semester, maybe, but thin enough to slip into my book bag without weighing it down. The size of a large novel, big enough to hold both words and pictures. Dad knows how much space I need. He's been buying one of these for me every summer since I can remember.

"It's nice. Handmade?" the cute boy asks, handing it back to me.

I nod, curious at his question and distracted by his lips. "It was a gift from my father. He likes pretty things, like shoes and hats and paintings and these books. His ex-boyfriend was a book maker and got him hooked. So, he spoils me with handmade sketchbooks." I say this all in one breath because my heart is racing, and my face feels hot from being so close to his.

Oh shit. I just spilled the gay beans. Dammit. I usually wait until I know how a person is going to take it. I couldn't just keep my big mouth shut. Baby Keanu is so cute, I am losing my mind.

Now he's not saying anything. He just stares at me with his mouth open. Usually, once I share the fact that my dad is gay with people, they make a certain face. It's somewhere in the vicinity of confusion and horror. Like when you think you're eating a grape, but it turns out to be an olive. But this Keanu dude is giving me something closer to sheer fascination, like he found a magical elf in the forest with a pot of gold. His eyes are squinting a little bit, but his mouth is still sort of smiling. He looks fundamentally delighted. I need to vacate this situation before I say something truly idiotic.

"Sorry, I . . . Thanks," I say, taking the sketchbook from his hands. "Well, see ya."

"Wait," he says, "which way are you walking? Can I walk with you and, you know, lend you the use of my arms here?"

I nod and say, "Sure, that would be great." My arms full, I use my chin to point toward the exit we should take, as he slowly takes one of the things I'm holding. I'm not going to lie, I'm glad it's the box because I would have to stop and shake out my arms.

As we walk, he keeps the conversation going, "Wow, what a day out here, huh?" I notice the afternoon light is pouring across the trees as golden and red leaves flutter down to the ground. Yes, it is a good fall day. Arthur called this "crispy light."

"So, you're new?" I ask him.

"Yes! Just transferred. Barely know a soul here."

"Oh, cool. What year?" Should I be asking him so many questions?

"Senior. You?"

"Same," I say. "Been here since ninth grade." I offer more than he asked. Is that OK? What is wrong with me? "My dorm is that way," I say, without thinking. I take the box from him, wishing he'd offer to walk me farther. God, why is this thing so heavy?

"Can I . . . um, can I see your art sometime?"

If only I could think of something cool and mysterious, but I just say, "Umm, maybe?" My flirting skills need some help. He looks hurt so I try to make a joke. "You seem so clean. I don't want you to, like, get weird toxic paint on your T-shirt." That wasn't funny at all, Danielle. Does this guy KNOW how cute he is? He must have to deal with people always turning into idiots in his presence.

He nods and smiles, "Well, nice meeting you, Danielle. I'm Marco."

I smile. "Like Polo?"

He scrunches up his eyebrows. "Yeah, yeah."

"OK, Marco Polo." Crap, he isn't smiling at that. I'm probably the thousandth person to make that joke. Man, things were going so well. "Thanks for your help." I jut out my hand for a handshake.

What am I, a businessman? "Welcome to the Baxter School for fancy boys and girls!" We shake and he laughs. Dear God, his smile is glorious.

I walk back to the dorm feeling like the world just changed. In reality, I just flirted with a super gorgeous boy, but I'm a teenage girl, for God's sake. I have no defenses against that level of cuteness.

Up in my dorm room, I slide the box onto my already disastrous desk.

Amy and I have lived together for the last two years, but let's just say that our tidiness levels have never been quite compatible. Her side of the room is perfect, with books organized by subjects then by authors' last names, pencils neatly stored in a cup, her bed made with hospital corners. Hospital corners! Some people who tend toward this level of neat-freakishness can be hard to be around, but not Amy. I mean, she'd clean my side of the room if I let her, but she also respects my way of living—or at least accepts me for my pigpen qualities.

Also, Amy's music collection is solid. She's currently going through a vigorous love affair with Lou Reed, so we've got the Velvet Underground on heavy rotation. Her dark curls bob up and down while Nico sings about love. She pretends not to notice that I've brought more junk into our room. She's scribbling in her notebook, likely updating her to-do list or planning her next week of schedules. It's only the first week of school, but I'm sure she's already got a list at least two pages long.

I'm not in the mood to clean or talk about music though because I can't get Keanu/Marco out of my head.

"Holy mother of God, I have something to tell you," I say, sitting down carefully because I am about to burst.

"Oh, I know. Ashley Norton got arrested over the summer for drunk driving, and she joined AA," she says, still looking into her notebook.

"Well, that is something, but no, something else," I say.

"What?" She finally stops writing and looks at me, wanting to know.

"There is a new boy in our grade, and he is so gorgeous that words in the English language fail to describe." I sigh, flopping down on my bed.

"Uh-oh, what? Where did he come from? Tell me everything."

I explain the whole mail room scene and then I make very important notes as we discuss this for an embarrassingly long time.

he may not be actually,
really real

Possible scenarios about the Great Handsome Teenage
Daydream, a.k.a Keanu Reeves's baby brother, a.k.a
Marco Polo:
He is not real. I dreamed the whole thing—I actually
bonked my head on the mailbox door and fantasized that
a perfect boy with a sweet voice just helped me pick up all
my mail.
He is a foreign exchange student from Paris (because only
French men are that handsome) with a perfect American
accent and he has come to Baxter to do a gap year before
attending UC Berkeley or Julliard or MIT. He is brilliant,
kind, and particularly loves tall girls with short black hair
named Danielle who drop their mail.
He is an international spy. Spies are devastatingly handsome.
He is a robot from outer space. How can any human be that
good-looking and nice?

"It's probably the first one," Amy says, peering over my shoulder. It figures. Amy doesn't believe anyone as cute as I've described Marco to be could actually attend Baxter. Next thing I know, she's on the floor doing sit-ups. Unlike me, she rarely sits still.

"So, are you going to spend the whole weekend thinking about this guy? 'Cause Noah and I are going to see *Working Girl* in the quad if you want to come."

This invitation is code for "I want to fix you up with one of my boy-friend's basketball friends and get you out of the house." Amy thinks that since I broke up with Brian last year I cannot survive without a boyfriend. I can. Quite well, in fact.

Since Brian, I've been on a journey to enjoy *not* dating anyone. That breakup devastated me and left me wondering what the point of love even was, aside from a gooey topic for pop songs. I was so focused on him. I tried so hard to get more attention from him—I stopped eating, I stopped sleeping, I stopped drawing. And it never paid back. He made me feel small. And now that I'm finally out of the throes of it all, I really don't want to get sucked back into anything. Even thinking about Marco, the mail room boy, is dangerous territory.

Dad unknowingly gave me really good dating advice about a month ago which came by way of the supermarket. We were in the produce section and someone had placed some bananas in the lemon section. He shook his head, lifting them and putting them back in their home on the shelf nearby. "Bananas don't do well next to lemons. It's just chemistry. It all turns to crap." This landed right in my core and stayed with me. Brian and I didn't do well together. Looking at it like this helped me feel better.

That doesn't mean I am blind to the cuteness of cute boys. I mean, chemistry works in mysterious ways, right?

Amy is staring and patiently waiting for a response to her double-date invitation.

"Um, yeah, thanks, but I've got to get working," I say. "I have a bunch of drawings to start for my RISD application."

"OK then, enjoy your toil!" She is refolding the clothes in her dresser. "I meant to ask, how was that postfuneral thing for Arthur?"

"The unveiling? It was fine." I leave out the AIDS discovery. Opening a can of worms with Amy is usually a commitment. I mean, we just spent like forty-five minutes talking about a cute boy. I'll get into it later.

"Yeah. Arthur was the best. Remember when he came to Parents' Day in ninth grade? That was amazing." Amy beams at the thought.

"Right. Wearing his shiny blue tuxedo!" I smile, remembering his pranks.

"God, Danielle, your family is just so . . ." Amy coos.

"Weird?" I roll my eyes at the stuff I haven't told her about.

"No, I was going to say interesting," she said.

"Whatever you say," I reply, shoving my clothes into the three drawers of the dorm dresser.

I get myself together and head to my studio in the gym building, a short walk from my dorm. This box feels no less heavy even though I unloaded it. If only Keanu magically appeared.

At the gym, in the basement, I find my key and unlock the door.

Once upon a time this place I call my studio was some sort of mechanical room. But last year, I was increasingly frustrated with trying to make art only during art class and only in the art room. Too many people, too few hours, and too little space. And Arthur always taught me that all an artist needs is time, space, and solitude. When I talked to him about this sophomore year, Arthur said, "Danielle, honey, no one is coming with all your wants and desires on a platter. You must advocate for what you need, don't wait for it to come wrapped in some pretty bow." So, I made requests for a studio space to my art teacher, to the headmaster, to whoever would listen, really. I was persistent, and eventually, the school relented and found this unused room in the gym, which is pretty disgusting but does have exceptionally high ceilings. And now, at least until I graduate, they told me it's all mine. I sometimes wonder if I should have asked for a bigger space for more people to use.

I can smell the dust. I may not get to any drawings today. First, I need to find a vacuum cleaner. I hear the pounding of footsteps above me and wonder if Marco plays sports.

5
"Keep on Loving You"

By week two, Amy really starts becoming my school mom.

"So, what's up with you today?" she asks while she does her hundredth morning sit-up. Last year this was how we started our Saturdays: Amy checking in on my schedule before she begins a day of field hockey practice and other highly productive activities.

"Studio," I mutter, glancing at the box overflowing with art supplies by the foot of my bed. I look at the clock; it's already ten forty-five a.m.

"Ugh, Dani, I don't know how you can be creative there." Amy flares her nostrils at the thought of it. "I won't be surprised when you get asbestos poisoning."

"Hey, I cleaned it. At least it's a room of my own." I'm shuffling around trying to find my toothbrush. "No offense," I say, realizing that maybe it sounded rude.

She smiles and pats me on the head as she leaves, "Oh, believe me, I'd rather you create elsewhere." Now she's putting on her sweatpants and tying her shoes. "I'm off to practice. See you later at the you-know-what!"

I nod. In truth, I don't know what she's talking about, but I'm pretty sure I don't want to go.

I slip into the cafeteria for something to eat. The campus is buzzing in that weekend way: no classes, but the social dial is up. Excited sophomore girls talk too loud about their new back-to-school shoes while freshmen boys look at them with no idea how to interact. I see Kyle and Daria, who wave to me as enthusiastically as a dry tissue. I grab a tuna sandwich and a package of chocolate chip cookies, shove them into my backpack, and head for the back door.

I see signs up for the thing Amy was referring to: the Mix-A-Lot, Baxter's annual welcome back celebration for clueless youths who like to dance to terrible music in a school gymnasium. Mostly younger kids go to it, or new transfer students. By the time you get to senior year, it's universally understood that it is not at all cool to attend the Mix-A-Lot. Amy, though, still goes because her love of dancing overrides a normal teenager's need to be cool. Also, she has a boyfriend, so it's a chance to do boyfriend-girlfriend stuff, I suppose.

Actually, I have the Mix-A-Lot to thank for meeting my number one girl. In freshman year, after ten excruciating minutes of standing around awkwardly, I saw Amy. She was rearranging the snack table while she thought no one was looking. She had a really cool haircut that angled up in the back, her black curls dangling perfectly around her face, and she wore a black turtleneck with a red miniskirt and black Converse sneakers. She looked like Molly Ringwald from *The Breakfast Club*, but less prissy, more mysterious. I went over and asked her for a cup, and she immediately launched into a whole thing about the punch and corn syrup and red dye number two and the wasteful overuse of plastic cups, and then, just when I thought she was basically yelling at me for asking for something to drink, she stopped, looked me up and down, and smiled. "I love those pants," she said like we were already friends. We later referred to them as my Scottish clown pants. We talked about everything that night: families, crushes, food, style icons. Hers were Aimee Mann and Nico, and mine were a kaleidoscope of Cyndi Lauper, Joan Jett, and James Dean. She said she liked my straight hair, I said I liked her curly hair. And that was that. Friends.

Back in my studio, I play Led Zeppelin on my boom box and put on my work clothes. Arthur taught me it helps to have a uniform. It's true. Like switching stations, I go into work mode with my paint-splattered pants on.

I flip through my datebook and count. November 15 is just eight weeks away. I feel a tightening in my chest. The stress is starting.

At the end of eighth grade, I discovered what Arthur called "art stress." At my middle school, all graduating eighth graders had to do dumb year-end projects the teachers all said were rites of passage. Reading from the Torah in front of a hundred people was a rite of passage. This was just bullshit. Believing I was already a full grown teenager, most of that year I spent counting the minutes until high school. My project was to draw all my teachers' desks. I must have thought it was some cool angle on portraiture, so I set myself the task of drawing six of them in the last three weeks of the school year. It was torture and took way longer than I expected.

One Sunday I was particularly worried about time. Arthur came over to Dad's for dinner that night. He was slicing apples for Dad's apple tart while I sat at the kitchen table freaking out.

"I have to finish an English essay, take a Spanish test, and do this biology team project, and I've only finished two of my project drawings, and I'm supposed to have them all done this week. It's bullshit!" I whined.

"What's bullshit?" Arthur asked, washing more apples and tossing a dish towel over his shoulder.

"All the projects are just . . . whatever. Other kids are, like, volunteering at soup kitchens for an afternoon or helping their cousins with math homework, and I'm doing this dumb project that's taking forever."

"OK, let me get this straight, young lady." Arthur opened the fridge. "You established your own goal for this independent project, right? No one told you what to do?"

"Yes," I said, admitting he was right.

"You conceived of a brilliant notion of creating portraits from the debris of your mentors, to personify them." He pulled a half-full bottle of white wine out of the fridge and immediately turned to the cabinet to find a glass. "Again, brilliant, but what did you expect? That they'd draw themselves?" Arthur poured the wine and let that just sit in the air for me.

"No, but, I don't know . . . It's just not fair," I repeated.

"What's not fair? That you have actual ideas in that pretty little head?" He said this while tapping his fingers on top of my head.

"No. I want to do the drawings, but why do I have to do all this other stuff? I mean, it doesn't even matter what my grades are. I'm already going to Baxter next year . . . Who cares about some dumb eighth grade essay on poetry, anyway? If I'm so brilliant, why do I have to do all this dumb school stuff?"

Arthur looked at me with his head tilted. Then he closed his eyes. He placed his wine glass gently on the table and sat next to me.

"My love, you are experiencing a particular condition we who devote our lives to creating art must contend with, I'm sorry to report. Regardless of your brilliance, a girl's got to eat, you know? It's art stress, plain and simple."

"What do you mean? What makes it different from other stress?"

"You make art because you love it, right?"

"Of course," I said quickly.

"And that's a beautiful thing. But, my dear, that does not get you off the hook for what I call 'human tasks.' All that boring life crap: buying groceries, paying bills, doing homework, and, eventually, getting a job. All the things that will sustain you so that you can make art."

He held out his hands like he was holding the sides of an invisible box. "See, most people have this much time to do human tasks. They wake up and make money at their job, then they spend their money on food, clothing, rent, and heat, and if they're lucky, at night, they love their family and friends and have some fun, or you know, make the world a better place. But we, my gorgeous Danielle," he paused and put his hands closer together, "we must find this much time in those same twenty-four hours to make art."

I looked at him, confused.

"So, if we need that much time for art," he began, "but we still have to do human tasks, what does that mean?"

"Umm, that we have less time to do human tasks than other people?"

"Right!" He smiled and took a sip of wine. "We have to do all that human stuff faster. You find a way, or else you either don't have money

and food, or you stop creating. This is just reality, my dear one. And sadly, it's not going to be easier later. It's the invisible burden of every artist. Some can get away with art all the time if they have a very useful or wealthy spouse or really rich and generous parents, I guess. But even then, you must organize your time so you can make your work and keep yourself alive."

"How do you do that? I mean, how do you squeeze the rest of your life into that little slice of time?"

He sighed and took another sip of wine. "For me, I had to get comfortable with three things: a small apartment, very boring meals, and being alone. I recommend you try to need fewer people around you. Some people fear loneliness. But the truth is, being alone saves a lot of time. People are time-consuming and frankly, exhausting!"

Just then, Dad came in to check on the apples, and clearly he'd eavesdropped on that last part. "Don't believe a word. Arthur loves people. His real secret is that he doesn't sleep like a normal person!"

"That's true. Learn not to sleep." He finished his glass of wine and went back to slicing apples.

Led Zeppelin ends on the CD player, and I suddenly remember coming home after school meant making myself grilled cheese sandwiches, watching TV reruns, drawing myself in a mirror, and listening to music. Since both my parents worked and Jake lived at boarding school, I was the typical latchkey girl, and I sort of liked it, even though I was sometimes lonely. But once I got to Baxter, I found it harder to really be alone—sharing a room, eating all my meals in the cafeteria, and art class with fifteen or twenty other kids. But now I can spend whole days in my studio and no one notices. It's how I squeeze everything in. I don't waste my time hanging out and gossiping or whatever girls usually do after dinner. I come here and make things.

I find an envelope filled with Post-its Arthur wrote for me when I began high school. I laminated them for longevity. Wherever I make paintings or drawings, I keep them close. I copy them down in all my journals, hoping they'll sink deep into my brain.

Resolving is Bullshit

After Jake went to college, I never heard from him. I'd sometimes write him letters or try to call. I'd see him at Thanksgiving and Christmas, but he stopped coming home for summer and seemed to be less and less interested in me and my life. Once I started Baxter, I loved feeling like I was already in college, sort of. I was busy having crushes on boys, trying out makeup, and hearing about making out from older girls in the dorm. Later, I was shaving my legs, plucking my eyebrows, piercing my ears, and dyeing my hair. I learned to navigate cliques and jocks. All while writing history papers and science lab reports, studying for math tests, and memorizing Spanish words.

Pay Attention to Everything

I take out my drawing portfolio and find an old sketch I made of my hands. I pin it to the wall. The lines look unsure of themselves. We'd been doing blind contour drawings last year. The art teacher, Mrs. Funk, kept reminding us of her positive-space lesson.

On the first day of art class freshman year, Mrs. Funk held up her hands with her fingers spread wide.

"Notice my hands, the shape they make," she said as she kept them still, like frozen jazz hands in front of her blue sweater. She looked around at all of us, making sure we were with her. "All right, now, I want you to look at the space between my fingers. My sweater, see the shape that makes." Then, she slowly started moving her fingers, saying "Now, don't look at my fingers. Look at the space between. Yes?" As she spoke, those spaces changed shape. Her fingers, of course, were still the same shape and size, but the space in between swelled and narrowed as she moved them around. "My fingers are the positive space. In between is the negative space. Sometimes we call it 'background.' But positive and negative spaces fit together and help you tell the whole story. If you only focus on one, you might get lost."

Remain calm

I spent my free periods in the art room, so I got to be friendly with older kids who seemed like they were born cool. As the months wore on, I realized that these kids were Baxter's fringe. They were the edge where norms of traditional boarding schools began to fray and disintegrate.

Baxter loves tradition, and it really loves everyone being the same. They only ditched uniforms about ten years ago but most students dress alike anyway. I don't try to change their minds, but as time's gone on, I long to be somewhere a little less stuffy, a little more messy, more colorful, more understanding that some people enjoy being different. More than understanding, maybe even encouraging?

Drown out the nonsense

But I play along, which is not always fun but feels necessary. I'm not spending the rest of my life here, so I'm keeping my head down 'til I can leave. I paint here under the radar, do my homework on time, and stay out of trouble. I don't join conversations about dads who play golf or moms who get nose jobs. Instead, I find a few people who are smart and open-minded and teachers who lead me down paths that wake me up instead of put me to sleep.

I find my own little path through Baxter's secluded woods, but I long for an open field where I can take a break from hiding.

Make it yours

Arthur taught me how to understand what I was seeing, to see the shapes that make up bigger shapes, and how drawn lines on a surface change the way things feel: shaky lines feel scared, big solid lines seem stubborn but sometimes strong. He showed me the horizon line, how the eye understands distance with perspective, and he pointed out the light near the end of the day and how it got softer and bluer. Artists need tricks up their sleeves to tell their stories. It's not quite magic, but sometimes it's close.

I pull down my pads of paper from the shelf. I place my brushes in the jars I left here last year. I find the rolling cart in the corner and set up my palette and paints in order: yellow, orange, red, purple, blue, green, and white.

I look through the art books Arthur gave me. Caravaggio was our favorite. Beautiful bodies, red and blue drapery, glistening fruit in shining silver bowls. A true master who made everything look like it was perfect. Arthur was fond of these. He'd sigh whenever we flipped through this book. "Insanely beautiful." Another book is about Eva Hesse, whose drippy globs somehow manage to be graceful. She's one of my favorite artists, and I always wonder what else she else would have done had she not died so young.

Irreverence is essential

I find the black portfolio in the box Dad sent me and start pinning my summer drawings onto the wall. This is the start of my RISD application portfolio. Sometimes moving to a different place from where you made something gives you a fresh take. Drawings of chairs stacked, empty hallways, Dad's den which is my summer bedroom, books in piles, glasses on a table. Clunky lines, small bursts of color, a shakiness alongside some more fluid marks.

I imagine Arthur standing beside me, staring from one to the other. "I see your trademark clunkiness mixed with those graceful lines. Some courage with the colors, but Danielle, my love, I need to ask: Where is the life?"

This cuts me deep. Even gone, he still surprises me.

Even as a young kid, I somehow knew his adult life was different from my parents' other friends. He was both softer and sharper than other adults, more beautiful, less angry. But there was something else I didn't grasp until I got older and learned that the world wasn't so kind to his difference. Some of the world, anyway, didn't see him as beautiful.

One summer, when I was seven, Arthur and I spent the day at the beach in Cape Cod. It was hot, and Arthur decided we needed to buy some Popsicles for everyone back at our house. As we walked through the store, he held my hand and carried the shopping basket in the other, looped in his elbow. Arthur wore his tiny leopard print bathing suit and an equally tiny tank top with bright green flip-flops. His hair was long then, and his wet ringlets fell to his shoulders.

"Popsicles, Popsicles, I love eating those Popsicles," he sang to the tune of the Spider-Man theme song. "What color do you want, my little love?"

"I want orange. It's a color and a flavor," I said with a wink because he taught me that joke.

"That's my clever girl. Good choice!!"

Just then, I noticed a large man in dirty clothes and a baseball cap, standing next to the freezer. He was holding a six pack of beer in one hand and a loaf of bread in the other. He stared at us, scanning Arthur up and down. His eyes flicked over to me, then back at Arthur, fixed and full of danger. I felt a pull in my stomach, deep and dark.

"What the fuck are you supposed to be?" he said in a low voice.

I did not understand the question. Arthur wasn't wearing a costume, and aside from the cursing, that sounded like something you'd say at Halloween. Then I saw Arthur's face, still searching the freezer for our Popsicles; he was puckering his lips tight. His nostrils looked funny, and I knew the man had said something terrible, something mean. But Arthur didn't respond. His hand held mine a little tighter and with the other, he opened the freezer door. As the burst of cold hit us, he just said, "Oh, Dani, look, they have orange!" And then he looked at me with his giant warm smile, grabbed the box of Popsicles, and said, "Shall we?" I nodded and smiled back. Happy to see him happy and excited about the Popsicles.

He never spoke to the dirty man. He never even looked at him.

I felt a new kind of confusion, and maybe even fear. Arthur was always so nice to everyone. Arthur wasn't doing anything wrong. Even though most people smiled when he was around, something about Arthur made certain people angry and mean. And that scared me.

I looked to Arthur to understand what to do. Should I be scared, or was everything fine? But Arthur acted like the big man simply wasn't there. At the cashier, I turned around and saw the mean man still staring at us, his eyes thin and angry, but he wasn't following us. Arthur held my hand, a bit tighter than normal. He paid the cashier and said, "Thank you, doll!" and looked down at me with his big warm smile. "Come on, darling, let's get these yummy pops home quick before they melt."

It is clear to me now that Arthur did all he could to make me feel safe. To make me feel like the world wasn't so scary, to protect me—because he knew better. Then, and later, he didn't want me to be afraid of the world.

I put in another CD. Miles Davis, *Kind of Blue*—one of Arthur's favorites. The light through the small window is dimming, and I switch on my desk lamp. I think I missed dinner. I dig through my backpack for the cookies left from lunch.

I had heard the word *gay*, when I was young, but like coffee and mortgages, it was all too adult for me to bother trying to understand. But once boys became less annoying and more interesting, I began to understand that liking guys wasn't just for teenage girls or grown-up women. I eventually understood that *gay* was something people rarely talked about in public. But it was often there, beneath the surface, un-aired, heavy, and dark. In later years, Arthur would sometimes make his summer visits with a man named Christopher, who had long eyelashes and muscular shoulders and called everyone Sweetie. And when Jake called him "Arthur's boyfriend," I remember thinking Jake was making fun of Arthur. I might have even cried.

Bravery breeds creativity

Dad says most people find it easier to travel down roads our world has already built. Smooth, paved highways going in the same direction as everyone else. It's easier to slide along and never question what you're doing, or why. Never listen to the voice that is screaming inside you. He says it seems like laziness but really, it's just not knowing you have a choice. *And sometimes*, he'd say, *fear keeps you from being honest.*

I hear REO Speedwagon playing above me. The Mix-A-Lot has started. I turn up my music and then hear someone banging on the door, and before I can get up, Amy opens it quickly, laughing. She's wearing a red dress and holding a small tote bag. "Oh my God, Dani, you need to come see what Kelly McGraw is wearing. She looks like a cross between a stripper and an astronaut."

I'm not in the mood and don't care what Kelly McGraw is wearing. "Yeah, I'm sort of busy here."

"Come on, Dani. You're going to turn into a swamp troll down here." She looks me up and down, shaking her head and quickly doing a makeover in her mind. She opens up the bag and produces not one, but two dresses from my closet. "You know you can't resist it. It's our last Mix-A-Lot!"

"Like a Last Supper?" I ask, smiling. OK, she's doing a good job turning me.

"Exactly. Without all the prophesying." She holds up the blue dress, making the decision for me.

"Ugh, I'm hungry though," I say, changing my clothes.

"You are a piece of work, Danielle Silver. Are you a toddler? You need a snack?" She's digging through the bag again, maybe for lipstick. A granola bar. She brought me a granola bar. I get on the blue dress, lace up my Doc Martens, and shove the whole granola bar into my mouth. "Let's do it," I say.

6

"I Wish"

"Do you listen to the same music as your parents?" Ms. Davis says, walking from the back of the classroom to the front, as we settle into class. Her tight black braids pulled back into a neat ponytail, she pulls out today's attendance sheet and hands it to Kelly in the front row.

Everyone laughs. The second week of class and Ms. Davis has hit her stride.

"As if," says Colin, grinning for attention. Oh, Colin, you have haunted me for three years. If I never had to see you again it would be too soon. Why did you have to pick this class anyway? I suffered with you through ninth-grade English, tenth-grade world history, eleventh-grade biology and homeroom, and now this.

"Sometimes they make me, but their music is pretty boring," says Harriet. I think of Dad and the car stereo.

"Right," Ms. Davis says. "When I was a kid, my mom used to listen to Dinah Washington on Friday nights when all I wanted was Stevie Wonder. I get it."

"Oh my God, when my mom drinks wine, she always listens to Frank Sinatra," says Harper. "It's awful."

Ms. Davis continues, "It's useful to approach art history as a series of generations. We think of certain artists as geniuses who moved progress along, but until fairly recently, generation after generation looked like, acted like, and painted like their forefathers. Change occurred really slowly. Rejection of your own culture wasn't a thing until everything started moving faster. Anyone know why?"

Oh, she's going to love my answer. I need to impress her so she'll write my recommendation, but so far, I haven't found a way to without seeming like I'm trying way too hard. I'll need to ask her soon, though, which means I better dazzle her this week. I raise my hand, but she doesn't see me. Colin raises his hand on the other side of the room and does his usual eager grunt, so she turns to him, "Yes, Colin?"

"The Industrial Revolution." He punctuates the last word like he's just cured cancer, like it's so obvious.

"Yes! Can anyone tell me why the Industrial Revolution impacted the world of art? Since that's what we're here for."

I raise my hand as fast as possible. She sees me and matches my enthusiasm, "Yes, Danielle!"

I know all of this from Arthur. "More people began earning money and wanting paintings in their homes. So there was a market, and new artists wanted to paint the world they knew, not what their parents' world looked like."

"Nicely summarized, but what other influences aside from the economy were at play at the outset of modern art?" she says, nodding. I can tell she's not really all that impressed. I really need her recommendation for RISD, and I'm not going to get it like this. Better up my game here.

Colin, again, beats me and everyone to the punch. Such a tool. "The advent of photography allowed people to see differently. The impressionists began a cycle of rebellion within visual art which then resulted in their obsolescence." Someone did the reading carefully.

"Well put, Colin," She looks at others in the room, realizing Colin and I are the only ones raising our hands. "Debbie, how do you think art goes from being a radical departure to the middle of the mainstream?" she asks.

"It gets old?" says Debbie.

Ms. Davis's face twists up, nodding slightly and trying to use this answer to keep the conversation moving. "Can anyone elaborate?"

"When enough people accept something, it becomes mainstream," says Kyle from the back without raising his hand, sneering at the final word like it was herpes. I turn to see him and smile. His eyeliner work is exquisite, and he lifts one eyebrow when he sees me.

Ms. Davis smiles and nods. "So, we're talking about the arc from radical to standard. Yes!" She claps her hands and moves on. OK, I need to get at least one more good answer to get onto her radar. Last year, apparently, when Molly Landsman asked her to write a recommendation, Ms. Davis said she was far too busy.

"What was radical can become standard when you add time and acceptance," Ms. Davis explains. "So now, a hundred years later, we see some boring old paintings, right? So. If we jump off from the impressionists, who can tell me where they see the history of modern art taking us? How do we go from Renoir to Jean-Michel Basquiat, or from Mary Cassatt to Cindy Sherman?"

Colin and I raise our hands at the exact same time. She calls on me.

"Well, the impressionists are a foundation for another generation. Each generation stands on the last one's shoulders. Within each one are the DNA of previous generations, and they tell the story of art history," I say. Pleased with myself, I sit back.

"Um, Ms. Davis, can I just say one more thing?" Colin again.

"Sure, Colin," she says, returning to her desk.

"While I get Danielle's point, I think Western art has mostly been told as the history of white European and American men making art. They've mythologized themselves as heroes, shaping how we see our own reality. But their story leaves out the stories of everyone else who influenced culture in the past century. Modern art leaves out a lot of nonwhite, nonmale artists." Where does he come up with this? Did he read ahead? He's totally right and, as usual, says everything I should have said. Ugh, Colin, you suck.

Ms. Davis takes a big breath in, nodding wholeheartedly. She claps once. "Yes, Colin, excellent point, and a very welcome and progressive take on this topic. Who tells our history can shape our present and future. So, this is actually a great segue." She walks over to her desk to grab a stack of paper.

I glance at Colin, who has the biggest shit-eating grin on his face I've ever seen. He really needs a punch in the nose.

"So, I want to introduce your semester project," Ms. Davis begins as a murmuring groan moves through the room. She looks up at us with a silent glare. "My dear students, do you honestly think you aren't going to have to work in this class? Come on now. Nobody needs to hear that." She passes out the sheets. "You will choose an artist from the past hundred years whose work speaks to you personally. As Colin just noted, artists of all kinds speak stories of worlds they know, imagine, or seek to create. Your task will be to find an artist whose work relates to some part of your own story and explore their art and its context. Bring ideas next time."

I walk up to her as everyone else rushes out.

"Hi, Ms. Davis. How's it going?" Maybe I start with some small talk and then dive into asking.

Looking at her watch, she doesn't respond. Instead, she says, "You know what, Danielle? I need to run to a meeting. Let's catch up next class, OK?" She throws her bag over her shoulder and heads toward the door.

Great.

I head to my next class, physics. Baby Keanu is here, as he has been since the first week of school. I haven't really been able to offer more than a quick hello and vague nodding. Every time we lock eyes, I get this wave of nausea and suddenly feel afraid I'm going to say something really dumb or actually vomit. And by now, every other girl at Baxter has their eyes all over him. He waves and I notice that he hasn't gotten any less gorgeous, and I wonder if there's anything at all about me that's genuinely attractive to him. It is possible I may not learn physics this year. I saw him a couple times these past few days but managed to run away like a dingbat before having to talk to him. As class ends, I see Tina Murray rush up to him to flirt by asking some physics-related question, so I make a quick escape. I can't compete with those pretty girls, even if I wanted to.

I grab another tuna sandwich in the lunchroom and find a sunny spot at the top of the staircase.

Plans get interrupted
Unexpected things happen
Rules change
People come and go, forget and ignore
Unreliable
Slippery
Like ice, mud, soap
But still, I need them
To help me find the exit from this place
I'm full of distraction
By that boy
And his face
Those lashes,
My word.

After lunch, I arrive early to advanced painting. It's a rainy day and thunder keeps rumbling closer, like a slow-moving train. I love being in this studio classroom when it's empty. The window gives me a perfect view of the storm.

Kyle shows up next. He sets his stuff near me. I still see traces of freshman Kyle, with his enormous wire-rimmed glasses and chubby fingers, like a child science teacher. Now, after a series of transformations, he has perfected a trademark sneer, keen fashion sense, and a veneer of cool rarely seen here.

"So, who are you going to research for art history class?" I ask him.

"Basquiat," says Kyle. I almost laugh. How does the work of a Black artist who was inspired by street art and James Baldwin and who died at twenty-eight of a drug overdose speak to Kyle, a rich white kid from Passaic, New Jersey? I don't ask though. Maybe I'm missing something.

Who am I to judge? Also, I've learned not to argue with Kyle. I prefer to stay on his good side.

"Cool," I respond.

"And you?"

"Undecided," I say. I actually have no idea.

"Cool," he says.

Mrs. Funk comes into the room, throwing her bag on her desk and quickly grabbing her apron. I love how she wears an apron like we're on a cooking show.

"Hello, Danielle and Kyle. How are we?"

Kyle looks at me and mouths, *The shoes*, with his eyes enormously wide. I look down and see her silver clogs catching the morning sun. I look back to Kyle who just puts his hand over his heart and mouths, *Love her*. I nod in agreement.

Mrs. Funk rifles through her desk as more students arrive. She always mutters to herself while she's doing things, narrating her tasks. "OK, somewhere, somewhere, I know I saw you just yesterday . . ." My money's on the class list. Baxter is strict about attendance, otherwise we'd probably all just sleep all day. If you have more than two tardies on your record you go straight to the top to see Headmaster Turner and someone calls your parents.

Kyle and I glance at each other and almost smile. Mrs. Funk pulls a fresh apricot out of a bag and eats it as she frantically searches her desk. I've been her student since ninth grade and she's what my father would call a "colorful character." Mrs. Funkelberg is about six inches shorter than me and has taught at Baxter for at least twenty years. I have no idea how old she is but she definitely dyes her hair. This year it's a lovely burnt orange. The thing about art class is that even as we make new things here all the time, there's a certainty about it—like, you know what you're getting with her and in this room. I have to admit that having this class year after year is better than a homeroom. It's like home.

"Ah-ha! Got you!" she says, lifting up a piece of paper.

Then she pulls an entire bag of apricots out of her tote and places them in a bowl in the center of the room.

We have a nice U shape of easels around our center platform which usually has either a still life or a model. Amy once modeled and she and I could not stop laughing. She never came back.

When we asked during the first week about Mr. Thorne, the teacher who didn't return, Mrs. Funk gave a long sigh and finally just nodded. It was clear she was not pleased about whatever happened. There's always an understood code of silence among teachers. Like we're not supposed to know what they really think, which is weird when I consider that they're teaching us to think.

"OK, everyone ready? Let's get started." She looks around the room and climbs up onto a stool. She looks again at what I assume is the attendance paper and I see a glimmer of worry in her face.

"Right, yes. All right, here we go." She looks around. "OK, well, so before we get started drawing today's still life, let's just get through a few announcements. As you probably have noticed, the timing for classes has shifted from previous years, so be sure to check your schedules and I will too! Apparently, the administration decided each period will be forty-three minutes so after-school activities can start earlier." She rolls her eyes as she shakes her head, which is exactly how we all feel because, for most Baxter students, after-school activities mean sports. I'm already drawing the apricots in my sketchbook because I feel we are wasting precious time.

"Next," Mrs. Funk continues, "we will, in the next couple of weeks, be moving our art room."

"Moving? Why?" asks Kyle.

Funk looks over the paper for what seems like the tenth time since she sat down and says, "It's unclear, Kyle. All I am told here is to give warning that the art room will be moved. Some major renovations happening in this building will make it impossible for us to have class here. So stay tuned."

"Fucking jocks," says Kyle under his breath.

I lean over to him and ask, "What are you talking about?"

"Obviously, the jocks are taking over the school." He heaves a big sigh matching the biggest eye roll I think he's ever made.

So much for my one stable thing. The space here just got smaller.

7

"Only You"

"Cool Ranch Doritos," I say definitively. At dinner, Amy and I play One Food: What's one food you'd live on forever?

"Gross. That powder is basically cancer dust," she says, shoveling green leaves into her mouth.

"It's seasoning. It's delicious dust that makes my mouth so happy. Where did you come from, not liking Doritos?" I ask.

Amy chooses broccoli. This girl and her antioxidants.

We laugh, just as the ogres roll past us. That's our name for Baxter's resident jersey-wearing, dick-joke-telling, girlfriend-using, test-cheating, paper-forging, body-odor-having douchebag bullies. In ninth grade Derek was this shy kid with pimples, obsessed with Dungeons & Dragons. Now he's six foot two and resembles a truck with arms. He winks at us as he whispers, "Lezzos," like he knows some secret about us. He laughs and slaps one of his buds on the butt.

Amy and I do what we usually do, which is to wrap our arms around each other like we're a couple. Since sophomore year when we went to the spring dance together, we've been playing this game with Derek. He calls us names and tells people we're secret lesbians, and we act it out, big time. Even though Amy's been going out with Noah for two years, and Derek totally knows him, he still believes he's insulting us. At this point, honestly, it's boring. It's just too easy to make his ugly face twist up into an ugly, gross knot.

"What would Derek do if he ever actually met a gay person?" Amy asks as he walks away.

"Maybe his head will explode? I mean, we can dream, right?" I say.

On my way to the studio, I check the mail, and finally, what I've been waiting for has arrived. My RISD application. In a gray envelope. Ordinary and easily mistaken for junk mail, it's here. I thought it would come two weeks ago, but I still have six weeks.

I head to my studio. It's practice time in the gym, and I hear whistles blowing and coaches yelling as I walk into my messy lair and shut it all out. I read the entire application, looking for the work sample section, and read the two sentences:

All applicants must submit ten to twenty images as a portfolio. These can be a collection of works or a singular project.

That's pretty vague, but I guess that's a good thing.

Arthur showed me that being an artist isn't about being cool or irresponsible or crazy. He told me it was more like being a monk or a scholar. A real artist, a *true* artist, needs to live apart from the rest of the world, to live differently.

Homework and RISD application. That's my focus. I put on my Yaz tape from a few years ago, which always keeps me going.

Drawings. Lines. Pen making marks. Thick bulky lines or delicate traces? Heavy color or drippy washes? The options keep unfolding, and I cannot always find where I think my center should be. Like picking a hairstyle or what shoes to wear or who to be friends with, how do you know you're making the right decision?

Working on a new drawing of the library staircase: the twists in the wooden banister, just so, needs a thicker line, and the shadowed stairs need more layers of darkness. I find my fine-tipped pens and start the details. It's painstaking, but I like how it's coming out. I'm distracted by a sudden thirst.

Walking down the hall to the water fountain to fill my water jar, I see Marco standing there like a commercial for himself—sweaty, sparkly, and gorgeous.

He's gulping down water. His eyes get wide, and he waves his hand as he finishes drinking.

"Hi," I say, wondering what was happening. Why is he in the basement? Is he lost? Was he at practice and felt my aura through the walls? I'm insane.

"Danielle, I found you!" He smiles. Wait, did he just say what I think he said? His teeth are enormous and bright and stupefying. He backs away to let me fill my water bottle and when I turn to go back to my studio, he skips to meet me, walking alongside.

I can't tell if he's following me or what. I stand outside my open studio door, and he looks past me into the studio like I'm some crafty witch and he's at the threshold of my cave of wonders.

"This is it, huh?" he asks with so much enthusiasm.

"This is it, yes. Um . . . What brings you to the basement? I mean, I am guessing by this look you've got happening that you're in the middle of football practice, maybe?" I look at his tight pants and giant shoulder pads, trying not to laugh. Sports uniforms are quite silly out of context.

"Football, yeah. We have a break and so I came down here to get some water 'cause there was a long line at the outdoor fountain and also you said you had a studio down here. So I asked around where I might find a girl with short black hair who paints. Someone told me your studio is down here with a picture of David Bowie in the door window, so here I am. Also, I was wondering if you'd like to study together for the test?"

"What test?" I have no idea what he's talking about, and he seems to note this immediately. It takes me another moment to absorb that he's just told me that he, in fact, remembered everything I told him weeks ago in the mail room and wants to hang out with me.

"The physics test. Next Monday?" He says all this with a look of hope that maybe some of these words would spark some familiarity in my mind, which they do not. "I take a lot of notes but I think it's easier to study with someone."

I realize I need to respond, and I've just been gazing at his perfect face. "Study. Yes, I will need to do that also." Why am I speaking like a robot? Oh my God, this guy's face is like a sculpture by an old Italian master, where all the proportions are perfect. Like Michelangelo's *David*, only he's not naked. Dammit, now I'm thinking about him naked. Stop it, Danielle! I very much want to touch his perfect lips but that would be super inappropriate.

He is just looking at me. Is there paint on my forehead? I need to say something else. Like it's my line in this scene and he's waiting for his cue. "Yeah, OK, um, sure. Study. Yes. Later? My room?" Oh my God, why did I just invite him to my room? He can't come to my dorm. He's a boy. "The Shaw Lounge. Did I say my room? I meant the Shaw Lounge." God, Danielle, get yourself together!

"Oh! Yeah, great. Tomorrow, seven fifteen? In the lounge with the candlestick!"

"Ha, Clue. Nice." I smile. He's funny too? How can you be that cute and funny and nice?

"Right. It's a date!" Then he frowns, "I mean, not a date but we have a plan. It's a plan! Later, Danielle." He waves, disappearing up the stairs.

Amy is going to flip out.

The next day is excruciatingly slow. I watch every clock. During English, I draw his nose, as well as I can remember. Over and over.

Dinner takes ages—why are lines always slower when you have so much to do aside from stand in a line? I inhale my plate of food and try not to look like I'm running when I leave the cafeteria.

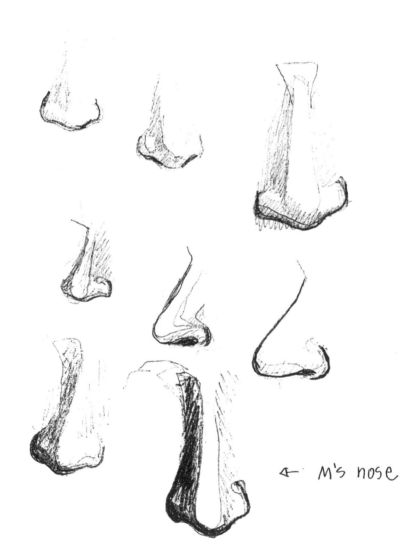

M's nose

After dinner I take a shower, shave my legs, and put on that orange shirt that Amy says makes my boobs look cute. We find some lipstick but decide against other makeup so as to seem, you know, casual, about my hanging out with the cutest boy in the history of the world. Looking in the mirror, I remember how he was scanning my face like he was looking for something. Do I need to pluck my eyebrows? Is a zit coming out on my forehead? I really can't tell what I look like. Can anyone?

Amy sends me off with a military salute. "Don't forget, you're the rock star. Let him work a little."

"But he's so . . ." I stare off into space.

"I know, Dan, he's a dish, but you must keep your shit together. Just 'cause he's got a cute face and an amazing body does not necessarily mean he's a good person who is worth your time. Let him show you who he is."

In the lounge, I grab the green sofa and start unpacking my notebook.

"Danielle?" I immediately hear a voice from across the room. Marco is standing on the other end, grinning. He's wearing a dusty blue button-up shirt tucked into his perfectly faded jeans. He got here before I did. It's seven ten. This is a boy who gets places early and tucks in his shirts. Am I hallucinating? "I'll come to you," he says, gathering all his stuff. As he rushes across the red-and-orange carpet, past wood-paneled walls and bulletin boards full of school notices, all I can think about are his broad shoulders. Keep it together, Danielle.

He sits on the armchair across from me, keeping his distance politely.

"You ready?" he asks.

"Sure am." I try to sound cool.

He opens an enormous three-ring binder that has, what seems like, thirty different colored tabs. Each, apparently, correlated to a different subject.

"OK, physics, physics, physics . . ." he mumbles, flipping past green, purple, and yellow tabs.

"That's some binder you've got there, Marco. Do you use that for everything?" I don't know why I just asked that. Clearly, he does. Why can't I just be like, "So, physics, huh?" My notes, on the other hand, are randomly stuffed into the attached folder of the Five Star spiral notebook I use for every subject so far. I am really not on his level.

He smiles. Geez, I hope it's a real smile and not an "I'm uncomfortable, but I've been taught to be nice" smile.

"Yeah, it's my life, really," he finally says.

"Well, OK, then. What color is physics?"

"Blue, well, light blue. Kind of turquoise." He runs his hand down a line of tabs that progressed through the color wheel. "Never mind, sorry. I got it." He opens the binder like a detective unlocking some mysterious clue.

"Cyan," I offer before I can stop myself. "That's the paint name for turquoise."

He raises his eyebrows. "OK, cool. I didn't know that." He seems pleased to learn something new.

"Speaking of physics, did you know that all colors are just reflections of light?" I ask him. Do I sound smart or pretentious?

"Yeah, the spectrum is just different lengths or something, right?"

"Yes! Like, an apple looks red, but it's just how the light interacts with it. Red bounces back to meet our eyes."

"Wait, did you take physics already? How do you know all these things about color, Danielle?"

"My uncle Arthur taught me all about it, and then in art class, you learn about warm and cool colors, and the color wheel is really just math: percentages, proportions, opposites." I'm rambling and staring out the window at a streetlight making the fall leaves throw shadows on the sidewalk.

I look back at his face, and his head is tilted, eyebrows raised, waiting. "Wow," he finally says, once I dart my eyes back and forth to let him know I was actually finished. Then he shakes his head and looks back into his giant binder.

"So, the first lab we did was about force. Equal and opposing. Remember that one with the weights hanging off the table? It was, like, the second week of class, I think."

"Right," I say, flipping through my own notebook which is a maze of words I heard in class: classic laws of motion: velocity, thrust, drag, torque, and a doodle of a cat for no reason I can recall.

He reads to me, "OK, let's review: objects at rest will remain at rest, and objects in motion will remain in motion at the same velocity . . ."

"Unless the object is acted on by an external force," I finish.

He looks up at me, grinning and nodding.

"I remember that by thinking about tipping a canvas while the paint is dripping. Exerting force," I say, not sure if it sounds cool or just obvious.

He continues, "The second object exerts an equal and opposite force on the first."

"Right, complementary colors turn brown when you mix them together: red and green, blue and orange. Opposites in equal parts make a neutral color."

"Nice!" he says, raising his hand across the table between us. We high-five. Does he actually like studying? Do I?

We get into relativity, even though it's not on the test. The spinning of the earth and how we perceive motion, time, and space.

"It's like one-point perspective," I say.

"What's that?" he asks.

I pull out my sketchbook and find the next blank page and make a dot in the middle of the paper.

"That's the vanishing point. Eventually, everything goes there," I say pointing to the middle of the drawing.

He looks confused. "Everything goes there and vanishes?"

"Kind of. Well, it doesn't vanish like a magic show, but according to our perception, yeah, it disappears," I say. Then I draw lines that meet in the middle, at the vanishing point, and some vertical lines to make it look like a street. Marco stares.

"Close to you, things are large, then they get smaller and smaller as they go farther away."

His eyes are wide, and then he gets it.

"Relativity!" he shouts.

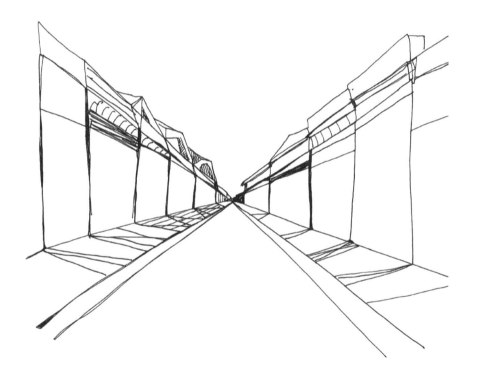

I nod. "Exactly."

"Your uncle taught you that?" he asks.

"Yes, when I was seven."

"Lucky kid."

I look at him and my stomach flips like a lulling ocean tide.

As he recites notes about Newton's laws of motion and universal gravitation, I imagine holding his hand or resting my head on his shoulder while we're on a date at the movies. He's probably a really good kisser. Sometimes people just seem like they're good kissers. His perfect lips plump, moving over his teeth, his tongue every so often licking the top corner of his mouth. I just want to . . .

"Uh, Danielle . . . You want to take a break? Or call it a night?"

I blink hard. "What? Oh, yeah. I guess so. It must be so late. Is it like midnight?"

"It's 8:32," he says, adjusting the Casio watch on his perfect wrist.

"Wow! Really? Um, yeah, I might need to pause and let my brain, you know, digest all this velocity."

"Cool." He closes his big binder but doesn't get up to go.

Is there more? Is he going to kiss me? Why am I sweating? Can he tell I'm sweating? I shift my weight on the love seat and try to move into a more comfortable position, but I'm pretty sure I look like a dog trying to settle down over and over in the same spot.

"Hey, are you OK?" he asks.

"Yeah," I say, finally sitting still.

"So, Danielle, do you know where you want to go next year?" He's staring at me, eyes squinting. I try to avoid direct eye contact.

"Yeah, well, my dream is to go to RISD." His eyebrows squinch up in a question mark. "Rhode Island School of Design. It's, like, the best art school in the country, and my uncle Arthur went there."

"Well, that's great, Danielle. I hope your dreams come true."

"How 'bout you?" I ask, remembering what Amy said about letting him reveal himself.

"Oh, I'm applying to Penn, Temple, Drexel, and, um, Swarthmore. Trying to stay close to home."

"Wait, are you from Philly!?" I ask, recognizing all those local schools.

"Yes! Are you?"

I nod, suddenly feeling more OK with this conversation.

"What part?" he asks.

"Center City. You?"

"Delco, hon," he says with a thick Philly accent which makes almost anyone sound like a nosy neighbor standing on her stoop talking shit about your cousin. "So, youse all fancy, I s'pose? You grow up in one of them nice brownstones?"

I smile. "Not that fancy, no. My parents just hated the suburbs."

"Well, you go to this fancy school, don'tcha?"

"Yeah, I guess. But so do you!"

"Oh, hon, I'm on a sports scholarship for football and wrestling, that's how come I gotta be at practice all the time." His accent was impeccable and terrifying at the same time.

"You came here to play sports? Didn't they have teams at your old school?"

He shifts how he's sitting, like the chair suddenly doesn't fit, and drops the accent. "Well, my dad got a job with lots of travel, so he needed to figure out where I'd sleep at night, so he found a boarding school with a wrestling scholarship. I was varsity for wrestling and football at my school in Philly."

"Parents divorced too?" I ask.

"Nope, my mom passed away a few years ago."

"Oh, I'm sorry," I say.

"Thanks!" he says way more enthusiastically than he needs to. I guess he's used to having to respond to *I'm sorry* which is weird to say cause it's not like I caused his mother's death, but everyone says *I'm sorry* when someone dies. I decide not to ask more. Sometimes people don't want to talk about death. I change the subject.

"So, sports, huh? At least you have something to fall back on. If you don't end up pursuing a career in physics, I mean, you can always be a wrestler!"

"Right, good point." He smiles, and then he miraculously says,

"Well, maybe we'll take the bus down to Philly together sometime?"
Amy once advised me that if a guy finds excuses to make plans, he's into
you. Could this be that?

"Sure, yeah, that would be super-duper," I say, stretching my neck
and shoving things into my bag. "Well, Marco, I thank you for your
kind assistance. It was a true honor to explore the physical world with
you tonight."

"Anytime, Danielle. Really. Let me know if you want a refresher the
night before. I think you're gonna rock the test."

'Cause I'm a rock star, I think to myself.

Is it too much to hope to think that maybe?
Maybe you?
Maybe I?
Maybe us?
Too much to feel that your hands might touch my hands
And your eyes might look into mine,
To silently tell me something sweet,
Something secret,
Something real?
I don't think I've ever seen anything as beautiful as you.

8

"Sometimes It Snows in April"

As class ends, Ms. Davis turns off the slide projector, turns on the lights, and waves everyone out. I've kicked this conversation down the road for four weeks already. It's now or never. I walk up to her desk, determined. I waited the past two classes because, well, I'm sometimes a dopey coward.

"Hello, Danielle, what's the latest?" she asks as she writes something in her teacher calendar and begins to pack up her things.

"Oh, hey, I liked those postimpressionists. Weird stuff."

"Yeah, what did you think of Rousseau? With the creepy animals?" she asks.

"They will haunt my dreams, I'm not going to lie." I laugh and am relieved to see her smile. "So, Ms. Davis, I wanted to ask if you might be willing to write me a recommendation for a college application."

She raises her eyebrows. "I guess it's that time of year. Which schools are you applying to, Danielle?"

"RISD," I tell her.

"And?"

"And . . . would you please write me a recommendation?" I say, overdoing the politeness.

"No, I mean, where else are you applying?" She smiles at my misunderstanding.

"Oh! Just to RISD, for early admission," I explain.

"Well, it's a very selective college with a limited number of spaces. We can't be certain you'll be admitted, right?" She sounds surprisingly like my mom, suddenly. The traffic light in my head goes from green to yellow.

"I guess," I say, hiding my sudden hurt at her skepticism.

"It's just more typical in the process to give yourself a few options, just in case," she explains. "I'm sure the college counseling office can give you advice."

"I know. It's just that I've always planned to go there. That's why I'm applying early."

"Well, I applied early to college too. I get it. Sometimes you just know in your bones, right?" As she talks, she pulls the small white framed slides from the slide projector and carefully places them into a box, checking that each is facing the right way. "I think I can write for you, but I'm pretty busy right now, as I'm submitting my own graduate school thesis in a few weeks. But I'm curious, why RISD?" she asks.

"It's the best art school in the country. And since I was little, my uncle Arthur told me stories about it. He said they taught him how to be an artist and that's what I want to do too."

"So, your uncle Arthur is an artist?" she asks, interested.

"Was. He died last year. Arthur Dreyfus. He's sort of famous."

"Wow, I'll have to look him up, but I'm sorry for your loss. Was he sick or was it sudden?"

"Both actually. He died from AIDS, but it happened fast," I blurt out, forgetting I am at Baxter. I suddenly feel a tightness, a fear I said too much, and she might retract, judge, or dismiss me.

Instead, her whole body softens. Her head falls sideways, in a sympathetic, defeated way. Her face grows kind and sad. She simply says, "Danielle, I'm really sorry."

Her tone sinks fast into me with some deep knowledge, and I want to cry. But I don't. This is not that conversation. I need to get her to say yes, and I cannot do that if I'm a wreck. I try another direction.

"Would you maybe want to see some of my artwork?"

She looks pleased with me, finally. "Of course, Danielle. I'd be happy to take a look. Is it all in the art room?"

"Actually, it's in the gym."

"You are full of surprises." She looks at her watch and seems to be doing some calculations in her head before saying, "I'm free now if that works for you?"

"Sure!" I say, gathering my bag and heading into the hallway with her.

Outside, we walk over falling leaves, and Ms. Davis asks me who my favorite artists are.

"Well, I like Caravaggio, Ingres, Van Eyck, and Van Gogh. I also like Robert Rauschenberg, Eva Hesse, and Cy Twombly." I could go on and on, but I don't. I stop talking.

"A nice range there, Danielle. Old, newer, clean, messy. Great choices. It seems your uncle taught you well to appreciate art giants. Did Arthur ever take you to galleries?"

"He did. Sometimes we'd take the train to New York, which has a lot more galleries than Philadelphia, where I'm from. We saw a Cindy Sherman show at a gallery in SoHo. We saw a show about books last year at the ICA at Penn, and a Jasper Johns show at the Philadelphia Museum of Art."

"Oh, I love the Tanner there. One of my favorites," she says dreamily. I nod and smile big because I know she's talking about *The Annunciation* by Henry Ossawa Tanner, an amazing depiction of the Virgin Mary being visited by the angel Gabriel, but instead of a man with wings and a halo, Gabriel is this bright, glowing mass of light.

"I love that painting too," I say. "I like how Mary's painted like a shy, almost mortified teenager."

"Exactly!" she says. "Have you decided who you will study for our class project? I'm just curious, now that I know of your art history knowledge."

"Well, I was thinking about Helen Frankenthaler or Eva Hesse. I'm sort of interested in how women made their way as artists in what was totally a male-dominated art world."

"Still is," Ms. Davis mutters under her breath. "What about a young artist working now?"

"I haven't thought of anyone I can relate to, I guess."

"Well, if you want some suggestions, I could offer a few . . . maybe after I see your work?" she says in a sweet tone.

"Sure," I say, wondering who she'll suggest as we walk into the gym.

"Where are we going, anyway?" Ms. Davis asks, looking along the hallway walls, like my art will be there.

"Downstairs. I have a studio space in the basement."

"Wow. How did you manage that?" She sounds impressed.

Pointing to myself I say, "Squeaky wheel."

"Good for you," she says quietly, like a secret.

As soon as we walk in, I'm horrified by how I've left the place. "Oh, Ms. Davis, I'm really sorry. I didn't know you were coming so I haven't cleaned in a while." I move magazines and CDs off the chair and clear chip bags and soda cans into the trash.

"Danielle, it's fine. I know this was last minute. I just want to see what you've been working on, and what you're thinking about for your application portfolio."

Showing people my artwork can be nerve-wracking. I watch them, looking at what I made, wondering if they are having some sort of epiphany. And then feeling like a real asshole for thinking my work is so amazing that someone would have an epiphany. It seems like a lot of people have a hard time really putting into words how art makes them feel. So you get, "Wow, this is amazing," which sort of means nothing, or "God you're so good at painting" or—the most common—"Cool," with some vague nodding. Or they think it sucks and are too polite to tell me. It's rarely satisfying to witness, but Arthur always said it comes with the territory.

Classes are different. In art class, the teacher makes people answer specific questions or gets the person who made it to talk about their materials or their process. Then you start a conversation about something and move past nodding and "Wow." Having my art history teacher here is something in between the two.

As we look at the wall of paintings and drawings, I explain my ideas.

"These are a series of drawings of interior spaces at Baxter . . . And these ones are me attempting abstract painting." I point to squares of paint, brown neutrals smeary and thick on small canvases.

"You show a lot of promise, Danielle. So, how does this speak to any larger issues you might be facing? I imagine you're thinking about leaving Baxter, forging a new world for yourself," she pauses, "or perhaps thinking about your uncle's death? I sense the notions of absence here with these empty spaces."

I'm quiet but feel pressure to say something impressive. "I've been thinking about absence, yeah. And about change too, I suppose." I wish I had more eloquence to share.

Ms. Davis nods at the canvases and finally says, "I love these shades. So warm and complex. And your lines in some of these drawings are just exquisite."

She looks around the room and sees Arthur's Post-its.

"Bravery breeds creativity," she reads out loud. "The Post-it's are wonderful. Where are they from?"

"My uncle," I say, smiling. "He made them for me to put up wherever I work."

"He would have written you this recommendation, wouldn't he?" she asks, softly.

I nod.

"All right." She turns back to my drawings and shifts gears, tapping her finger to her lip. "I wonder how much of what you're doing here is about losing someone. All this emptiness. Most artists use their own lives as a source to make their work. They are moved by what they're living through and the questions they have."

"Right. I guess that's why I'm not sure what artist to choose to research for class. If we are supposed to relate to them somehow, I don't know an artist who is wondering about being a teenager in 1991, thinking about death, AIDS, and loss."

"Well, you might find some of that, if not an exact mirror of you. There's an artist named David Wojnarowicz you might appreciate. I see you have some writing up here." She points to a poem I wrote and pinned to the wall. "He's also an artist who uses writing. And he's very interested in AIDS and politics. He sees his art as a platform to spark conversation, to raise awareness. Might be interesting to you."

"Is he the guy who sewed his lips shut?" I ask, remembering an image I saw in an art magazine. It is hard to forget that image.

"Yes! It's a photograph titled *Silence=Death*, which is the phrase used by ACT UP. Maybe you've seen it on posters or elsewhere?"

Robert's T-shirt. Yes!

"Yeah, sure. Did he come up with that phrase?"

"No, that was a group of graphic designers who were making posters early on in the AIDS activism scene. It just caught on, and Wojnarowicz quoted it."

How does Ms. Davis know so much about contemporary artists dealing with AIDS? I need to go find that copy of *Artforum* now. It might be here in my studio somewhere. I have a whole box of them. Hopefully, I haven't lost it.

Ms. Davis picks up a CD case on the table by my paintbrushes and sighs. "Prince's *Parade*. I love this record." She takes a deep breath, seeming to remember something as she tilts her head and reads the song list on the back. She nods and says, "'Sometimes It Snows in April' is one of my favorites."

I remember the song. It's sad and beautiful.

"Well, Danielle, I'm thrilled you allowed me in here. And I'd be honored to write you a recommendation. Bring me the form and an addressed envelope when you can. Deadline is the middle of November, right?"

"Yes. And thank you!"

"Anyone coming for Parents' Day tomorrow?" she asks, collecting her things to go.

"My dad's coming. I think you maybe met him a couple of years ago when I was in your world history class? He loved that class."

"Oh, sure. How can I forget Mr. Silver? He gave me a run for my money on Maximilien Robespierre." She laughs as she heads out the door. "OK, I'll be ready for him. See you both tomorrow."

9
"Whatta Man"

Dad arrives after second period, looking spiffy in a yellow polo shirt and a baby blue sweater. He brings me a goodie bag from Di Bruno Bros.: rosemary crackers, candied walnuts, and chocolate-covered raisins. As we walk to my third-period class together, I notice he's limping again. Just a little. Maybe he twisted his ankle? I'll ask him later.

In place of fourth period today, we all head to the gym for a special assembly. On the way there, we see Marco, and I introduce him to Dad before he dashes off to get into his uniform. Dad turns to me with his jaw dropped once Marco's gone. "Major cute," he says. I roll my eyes but deep down I am in total agreement.

The assembly is like a redo of the first one a few weeks ago, but this time for the parents so it's completely packed. Somehow a military parade comes to mind. Each sport team marches out in their uniforms, walking between two lines of cheerleaders, and the headmaster gives a maniacally enthusiastic speech about the glory of competition. I want to barf. Dad leans over to me and says, "Are we at the North Korean Olympics?"

I shake my head, "I honestly have no idea what is happening. I tend to zone out during these things. Thankfully, someone bought me this . . ." I say, taking out my sketchbook.

"Why didn't you tell me to bring a book? Do these pep assemblies happen often?" Dad asks, looking around slightly suspiciously.

"I think they're trying to raise money and, you know, win everything," I reply flatly.

"Geez, Baxter is really changing," he says, dumbfounded.

The cheerleaders spell out B-A-X-T-E-R and jump up and down. Then all the teams begin chanting together: "Baxter pride, strong and true—Baxter promise full of hope—Baxter triumph heart and home."

"Yikes," I mutter so only Dad can hear.

He checks his watch, eyes wide, as bored as I am. "Is it lunch yet?"

An hour later I'm sitting in the cafeteria with Dad as Marco and Amy join us. Marco's father has to travel for work, and Amy's parents are on a bicycle trip in Spain. So I share Dad. We sit in the corner of the cafeteria at lunch and discuss:

The Treaty of Versailles: Amy just finished a paper about how the treaty's harsh treatment of Germany left a bitter legacy.

Newton's first law of motion: "Every object," says Marco, "in a state of uniform motion tends to remain in that state of motion unless an external force is applied to it."

Dad replies, "Ain't it the truth?"

Thanksgiving: Amy is going to her great-aunt Paulie's house on the Upper West Side of Manhattan. Amy says she was once a vaudeville dancer. "The food is terrible, but her stories are amazing." Apparently, Aunt Paulie had a great love affair with Charlie Chaplin. "No one knows if it's true, but we don't care."

Then Marco tells us about his big family and all the Cuban food they eat on Thanksgiving. "Basically, we eat pork instead of turkey." When Dad learns that Marco lives in Philly he immediately invites him over for dessert at Thanksgiving.

Music: Dad asks us what music we're listening to, and Amy mentions Salt-N-Pepa. Dad cannot fathom that there is a band named for table spices. Amy, Marco and I sing a verse of "Whatta Man."

Oyster crackers: I ask, "Are they made of oysters or supposed to resemble them?" We debate this for what seems an excessive amount of time.

Dad has a particular talent for not treating me or my friends like kids, but just like people. And Marco is completely in Dad's sway as soon as Dad asks him about his family and his interests.

After Marco leaves for class, Dad looks at me with his mouth hanging to the floor and says, "Wow, Dani, I like this one." I don't even know where to start with this, so I just smile. I mean, my dad talking to me about boys is kind of beyond what I can handle. I cannot find the words.

Suddenly, angry voices carry from the other side of the cafeteria, where Marco is dumping his tray into the trash and walking out faster than usual. Derek and Donald are standing near him and turn to watch him go, flopping their hands in his direction, but I can't quite make out what they're saying. Mr. George, my English teacher last year, goes over and talks to them, pointing with his finger, eyes wide, face red, by which time Marco is gone. Everyone is staring, and Dad has noticed too. Then Mr. George finally walks off quickly, and Derek and his sidekick turn to each other and laugh and walk across the cafeteria, passing us.

"What a faggot," Derek says loud enough for us to hear. Donald just laughs.

I sit frozen as my head begins to burn with rage. They've already stormed out the door, but my eyes are still fixed on the spot. Dad, though, seems unfazed. He simply takes his napkin and dabs the corners of his mouth, as if to rise above this juvenile display of homophobic nonsense. I'm stunned and horrified he heard that. Also, I'm scared of what they said to Marco and embarrassed that such shitheads go to my school. I want to scream, and I want to cry and turn back the earth so that it never happened. But nothing seems to come out of my mouth. Did Derek run out of people to bully, so he found fresh new meat? Why Marco? I mean, it's one thing to call me a lesbian; he barely knows me. But Marco is like a super jock. Maybe Derek feels threatened by a new senior on the football team.

Dad finally places his napkin on his tray and smiles at us, raising his eyebrows. "OK kids, what's next?" He is a master of this, moving on. Sometimes it's infuriating, but other times, it's exactly what is needed. In one fell swoop, he's saying we're all above it, and the time has come to get along with our day. Amy nods, approving of my dad's directive, and we get up to clear our plates. I am not so quick to recover. My feet are dead weight; there is a volcano in my gut, and I'm really hoping it doesn't erupt.

We finally get outside, and I feel a reset. I'm grateful for fresh air and a change of scenery as I try to shake off Derek's actions. Amy leaves for class, and Dad walks with me to my studio, which I cleaned last night, especially for him.

All across the wall, I've hung paintings with smeared textures and brown squares. But Dad knows me and he knows art. And it never feels like he's scared to talk about it.

"So why the neutrals? Are you referencing nature or abstract expressionism or something?"

"I guess I felt like bold colors were too decisive. I mean, I've been thinking about how life is sort of a mush of confusing things. I put together complementary colors to make these brown tones—like the good and bad all mixed up leave you with these softer, richer colors to sort of swim through."

"Something comforting in combining opposites, maybe? Like they get along somehow?"

"Yeah, I like that. Ms. Davis said perhaps I was thinking about loss and death. I told her about Arthur and how he died."

Dad looks at the floor. Either consumed by this thought or completely distracted. He doesn't say anything except, "Yes. Well, perhaps that's something to consider." Something about his tone feels weird.

Dad checks his watch and informs me I have five minutes to get to class. He's not joining me; he says he needs to go make some calls. "Frankie's at six?" he says.

"Yes, sir!" Picking up my bag, we walk out into the chilly afternoon.

"I know sometimes you invite your friends, but how about tonight it's just us?"

"Oh, OK, sure." I think I did ask Amy, but I'll just tell her I made a mistake.

"Perfect. See you then, Bunny." He kisses my cheek lightly. "Go learn things!"

10

"O mio babbino caro"

Uncle Frankie's is not as crowded as usual. I'm already salivating over the thought of the lasagna. As I walk in, I hear a soaring opera soprano sing like she's flying through the sky to dive to her death.

I arrive before Dad, which is possibly an all-time first. Dad is always early. He used to make us get to the movies forty-five minutes early, and we'd just sit in the empty theater. They seat me at a corner table.

Dad walks in five minutes late, irritated by the existence of cars and traffic and other people. He is not his normal composed self. My stomach tightens, and I scan my mind for what I might have done to make him angry. Should I have picked a different place? Is he upset that I told Ms. Davis about Arthur's death? Was he covering it up all day and now he's going to let me have it? He's always been a master at shoving his anger down when it's inconvenient and then unleashing it when he can maintain control. But he doesn't really seem controlled now.

We sit down, and he is quiet. There is something unsettling about how he is studying the menu. He always gets the lobster ravioli. He smiles at me, finally.

The waitress takes our order, and when she walks away, he looks at me and takes a long breath in and then a long breath out. Then his face goes down as a clown goes from happy to sad. But slower. More like he can't help it. He can't pretend anymore.

"I'm so sorry, Danielle." What? Why is he sorry? I thought I did something wrong and now he's apologizing? "Honey. I'm so sorry, but I have to tell you something."

I suddenly remember, in my bedroom at age ten, my parents telling me and Jake that they were getting divorced. But that already happened. And then how he told us he was coming out of the closet. That already happened too. My heart starts pounding.

"Danielle, when we talked about Arthur's illness after the unveiling, you asked me if I'd tell you if I was HIV positive."

No. No. No. My heart thuds so hard it actually hurts.

"I wasn't honest with you."

No . . . No . . . No . . .

"I am, honey. I'm HIV positive."

Here it is. This hard, icy fact. He *was* limping. Was that from HIV?

"Danielle?" He puts his hand on my hand.

My mind races: When did you find out? Were you lying to me then? How did you get it? What am I supposed to tell people? Are you going to die? Everyone dies from this, right? Everyone dies. You are limping. Why are you limping?

"But . . . you said you were fine," I say finally. "You said you'd tell me. Are you? I mean, do you have AIDS? Is that what you're saying to me?" I try to keep my voice quiet.

"There is a virus in my blood." He speaks calmly, like when I skinned my knee when I was little and he wanted me to calm down. But now instead of wailing out loud, it's all just swelling up inside me. "The HIV virus is related to AIDS, and when you have the virus, you are considered 'HIV positive.'" He takes a deep breath, then he says, "There's no way to get rid of the virus. Having AIDS is a later stage. I'm not there at this point."

"I just don't . . . I just . . ." I don't even know what to ask. He's holding my hand. Should I be touching his hand? Of course, it's OK. I know it's not contagious that way, and I suddenly feel guilty even wondering that.

My words sit in the air, foggy clouds sagging with their own weight. I wish they would blow away, but they don't.

"I am HIV positive," he says, "but I am not sick. I may live to be a hundred." He says this last part like he's trying to convince both of us of something he clearly doesn't believe.

"And no, you cannot get it from me by holding my hand. It's OK." I quickly look down at my hands, which are back on my side of the table.

"I know," I whisper, still not moving.

Since I still can't form a sentence, he explains his T cell count. "They're good cells, the white blood cells, the fighters that keep away infections. The more you have, the better. But those are the cells that HIV kills. It's a virus. As the HIV gets worse," he explains, "the number of T white blood cells declines. When the T cell count eventually drops below 200, a person is diagnosed with AIDS. A normal range for T cells is 500 to 1500. My T cell count is 650. Good, but not great."

"How long have you known?" I ask.

"Two years," he confesses after a long pause.

I do the math. He has known for 730 days, and he didn't tell me. I squeeze my eyes shut to keep from screaming. For 730 days he chose not to tell me this.

"I didn't want you to worry. I'm not really sick, so you'd sort of be worrying about nothing."

"Nothing? What? I mean, it's not nothing, Dad. I don't understand why you wouldn't tell me."

"Well, Danielle, I also . . ." He pauses and looks down at the table. "I didn't want you to be ashamed of me."

"Ashamed of you? I'm your daughter. How could I be ashamed of you?"

He just looks at me with a sad smile.

"It's been a lot for you." He begins to explain, "The divorce, my coming out. Then losing Arthur. You've been so accepting of me and all the changes you've had to endure. But this. I know it's heavy and I know you'll have questions and feelings."

I don't know what to say.

He continues, "Come on, honey, you must know how this disease is judged and people living with it are ostracized. I didn't want you to judge me or feel like you had to protect me from other people."

"So, what changed your mind? Did something happen?"

"Well, I've had a lot of friends get sick the past few years, and some have died without ever sharing their diagnosis, like Arthur. It just seemed like such an awful, lonely road. And after I saw how much it hurt you that you didn't know about Arthur, I guess I didn't want to do that to you too. You mean the world to me, and ever since I came out of the closet, I've tried to be honest with myself and with the people I love."

He takes a big sip of water and rearranges the silverware on the table just as the waitress delivers his Caesar salad. He watches as she walks away, out of earshot.

"I thought I was being a good parent by not telling you. Not burdening you with something heavy and horrible." He takes another deep breath and then continues, "But after Arthur's unveiling, I realized it was selfish; it isn't fair to you. You're not a kid anymore. I know that as much as you need me, I need you back right now. I don't know what will happen, but I'd rather be able to talk about it with you."

He starts to cry. I realize there are already tears on my face.

We're holding hands again.

"I'd rather that too." I finally say.

"Plus, hospital food is disgusting, so I'm going to need you to go out and get me something delicious from Di Bruno Bros."

"Wait, are you going into the hospital?" My stomach drops.

"Oh no, darling, not today. I mean, I hope not." He smiles, bashful at his attempt at a joke. "But it is hard to tell with HIV. Some people are able to shake things off, and others aren't. There are different strains. Every person's response to the virus is different. I don't know what will happen."

"Did you tell Mom?" I ask, assuming he did.

"No, but you can tell her if you want. I mean, if it helps you in any way. I don't mind. But I don't need her to know for my own sake."

Am I supposed to actually decide that for the two of them? That can't be what's actually happening. I cannot really process that on top of everything else this instant.

"Um, OK," I say, still not sure he actually just said that. "Does Jake know?"

"Not yet. I'm going up to Massachusetts tomorrow to have a similar talk."

He told me first. It almost makes up for not telling me about Arthur.

The conversation pauses as the waitress asks if we need water refills. I watch the candlelight flicker through the glasses, ice cracking. I suddenly look around to see if anyone is sitting close and has heard our conversation. Or if anyone from school is here. I want to look around more, but then wonder if Dad will think I'm ashamed of him. It suddenly dawns on me that this whole thing happened out in the open and that this conversation would seem startling to most of the people in this restaurant. And what if people at Baxter find out?

"I'm so sorry, darling. I'm so sorry to do this to you."

I want to say, "It's OK," but I stop myself. This isn't a passing thing. This is the new world I am joining him in. But there's a look in his eyes that is unfamiliar. A sharp hint of fear I've never seen on his face before. Uncertainty. Without thinking more, I say, "It's OK. It's OK, Dad." I hold his hand. "I love you."

"I love you too, more than you can imagine." He looks like a scared, embarrassed little boy. "I'm so sorry," he says again, not looking at me.

"Dad. I don't think it's your fault."

"Thank you, Bunny." Dad has called me Bunny since I was a baby. It always made me feel like he could protect me. But it doesn't sound right here. Not now.

"Will you tell me when I need to worry?" I ask.

He takes a long look at me, sizing up whether we are both up to such a request.

"Yes. Of course."

I tilt my head and grimace. "OK, well, remember I'm the one who knows which pasta salad you like. Jake never remembers. You better stay on my good side."

"Oh, I will do my best." He smiles and dabs the corners of his eyes with a napkin.

We sit there not sure what else to say. Do you chat about the weather after learning about a life-threatening virus? We muddle through some small talk. I tell him about *The Awakening*, which we are reading in English. The Italian opera continues in the background. He eats his salad, and I dip some bread in olive oil.

Later, when we say goodbye at the edge of campus, he says, "Be good, my sweet Bunny. And call me anytime if you want to talk more or ask me questions. OK?"

He hugs me longer than usual, my face buried under his neck, listening to his chest. His heart thumps loudly against my body, and suddenly it's like I'm two years old and curled up in his arms. Coffee breath and the cologne he put on this morning are trying their best to calm my panicked nerves, to make the world stop spinning. With a quick kiss on my head, he gets back in the car and drives away.

I stand at Baxter's main gate, not really wanting to move because then it would be that part. The next part. The part where I know this terrible true thing will linger all around me and not go away. I end up standing here for so long that the sky begins to change, growing darker as the sun sets. Just walk, Danielle. You can do this. But as I step one foot in front of the other, it's like I'm moving in slow motion, the light also caught up in this time warp.

Everything is slowly getting covered in something dark and terrifying. Everything I've known and been distracted by flattens like cutouts inside my heart: high school angst, college applications, term papers, haircuts, boyfriends, crushes, physics class, final exams, announcements, detentions, roommates, pimples, passing notes, cutting classes, how clothes fit, why teachers can't use slang, homework, periods, tampons, bleeding onto my sheets, how that boy looked at me, whether my boots were cool or lame, getting papers printed in the computer lab, phone calls, care packages, friends, having enough toothpaste or shampoo, gym sock smell, growing my hair and cutting my hair and dyeing my hair, music that makes me dance and music that makes me want to paint, and missing breakfast over and over and over and over. It's all shrunken down under this cloud. HIV smacks down everything into one question: Why care about all that nonsense when my dad is going to die?

I hope Amy is in our room. I don't know what I'm going to do by myself. I open our door and she is sitting on her bed, sorting three-by-five cards. She takes one look at me and says, "What happened?"

"My . . . my dad . . ." I manage before crumpling to my knees. We sit on the floor and she is patient while I tell her everything. I feel like a pendulum swinging from intense fear to utter numbness.

She gets out Grandma, her quilt, comforting, soft, and old, and drapes it over me.

I stay on the floor, while Amy starts making tea with her electric kettle. "So, he's not sick?" she asks.

"Right," I say, poking my fingers through the holes in the blanket.

"Is there any way to know when he will get sick?" she asks, bringing me a steaming cup of mint tea.

"Not really. I mean, he'll keep track of the good blood cells, called T cells. But it's impossible to know when he'll get sick. Or if he'll get sick, even."

"So . . . can you, like— Well . . . I'm wondering if you ought to put this on the shelf, like, set it aside for now?"

"What do you mean?" I ask.

"I mean, worry when you have to, but not before. He's healthy now, so can you just, like, maybe not worry too much about it?"

What is she talking about? HIV is attacking the immune cells that are keeping him healthy. It takes out the soldiers, so the battlefield is its own. How can I look away while a war is raging in his body? Would she be able to just put it on a shelf if it were her dad? I don't say a word. Instead, I get up and move to my bed. "Thanks for the tea. I think I'm just going to take a shower."

She looks surprised and then says, "Yeah, OK. I'm going to meet Noah in a few minutes. Unless, you want me to stay?"

"No, thanks," I say, sort of glad she's leaving. Sometimes her can-do spirit isn't what I need.

Put it on a shelf. It would have to be one big-ass shelf.

After a hot shower, I get back to the room and listen to the silence. I drink the now-cold tea she made. The quiet is no good either. My noisy thoughts come rushing in, cold and sharp.

Don't let him get sick Don't let him get sick
Don't let him get sick Don't let him get sick
Don't let him get sick
Don't let him
Get
Sick

I dream that Arthur and I are strolling through an art museum holding pineapples in our arms. All around us are paintings full of colors and lines and washes and drips. We are laughing. He says something hilarious, then he falls asleep on a bench, and I cannot move him or wake him. I start crying.

I have tears in my eyes for real when I wake up. I go to the bathroom. It's midmorning on Saturday. In the hall I stare at the brownish reddish carpet as I walk. I pee, wash my hands, and throw water on my face. I pat my face with my T-shirt and shuffle back to my room. I yawn and start changing from one pair of sweatpants to another.

Taking breaths, I wonder how many times we breathe in our lifetime. A billion? A trillion? I think about the constancy of the action, about the breaths we take without realizing it most of the time. All my breaths. All his breaths.

"Breakfast?" I say to Amy, who is up and looking ready to move.

"Sure. Of course." She puts on her running gear and quickly ties her sneakers. I walk past a mirror and choose not to change my clothes. I wear slippers and my puffy coat. Walking across campus, we pass circles of girls gossiping and boys hacky-sacking. Can everyone see the HIV cloud around me? Do these kids even know what AIDS is?

I once had a fight with a friend in seventh grade. She'd been so mean to me and I didn't know why. Later I found out her dad left their home in the middle of the night without telling anyone and never came back. When I told Dad, he said, "Everybody's got a bag of rocks, Bunny. Sometimes you can see what they have to carry, a disability or illness. But sometimes it's invisible. Difficult family, health problems, financial troubles, addictions—who knows? But believe me, everyone carries something big and heavy and terrifying which sometimes prevents them from being bouncy. So, it's best to be patient and kind, especially when you don't know someone's whole story. Try to remember this when people are rude or mean. Everyone has some kind of bag of rocks. *Everyone.* And those rocks make people cranky."

I guess, now this is mine.

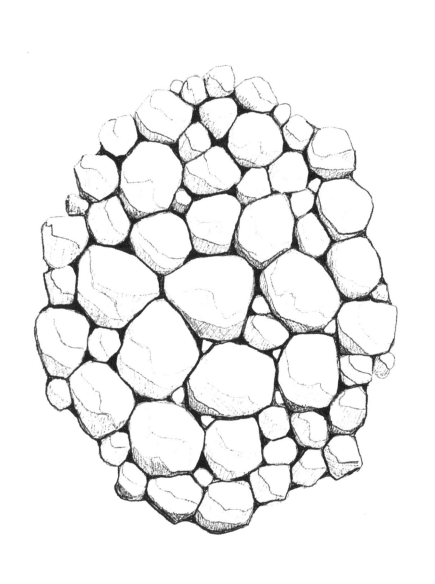

11

"River"

After wasting all of yesterday lying around, I get up and force myself to go to the studio. Maybe feeling productive will help. But as I look over my portfolio drawings of spaces on campus, they all seem cold and empty. I wanted to make them feel so close to the real thing that the picture felt like it was popping out. Like Vermeer. Or Caravaggio. Arthur taught me the magic of precision and these drawings are precise. Finely tuned. Delicately exact. But now they feel so fragile, like ice.

It is painfully clear that I am not Caravaggio.

Panic swells in me, like a sneeze coming up. I cannot control it.

I wanted these portfolio drawings to show empty spaces, the details of corners and staircases, tables and windows. But now there's a flatness to them, a lifelessness. Maybe there are too many mental steps between these drawings and my ideas. Maybe I am not connecting the dots enough. Or maybe my ideas are just dumb: of course, empty spaces lack warmth.

Being an artist in an art studio occasionally feels like standing naked in a hall of mirrors. Sometimes it is hideous.

I find in one of my folders a portrait I made of Arthur from last year. That was a good day. We'd been sitting in a coffee shop near his house by the window, sunlight streaming in. I was drawing his face, noticing the way the corners of his mouth curled up, a smile waiting in the wings. And how his eyes were so round and curious, like they would pop out of his head if he saw something particularly interesting. Drinking his decaf, he said, "Danielle, I love watching you draw. To see how you observe the world is such a delight."

Glimpses of dinner at Frankie's keep flashing in my mind. The drops of water rolling down the glass as Dad tells me about his HIV. The sorrow in his eyes, explaining why he hadn't told me. If it was cancer, I could tell someone in some office here, and they'd give me extensions for schoolwork. The school counselor could give me pamphlets about cancer or grief or something helpful. But at Baxter you don't say, "My dad has HIV." I mean, I've never tried to, but my hunch is it would be akin to telling the nurse I have leprosy.

It's hard to even talk about my dad being gay. After he came out, so many people asked, "Was he always gay?" and "Did he always sleep with men?" I mean, come on, who talks to their parents about their sex lives? Not me. Just saying the word *gay* seems to immediately make certain straight people think about sex. I really don't know how to mention it casually around here. It's too far away from what people here can imagine.

I guess if Dad could keep being gay a secret for, like, decades, and Arthur could keep his HIV status from me for I don't even know how long, I can certainly keep a lid on Dad's status while I'm at school. I mean, besides Amy, why would I need to tell anyone?

OK, focus, Danielle. What do I need to do? Art history . . . and I recall the artist Ms. Davis mentioned and that image with the lips sewn shut, and I start flipping through my *Artforum* magazines. It wasn't that long ago I saw it.

In the fourth magazine I look through, I find the article from last spring on Wojnarowicz. I read about his childhood, his abusive father, and how he ran away and lived on the streets. And now he's HIV positive and making art about it. He is losing friends to the disease, and the queer community he is part of is increasingly angry at the government's neglect of this health crisis. His artwork is so many things:

collages, paintings, poetry, performance. There is something raw about it, unpolished. What did Arthur think of his work? I wonder. I imagine he'd think it was rough, maybe even ugly. I mark the pages to use later.

Out in the hallway, it smells like rubber and sweat; there's volleyball practice down the hall. I use my prepaid calling card at the hallway phone to call Dad and get his answering machine. No one is around so I feel OK to talk.

"Dad, hey! I'm just calling to see how you're doing. Just want you to know I hope you're all right. And I'm not ashamed or embarrassed or anything that you have HIV. I just want you to know I'm, like, OK. I'm, well, fine . . . And I'm here, and I'm glad you told me. And I love you." There are tears on my face by the time I hang up the phone.

I hate using a hall phone. Anyone can walk by at any time. But that's basically all we have at Baxter.

I lock my studio and go back to my dorm to study for tomorrow's physics test.

Focus.

I lie in bed and simply cannot read my physics notes. I need to listen to Joni Mitchell and draw instead. I'll look at physics later.

The trouble is,
When I close my eyes, it's here.
Sticky, bitter goo
Filling me from the inside, looking for ways to get out.
This virus seeps and alters him,
Finding places to make him sick.
It doesn't care about his value or his intentions.
It just wants to multiply and take over.

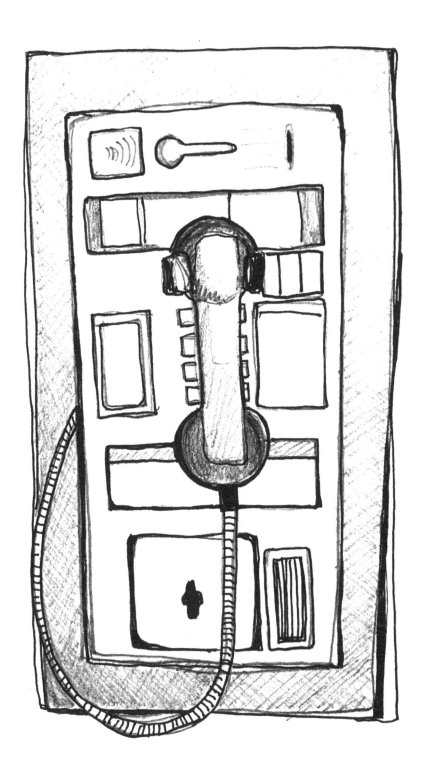

The next morning I rush into the physics classroom a few minutes early for the test, swallowing the last of the muffin I grabbed on the way. There's Marco, looking like he's been awake and organized for hours. I sit down two rows behind him while I take out my notebook for one last glimpse. He turns around and gives me a big smile and two thumbs up. "You good?"

"Yeah, thanks."

There's not a world in which I'd describe my state right now as good. Nervous, terrified, exhausted, and clueless would be far more accurate. The truth is I barely cracked a book last night, and I mostly hope to remember what Marco and I reviewed the other night. But it feels like months ago now. My brain's space for velocities and force has been invaded by a humming of worry about AIDS and Dad. Maybe the test will be easy. Maybe my mind will put it together anyway.

Or maybe not.

I struggle through each question like I'm translating a language I've never learned. I know what most of the words mean, but all together they make no sense.

A voice inside my head keeps repeating, "Don't let him get it." I don't even know who I'm pleading with.

I answer what I can and hit a dead end. I look at the clock. There are ten minutes left, but no amount of minutes would give me the clarity of mind to calculate the velocity of a marble falling out of a skyscraper.

"Pencils down," Mrs. Capshaw announces, finally.

Oh boy. My stomach is churning like a slow flush. Will RISD care about my physics grades?

Out in the hall, Marco says, "So? Not so bad, right? I mean that marble problem was a head-scratcher, but we did an acceleration problem like that one about the airplane, right?" His face is sweet and concerned and impossibly adorable.

"Oh, Marco, a lady never tells." I try to be coy, which is ridiculous. I look up and his face has dropped, frowning.

"You bombed it, didn't you?"

"Thanks for the vote of confidence, friend!" I will fight this one. Why will he ever need to know?

"I can see it in your face."

Damn. I drop the act. "Fret not, you did all anyone could do, really. It was all me, Marco. I'm my own woman." I pat his shoulder with pitiful reassurance.

We are walking down the hall, out the door, and toward my studio. At least I am, I don't know if he's heading there for the gym or following me.

"But I really wanted to help you! I feel awful." He's still talking to me, and now it's starting to bug me.

"Seriously, man, you're so nice. Don't blame yourself. I am in sync with neither vectors nor velocity . . ."

"Maybe other stuff is distracting you?"

"What are you talking about?" I stop walking and look at him. I never told Marco about my dad. It dawns on me that I've sort of avoided him since Dad was here.

"I overheard you," he says quietly. "On the phone . . . in the hall . . . last night at the gym. I didn't mean to pry or anything. I just heard what you said and if you need someone to talk to or something, I know it's hard to have someone you love be . . . sick."

I stare at him. Nope. I can't do this. I get that he's trying to be nice, but I'm not doing this now, here. I can't be some sad kitten in a tree he's going to rescue. "I gotta go," is all I say to him. I feel the hardness of a shell forming all around me. He nods while looking at me with squinted eyes.

"OK. Well, if you want to grab dinner, I'll be in the library after seventh period."

I'm a giant creep. If I keep standing here, I'll crumble into a pile of ashes right before his eyes.

Instead, I lie to his beautiful face. "Yeah, I have to do some stuff in my studio."

"Oh, sure, I get it," he tries to seem breezy and understanding but clearly looks dejected. "Let me know if you get hungry . . ."

Just then, Amy walks up and raises an eyebrow which communicates precisely, *Well, what do we have here?*

I start walking and she follows me.

"Danielle Florence Silver! What was THAT?"

"Just Marco asking about the test."

"No, for real, you must have noticed how he was looking at you! And did I or did I not hear him ask you to have dinner?"

"I guess . . ." I say, shrugging.

"Dani, seriously. I am going to smack your face. Don't you want to go out with him? Geez, let that hot dude cheer you up. You guys could go to the homecoming dance with me and Noah. A double date?"

"I just . . ." I'm not sure what to say. I can't get involved with someone right now? I can't open up and be all cutesy and romantic inside this turtle shell I need around me for safety. I can't be a normal kid. But I say nothing and stare at the ground.

She understands. She nods.

"Let's talk later tonight, OK? We'll have girlie teatime?"

I roll my eyes. She knows I hate that title. But I do like tea. And her.

In my tower alone, I am fine.
Better than fine, really.
Cute boys don't solve problems.
I don't need pity or questions or that sparkle.
What could he possibly say that would make anything better?
This dread is a slow-moving train coming for me.
Unpredictable and heavy and sure.

I go to dinner late. I sit in the corner of the dining hall with my sorry chicken noodle soup and a tiny bag of oyster crackers and my history reading to keep me company. Marco sees me and comes over.

"Hey," he says, like he's interrupting me.

I suddenly remember him asking me to have dinner, and I suddenly feel guilty and angry, which is a fun combo. This is how it feels to keep it in and push it down and not share. You stare honesty in the face and simply say, "Nope." Is this what putting it on the shelf feels like? It just feels like lying.

"Hi there." My body feels weak, and I know I'm failing miserably. "Can I join you?"

"I guess. I mean, I kind of need to read," I say, doing a terrible balancing act of lying and avoiding eye contact.

"Oh, yeah, OK. I can go." He doesn't sit down. I want him to sit down and I want him to leave, and my confusion is even making me queasy. I don't imagine it's fun for him either.

He turns back just as he's leaving and says, "I'm around. If you need to talk." He nods, looking at me, maybe waiting for something more, but I just stare at him. Finally, he turns and walks away.

I feel like I'm in that nightmare where you're on stage naked and don't know your lines. Only I'm sitting here with cold chicken soup and no idea how to talk to a cute boy who wants to talk to me. Now I can't read and I feel awful and I just need to get out of here.

Back in my room, I find Amy, already boiling water.

She presses play on the stereo and my CD picks back up. Joni Mitchell sings like a lullaby, as Amy hands me a steamy cup of ginger tea. I wish I had a river too.

"OK, spill it." Amy doesn't beat around the bush.

"I don't know." I take off my shoes and sit on the bed.

"Yeah, you do. Come on, Dan. Talk to me," she says quietly.

"I don't think I can keep this on the shelf. I know you think that's, like, the best thing, but I don't know how to keep it there. It's too big. It doesn't fit. I can't pretend."

Amy gets me a tissue when she sees my eyes start to well up. I feel all these thoughts just seeping out of me.

"There's all this other stuff I'm supposed to do, you know?" I continue. "I have to read books, and take tests and finish applying to college, and be nice to people, and get boys to like me, and all I can think is that my dad's got this horrible disease I cannot even mention out loud. And I don't know what is going to happen to him. And I don't know what to do."

She sits still and lets me turn into a puddle.

"It's here." I point to the spot right between my eyebrows. "It's constant and heavy, and I don't know how to put it down."

"OK, OK," she says using her calm, smooth, I'm-here-for-you voice. Teardrops fall into my lap. "Dani, look at me." I do. She is looking into my eyes—this thing she does when she wants someone to really pay attention. It's eerie and it works.

"Take a breath," she says calmly.

I do. It hurts.

"I know you feel like you're losing your mind, but honestly, I don't think anyone else would react all that differently. I wouldn't. It's scary. You're human, and he's your dad, and you love him. Not everyone is lucky enough to have a dad who loves them like he loves you. But that's making this so much worse. How you're reacting seems totally normal— maybe that's sort of helpful?"

I keep trying to breathe but everything is too tight. Amy hands me the tissues.

"What do you need right now? Let's think of something." Amy knows the right questions to ask in order to do what she does best: move forward.

"I just don't know anything about this disease, like about what's going to happen to him, and I don't know how to deal with that."

"Well, what are the options? You can accept you don't know anything about HIV, or, like, learn more about it so you do know something. I mean, you can't tell the future, but maybe if you learn more, it might feel less scary?"

I nod. I manage to say, "Yeah, that sounds good."

"Knowledge it is, then. We're going to the Playground tomorrow. I have an appointment and you're coming with me."

12
"The Weight"

After seventh period, Amy and I walk to the main office where we get our off-campus passes. I've been her off-campus buddy for her thyroid tests at the women's clinic before, so it's nothing new for us or the school. Going off campus is like taking a tiny vacation. We always get milkshakes from Bennigan's on our way back.

Amy calls it the Playground because the clinic is next to a real playground, so we get to swing on the swings and pretend we're six for a minute or two. We have about two hours off campus or else Baxter sends the Coast Guard after us or something. As we get close, Amy explains her idea.

"So, in the waiting room, there's all kinds of pamphlets. I usually ignore them, but I think some had HIV and AIDS on the covers. How about when I go in to see the doctor, you just take, like, one of each? Then we can see what they say."

"What if someone sees me?" I ask.

"Um, you'll make them super jazzed because no one ever takes those pamphlets," she says, emphatically.

As Amy checks in up front, I go to the table with the pamphlets.

Safe Sex & Your Body

What AIDS Is

Do You Have An STD?

You know that feeling when you're watching a fire on the news and then you realize the fire is happening in your neighborhood? Not only can you see it on the TV screen, but you smell it through the open window and you hear the sirens? Yeah, that's how this is.

"See?" she whispers. "It's all here. Take them. I'll be back." She heads to the exam room while I sit with the fish tank and the pamphlets. I mouth the words, *Thank you*, as she leaves.

The pamphlets seem to understand just how terrifying this is, and like a Sesame Street character introducing math, they ease you into it with silly pictures and simple words. As I read, I write notes in my journal to keep for later. One has a close-up photo of the actual virus. It looks like an alien fruit.

AIDS is spread when you have unprotected sex, receive blood from a transfusion, or share needles intravenously. It is in bodily fluids: blood, semen, preseminal fluids, rectal fluids, vaginal fluids, and breast milk.

HIV transmission is only possible if these fluids come in contact with a mucous membrane or damaged tissue or are directly injected into the bloodstream (from a needle or syringe). Mucous membranes are found inside the rectum, the vagina, the opening of the penis, and the mouth.

AIDS, Acquired Immunodeficiency Syndrome: a state in which the immune system's ability to fight infectious disease is compromised or entirely absent.

HIV, Human Immunodeficiency Virus: any of various strains of the virus that cause AIDS by infecting the body's immune system.

But how do you fight it?

They say all these things you can and can't do, but still, nobody can stop it once it's in your body? Why aren't all those scientists and doctors trying harder?

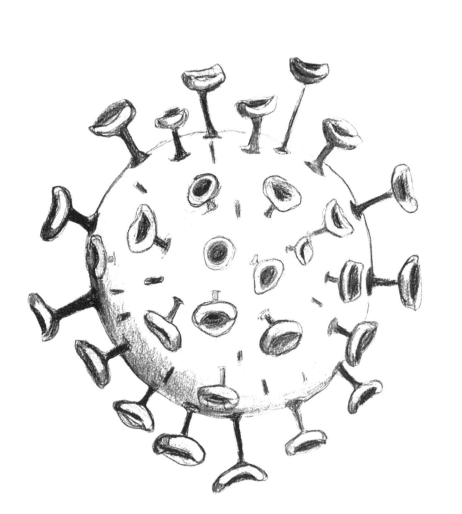

I suddenly remember last year over winter break when Brian and I had sex and the condom broke. And all I worried about was that I might get pregnant. How did I not even think about this? I mean, I knew HIV was out there. Why didn't I think it would get to me? Did I assume it was some faraway thing that would never impact my life? I guess so.

The pamphlet says that people can look healthy but still have HIV. Arthur looked fine even a month before he died. I guess that's how people keep it a secret. Until they can't.

A woman comes into the office waiting area. Pearls, headband, perfect hair and nails. I shift my chair so she can't see what I'm reading. AIDS is so far away from this New Jersey golf-playing suburb. She does not seem at all ready to have a conversation that could involve the word *rectum*.

Since I was twelve, I knew AIDS existed. It was in the newspapers and on the radio and sometimes they'd mention it on TV, but I didn't pay much attention. And I know how terrified most people are of it, too scared to talk about it. Even Arthur didn't want people to know.

All at once, the world feels like a giant pile of sand, and we've all buried our heads. But also, is this really my job? I mean I'm only seventeen. Am I really supposed to take this on? To know and teach others and, like, be responsible?

When I was little, I thought adults all knew what they were doing. Now, I'm not so sure they do. It seems to me that people who are gay, or poor, or Black get abused by the government and ignored or sensationalized by the people making TV shows. But AIDS can kill anyone—any human who's been exposed—so why would they make it about being gay, instead of about being sick? Silence=Death makes more and more sense to me.

Amy emerges from the exam room.

"All done?" I ask her, suddenly aware that she too must worry about her own health.

"Oh yeah, it's the usual: they take blood, ask me how I'm feeling, and give me a new round of pills."

"OK, I just never hear you talk about it." It's started raining so we skip the playground and start walking to Bennigan's.

"There's not much to say. Since I got diagnosed with this thyroid thing, they just take blood every three months to make sure my levels are good. An extra bonus: they check out my female stuff, make sure my diaphragm still fits, and give me all the condoms I want."

"You talk to the doctors here about sex?" I had no idea.

"Oh, sure. The doctors here are awesome. I sure as hell can't talk to my parents about sex, can you?"

"No, not really. I mean, I think they both tried but it was just mortifying."

"So, did you get the skinny on the you-know-what?"

"Yeah, I did. Thanks, babe." I learned a bit more so I feel lighter.

We walk into Bennigan's, and she starts her usual debate: Chocolate or strawberry? We both choose strawberry.

Afterward we walk up the hill to Baxter, singing the Aretha version of "The Weight."

Put the weight on me.

It's been a few days since I last saw Marco in the hall outside the cafeteria. I don't make eye contact. I don't want to talk to him about my dad, but I can't ignore it. I want him to like me, but I think I might explode into a nervous wreck if I start talking to him just now.

I pivot. I redirect. I do that thing I need to do when I've been too distracted. Focus. I throw myself into my portfolio drawings of Baxter's corners and crevices. I look for the places that spend their days being ignored. I focus on the light hitting the floor or the way my closet door frame is not at an exact right angle. I've always liked the way spaces leave me to wonder who might fill them. Like, when you see some old house or a reconstructed room in a museum. Who was here? What happened in this room? And what might happen later when I'm gone? There's something eternal in these spaces.

I'll need twelve drawings for my application portfolio. I have eight.

The dining hall: once a fancy hotel, this room must have housed parties and will one day be filled with high school kids who are not yet born.

The library: Before Baxter went coed, only boys were allowed here. There was a time when only boys were taught to read.

My dorm room: How many other students lived here? And who will be here after I graduate and get old myself?

My history classroom: How do we tell ourselves stories of what came before us? What do we pay attention to?

The second-floor landing in Old Main: I once heard about someone seeing a ghost here, crying and holding a letter. When this was a hotel, it must have had all sorts of stories within it—romance, intrigue, maybe murder?

The gym: Ugh, the gym. Maybe I leave this out.

The girls' bathroom: Above the garden, which oddly has maybe the best view of the campus green. Did the architect plan this? I mean, was some old guy architect thinking about looking at a view from the bathroom?

The fireplace outside of the alumni office: I'll be an alum soon enough, but will I ever come back here? I cannot imagine.

I read over the list in my sketchbook and wonder if I'm just some weird loner who can't be with people. I should talk to Marco. I mean, I don't have to tell him everything and vomit all my problems all over his exquisite face. I can just, like, hang out. Be nice, at least. Yeah, I should.

I quickly rip out a page from my sketchbook and write on it before I lose my nerve.

If you're free after first period tomorrow, meet me at the top of the pretty stairs. —D

I fold it up and write *M* on the front and slip it into his mailbox after I check my mail.

I call Dad. He keeps coughing. He says it is a cold. He's had that cold for a while now.

13

"Freedom! '90"

I'm drawing the staircase again. Trying to get it right: accurate, convincing, communicating with lines, the exact angles, the precise time of the morning. Arthur used to say that painters like Vermeer ("of which there were none others, really") could convey the weather, the time of day, and even the month of the year just with the light coming through a window. I'm trying to convey a bright October day with the staircase in the library, but it's not really working out. I'm rushing. The lines are wrong. I'm missing something, even though it is all literally right in front of my face. Then, suddenly, there are two big white sneakers blocking my view. One foot is tapping. Shoes, baggy pants, a book bag hanging low, a long green sweater, and that shining face. Those lips. My stomach makes a slow somersault.

"Hey," he says. He's hesitant. Or confused, maybe? Like, scared or nervous or something. He does not smile.

"Marco . . . what's up?"

"Oh, you know, just coming from physics."

My heart is pounding, and I nod and try to act nonchalant. I'm trying to remember what I thought of last night. Instead, I try to act cool, which doesn't seem to be charming him like I'd hoped. "Oh, cool . . ." I say, realizing I hadn't even heard what he said.

"Are you on some self-imposed break? No need to go to class?"

I looked at my watch. "Oh shit!" I say, managing to spill my pencils all over the floor. It's nine thirty a.m. I've been sitting here since breakfast and completely forgot to go to physics. I stare at him, shaking my head. He barely contains a grin and tries not to laugh. Is he mocking me, or am I genuinely amusing him? Either way, his smile sends a wave through me.

"I guess I got sort of sucked in," I say, biting my lip and grimacing. "What did I miss?"

"Not much. Just got our tests back and started a unit on Newton's laws. Nothing important."

Funny. He's funny.

"So? Why have you beckoned me atop this grand staircase?" he asks.

Here goes nothing. I stand up and face him and take a deep breath before I begin. "So, when you asked me how I was, I freaked out a little. The truth is, I'm kind of a wreck. My life is confusing, and I don't really know how to talk about it. My dad has a disease, and he isn't sick, but he isn't well. It's complicated. And I recently found out that it also killed my uncle last year. It's just been a shock. So, I'm trying to keep it on a shelf and not talk about it because, well, I guess I've gotten used to not talking about Dad. Here. I usually don't talk about him here." I look around at the dark wood walls, the carved banister shiny with years of hands running along it, and the stained glass on the landing.

Marco stands next to me and we both instinctively sit down. I keep going. "But you overheard me on the phone and then you asked me, and you knew something about me and my instinct was to run away and hide."

He closes his eyes and nods his head slightly, like he's connecting the dots.

I continue because if I don't spit it all out now, I never will. "I think you're spectacular, and I don't want you to think my weirdness has anything to do with you. You're kind and you organize your notes in the

colors of the rainbow, which is overwhelmingly adorable and slightly in-
timidating, and you care that I probably failed my physics test and . . ."
I don't know how to finish. Maybe I should have written this all out.

He's just staring at me, so I keep going.

"I just wanted to say, you were kind and I was shitty. I do want to
talk about it, if you want to know, but also I don't want you to think
I'm super needy and then have you never talk to me again."

This is a disaster. Does talking to cute boys ever get easier? It has to.

Maybe if I keep talking, we'll get past this horrific moment and
onto something less awful. "I just don't know how to do all this, and
I like you, and I want you to like me, but this isn't what I want you to
see." I wipe my eyes with my bare hands, smearing charcoal on my face.

"I do like you, Danielle," he says softly, as he pulls a tissue packet
out of his backpack.

"You do?" I look up at him, take the tissue he hands me, forgetting about the smears on my face and taking this in. Wait, he likes me?

"Yes, and you don't have to hide to make me like you more."

"I don't?" I say.

"No, you don't. You don't need to, like, pretend to be happy either,
if you're not."

I look at him and wonder where he came from. I've never met a
boy like this. "I don't think anyone's ever said that to me before," I tell
him, quietly. "I thought boys hated drama."

"Well, um . . . I'm spectacular, remember?" he says, his smile beam-
ing at me like the brightest sunshine.

"You are, indeed, Marco Polo."

"Not actually my real name, Danielita." My heart calms down. My
breathing feels better.

"What is your real name then?" I ask in all seriousness.

"Marcello," he whispers.

"Marcello? That's your real name?" I blurt out.

"Yeah. Marcello Claudio Fernando Díaz." He says it with an air of
pride.

"That's your actual full name?"

"Yes." He has bowed his head toward his chest.

"Are you a king in ancient Rome?"

"Ancient Spain, actually. But yes. I am." He stands up and straightens himself very tall, like royalty.

"Very well, Your Majesty." I stand up too. "I offer you my sincerest intentions to be an unhappy mess at my convenience, as per your ruling."

He scans my face, waiting for me to break.

"His Majesty will allow it." He taps my shoulders one at a time with his rolled-up physics test.

Watching him do this, I ask, "Did you just knight me?"

"Yes. But you're a lady knight. You're now Lady Danielle, um . . . What's your middle name?" he whispers.

"Florence, for my great-grandmother," I say.

He smiles and straightens back up with acceptance. "Lady Danielle Florence Silver, I bestow upon you freedom to display unpleasant and even annoying feelings! May you breathe the sweet relief of not needing to pretend." He taps my shoulders alternately a few times, then bows.

We stand there staring at each other. It's not awkward, it just feels like a necessary part of the conversation.

"Well, you better get back to your staircase," he says finally.

"Yes, sir. Would Your Majesty consider dining with me?"

"Sure, see you at six fifteen, m'lady." He walks carefully around my pile of stuff and bows in my direction.

"Six forty-five? I tend to run late."

"OK, let's live dangerously." He waves goodbye.

―――――――――――――

Marco carries toothpicks in his bag. Just something else I learn about him at dinner. I pick my teeth to get spinach out as we talk in front of our finished meals in the dining hall. Also, he's really into George Michael and spends about ten minutes telling me about the song "Freedom! '90" and why he listens to it almost every day. "Seriously, it is life-altering."

Eventually, I tell him everything. First Arthur, then Dad. I'm careful

to be quiet, but we're seated away from other people, and dinner is almost over, so there aren't too many busybodies nosing about.

"Wow, Dani, that's so much," Marco finally says.

"I guess . . . I don't know." I try to diminish what must be sounding awfully dramatic.

"No, it is." He nods. "A sick parent is heavy. It's unnatural, sort of. They're supposed to take care of us until we grow up. They're not supposed to get sick or die when we're still kids." He widens his eyes, like he's remembering it all over again, and then digs into his carrot cake.

"So, was your family around when your mom got sick?"

"Oh yeah. I mean, I was pretty young so my older sisters sort of took over. They cooked and cleaned and put me to bed and all that. It was an adjustment, but it also was nice, I guess, for my mom. She could just enjoy all of us being there together."

"Big family?" I ask, picking at my apple pie.

"Yes," he explains, "I have two sisters and three brothers. I'm the youngest. And my parents both immigrated from Havana in the 1950s during the Communist Revolution."

"You're Cuban?" I ask.

"Well, my family, yeah. I was born in Ohio."

"And what was your mom like?" Also wondering if he was as unbelievably cute as a baby, but it seems really wrong to ask him that. Also, of course, he was.

He grins, thinking of her. "She never sat still, my mom. She was always going. I swear I never saw her sleep. Well, not until she got sick. There were six of us and she kept everyone fed, loved, and challenged, you know? She loved to dance, and she was a great cook, and she just seemed to love being our mom. It sounds so cheesy but really, I believe that."

"You must miss her, huh?"

"Yeah, losing my mom shook everything else loose, and that was hard."

"Like what?" I ask.

"Well, my siblings were all pretty grown-up and moved out by then, so I was the only one left. I was only thirteen. And my dad, he didn't really get over it. I think he needed to just be somewhere else because being in the house was too sad. He got this job with IBM and had to travel a lot, so I got shuffled from aunt to aunt until I finally came here to boarding school."

"So, wow, yeah, a lot changed for you, huh?"

He nods his head. "But anyway, I'm sorry about your uncle and about your dad too. I really like him, by the way. He's amazing. I love meeting friends' parents. It's a way to see the ingredients that made them, you know?"

I smile. "Yeah." Imagining how much of me comes from Dad, like cups of brown sugar in cookie dough.

"Danielle, for what it's worth—and I hope this doesn't freak you out—it sounds to me like what you're dealing with is for real scary. I mean, AIDS is, well, serious. Don't they call it a 'death sentence'?"

"Yeah, that's what I've heard too." I say, "Some people are taking this new drug called AZT, but it also has a ton of side effects, and it's expensive for people who don't have insurance."

"And it's spread more by gay people, huh?" he asks quietly. Like it's some sort of secret.

"Well, it's spread through sex and needles for drugs and blood transfusions, but since it really took hold among gay men, that's how people think of it."

"So, is the drug research slow because it's mostly gay people who are sick?"

"Yeah, I bet that's true. I read this great quote from this artist, David Wojnarowicz. About how things won't change until the straight world is threatened and speaks up."

"And in the meantime . . ." Marco doesn't finish the sentence.

". . . people are dying," I finish it for him.

"Danielle, I'm so sorry. If there's anything I can do, just tell me, OK?"

I look up at him still devouring his cake. He suddenly looks different. More complete somehow. I don't feel like I'm talking to some cute guy now. Maybe I don't have to hide anything either or worry about how my hair looks.

After dinner, he has to go to football practice.

"Hey, Danielle, thanks," he says as he gathers his stuff.

"For what?"

"For this. You're super cool and I'm glad to, I don't know . . . be friends."

"Same here, Your Majesty."

He smiles and throws his arms around me and kisses my cheek. He looks at me once more with a smile and turns and walks away.

Oh my God.

Your hands are too perfect
When you open a bottle or butter your bread.
They seem like marble, smooth, flawless,
Bone by bone someone perfected them over a long time.
Your shoulders can't be that broad and strong—
Perfect proportions of man.
I cannot fathom the mathematics of your frame,
And inside your head lives so much kindness
and care, and sweetness, and light.
How can anyone be all these things?
You held it, my bag of rocks
Easy, like you already knew how.
And I could breathe again.
When you smiled at me,
everything got brighter.

In the morning, I walk to class in a daze. It's a gray, cold fall morning, but I feel like Maria in *The Sound of Music* when she realizes she loves Captain von Trapp and she runs through hills and glens with her guitar swinging side to side. I float to class, humming, "The hills are alive."

Wait, am I in love?

Oh God, Danielle. Take it easy.

After art history, I tell Ms. Davis that I read about David Wojnarowicz. I thank her for the project suggestion.

Out in the hallway, Marco yells, "Danielle! Yo! Lady Danielita!"

"Oh, hey." I almost tell him I was just thinking about him, but the reality is I've been thinking about him ever since last night. I cannot possibly tell him this. He falls into stride next to me as I make my way to math class.

"Guess what?" he says with a silly grin on his face.

"What?"

"I just learned that there's a homecoming dance in two weeks!" He says this like he's just told me he's getting a puppy for Christmas.

"And?" I ask. It's just going to be another Baxter dance disaster. Only three weeks since that last one. I must not have adequately informed Marco of the irrelevance of such social gatherings.

"And, I've never been to a Baxter homecoming, I missed the Mix-A-Lot because of a football scrimmage, and I'll never have another chance, and I want to go!"

"OK, cool. Have a blast, nerd." I keep walking.

"Wow, you are impossible." He stops short, and I moonwalk my way back to him in slow motion.

"What?" I ask. "What's wrong?"

"Danielle. Will you go to the dance with me?" He opens his eyes wide 'cause I'm being super dense.

Oh, wait, what? He's asking me to the dance. Say something. Say yes, idiot!

"Well, I think your dance expectations might need some adjusting, but sure. Yes, Marco. I will go with you to the homecoming dance."

"Finally! OK, great. See you later!" He gives me a hug and dashes off.

Holy mother of God. Are we dating?

14
"When I Was A Painter"

We did not plan this out too well, blindly following Kyle's directions. At the end of art class, he reminded us about his next "Statement Piece." Kyle sees these solo performances as commentary on society. Last spring he read an entire chapter of Camus's *The Plague* in a French accent from the window of the French room. In the winter he sang Dolly Parton's "Telling Me Lies" from the chapel pulpit while wearing what looked like a nun's habit and a fringe dress.

Usually, Kyle's audience includes three art students and a kid named Jared, who clearly sees Kyle as a god. Kyle takes his Statement Pieces seriously, and he's super professional about them. He makes gorgeous hand-drawn invitations, and each piece has a theme, like "the vulgarity of capitalism," and "the beauty of mortality."

Tonight's invitation reads: Meet at 10:45 p.m. at the epicenter of artistic demise (the football field). Tonight's Statement Piece will be a critique of the arts and athletics at Baxter.

We are sitting in the grass in the moonlight in the center of the field, waiting. Daria is here with Simon and Jared. And I brought Marco. I've told him all about Kyle's previous Statements Pieces. Marco has never experienced performance art and seems genuinely intrigued. Selfishly, I thought this could be a quasi date. It's weird to date at boarding school—mostly you just have to call things dates because we all live together.

Ever since Marco asked me to the dance, I haven't been able to focus on the same thought for more than a few moments. One minute, I know we will spend our lives together because we are truly, deeply bonded and always will be. But the next minute, I am, as Amy puts it, "worsting." He doesn't really like me, he just wants to meet my friends; he doesn't think I'm pretty, he just likes my jokes.

So I'm sitting here on the football field thinking Marco should have his arm around me, and he doesn't. He should be trying to sneak off with me into the bushes to make out, and he isn't. He hasn't even kissed me yet. I shove all those thoughts way down and smile. Hope they're just stupid feelings and that we will live in a beautiful Lower Manhattan loft one day and have a puppy named Oscar and throw glamorous dinner parties.

"It's fucking freezing," says Simon, who is now rolling a joint. The field is only lit by the almost full moon and two lamps. The early November chill hits me as I shove my hands into my coat pockets. It's rare I'm ever on the football field, but it's also really magical at night. You can lie on your back and see the stars, and when there's no game scheduled, it's so quiet. Simon takes a hit off of the joint and passes it to Daria, who does the same. Then she passes it to me. I sneak a glance at Marco and say, "No thanks." I don't really smoke pot much because mostly it just makes me lazy and dumb. But tonight, I declined because I saw Marco's horror-struck face. I remember that this field is where he practices, and with his scholarship, he's got way more to lose than the rest of us. Jared happily takes the joint and giggles, passing it back to Simon.

Finally, Kyle comes out from behind the bleachers, wearing a cheerleader uniform. Where did he get that? It looks so good on him. He stands in front of us and sings the Baxter fight song in a creepy slow, sultry way while shaking pom poms in slow motion. It has the effect of a mime in protest. I think it's funny, but I look around and no one is laughing. Marco looks simultaneously frightened and impressed. I guess

Kyle is a particular taste. Personally, I think he's onto something. Even though I get exhausted from his need for attention, he provides some excitement for those of us who don't really like football games.

"Let's see if we can get into the kitchen and find some snacks," says Simon after Kyle finishes with a flourish and slow-motion curtsy. We walk as a group across the field, headed toward Old Main.

"Hey!" someone yells from the shadows about twenty-five feet away. Crap.

"Hey! What are you doing?" It's Mr. Tate, a Spanish teacher. "It's after curfew. What's going on out here?" he shouts.

Daria puts her hand up to the rest of us as if to say, *Allow me.*

She walks over to Mr. Tate, out of earshot of the rest of us, and has a brief conversation, after which Mr. Tate glances over at Simon and says, "So sorry for your loss. But please, all of you, get back to your dorms. Now."

We all nod and turn around. Daria comes back over and links arms with Simon and Kyle. "You heard the man, let's away!"

Marco can barely catch his breath. "Wait, what just happened?" he asks. "Are we getting detention?"

"No. Daria fixed it. What was it, Daria? Cancer?" Kyle explains.

"Heart attack. Simon, your grandpa died. He loved football so we were paying tribute." Daria announces the lie she'd told.

"And Mr. Tate bought that?" Simon laughs.

"Oh yeah. Paid full price," says Daria.

Marco looks at me, still shaken. I put my arm around him. "Hey, you all right?"

He turns to look at me, like he just got caught in a raid, and says, "Do you guys do this all the time?"

"Usually we don't get caught," says Daria. "So that makes it less stressful," she jokes.

"Kyle usually performs in daylight, indoors. We don't generally break rules for art." I say. God, I don't want him to think I'm trouble.

"We should though," Kyle says. "Otherwise, what's the point?"

We let that linger as we keep walking.

At the fork, the girls peel off to the left, and I go to give Marco a hug goodbye. He's being weird so I just say, "Good night." He nods, looking at the ground. "Night," he says and turns and walks away. Did I ruin everything bringing him along?

Daria walks beside me. "What's the deal with you two?"

I shake my head and shrug, saying nothing.

"He's cute, but I'm not seeing sparks." Daria is a blunt object, always.

"Shut up, Daria. This just isn't his thing."

"I wonder what is," she says, raising an eyebrow and walking into the back door we'd propped open.

From the front row center you can see everything.
Nothing stands in your way.
No flyaway curls block your view of the action, or long-
torsoed men obstructing your access.
Those front-row girls get all the perks, all the glances, all
the love.
Me, I'm somewhere near the back. On the side. Behind a pillar.
I can pretend I know, but I don't.
I can talk my way to sounding like a front row center kind
of girl
But it's just an act.
Thinly veiled and overplayed.
Adorned with hair dye and neon-colored earrings, wearing
secondhand fake fur and big boots, I can distract enough
for attention. Or hide altogether so no one knows I'm here.
But the boys, I think, the boys want front-row girls who
dazzle and delight and hold all the cards.
Hold all the power.
From the back, we cannot even see, much less hold
anything.
I can try, but he will probably not love me.

After third period, I head to my studio. I feel the note folded in my pocket from last night. Call Your Dad. It was so late when I came in, I didn't want to wake him up. He always calls on the pay phone down the hall, but I'm never around when he does. I don't think it's urgent. Deep down, though, a small voice is screaming songs of panic: Maybe he's in the hospital! Maybe he's dying! What are you waiting for? The rest of me stays calm and knows I will call him and everything will be fine. It doesn't say *emergency* on the note. I read it five times. It's probably fine. I breathe in. I breathe out.

This English class is really dragging. It's Monday again. I have ten days to get my application done and sent. I need to make more drawings and start my essay. Inconveniently, I also have to go to classes which increasingly feel like a waste of my precious time. I hear Mrs. Fox talking but the words aren't going into my brain.

I'm tired. OK. Breathe in. English, history, gym. Classes finish today at two forty-five, so I can spend, like, four hours before dinner and four hours after, maybe. Or three. There's something I'm supposed to do for English, I think. And I have to write my outline for art history.

Marco wasn't at breakfast. Does he hate me now? I mean I almost got him kicked out of school. Does he think I'm some juvenile delinquent who hangs out with crazy pothead artists on football fields? I guess I would if I were him.

And then there's the dance on Friday. I guess we aren't actually going together. I don't know.

I'm searching for my college application notes. I had some ideas I wrote down, but now I can't find them. Did I write them in my English notebook or physics? I'm aware of trying to look like I'm focusing on something school-related, when in fact I am doing nothing of the sort.

"Danielle!" Mrs. Fox says loudly, as my brain suddenly returns to the room.

"Yeah?"

"Do you have your essay?"

"My what?" Does she mean my college essay? What?

"Your essay on the T. S. Eliot poem we read?"

As I shake my head slowly, I say, "Oh, sure, yeah. No, I have it. I just left it in my room. Can I bring it to you later?"

She looks at me like I just asked to take a crap in her handbag but says, "Sure."

Add that to the list. I'll be fine. I'll just stay up tonight and bring it tomorrow. Who needs sleep? Fine. It's fine. I can deal. It's just an essay.

At lunch Marco is sitting with Amy, talking about the dance. Amy has this idea that we should double-date or something. I feel like she's putting way too much pressure on this situation. It seems like bad luck or something. She reads too much Shakespeare, I swear. I was so excited to just have an actual date, a real moment of boy/girl stuff with Marco. And now she's making it a big social thing, and he thinks I'm some sort of criminal, and he'd probably prefer to just date a girl like her. God, what was I thinking? The only boyfriends I've had were because I helped them with their papers and put up with their bullshit.

I need to leave. I can feel my brain spinning into a frenzy. "Gotta dash, y'all," I say with a fake smile, ignoring Amy's plan-making.

"You're welcome for planning your social life, Dani . . ." Amy sneers, but I wave and head straight to the studio.

I feel like I'm in a crowded room, but instead of people, it's all these responsibilities demanding my attention. I can't keep up. If I focus on my homework, I can't finish this studio work. If I finish this studio work, I'm ignoring my friends. If I hang out with friends, I'm avoiding learning more about HIV and checking in on my dad. It's an endless chain of obligation and guilt. And I thought Marco liked me.

I feel the crumpled-up note in my pocket and stop at the pay phone in the gym. I dial Dad.

"Hello?" he says, sounding smaller than usual.

"Dad? It's Dani."

"Bunny, how are you?" His voice is all gravel and sand. "Sorry, I must have fallen asleep."

Asleep? It's almost three p.m. Dad doesn't nap. Aside from sunbathing naps that is.

"Oh, sorry," I say, feeling a need to apologize for waking him up. "Are you OK?"

"Oh, sure," he coughs suddenly. He doesn't sound OK.

"What's wrong, Dad?"

"Oh, Danielle, nothing, really," he says sharply.

"I got a note that you called?"

"You did? Oh yes, I called to see when you're coming for Thanksgiving."

"Thanksgiving? That's not for three more weeks, Dad." I laugh, thinking maybe he's joking.

"Really?" He's not joking. Does he not know what day it is?

"Dad, it's November 5." I say, as calmly as I can.

"Of course, it is." I hear him cough. "I just want to know if you're coming back early to help cook."

"Yeah, I'm pretty sure. There's a one p.m. bus that Wednesday I usually take. I can be there by three thirty."

"Sounds good. Whatever you need to do."

Why is he so confused?

"Dad, are you . . . I mean, is everything OK?"

"Yes, Danielle. I just lost track of the date. I've had this weird stomach bug, and it's made me a little foggy, but I'm OK. Really, really. Wednesday. Wonderful. We can make our pecan pie." He is trying hard to sound cheerful and I don't believe it.

"Sure," I say, not wanting to add fuel to this strange fire.

"OK, sweet Bunny. Getting everything done?"

"Yes, Dad," I sigh deeply. "Getting it all done." Lies.

We say goodbye. I feel my heart racing. He is not all right, and I have no idea what to do about it. Should I call someone? Who would I even call?

Inside my studio, I change my clothes and turn on the CD player to listen to the Breeders. I turn it up loud, sit down, and close my eyes. I try to shut out everything else.

I see his virus spreading. Latching on with its flowery tentacles all through his bloodstream, multiplying and invading everything. Taking over his brain, my favorite thing about him.

And now I see more, multiplying every minute. More people, more virus, more illness, more death. All those condoms and pamphlets won't stop the virus from spreading inside Dad's body. And I'm just sitting here, doing nothing. What should I do?

I turn up the music even more and start drawing. Pencils break, pens run out of ink. I am scratching so hard, there are holes forming in the paper. I should be doing something else. The heavy guitar sounds like muscles shredding.

What am I even going to art school for? I mean, am I really doing this with my life? I look around and everything looks like garbage that just hasn't been thrown away yet. My clumsy hands forget the language they've been so fluent in, and everything suddenly feels terrible.

Drown out the nonsense, says Arthur's Post-it. I don't know how to right now. School, portfolio, Marco, AIDS, Dad, friends, life. Is that nonsense, or just my life?

All this energy, all these pens and paints and paper and canvas. It could disappear and literally no one but me would notice. Finally, I understand why people laugh at art. It is so fucking stupid. How can sitting in a room, drawing lines on paper, matter when people are dying? When there's so much violence and hatred and carelessness? What possible difference can this make when our own president doesn't care about the citizens of this country? Not all of them.

Nothing matters more than art. That's what Arthur taught me. *It frees the mind and opens possibilities and makes the world better*, he told me. But now, I'm sitting on the floor of this room in the basement. What for? How is this helping?

The song ends on my CD player, and I sit in silence. It sounds endless.

Piles of drawings lay all over, flat and still, doing absolutely nothing. Making nothing happen, at all. Materials that held poetic potential have become garbage before my eyes.

I look at Arthur's Post-its.

"Focus," Arthur whispers to me.

"Why?" I say out loud. "What's the point? If I get an angle perfect, will that make Dad better? If I find the exact right shade of blue, will the government actually care about gay people, or poor people, or people with AIDS?"

Arthur doesn't respond. Because he died from a disease that makes everyone afraid. He thought artists should stay out of political issues. He thought art and politics were oil and water. "Art's impact is emotional," he used to say. "Politics are not emotional, they're devoid of humanity, removed from the heart."

Removed? I wonder how that can be? Don't governments do what they do for people? The government determines so much of how we live our lives: how schools are funded, which streets to fix, and what medicines are available, right? How can these decisions be separated from our emotions? Wojnarowicz doesn't see them as separate. I don't think I do either.

All of Arthur's artwork was about some dreamy idea of life: beautiful landscapes, images of perfect boys on perfect lawns, gardens, flowers, dogs, houses. All disconnected from the real world. Beautiful. Still. Silent. It never occurred to me to even ask him what his own paintings were about. I was always more interested in how he made them, not why. That's what he told me was important.

I am sitting on the floor and everything around me feels dead.

Dead or dying. Silent and useless.

It is eleven p.m. My application and portfolio are due in ten days. I look at my drawings. They do nothing. I had wanted them to be about spaces on campus, vessels for history or something, but everyone who should be there is missing. Everyone is somewhere else. Who will want to look at pictures of empty spaces? What a dumb idea. I don't even want to look at them and I made them. I'm no more interesting than I was in eighth grade. How do I manage to convince myself that my ideas are worthwhile? What a joke.

I take a drawing from the pile and hold it in my hands. A history classroom with no people. Tables, chairs, windows, classroom clutter. The light is well handled, and the lines are smooth and confident, but who will care? Useless. Silent. Empty. I slowly bend the thick paper. One fold will ruin it.

I fold it.

All that time, gone. Over. Done. No longer precious. Just ugly and pointless and difficult to fit into a trash can. I open the drawing up, and I tear it right in half. It's thick and rips unevenly. But now it fits in the garbage where it needs to go.

It's a terrible thrill. This destruction. A thrill to be able to decide something and just fucking do it. Not to be afraid. Just let it rip.

And then, nothing happens. The room is still silent. The world does not stop turning. It doesn't matter one bit. I made it, so I can destroy it. It feels like fireworks inside this dark room.

So, I take another drawing: the gym.

Fold. Rip.

And another: the girl's bathroom.

Fold. Rip.

The fireplace.

The dining hall.

The stairwell landing where Marco knighted me.

My dorm room where Amy and I talked about boys and listened to music and laughed so hard we cried. But no one would know that but me. RISD won't know. And they won't care.

It hits me that life will go on if I don't finish this application. In fact, no one but me will even notice. I find my journal in my bag. I need to interrupt myself.

Blood in your veins,
Menacing your arms and legs and heart.
I cannot remedy this.
I cannot draw my way out of this nastiness.
This meticulous work is useless and small.
This AIDS monster snarls and drools its contagion in every corner of every room, in every line I draw.
And I do not see the point of these lines and swirls and perspectives.
All this meticulousness will do nothing for him or anyone.
Arthur was wrong.
Who do I listen to now?

I leave the torn paper piled in the middle of the room. I'll deal with it later. If I stay here too long, I'll set the whole place on fire.

It's been three days now since I've been to my studio. I keep my sketch-book on me, a pesky companion reminding me of the mess I made. A vessel for me to spill my dumb guts. Just words; I can't draw right now.

The deadline gets closer every day, and I am stuck. Marco keeps talking about the dance, and Amy keeps talking about Marco, and I am frozen. I make it to all my classes and I try to read, but the words all mush together. I try to add numbers and finish physics homework, but all I can see is a pointless road.

We who see, don't get to look away when things get ugly.
We don't benefit from this sort of convenience.
We have to see the whole picture.
Every crack in severe focus.
Every word, a knife in our heads.
But sometimes it's too much
We long for fuzziness or a blank space
To relax,
To forget,
To escape from seeing it all.
I should be done with this project by now.
And instead, I am nowhere.
Perhaps the worst part is that no one will notice.

15

"Is It Really so Strange?"

First-period art class is really never a good idea. It seems clear to me after nearly four years of high school that artists are not morning people, and drawing isn't something you want to do when you're still asleep. Aside from the occasional yawn, it's dead silent today as we draw the still life: a clay rabbit, a glass bottle, and three lemons.

This is the first thing I've drawn since my studio massacre five days ago. It feels pointless. Even now.

Mrs. Funk walks around the room as we all stare at a very uninspired still life. She gives us tips on our progress. We are not supposed to lift our pencils from the paper. Contour drawings make you follow each edge like you're an ant crawling ever so slowly. My eyes keep closing. I tap my cheeks with my left hand.

"Danielle, are you OK?" asks Mrs. Funk.

"Oh, yeah, perfect." I say, trying to brighten my face by widening my eyes.

"OK, watch your negative space," she says.

"Yup," I say, barely concealing a sigh.

As the period nears an end, Funk addresses the class. "Everyone,

listen up. After this week, our class will be meeting in Clark Hall, in room 104. This building is going to begin renovations over Thanksgiving break and the administration is moving some classes to other spaces on campus."

Kyle makes a face. "Clark? Where the library is?"

"Right," says Funk, busying herself with papers on her desk.

"But that building is tiny. Where are we going to set up and paint? Are there even windows?"

"We will make do. Art can be made anywhere. We'll scale down our size and adapt." Funk is trying to keep us calm, but the sharpness of objections take on a menacing tone.

"Do we need to move all our stuff?"

"Why don't they wait 'til the summer?"

"This school sucks."

"It's because of the new gym," says Daria flatly, closing her giant pad of paper.

"Really?" I ask quietly.

"Yeah, they want this building's renovations done in the winter so the gym can be under construction in time for graduation. That way the families see the work half done and give them more money. Rich people hate mess. It's 'show' business." She air quotes while her eyes do an Olympic-level roll. Daria is a trusted source of inside scoops. I have no idea where her intel comes from, but it tends to be true. She always knows which teachers are leaving, dating, or lying. I swear she has an adult antenna.

Funk avoids her, frowns, and tries to shift gears. "Anyway, you will need to pack up your supplies by Friday, and starting next week we'll meet in the new space."

"This is some serious bullshit," I say far more loudly than I intended.

"Excuse me, Danielle! That's not how we speak here," Funk says sharply. She's never gotten mad at me before, but I don't even care right now. It is utter bullshit.

"Why is art disposable? I mean, they didn't bring back Mr. Thorne, and now they're shoving us into some tiny classroom so they can build a gym? Why not just cut the entire art program?"

"While I agree that art ought to receive adequate support from the school, we can only do so much to change the decisions made by the administration. This isn't only an art school. Large gym spaces attract students, and whether we like it or not, boarding schools are private businesses. They need to stay competitive with other schools, and that's life."

"Capitalism is murder," says Kyle, like it's a fact of life.

"Well, Kyle, that's a bit overblown, but I respect your opinions and your feelings. Believe me when I tell you there's only so much we can do." Funk goes back to her desk and sits down, indicating the end of the conversation.

"I can't believe it," I say to Daria, feeling more than a little guilty that I have my own studio space and my application project torn to shreds on the floor.

"I don't know why you're so shocked, Dan," she says, as she slides her pencils into a case and wads up her gray eraser. "Baxter is a breeding ground for captains of industry who tend to spend their high school years playing football and their adult years making money."

At the end of class, Funk comes up to me. "Danielle, I know your application is due soon. I sent RISD the recommendation you asked for. Let me know if you want me to send copies to any other colleges. Are your essay and portfolio all set?"

"You bet." I am not in the least bit set. I should have an entire application ready to go in the mail in two days and instead I have a pile of garbage.

"Want me to take a look at anything?"

I shake my head, holding it all in, "Nope, I'm good. Thank you for the letter."

"You're welcome. And I'm truly sorry that we have to relocate." She looks around the room. "I wish there was something I could do." Then she whispers, "You're right that it is some serious bullshit."

I should be nearing the finish line, but it's like I just came around the bend to realize there's a whole lot more to this race than I thought. I just want to get out of this school, and now I've made it worse.

I walk back to my room and throw my bag down loudly, and promptly stub my toe on the bed frame. "Fuck me," I shriek.

Amy is at her desk and gives me a sudden glare.

"Hey, Dani, what's your problem?" she says, clearly offended by my loudness.

"My toe . . . and they're moving advanced painting to Clark Hall, to some tiny office. The art room will disappear so they can renovate the gym. We're going to have to make micro paintings now. Thank God I'm leaving this fucking school. All they care about is sports, I swear to God."

"Are you kidding me? Don't be so dramatic." Amy hates when I complain about Baxter's obsession with sports. Here it comes. We hardly ever fight, and when we do it's about two things: me leaving my clothes on the floor and the sports-arts divide at Baxter. But I'm in no mood to keep quiet.

"Are *you* kidding *me*?" I know I sound like a lunatic, but I need to let this out. "Look at the gym: they're renovating it and they're planning to build a new one. When was the last time you went into the theater? Or the music room? They're small and old, and the windows are cracking. But hey, we must amp up the sports! Biffy and Skip need another perfect football field! We can't have them uncomfortable while they make us all proud with their perfect, athletic bodies that are destined to get married and join golf clubs. There are eleven gym teachers and about forty coaches. There are two music teachers, one art teacher, and a part-time drama teacher. It's obvious what the Baxter School cares about: jocks and jerks."

Amy stands in the middle of the room staring at me. I stare back. We've been best friends for four years and I suddenly feel a million miles away from her.

"OK, Danielle. So now everyone who does sports is just some ignorant jerk? Noah? Me?"

"No! I'm just saying, sports shouldn't be the top priority, all the time. Playing sports won't help the world or make you think more deeply about things that matter. It's not training you to help other people. It's just about winning. It's like all anyone wants is to conquer your opponent and buy a big house in the suburbs."

"What about your boyfriend, Marco? Isn't he a jock?"

"He's different. He's on a scholarship. He has to play sports to stay here to get an education," I say, excusing him from the ranks of the jocks. I don't include that he's not technically my boyfriend. I mean, I don't think he is. Yet.

"OK, so you only hate the rich jocks because they're a bunch of worthless assholes, and they're going to grow up to be bigger assholes who hate you?" God, why is she being so impossible?

"Hate me? Yeah, and my dad," I say flatly. "If we're being honest—which it seems like we are—yes, I think most of the people here at Baxter will grow up to be people who will hate us, and if they knew about my dad being gay and having HIV, they'd probably be so freaked out they'd want me gone."

"Wow, so, is that what this is about?" She changes her tone. Softer. Weirder, somehow.

"What? About my dad? No! This is about Baxter having fucked up priorities," I say quickly. It's nothing to do with my dad.

"Are you sure about that?" I just glare at her and decide I need to get out of here. I throw on my coat, grab my journal, and slam the door behind me.

Outside, the cold air smells like a fireplace somewhere nearby, maybe in the headmaster's house? I wish I was in a house right now. Curled up on a couch with people who get me. It's so exhausting here.

Overboard I go.
Far away from my life preserver.
I hurl myself over to the cold, dark water
Because this life vest doesn't fit.
The water is cold and murky
And I'm trying to keep my head up,
But this bag of rocks keeps pulling me deeper and deeper down
I never knew how tiring treading water could be.

All weekend I avoid everything. I find a book in the library about a serial killer, get a big bag of pistachios from the school store, and hide in the lounge cracking shells and getting thirsty while imagining being kidnapped and murdered in a basement. I go to my studio only to clean up. I throw the shredded drawings in a plastic bag and toss them in a dumpster. I feel like I murdered someone. I barely do my homework or talk to anyone. I listen to the Smiths' *Louder Than Bombs* on repeat. The days are mercifully shorter and shorter, and I go to sleep early.

Amy and I haven't spoken in four days. We are doing a really good job not overlapping during waking hours. By the time I wake up in the morning, she is already out.

Walking this morning to our new art classroom in a daze, I feel something similar to when Arthur died: a sense of loss but everything around me is weirdly the same as always. Like there's a bubble over me no one can see, but its pressure, heaviness, and dread weigh on me all at once. Like a cartoon where the rain cloud is only raining on me.

Today's the last day to send in my RISD application. After that, I go into the regular application pool and there's less of a chance I'll get in. Destroying those drawings feels like the end of something. Hope? Excitement? Possibility? My plan? Art was the most important thing in the entire universe, and now, I feel flat. Hollowed out.

Art class is tinged with everyone's collective annoyance at our new space. No one can settle, and Mrs. Funk is obviously over our whining.

"Make do, for God's sake," she finally tells us.

Make. Do. For God's sake.

Outside Clark Hall, Marco is sitting on a bench and gets up quickly when he sees me. Was he waiting for me? We haven't spoken since last week. I managed to hide all weekend.

"Dani, hey."

"Oh, hey." I look up at him, feeling like I should be something I am not. Sweet, or thankful, or funny, or cute. Something else. And somehow, he reads my mind.

"Are you OK? I haven't seen you around." He's reading my face. I don't want him to read my face. And I can't break down.

"Yeah, I'll be OK. I'm just late for English; I have to go."

"Yeah, of course. I'll catch up with you later." He puts his hand on my shoulder. It makes me a bit dizzy.

The next period begins. I slip out the side door before it really starts, and no one notices. I just can't sit through forty-five minutes of James Joyce. I get back to my dorm and call the nurse. I say it's diarrhea. She buys it. They always buy that. No school nurse wants a kid with diarrhea wandering around. Something is always going around at school. I lay down on my bed and pull the covers up and close my eyes.

I wake up an hour later to Amy walking in, jumping out of her skin when she sees me in bed.

"Dani! What are you doing here?" She looks at me like I'm a burglar.

"Diarrhea." I half smile while making air quotes with my index fingers. I don't think you're supposed to make jokes when you're in a fight, but diarrhea is just funny.

She looks at me and understands. "OK, well, I'm just here to get my math book." She goes to her desk and grabs the giant textbook and puts it in her bag.

I turn over in bed to face the wall. She leaves without a word.

Staring into my bowl in the final half hour of dinner, I wonder how they make cereal. Like, where is this even created? Whose job is it to decide the colors and shapes? So many colors. Looking around the dining hall, it's like a layer came off and I'm seeing details I never noticed before. Splinters in the floorboards, cracked paint around the windows, years of dishwasher dents on the spoon. Someone clears their throat next to me. Marco.

"Hi," I say.

"Hi. What's up?" he asks, noticing my deep pondering of the cereal.

"Who makes these little O's?" I ask quietly.

"The cereal?"

"Yes. The cereal. Who makes them?"

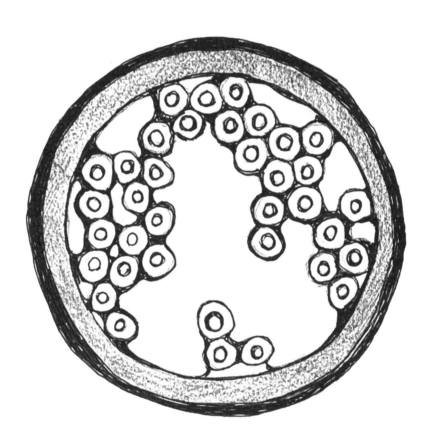

"Machines?" he suggests.

"Machines? That's disappointing. Where's the magic in that?" I say.

"Dani? Seriously, what's up? I didn't see you in class today. Are you sick or something?" He looks at my pajama bottoms, like I'm an escapee from a sick ward.

It is absurd to lie to him. "I didn't send in my application."

He sighs quietly, more of an *I get it* than *What a loser*.

"You didn't, huh?" He doesn't use exclamation points. He is quiet, accepting as he sits down across from me with a bowl full of salad.

"Nope. And I ripped up my portfolio drawings," I confess quietly, speaking into my cereal bowl.

He nods, like he's summing all of this up.

"Yeah, that sounds about right," he finally says.

"It does?"

"Sure. You're making the bed in the middle of a tornado."

"I'm what?" I ask, finally seeing his face as he sits beside me.

"You're in a terrible situation. You're taking control of something. Making the bed."

"But it doesn't help," I say, feeling worse.

"Yeah, but until you get through this part, you won't be able to be, like, stable."

"What part?"

"The shock, the surprise. It's like you just woke up and saw this hideous monster devouring your father, but not quite killing him, leaving you worried about a thing you can't be sure about. It's a nightmare in real life." It all sounds so logical when he says it.

"And then what?" I feel like Marco is showing me some supersecret, magical map, a way through this murky forest.

"Well, you have to stay strong, stay open, and fight what you can."

Fight what I can.

"My *tía* Sophia always says, 'Put your oxygen mask on your own face first.'"

"Meaning?"

"Meaning, take care of yourself so you can take care of everything else. Do what you need to do to stay strong for him, to be ready if the monster bares its teeth."

Maybe Dad will recover and be OK again, and the medical world will find a cure. Maybe he'll get on some perfect trial drug, and it will be a miracle that saves millions of people. Maybe.

I like that Marco said *if* not *when*. Even that feels like welcome hope.

"Marco?" I finally look away from the soggy cereal.

"Yeah?" he says, shoving some salad into his mouth.

"Thanks."

He puts down his fork and looks at me. "Anytime, Danielle."

Anytime. What a beautiful word, spoken by an even more beautiful mouth.

"Now, I have a really serious question," he says.

"Will I have a serious answer?" I reply.

"You better. The dance, is it formal? Do I need a suit or a tuxedo?"

I make a scared face. "No. But you can't wear a T-shirt either."

"I only have one button-down shirt with an actual collar, and it's purple," he admits.

"Let's go raid the costume shop in the theater tomorrow."

"Is that a thing people do here?"

"I do! I wore a 1950s cocktail dress to graduation last year. They never lock that place, and no one seems to care. Don't you worry, Mr. Díaz. Meet me outside the theater at four fifteen. We'll get you suited up!"

He brightens up, surprised by my sudden enthusiasm.

"Well, well, well, look who's got a project?" he laughs.

16
"When You Were Mine"

I get dressed in the theater bathroom. I don't want to be in my dorm room with Amy glaring at me, and I don't want to fight. I want to go to the stupid homecoming dance with a boy I have a crush on and not be angry or sad.

I zip up my red satin dress with little silver beads lining the scooped collar and lace sleeves to my elbows. I tie my boots up and step outside to find Marco all decked out in the blue tuxedo we found, a white tuxedo shirt, and a gray cummerbund and bow tie. Even in this Franken-suit, he is flawlessly handsome.

"You look like an evil punk prom queen!" he says, his eyes wide with excitement.

"You look like the son of a preacher!" I say, pulling on a pair of long black gloves.

"Yes, I do. Thank you!" Marco takes most things as compliments.

The dance has a theme we don't quite understand. It's like Mardi Gras and a Hawaiian luau are trying to be a Bat Mitzvah, all at a sporting event. Giant cut outs of palm trees line the gym and tissue-paper flowers decorate the walls. Handmade posters with Go Lions are scattered

everywhere. From the ceiling, disco balls bounce beams of light across the room so it looks like a space movie. It's too bad the sports part of Baxter doesn't talk to the arts part. We could really help them out in such circumstances.

As we dance to bouncy pop music, I feel like a normal girl. There's an actual band playing cover songs like "Celebration" and "Joanna," and instead of recoiling from its cheesiness, I love every minute. For a moment I feel an open space where my hurt and fear and anger usually sit. Air rushes in. For a moment I forget to worry.

I notice girls like Kirsten Floyd looking at me and Marco with the particular blend of envy and disdain that only high school girls are capable of, and I wonder if they are actually jealous of me? It seems so unlikely, but then again, look at this guy.

I see Amy with the jock crowd and avoid eye contact. I don't want to share this moment with all of them. For a little while, I forget to be sad, or worried, or just generally feeling like a twisted mess. Marco holds my hand. I try to keep my cool.

When the band takes a break, Kyle walks over to Mr. Fox, who's the teacher in charge of the dance, and hands him a cassette tape. Since they play a tape anyway while the band goes to smoke, Kyle and Daria always make a mixtape and persuade the teacher in charge to play it. Tonight's is a robust blend of the Cure, the Sugarcubes, Bananarama, the Smiths, and Cyndi Lauper.

All the jocks clear off to drink punch or whatever, and the art kids dance to our music. Marco and I join them. He knows how to make everyone feel joy, even this surly gang. He twirls Daria around and around and shimmies with Kyle. Every moment makes me crush harder. When Cyndi Lauper's "When You Were Mine" plays, I laugh inside thinking about how the lyrics are about a girl pining for a guy going out with another guy. Kyle has a triumphant grin on his face. Making the Baxter crowd listen to music about things they'd never talk about feels doubly excellent.

Eventually, the band comes back and the slow songs begin. The dance floor is flooded once again, and people are coupling up like penguins, swaying awkwardly, living out the romance. It's too much for me. "Let's go get some air outside," I whisper into Marco's ear. He makes a thumbs-up gesture.

We sit on a bench. Our breath shoots out of our panting mouths in thin clouds, and our faces steam from sweat.

"So, how does this compare to your old school's dances?" I ask.

"Let's see. We never had a live band, and there were so many more people there. It was always crowded and loud and chaotic."

"That doesn't sound fun," I say, scrunching up my nose. Am I being too cute? Or just cute enough?

"I wasn't that into it. I mean, I tried. I wanted to be, but well, yeah . . ." he trails off.

"If you ask me, this is the best dance at Baxter so far."

"You think so? Of all the dances over all the years?"

"Sure," I say.

"How many dances, exactly, have you ever been to?" He squints at me, skeptical.

"Um, a bunch."

He looks at me, waiting for me to stop lying.

"OK, three."

"Three? Aren't there, like, three a year? What were you doing? Being artistic and cool in your studio alone?"

"I don't remember," I say, trying to get the image of my ex out of my head. Brian never wanted to go to dances, so I just stopped going. Looking back, I'm embarrassed about how I followed Brian around like a love-starved puppy. Being with Marco feels so balanced. I am not running after him or waiting around for him. He's just here, smiling at me.

We hear "More Than Words" sifting through the door out into the cold.

"Yeah, this is the best dance by far." I tilt my head back and forth. "Because of you."

"Aww, Dani, that's so . . ."

And then it happens. Maybe it's the cold air. Maybe it's the sappy song. But all of it rolled into one thought in my mind. We have to kiss.

I lean right over and shove my stupid lips on his perfect face. I kiss him.

Immediately, his face sort of closes. He holds still but doesn't kiss me back. After a few moments, he pulls his face away. Holding my arms with his perfect hands, making space between us. My stomach flops like a dying fish, my head hot with shock. Everything is wrong. I've made a massive mistake.

"Danielle," he says slowly, like he is afraid to get the words out. The awful, sudden knowledge of misjudgment crashes into my head. This rejection is pounding inside me over and over. I should have stayed alone in my room.

"No, it's OK. You don't have to say anything," I say, my body wanting to go as far away as possible. "I'm sorry. I thought . . . Never mind. I'm sorry." I move his hands away and get up and go.

I run across the grass to the library. The cold air filling my chest, seeping across my body. I get to the door and it's unlocked, thank God. Inside, I walk through the dark hallway into the main library room, and sit under a table to try to make the awfulness disappear.

I thought he liked me. I thought he was spending all this time with me and helping me with homework and talking to me about death and loss because he liked me.

I'm so stupid.

He's way too cute. I mean, he'd want me as a friend, not someone to kiss. Amy always tells me that girls are supposed to wait for boys to kiss them or ask them out. I never remember this. I never wait. I kissed Brian before he kissed me. I just thought you had to do that 'cause boys are sometimes nervous or dense. But the truth is, I think they'll never kiss me otherwise. Clearly, there is something deeply wrong with me, and maybe there always will be. I'm not pretty enough to be his girlfriend. I'm not an athlete. I'm not his type.

I hear the door to the library open and then close. I see the black sneakers he thought could be disguised as fancy shoes walking toward me. The blue tuxedo pants drooping.

He sits down just outside my little cave.

"Danielle?"

"Yes?"

"Can I come in?" he asks quietly.

I wipe my face with my hands. "Sure."

He crawls under the table with me. He curls his body and sits cross-legged, looking straight at me. He takes a deep breath in.

"Danielle, I'm sorry," he says.

"It's fine." I stare at the floor. I cannot look at him. This is excruciating.

"No, it's not fine. I think I gave you the wrong impression."

I finally look up at him. Now he is staring at the floor. I knew it. Of course, he doesn't really like me like that.

"I need to tell you something," he says.

"I've heard this one before, Marco, really, save your breath."

"It's not what you think."

"It's not?"

"No Dani, I'm . . . I think I wanted you to like me so I wouldn't seem . . . Well, no one would think . . . no one would know . . ."

"That you don't like me? I get it. Like I said, I've heard it before."

"That's not it. I do like you. But you deserve the truth."

"What truth? That you don't want to be my boyfriend. But then why be so intent on this stupid dance? I didn't even want to go."

"I've never told anyone this, and I just need you to keep it a secret . . ." He pauses and takes a deep breath.

I wait, staring at him. Somehow I sense he isn't just telling me the same old boring bullshit a boy says to try to make a bad situation better

He takes another big breath and closes his eyes as he says, "I think, well, I pretty much know . . . Danielle, I'm gay."

This fact lands slowly and certainly, like a parachute has opened and is drifting down to a landing.

"You're gay?" I repeat, making it slightly more real.

"Yes. I mean, I feel like I am. But yes, I think so."

We sit in silence for a long time. My mind is playing a reverse montage reel of every single moment, starting tonight and ending with us at the mailboxes when school started, and trying to add this all up.

"You flirted with me, though, didn't you?" I have to ask. "I mean, it felt like flirting. Was I just being clueless?"

He continues, "I'm a guy, and well, I'm supposed to have a girl-friend and take her to dances, and I guess it's been so long I've been on autopilot, I just keep it up, even though I know now—like pretty much positively—that I'm different. And you're not just some girl, Danielle. You're . . . amazing, smart, creative, funny, and . . . you get it. You get me."

"Obviously not, Marco." I shoot back, hard. "Obviously, I have no fucking clue. Plus, is that all you cared about, that I get you? How was this supposed to go? I was going to hang on to the remote possibility of your liking me back and just sort of pine away for you and take whatever tiny fragments of affection you can stand to share until we graduate? But as long as I *got* you, that's all that would matter? What are you even talking about?"

"I'm just— I'm trying to be honest with you. I've never talked to anyone about this before. I've never told anyone. Ever. I thought maybe you'd understand. Because of your dad and everything."

"Wait, you thought I'd be OK with you pretending to be my boy-friend because I have a gay father? Are you serious?"

For an instant, I see my mom's face as she raged at my dad. This is it. This is why she lost it on him. He was using her, a veil to conceal his real self. Then he rejected her.

This is the last straw for me. I need air. I crawl out from under the table, and walk out of the library.

I head back to my dorm room, grab my journal, and go sit in the lounge.

I tell myself it's better outside,
Cooler, more daring, more real.
More like my heroes who faced life unfiltered, loud, painful, strong.
But did they ever feel unhappy, lonely, left out?
Or did they just feel free?
Surely, they kept their armor on, deflecting this sort of nonsense.
But I am bare, torn, weak,

My soft parts exposed,
Foolish beyond measure for holding hope.
Imagining myself
Past this book, these hands, this room,
inside a world I cannot escape,
Pining for a world I cannot enter
Where love happens.
Where endings are happy.
But still, I'm here,
Wondering why I ever entertained fairy-tale dreams
When I ought to know better.

I open the door to my room, remembering that Amy and I are fighting, and wishing we weren't. This is that moment when I need to fall into her lap. Collapse and have her hold me together.

The desk lamp is on, and there's some quiet music playing. Lou Reed sings warm and gentle, like a lullaby. But I don't see Amy right away. Then I notice her bed is a huge pile of blankets and a big lump. She's in there. I try to be quiet while I take off my dress and change into pajamas.

"Hey," I hear her say from under the covers.

"Hey. Sorry if I woke you." I remove my gloves and my boots. I catch myself in the mirror, mascara smeared and lipstick gone.

"I wasn't sleeping," she says from inside her bed.

"Oh, OK." I start putting my earrings and necklace away.

"Did you have fun at the dance?" she asks.

"No. Not really," I say after weighing the odds of lying.

"Baxter dances suck," she says, not sounding like herself.

"What happened? Homecoming dances are your thing." I say this kindly but realize it might sound bitchy too.

"Noah and I had a fight," she says, her face emerging from her cocoon.

"Oh, really?" I'm relieved she didn't snap back at me, but now I'm suddenly concerned she's actually hurting.

When she uncovers herself, her eyes are puffy and red. She's still wearing her dress. She's been crying too. Sadder than me, it seems.

"He wanted to get high before the dance. With his friends. Kenny had a joint and wanted us all to sneak into the gym locker room and smoke weed."

"And you, of course, said you didn't want to." Amy says pot makes her chest hurt and her head full of scary thoughts. I get it. Also this girl is nothing if not a rule follower.

"Right, I didn't. So then he started saying all this stuff about how I'm no fun anymore, and his friends all say he's turning into a boring old fart 'cause he's with me, and that maybe we should take a break."

"'Take a break'? What are you, married?"

"That's what I said!" she says, sitting up straighter, shaking off the covers from her shoulders. "I mean, if you don't want to date me, just say so!"

"Did you say that to him?" I ask.

"Yeah. And he said, 'Maybe I don't.'" She starts to cry. I grab the box of tissues and sit next to her. I wasn't Noah's biggest fan, but they always seemed so solid, like they would one day co-own real estate and adopt a slew of shelter dogs.

"I'm sorry, Ames," I say. Her problem is the one we need to take care of right now. Not mine. In fact, I'm relieved to focus on her.

I make us chamomile tea, and we wrap blankets around ourselves and sit on her bed together.

"It's been like this since we got back to school. He's been different. More controlling." She tells me, like she's confessing somehow. Like she hadn't wanted me to know this.

"Really? I'm surprised. You seemed pretty happy," I say.

"I know. Well, it's not like we don't love each other. It's just, well, he hates all the movies I want to see. He's just, like, into his team and his buds. He also wants me to apply to the same schools as him."

"Really? But you've wanted to go to Berkeley, like, forever," I say, also trying to be calm about all of this even as it sounds weirder and more disturbing.

"Yeah, no." She pulls her hair into a quick bun as she perks up, sharing details with me. "He wants me to apply to Dartmouth and

Wash U—his top two schools—but it's a moot point now. I mean, I guess I was thinking we'd just do long distance . . . I don't know. And if I'm being really honest, I guess I was sort of looking forward to after graduation because then it would be easier to be . . . apart."

She was avoiding the big bad breakup. My efficient, neat, and tidy friend was dealing with a mess the best way she could. I just nod. She takes a deep breath and sighs. Then she looks at me, at my dress in a pile on the floor, and back to my eyes. "Wait, why are you back so early? What happened with Marco?"

"Well . . ." I don't know what to tell her. Do I tell her about the kiss? Or the rejection or what we talked about under the library tables? Am I sworn to secrecy? Or does it not count when it's your best friend and you're heartbroken? I mean, I'm mad at him, but also, this is, like, a big deal thing to spill to someone else. But it's not just anyone, it's Amy, and we're actually, finally, not fighting. God I've missed her.

"You have to promise not to tell anyone," I say quietly, like someone's listening.

She squints her eyes and brings her face closer to mine. "I promise. What? Did you guys have sex?"

"Um, no." I nearly laugh. "I tried to kiss him, and he pulled away, and I freaked, and then he told me . . . he's gay."

Her eyes open up big, and she sits up straight, inhaling sharply.

Then she relaxes and nods about six or seven times slowly.

"Yeah. Totally. I see it now. Thoughtful, well-groomed, smells amazing, and has a more organized binder of notes than me. Dammit, how could I be so blind?" I love how she somehow feels responsible for this oversight.

"Well, I sure didn't see it," I say.

"You had a crush on him, so how could you? I mean, his beauty blinded your delicate little heart."

We sit there for a minute, talking through our eyes. It's such a relief to be with her again. Like drinking a glass of water after eating too many chips.

"I'm sorry, Ame. I'm sorry for everything I said yesterday. I just . . .

well, I've been freaking out and just unhinged. Everything feels so shaky, and I guess it felt like you weren't on my side."

"I know. I wasn't. I thought you were being unfair to Noah, and I wanted to defend him . . . which seems especially dumb now," she says, playing with the hem of the blanket.

"It's not dumb."

"It was kind of. I mean, the reality is I totally agree that this place thinks sports is the most important thing in the universe, and they're a bunch of uptight, traditional assholes who just want to win trophies."

I smile at her. "Trophies are awfully shiny."

We laugh. She hugs me. "I love you, Danidan. I'm sorry I called you an ass," she says.

"It's OK, Amela, I was being one."

"You were a little, but I love you anyway," she says, still wrapping her arms around me.

"I love you too."

"And I'm sorry things with Marco aren't what you thought," she says delicately, sipping her tea.

"Yeah, well, just my luck, right?"

"Well, you're still going to be friends with him, aren't you?"

"I sort of wigged out after he told me. I don't know where this is going to end up, honestly."

"But it's not like he's going out with another girl. Isn't this better, in a way? Like, it's actually not at all about you."

This hits me deep. She's right. It's not about me at all. He didn't reject me because he doesn't like me, he's just not attracted to girls.

"Did you storm off in a classic Danielle huff?" she asks with her mom face.

I frown a little and admit, "Totally."

She sighs another sigh and shakes her head. "Talk to him. Don't be the asshole here. He's a good guy, and you of all people must know how scary it is to come out."

"But I've never done it."

"Yeah, but you are so careful about how and when you talk about your dad here. Like, you know this place will go to pieces if they have to accept someone being gay! How do you think Marco must feel?"

Oh, Amy, teller of truths. I hadn't even thought about it. I was so concerned with my own feelings and seeing this as some kind of massive heartbreak, but it isn't that. I should be supportive, not self-absorbed.

I mean, isn't that what friends do?

17
"Protection"

Saturday morning is good library time. Everyone else is either sleeping or serving Saturday detention. Ms. Franklin is here until noon and always ready to help with any sort of detectivelike research. I swear she was born right out of a Nancy Drew book, a redheaded sleuth.

"Well, Danielle, how goes it?" She pulls off her reading glasses and lets them fall on their orange beaded chain, down onto her mighty bosom.

"Hi, Ms. Franklin. How are you? How's Poppy?" I glance at her bulletin board and the photo of the miniature poodle. Unlike Lloyd in the mail room, I've found the way to Ms. Franklin's heart.

"Oh, she's getting on, Danielle. Some digestion issues, but she's still got a few good miles left. Thanks . . . So, what's cooking?"

"Well, actually, I'm looking to do some research and not sure where to start."

She pulls out a yellow pad of paper and a pen to make some notes. She's ready. "Well, you came to the right place. Shoot!"

"I'm researching an artist for art history class."

"Wonderful! What's their name?"

I open my sketchbook to spell it out for her. I even learned how to pronounce it: Worn-a-ro-vitch.

"Hmm, I've never heard of him. Is he European? That name seems . . . Polish maybe?"

"American, actually. He lives in New York. I think he's in his thirties?"

"All right, let me see what I can find. Looking for anything in particular?"

"Articles, essays, anything really. I already found an article in *Artforum*."

"So, Ms. Davis's class? Lucky you. She's a gem." Ms. Franklin finishes writing and looks back at me. "Got it. What else?"

"Well, I want to read more about, um, AIDS, actually."

She tilts her head up and bites down on both her lips like she's keeping herself from speaking.

"Oh," she responds as though I've just asked her to research the smell of urine.

I know talking about the world outside our ivy-and-stone walls is usually a tricky proposition, but getting into subjects like AIDS is just fully risky to the sensitive folks at Baxter.

"No. I just want to, you know, learn more about what Wojnarowicz was making art about."

"Phew, you had me worried there for a second." She sighs with deep relief; maybe glad she isn't two steps from the dreaded disease? If she only knew.

I'm not lying, but it feels like I am.

"I hear the news sometimes," I continue. "But I don't really read the newspaper, like, all the time, so I'm looking for recent news about what's been happening. Like, what are the most successful treatments? How many people have died? What is the government doing about it? To, you know, better understand his art."

She gives me a long look and finally breathes in the air of my evident scholarly curiosity, a librarian's dream. "Good. Great. Love it. The *New York Times* should give us what we need. In fact, I did see something recently."

She turns to head deep into the area behind the desk. After a minute she brings out a stack of newspapers.

"Are we looking at this year only? How far back do you want to go? We'll need to use microfilm for articles older than a year, so let's work our way backward."

There's no map here. There's no lesson plan. Only me and Ms. Franklin, alone in the library. This is how I learn about the disease coursing through my father's body.

"So, I saw an article last winter." She continues. "Maybe January? About the death toll. I remember because I read about how Princess Diana sat with AIDS victims when she visited New York, and there was that actor who died. Rock Hudson, wasn't it? Anyway, let me see . . ." She flips through the stack. Looking over her shoulder, I'm shocked at all the news I don't read. I see a lot about Kuwait and Iraq and President Bush and abortion rights. When do you go from being a kid who stays blissfully away from the news to a person who actually cares? For me it's right now.

"Ah-ha! Here it is. January 1991. 'U.S. Reports AIDS Deaths Now Exceed 100,000.'" She scans the article and tells me, "One-third of them happened last year." She hands me the paper carefully and shakes her head. "It's on page eighteen of the first section. After an article about stamps." She's saying it like there is something wrong with page eighteen.

"Is that bad?" I ask.

"Well, a hundred thousand dead Americans seems more urgent than postage stamps," she says coldly.

I agree. It seems strange that even after all these years of AIDS being out there and covered in the news, this isn't a bigger deal. Is that because mostly gay people get it?

"And, I think, there was just recently an opinion piece. Let me see."

She flips back, closer to the most recent issues. "Ah, here it is. Opinion section. September 30, 1991. That's less than a month ago. The headline is 'Dithering About AIDS.'"

I look at her, uncertain what all that means but not wanting to come off as ignorant.

She smiles at me. She knows high school students don't read the newspaper. But she's kind enough not to make me feel stupid. "Most newspapers publish opinion pieces. They're not strictly reporting the news as much as discussing an issue and having an opinion about it. This article talks about how the federal government is 'dithering,' or wasting time, not addressing a major national health crisis."

She scans the page of the *New York Times* then reads aloud: "But high-level leadership is missing. 'In the past decade, the White House has rarely broken its silence on the topic of AIDS,' the AIDS commission lamented. President Bush has made only a single speech on AIDS, to an audience of businessmen. President Reagan also ducked the issue, which touches on homosexuality and drug addiction and thus inflames many conservatives.'"

"Do these articles actually change people's opinion?" I ask.

"Well, perhaps. It's a way for the newspaper to say, 'Hey, this is something we're seeing that's a problem, and we don't want to stay silent about it.' Now, you can also criticize the paper for ignoring it themselves . . . as we saw in that article from January. It's complicated. But interesting, don't you think?"

I read the article, and I recall modern world history, learning about the devastation of the 1918 flu. And I think about how we get vaccines now for the flu, as well as measles, mumps, and polio. I assumed the medical world had all the answers. Shouldn't the government want scientists and doctors to find cures as fast as possible if hundreds of thousands of people are dying? Last summer, NPR talked about how AIDS is simply untreatable, how it baffles modern medicine and there's no way to cure it. But this *New York Times* article talks about education to prevent the spread of HIV, which if done right could save a lot of lives. There's so much more we can be doing.

"Now, as for that artist you mentioned, I'm going to need to call in some backup. Want to check back in with me Monday? I should be able to find you something by then."

She takes the two newspapers and goes into the back to copy the articles on the Xerox machine.

"Here you go," she says, returning. She hands me a stapled bundle of paper. "I hope this helps, dear." She plays with her glasses chain. "It's a terrible disease and such a sad time for all those families." She again shakes her head.

I shudder. Does she know about my dad? "Families?" I ask.

"All those young men have parents, grandparents, aunts, and uncles. I know some are rejected for their lifestyle choices, but still, their families must be wrecked. From what I've read and seen on TV, it's an ugly thing, this AIDS."

Their families, as she's describing it, consist of the parents, the aunts and uncles. I love Ms. Franklin, but I can see by her face that she cannot fathom a person with AIDS having a child, much less being a Baxter parent. I nod to agree with her, hoping to cover up any emotions that might have sneaked across my face. "Yeah, well, thanks for all your help," I say.

Walking across campus I think about all those "young men" and how Ms. Franklin seemed so worried about all the people who care and worry about them. When you think about it on a human level, worrying about someone in pain seems such an obvious and true act.

And then I remember Marco, the dance, and the kiss. I realize how scared he must be, being gay, here, now. And when we live in a world with AIDS. How terrifying. A double-decker sandwich of fear of rejection for who you love and fear that that love might kill you. I sit in the cold, find a spot of sunshine, and take out my journal.

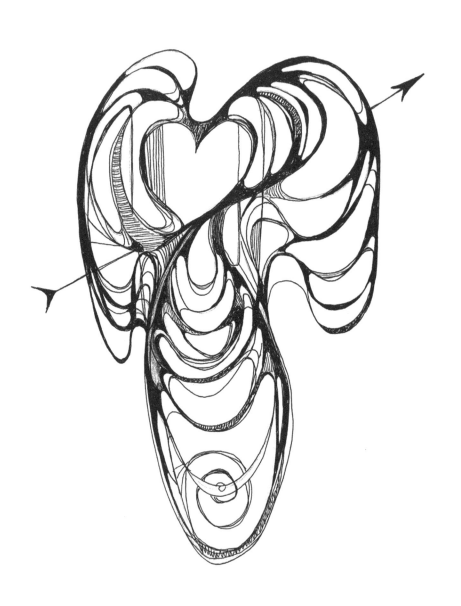

It's easy for me to think you don't have a monster chasing you,
You, the dashing prince in silver armor.
You shine so bright; how could dragons do you harm?
Surely, the screaming makes a way into your heart,
which must be tender
And into your mind, so fast and seeing.
Of course, there is fear.
I could be your warrior.
Fight any monster with you
Or tear their power down.
I could carry your rocks, like you carry mine.

"Danielle, can you please say something? All your note said was, 'Let's talk after dinner.'"

Marco and I are sitting on a bench at the back of the cafeteria. After dinner is always a quiet time here, Sundays especially. Everyone is in their rooms cramming in their weekend homework or off breaking rules and earning detention.

We stare into the trees off in the distance. It's so weird that humans feel so much shame about who they are. Do birds wonder about their looks? Do dogs judge each other for their bark or their fur? My mind wanders as I try to figure out how to start.

"So, I've thought a lot about this," I say slowly, remembering the dragons and monsters.

"OK. What is it?" he asks, clearly a little unsure and impatient with me.

I put my arm through his, quietly. I try to get him to look me in the eye, but he won't. "I'm glad you told me. And I'm grateful you trust me. I felt ashamed for liking you and kissing you, and I felt rejected more than anything. But that was just some selfish stuff I had to sort through. You deserve better than that from me. And I don't want you to have to keep everything all to yourself. It's OK."

"It's really not, though," he says. "The football team will all but boot me out, and wrestling starts soon, and they won't let me even practice if they knew. And I need to play or . . . I can't stay here. Everyone's going to be weird to me if they find out. They'll treat me differently, and let's face it, it won't be better."

"Not everyone will." I smile into his face 'til he looks into my eyes. "And you're still Marco: the guy who helps total strangers study for tests, who scores touchdowns and understands physics; the guy who dances to stupid music and wears ridiculous tuxedos, who organizes the living crap out of a binder with colorful tabs; the guy who comforts people when they're scared. And I'm guessing there will be more and more people you meet who like you for who you are, not in spite of it. But seriously, who could ever hate you once they knew you?"

"Oh, you know, my family, the government . . . every single person here, except you."

"And Amy!" I chime in, not thinking.

"Wait, did you tell Amy?" His eyes wide, full of shock and fear.

Oh, Danielle, you moronic dingbat.

I instantly fess up. This is not a time for lying. "Yes, I did. I needed to talk about it too. For what it's worth, she helped me be less focused on myself and more understanding toward you. If it weren't for her, I might still be the shithead with her head up her you-know-what?"

"Butt?" he asks, still looking at the ground.

"Right. Butt." I say.

"Huh, I guess that's nice. But what if she tells other people?"

"Don't worry. She won't tell a soul. Amy's way better at keeping secrets than I am. Plus, she had a huge fight with Noah, so it won't get to him. She's way more fond of you than him at the moment."

His brow crunches together, trying to solve a puzzle that is too confusing, and I say, "Marco, she thinks you're amazing too."

He stares at the floor, clearly still shaken.

"There's a lot more people on this side of the river than you think," I say to him, squeezing his perfect hand.

"The river?"

"Oh yeah, that's what I call the divide in the world. On one side, people don't question things, never challenge what they're told. They look alike and talk alike and live alike. And on the other side, where people like you and me live, there's more questioning, I guess. We wonder why women are expected to cook and clean and men are supposed to be big and violent and always, always, always be in charge of the entire world. Why should someone's skin determine their value, their abilities, their potential? Why are people who are different made to seem bad or wrong? Why is it wrong to be weird? What is normal anyway?"

By now, he's smiling.

I keep going, only because seeing him smile is making me happy. "So, on our side of the river, we're these silly creatures who ask a ton of questions. Our world, or the one we want anyway, is a place where we can investigate and be curious, feel our pain when we need, or celebrate joy and frolic without fear of being judged. Well, maybe judged a little for questionable haircut decisions, but judged with love."

He smiles at me. "Danielle." He stops, getting choked up.

"Marco, I know I was being a selfish douche on Friday night, but I'm really, very glad you told me the truth. I mean I wish you'd done it before I smeared my lips all over your face, but well, now it's out in the open—at least between us. And you can't hide behind me because that won't work, but I'll stand next to you and be your friend, if that's OK."

"That's very OK." He nods, tightening his arm in mine. "You're not mad?"

"No. I'd be mad if you were straight and rejected me for some boring, pretty girl."

"Oh my God, stop. You're beautiful, Danielle. If I were straight, I'd— Well, honestly, I don't know what, but you're gorgeous, and I am not rejecting you. But I should have told you before. You're the first person I've ever met who I thought I could tell."

"Well, I am honored. Really. Really, Marco Polo."

"Thanks, Danielita."

As we hug, I can smell his clean shirt and feel the softness of his coat on my cheek. He says, "Everything's better with you."

We look out the window, and someone comes in and starts putting turkey decorations on the wall.

"Oh Lord . . . Thanksgiving. What's your plan?" Marco asks.

"It's Dad's year," I say with a smile reflecting the enormousness of that statement. And then I take a deep breath and smile at him.

"Right, of course. He invited me for dessert? Maybe I can come."

"Absolutely, come over. This year's guest list is particularly fabulous."

"So, that's what, in two weeks? We'll take the bus Wednesday after class?" he asks.

"Bring snacks. I'll definitely miss breakfast."

"Of course."

18
"Heartbreak Hotel"

It's my biweekly call with Mom. We have this deal that every other Sunday, I call her with the Sprint phone card she gave me.

She still doesn't know Dad is HIV positive, and I don't know if I should tell her. Before I dial, I look at last night's notes in my sketchbook.

> Stay calm, keep it simple.
> Dad isn't sick
> Yet
> New medicines could help.
> He has good doctors.
> AIDS is not a death sentence.

This is not a situation I ever saw on an after-school TV special: *Should I tell my mom that my dad has AIDS?*

As soon as she picks up the phone, I hear it.

"Yes, dear?" she says fast and brittle, and I know she's stressed or rushed.

I can't do it.

"Oh, hey, Mom," I say, pretending there is no enormous piece of news I need to share with her.

"What's up?" she says quickly, like I'm keeping her from something.

"Oh, you know, same old same old. Homework, school. The usual." I think maybe I'm trying too hard, but she doesn't notice. "How are you this week, Mom?" This usually works, I just pivot to her and then the pressure subsides.

"Well, I was at the most incredible dinner last night at the dean's house. My God, you should have seen her ceramics collection. Some of my colleagues were there and dinner was amazing. I honestly don't know how she leads the school and has time to make beef bourguignon like that."

As she talks, I'm thinking, Why does it have to be me? I don't want to deal with other people's feelings about Dad's disease. I can barely handle myself. Maybe Jake will tell her, but I doubt it. I don't even know if they talk on the phone like we do.

Looking out the window from the hall phone as she talks about some Japanese movie she saw, I see the front gate of the campus and remember when I first arrived at Baxter. It was Jake's last year and my first. Mom and Dad decided to make this big show of unity, and we all arrived on move-in day together. I was nervous and scared about starting a new school and about being away from home. I'd been so excited about it, but when the actual day came, it hit me: I have to live here? Like, every day." My freshman roommate, Betsy, barely spoke when I met her so I thought she didn't like me. As we carried my crates and bags up the stairs, the kids all looked stressed and the parents all sounded angry. The hallway was dark, smelled musty, and my room didn't feel magical; it just felt old. We made a second trip to the car together, walking across campus to the front gate. Dad put his arm around me, and I started crying. Immediately, Mom asked what was wrong.

"I don't know, I just feel scared, I guess."

"Scared?" She nearly shrieked. "What is there to be scared of? This is a wonderful school in a beautiful place, and your big brother is here

to protect you." She actually laughed. She smiled at Dad and Jake for agreement. Neither of them were smiling.

"It's normal to be nervous on the first day," Jake finally said to me, breaking the awkward silence. "Dani, you'll make friends here really fast, you'll adjust quickly." His voice was almost comforting. I began to sob. As much as I hated eighth grade, I missed it terribly at that moment.

"Danielle, dear, do try to keep yourself together. We're in public," Mom said, looking around, like she was far more concerned with people seeing me cry than with my crying. I wanted to crawl into a hole and disappear.

"Laura, please," Dad said, putting his arm around me.

"She's fine," Mom insisted. "You're the one who always says, 'This is why God made boarding schools.'"

"Dammit, Laura, would you stop it? She's obviously upset."

"Well, so am I." Mom sneered, almost whispering, as we stood outside the gates. All day I'd been waiting for this. For her to explode at Dad, and here it all started because of me. "I am rising above it." She continued, "That's what it is to be a grown-up, Danielle. You hold your head up. You handle things."

"She's fourteen," is all Dad said.

That is a day I wish I could forget.

I know how my mom handles things. When I was twelve, it was just the two of us in the house after Dad left and Jake started Baxter. One night we'd been working together to update her work Rolodex, transferring her contact cards to the bigger ones and making changes. Mom always had me do little helpful projects, like cutting up tiny pieces of paper and taping them to cards, alphabetizing files, pasting newspaper clippings into her journalism portfolio. It used to feel fun to do these grown-up tasks. Like the mysterious grown-up world was being opened to me. That night, after about forty-five minutes, she sat up straight and said, "I think we need to make some cookies!" I was so relieved; my eyes were hurting, and I was getting bored.

In the kitchen we listened to Elvis Presley. Mom's messy bun had flour in it, butter wrappers and sugar and flour containers covered the kitchen counter. Dad was the neat cook. When Mom cooked it was like a bomb exploded. As we rolled the dough into golf ball blobs, she swayed to the music and bumped hips with me. "Heartbreak Hotel" came on and she closed her eyes and said, "I had my first kiss to this song."

"Really?" I said, wondering if she'd tell me about it.

"George Harmon," she sighed his name. "I was in ninth grade and he was in tenth, and he played baseball and had these big blue eyes." Then she paused, lost in memory.

"So, wait, what happened? Tell me the story." Her face always got soft and gooey when she talked about being a teenager in the 1950s. At twelve, I hadn't had my first kiss yet, but of course, it was a huge topic of conversation among my friends. I also loved imagining my mom as a younger version of this person I knew.

"Well," she was scraping the nearly empty bowl of cookie dough with her finger, "we were both on the school newspaper, and we'd worked on a story together about the football team, of all things. He was a terrible writer, but he was so cute. I didn't care. To my surprise, he asked me to the spring formal. I was so nervous, I nearly passed out before he picked me up, but maybe it was all the hairspray in my hair and that god-awful girdle my mother made me wear. I wore a yellow dress with a white collar. I looked like a daffodil. But I made it out the door, and we danced and had a great time, and at the end of the night, he kissed me!"

"Just like that? Out of nowhere?"

"Well, it wasn't completely out of nowhere. We were at the dance, after all." She was licking her finger, still moving to the music.

"Was it nice? The kiss?" I asked, hesitantly. I was so curious, but also, ew—who wants to think about their mom kissing someone?

"Oh, sure. It was a sweet little peck. He was a nice boy. It wasn't like full of tongue or anything."

"EW, Mom!"

"Sorry," she giggled.

"So, what happened to George? Did you, like, go steady?"

"We might have gone to the movies once or twice. My mother called him Motormouth because he'd get nervous around her and babble. But we just kind of drifted apart. He stopped calling and then he got serious with another girl, Marian something, a cheerleader. Her parents belonged to the local country club, and he was a boy destined for the golf course." She offered me the rest of the bowl to lick and started washing up.

It struck me that my mom might have been dumped in high school. Maybe her heart got broken. She didn't look sad, but I imagined her, fourteen years old, crying into a pillow. And then it struck me that Dad dumped her too.

Then, as I washed the bowl, the phone rang. Mom wiped her hands on her apron and picked up the receiver. Faintly, I could hear Dad's voice on the other end. Immediately, her face changed its shape and her eyes got narrow. She turned her body away from me, and I pretended to clean up, stacking bowls and closing containers. I heard her murmuring in a sharp voice.

"No, we said twelve thirty, not one thirty, Benjamin . . . Well, that isn't my problem . . . I didn't say that, I said it was precisely what I didn't want . . . No. No. Well, you might have thought about that before now. I cannot rearrange my schedule just to make life easier for you." She was nearly hissing.

I froze and didn't want to call attention to myself; I didn't want her to know I'd heard; I didn't want her to know I was there. It was only three months since Dad moved out, and they were still negotiating their divorce—who got what, who paid for what, all that grown-up stuff. All I wanted was my cookie-making, dancing mom who talked about boys and kisses. Dad's call stopped her cold.

She finally hung up the phone and ran her fingers through her hair. When she turned around, her eyes were red and her face full of rage. I didn't know what to do.

"Honey, I'm, um— Yeah, I need to go to . . . um, I need to . . ." And then she burst into tears. Her long fingers covered her whole face, and she just cried.

"Mom, I'm sorry," I said quietly, not knowing why I said it, just thinking maybe it would help.

Mom moved her hands from her face and found a towel to wipe her wet eyes. "You have nothing to be sorry about. It's just all so much, and it makes me so angry and then I get so sad, and I want to scream and punch things, and I'm just . . . I'm sorry, this isn't your fault." She said in one long breath.

"I know," I said. "But it isn't anybody's fault. I mean, Dad's just doing his best . . . like all of us."

And that's when she looked at me, the sadness vanished and a cold icy stare took over her face. Immediate regret filled my entire body.

"No," is all she said. And then she walked out of the kitchen, into her bedroom, and closed the door.

I never knew what she was saying no to. But I knew then to never talk about Dad with her. It only made things worse. Like my crying only made things worse on move-in day.

I know she looks forward to us eventually doing grown-up things together. I imagine she's waiting for a time when we will sip martinis and talk about current events in an adult way. Her move to San Francisco placed a useful and enormous space between us. We can talk about neutral things. That's fine. It usually works. We get along great. It was like letting a garden grow.

At this moment, I decide to keep Dad's virus a secret a little longer. There's no need to stir the pot.

"So, Danielle, my darling, is it done? The big application?" Mom asks, expecting an equal dose of enthusiasm. I'm so focused on not mentioning Dad or HIV, that I'm not really listening.

"What?" I ask, trying to get back to the here and now.

"Your RISD application? Hello? Earth to Danielle! Wasn't it due last week?"

I take a deep breath and magically weave a story about the admissions at RISD being different and how I got it wrong—so kind of admitting I was wrong, but not, you know, entirely. I make up some lies about the timeline and how I'll be in a better position to send in a more developed portfolio for the regular January deadline. That's partly true.

She questions nothing and says, "Well, good luck with everything. I

letting a garden grow

still want you to consider some other options." She has said this ten zillion times before, so I don't even answer her. "Oh, dear, it's late, I need to get going. Listen, I'll be in Philadelphia over the winter holiday, so I'll let you know and we can make plans, go shopping or something, OK? You'll be at your dad's for the holiday?"

"Yes, I will."

"OK, darling. Love you so much!"

"Love you too, Mom. Bye." I hang up feeling that I conned her doubly: not telling her the truth about the application or about Dad. Keeping secrets is messy and makes my belly hurt.

I call Dad right after. He's home, reading and making pasta sauce. He usually spends an average of four hours making bolognese pasta. "Tomato sauce cannot be rushed, Dani, like wine or poetry."

"Is everything OK, Dad?"

"Oh, sure, yeah. Robert came over today and brought me some delicious lemon bars. He's training volunteers for an upcoming ACT UP action in Philly."

"Really, what is it?"

"Something about using state funds to give out condoms, but the new volunteers need training."

"Robert trains people to give out condoms? Is it that difficult?" I ask, actually curious.

"They train people to protest peacefully," Dad explains. "That includes how to get arrested, what their rights are, what to say to journalists, all that. It's pretty intense, actually."

"Wow, that's cool. Has he been involved with ACT UP for a long time?"

"Yes. A few years. You know, as his friends have all been dying around him, I guess he felt like he couldn't sit idly by. It's important work. A cure isn't going to find itself, and we need to get pushy to make change happen."

"Do you ever go to protests or anything like that?"

"Oh, I've been to a few here in Philly, sure. But you know me, I don't like big crowds. I've been offering free legal advice to people with HIV at the AIDS Law Project here in Center City. That feels like a good use of my skills. It's mostly AIDS-related discrimination cases."

"Like what sort of cases?" I ask, feeling like I found a room in a house I thought I knew.

"Often it's workplace discrimination. Someone gets fired or doesn't receive a promotion they deserve and they believe it's due to their HIV status or that they're gay. Sometimes it is. So I help to settle these sorts of disputes," he explains.

"That's awesome, Dad. I didn't know that."

"Thanks, kid, I'm glad you think it's awesome. I think you're awesome," he says with a laugh.

"You know what else is awesome? Thanksgiving!"

"Yes! Let's get our menu together, shall we?"

"Yes. Turkey, stuffing, cranberry, pie," I suggest.

He laughs some more. "Yes. Oh boy, I'm looking forward to seeing you, sweet Bunny!"

He coughs as he says goodbye.

I know it's there—
With every cough, a dark space grows.
What if?
So I proceed with my day, do my homework, make my artwork
But doubt and fear are my constant visitors.
They won't let up.
Because the truth is he has the virus,
and it's only a matter of time.

19
"War"

The sky is heavy, leaking, and gray. From the back row of art history class, I watch the drips on the window fall, finding each other on their way down.

Ms. Davis is reviewing assignments and deadlines. Our outlines for the artist project are due Monday after Thanksgiving break.

"Now then, who knows this famous painting?" She switches on the slide projector to show gray and black shapes and half faces of people and animals in a blend of pain and torment.

I raise my hand and she nods. "It's called *Guernica*. By Pablo Picasso."

"Thanks, Danielle." She walks to the back of the room and asks, "What do you all see?"

"It's chaotic," says Sam.

"All the gray tones. Looks dead," says George.

"I see a bull," says Pam.

"And that guy looks like he's screaming," says Harriet.

"There's a woman holding a dead baby over there . . ."

"And that horse is walking over that guy on the ground . . ."

"And there's a newspaper . . ."

"And the sun is a lightbulb?"

Ms. Davis holds up her hands to quiet everyone down. "OK, great. So, what is this painting actually about? Can you guess?"

"War," says Kyle, sounding more engaged than usual.

Ms. Davis nods. "Yes, the Spanish Civil War. It depicts part of the 1937 bombing of a town in Spain called Guernica . . . Heads not attached to bodies, anguished expressions, screaming or dead. It was like a painting of hell. But it wasn't hell. It was war." Ms. Davis explains and adds, "The people in the Basque region of Spain wanted their freedom, but Franco, the dictator of Spain at the time, did not allow this."

"So, they got bombed?" Sam asks.

"Yes. Not armed rebels. Civilians."

"Their own government dropped bombs on a town?" asks Sam, sounding like such a preposterous idea couldn't possibly be true.

"Yes." Ms. Davis goes on, "Several hundred people died. And what was a national tragedy turned into a call to action for Picasso. He not only made this enormous painting—which was really a public admonishment of the government's violent actions—but he later donated the money he made touring this painting around the world to refugee causes. Over time, this explicitly violent painting has become a symbol for standing up against injustice, against war, and against genocide."

I suddenly imagine these twisted, screaming figures as victims of AIDS instead: too thin, faces covered with strange purple spots, alone and frightened. A slow-motion attack. The government has a vision, and they don't fit into it. They're dying, and their government is doing almost nothing. A quiet, terrible bombing.

I remember the sewn lips. The pink triangle. Silence. Death.

So, is it enough to make art? I guess Picasso could make money and give it to needy groups. I want to be useful too or find a way to make my art useful. To make the world better in whatever tiny way I can. Don't I? But in the face of pain and injustice, how can I think that making art will help? I'm not Picasso.

"So, isn't this just, like, another historical war painting?" asks Colin.

"It's not just another painting. It's a masterpiece," I snap back at him. God, Colin is annoying.

"Right, but how am I supposed to relate to this?" Colin continues. "Especially if I'm someone who doesn't know this whole story?"

"Presumably, because you are a human being with a heart and you'd care that people were suffering? Their own government did this. Their own government bombed them and watched them die," I say, sharpening my tongue like a knife. I'm so over this dude.

Ms. Davis gives me a look and takes over, proceeding with the lesson. As class ends, she comes up to my desk and asks, "Danielle?"

"Yeah," I say, looking at the ground.

"Is something up? You seem a little jumpy."

I shrug and shake my head. Where would I even start?

She dismisses this and continues, "Hey, I forgot to ask last week, you got your application in, right?"

My chest thumps with nerves and I just stand there, hot with shame and guilt and dread. I finally lock eyes with her and she seems to understand.

She puts her hand on my shoulder and says, "OK, it's all right. You have another shot with the regular January deadline, right?"

"Yeah," seems to be all I can say.

"Don't worry, most people apply regular . . . How's the work? Need me to come take a look?"

"Not yet. Thanks. I'll let you know," I say, finally looking her in the eye.

"OK, please do. And, also, who did you decide on for your project?"

"David Wojnarowicz. You were right, I really like him. Ms. Franklin is helping me research."

"Great." She nods. "I look forward to hearing your thoughts."

"Cool." I glance at the clock, realizing I told Ms. Franklin I'd come back before lunch. "I actually need to get to the library."

Across the green, the rain is so close to snow that tree branches look like glass. Ms. Franklin is putting on her coat when I arrive, but she brightens up when she sees me. "Danielle," she sings, "I found something for you: A *New York Times* article." She hands me the Xerox and reads the headline, "'An Artist Who Seeks Every Opportunity to Unnerve.' I hope that's helpful, dear." She buttons up her coat. It's a long article all about Wojnarowicz.

"Thank you, Ms. Franklin!"

"All righty. You let me know if there's more I can help with. Right now, I need to get going to check on Poppy. She's still having digestion issues."

"OK. Thanks again." That Ms. Franklin never fails.

I sit at a table and read about Wojnarowicz's show in New York, and I wish so much I could skip ahead and just be there already. Skip all of college entirely and be with the people making things, speaking out, acting up. It's not like David Wojnarowicz went to college, right? Or did Andy Warhol? Maybe I should just skip it?

"Don't be ridiculous, kid," I hear Arthur say.

20
"This Must Be the Place"

The bus to Philadelphia is packed. Marco and I squeeze into two seats near the back, bags on our laps. We both plug our headphones into my Discman and listen to the Talking Heads. I take out my physics notebook and tear out a sheet. I fold it up and we make an exquisite corpse drawing, where I make part then he makes part, then we trade back and forth until the page is done.

"Who's coming to Thanksgiving?" he asks, drawing hatched lines on the page.

"Well, Dad, and some unknown number of his loud and kooky friends."

Marco laughs. "Sounds like dinner with my family."

"You're welcome to join us. Anytime. Dad wanted me to invite you, again."

"My *tía* would kill me if I didn't come to Thanksgiving! But thanks, Dani. Maybe I can come over after dinner. Second dessert?"

Two hours later we are standing in Center City at Eleventh Street, pulling bags onto our shoulders. I write Dad's phone number on the back of Marco's hand.

"Perfect. Good luck out there, lady!" He hugs me close. I inhale the clean detergent smell on his sweatshirt. He is seriously the cleanest boy I've ever known.

Walking up Chestnut Street to Dad's place, there are turkey decorations everywhere, red and brown leaves fall onto the sidewalk, and I regret my jacket choice. It's a thin fake-leather jacket I bought at Second-Hand Rose thrift store here last year. It's orange and seemed like a good idea this morning, but now I'm freezing. It's colder than I thought it would be.

At Dad's apartment, I can't find my key. I knock and remember all the times Jake and I came to see him after the divorce. Standing in that doorway was like being on a threshold of a different world. Not the one of my childhood. It was a world where a whole other way of being was possible. It was like walking into a sigh of relief. I guess it still is.

"Bunny!" he says, standing there holding the door open for me. I drop my bags and hug him. I feel the bones of his ribs and smell his cologne. His face looks different, eyes rounder, cheekbones larger somehow. He's thinner, almost frail, but his face is happy. "How was the ride?"

"It was good. Marco was with me. He might join us for dessert tomorrow," I say. For a moment I want to tell him about the dance, everything, but I immediately think better of it and keep it to myself.

He smiles and backs up, letting me in.

I settle into his den again, unpacking books, boots, and toiletries all over. Dad knocks on the door, and when I open it, his hand is covering his eyes so as not to see the disaster I've instantly turned this room into.

"Ready?" We're going to get Chinese takeout and rent *Auntie Mame* from the video store on his street.

Outside I notice myself slowing down to walk at his pace. And he's coughing. But he's cheerful, so I don't want to ask him about it. I don't want to worry him. Worry is contagious.

We chop vegetables for Thanksgiving at the dining room table with the movie on in the living room. We've watched it at least ten times. Later, we eat chicken in black bean sauce and egg rolls while Mame redecorates her way through the ups and downs of life with her nephew. Dad knows all the lines. He lovingly mouths his favorites in synch with Mame herself, with a hand over his heart.

Darling . . .

it's time to eat

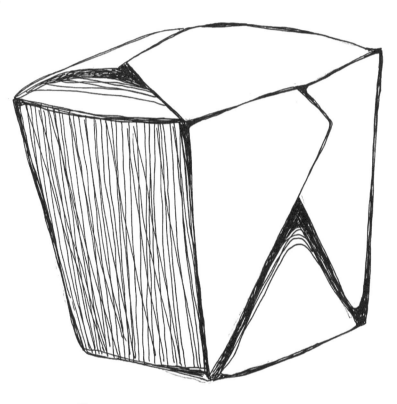

Life is a banquet

Let's have it!

After we've prepped the stuffing and cut the green beans for tomorrow, I put on my pj's and brush my teeth. As he takes some pills out of a jar, he says, "Good night, little Bunny. Need anything?"

"Nope, I'm fine. Thanks, Dad. I love you."

I put down the rocks and go to sleep.

In one rush, it hits me.
Now is all we ever know, really.
Seems stupidly obvious
But I breathe this in, a safe feeling of now.
As the monsters roar outside, in the future, aiming to terrify,
I pull the blanket up to my eyes.
I breathe,
Knowing he is safe.
For now.

Dad wakes up at seven to start cooking. I try to go back to sleep, but he's listening to Sondheim's *Follies*. If I opened my door right now, I'd no doubt see him swaying his hips as he cooked. I close my eyes and listen to the music.

I roll out of bed around ten, and he is sitting at the table drinking coffee and doing the crossword. The smell of fresh coffee permeates the air and tinfoil-covered bowls line the counter. Dear God, he is organized.

"Morning, Bunny. How'd you sleep? You hungry?" he asks as I pour myself some coffee.

"Um, yes. I am. Can you make that toast egg thing?"

"You got it." He slowly gets up, with effort. He coughs a little bit and then excuses himself to go to the bathroom.

I sit with my coffee and look out the window. From the nineteenth floor I can see all the way to New Jersey. I hear him cough some more through the bathroom door. I decide not to wait and make myself toast.

When he finally comes out, he seems to have forgotten about my breakfast and says he needs to lie down. "I'm just a little dizzy. I probably just didn't sleep enough."

I stare at my toast and feel a burning in my stomach. Is he getting worse, or am I just being paranoid? I eat, shower, and get dressed. Then I check in on Dad. He's reading in bed.

"What can I do? Need anything out in the world before the crowds arrive?" I ask.

"Yes. We need candles, parsley, limes, and half-and-half."

"OK, when is liftoff?" I ask, putting on my coat.

"The throngs descend upon us at three p.m., so maybe be back by two?"

I walk through Center City. It's hollowed out for the holiday. I imagine everyone has gone to suburban houses with large fireplaces, lawns, and TV rooms. Only a few stores are open. After getting the groceries Dad requested, I stop by Second-Hand Rose to see if they have any sweaters or warm coats on sale because I'm still freezing. They might actually be open on Thanksgiving.

Sure enough, Rita is there, working away. She's got the Ramones playing on the stereo.

"Danielle, my darling! How goes it?" Her hair is piled up high on her head and one pair of glasses is nestled into it, while another pair sit on her nose. In a red plaid flannel shirt, I can see her rose tattoos peeking out on her forearms. Rita's a rock and roll grandma.

"Hi, Rita! Happy Thanksgiving!"

"Fucking Thanksgiving. It's always so quiet on this goddamned holiday," she grumbles, and I laugh. Rita is a particular flavor of saltiness that sort of goes with everything. "I better make a sale sign for tomorrow. Dammit. That's when the crowds invade. I was hoping to make some progress on my book." The way she talks, it's not clear she wants customers at all.

I look down and see an enormous paperback sitting on the counter, *Interview with the Vampire*. I smile at her. "Good book?"

"Oh yeah. Super juicy. Hey, how's school? What year are you in now?"

"School's fine," I say, picking up some black rubber bracelets by the register. "I'm a senior."

"A senior? Come on now. How is that possible? No way! I remember the first time Arthur brought you in here. For your Bat Mitzvah, I think. You got that cute pink dress. So, are you getting tired of high school or is it, like, fun to be the oldest?"

"Eh, I'm pretty much over it," I go to the coat area and flip through the plaid men's coats.

"Boy, school gets old fast. I remember that feeling. Are you still making paintings? Still going to go to an art college, like Arthur?"

"That's my plan," I say.

"I saw your dad in the grocery store a few weeks ago. How's he doing? He looked a little under the weather." She stares at me with this look, like she's trying to tell me that she knows what I know. I feel like I'm in a weird dark comedy all of a sudden.

"Oh, he's all right; getting ready for the guests." I decide to change the subject fast. I find a black peacoat that fits me perfectly, a bright orange sweater, and a Velvet Underground T-shirt in the dollar bin for Amy.

She rings up my purchases. Eleven dollars and fifty cents. "Well, happy Thanksgiving, Rita. I'll send your love to the boys."

"Oh yes. Do that, sweet girl. And tell Robert he still owes me five bucks!" Handing me a receipt, she also gives me a mini Reese's peanut butter cup.

Back home I set the table while Dad whips mashed potatoes. I put on my new sweater and try to manage my hair into something presentable. Just after three the doorbell starts ringing and doesn't seem to stop. I put on Duke Ellington, and Dad starts warming things up, neatly filling the oven and humming along to the music.

Susie makes old-fashioneds and a Shirley Temple for me. Robert brings apple and pecan pies. The guests include Peter, the literary agent; Scott, the lighting designer; and Frankie, Scott's boyfriend who looks a lot like an Italian Richard Simmons. Scott met Frankie while singing in the Philadelphia Gay Men's Chorus. I don't know what Frankie's job is, but he sure has a lot of energy. There's also George, the librarian; his cousin Bernie, who came from Tenafly; and Rula, who volunteers with Dad at ActionAIDS. Each of them gives me hugs and asks me various questions about food, tasks, and drinks.

thanks!

With a flurry of tinfoil revealing dishes, there's a chorus of *oohs* and *aahs* from the group as they are each laid down, like offerings to the gods. It's hilarious that so much of the straight world somehow thinks gays are crazed heathens who just have sex parties all day and night. These people are very serious about food and traditions.

Once everyone fills their plate and finds a seat, my dad raises his glass. "I'd like to propose a toast!"

"'To the ladies who lunch!'" says Peter, mimicking Joanne from *Company*. Everybody laughs.

"Let's have a moment for all our loved ones who couldn't make it to this joyous day," says Dad. "We remember you and we continue to work toward a day when this disease isn't stigmatized but tended to with care and adequate federal support. We miss you, darlings, with a special kiss to our dear, sweet Arthur."

"Amen," says Susie.

"Rest in power!" says George, taking a big gulp of white wine.

"And," Robert continues, "let's send some love to all our sisters and brothers fighting the good fight, trying to make this world a little more—just a *little* more—kind and beautiful!"

"Yes!" Dad raises his glass higher.

"Hear, hear!" says Rula.

Everyone clinks glasses. Frankie and Scott are sniffling, and a brief silence falls over the room. In the face of an epidemic, our thanks feel more like a mourner's prayer. We sit in silence for a minute. Some hold hands. Others dab their eyes with a napkin.

"Dig in, everyone," Dad finally says as he gets up from the table and goes into the bathroom.

The clinking of dishes and forks fills the space as we all focus on the food. Rula's lentil salad with currants and tomatoes, Peter's biscuits, George's sweet potatoes. I keep my eye on Dad as he returns, blowing his nose as he slowly walks back to the table.

"So, Danielle, what's the latest? How's fancy school?" George asks me, elbowing Robert to his left. Peter snickers, and I shake my head and smile.

"It's fancy, Mr. Freeman," I say with a snide smile. George hates it when I call him that; he says it makes him sound old. "Homecoming was last week, and the semester will be over soon."

"And are you planning for college? Or just going to go kick around in a van with some hot boy?"

I shake my head and flare my nostrils and smile. "Sadly, that is not my plan."

Dad jumps in. "Danielle will attend the Rhode Island School of Design or the earth will cease spinning," he declares dramatically.

George nods his approval at my audacity, raising one eyebrow. "Well, all right then. Arthur's footsteps are deep. The best to you then, Danielle!" He raises his wine glass, I raise my water, and we clink.

An hour later we've piled dishes in the sink, and the doorbell rings. I run to the door to let Marco in and then I introduce around the room. After nearly every introduction, the guests look at me with a raised eyebrow and wink. I roll my eyes repeatedly. Dad gives him a sweet hug and says in his ear, "Glad to have you, Marco."

We play Pictionary. I get *fantasy*, and draw a dragon and a wizard and nobody gets it. The guys laugh, realizing how different their pictures would have been. Dad gets *political*, and draws an ACT UP flag and a voting booth and everyone gets it. Marco gets *camp* and he tries to draw kids in shorts and tents until Bernie puts it together and says "OK queens, think Carmen Miranda on the toilet!"

And they all yell "CAMP!"

Dad is laughing, tears in his eyes.

Later we have a *Sound of Music* sing-along. George fast-forwards all the talking scenes on the VHS tape ("So boring!"). We all know every single line. We sing "Sixteen Going on Seventeen" with Liesl, swoon at the captain's eyes, hiss at the baroness, and cheer when the nun cuts the car wire. Marco is eating it all up. I love how happy he is here.

These holidays used to remind me of what I wasn't. TV commercials showing families with a mom in the kitchen and a dad in a lounge chair watching sports never looked like my family. It was as though we had been left out of the "family" picture. Even before Dad came out, we weren't like everyone else. My mom watched baseball and worked all the time, and Dad put my hair in braids, did the grocery shopping, and made our meals. TV commercials only ever told me we were not normal. They used to make me think I should be normal, have a different family, be different from what we were. But now, everything has changed. Why would I ever want to be closed in like that, when I can be on this side of the river, where we laugh until we cry?

So much more is possible.

Any group of people who love each other can make a family. It seems so obvious to me. So there, normal world. We dance and cook and don't think about what we are not. We are too busy eating pie.

I take a picture of the moment in my mind. I know that even as this night has kept my heart in safekeeping, soon the monster will likely come back. This is what the commercials ought to show. It's messy and chaotic, but it is real and full of joy. I know this is one way to take care of myself. To know there's a place like this.

After everyone leaves, Marco and I put away leftovers and start doing dishes. Dad tells us to stop, to leave it for the morning. "I'm heading to bed. You kids behave yourselves." He kisses me on the head, then does the same to Marco.

"Dani, oh my God. Thank you!" Marco whispers after Dad closes his bedroom door.

I smile. "Yeah, well, I thought you needed a trip to this side of the river."

"Yeah, for real. I like it over here!"

We make Marco a bed on the living room couch. We brush our teeth side by side. He's wearing an enormous RELAX T-shirt and boxers, and even brushing his teeth he's beautiful. He may not be my boyfriend, but I'm glad he's in my world.

In the morning, I tiptoe over to the kitchen to start on the rest of the dishes. Marco gets up and rushes out to meet his father at the train.

Before he goes, he thanks my dad, like, ten thousand times and gives me a hug.

"Thank you, Marco Polo," I say back to him.

After he's gone, Dad smiles at me. I take a shower and wonder if Dad can tell Marco is gay or whether he thinks he's my boyfriend.

When I get out, Dad is sitting at the dining room table, taking his pills. A series of multicolored nuggets filed meticulously into little plastic boxes.

"What's this?" I ask, sitting down next to him while I peel an orange.

He gets up and takes a plate out of the kitchen. Handing it to me, he says, "They call it a cocktail, all these pills taken together. I have a whole schedule: Some I take first thing in the morning with no food. Then after breakfast, I wait thirty minutes to take another round. Then I need to take more before my next meal. There's a chart in the bathroom."

"What do they do?" I ask, sweeping orange seeds and peels with my hand from the table onto the plate.

"Mostly they make me nauseous. But they're supposed to help my body keep the good parts of my immune system intact. It's a very mysterious virus, and the drugs are all pretty new, so there are side effects even if the drug itself might be working. Some make you sleepy, some make you antsy, some hurt your stomach, some make you not want to eat food. And some have to be kept refrigerated."

"How many do you have to take?"

"At the moment, it's eighteen each day," he says before taking out five pills from the box. Eighteen. That seems like an awful lot. I think of how Amy has to remember to just take one each morning for her thyroid condition.

"Does it feel like they're helping?" is all I can manage to ask.

"It's difficult to say. We'll see how my numbers look in a couple months, but it's what my doctor recommends right now. So, we'll see." Embarrassed at my ignorant question, I decide not to ask more, but I'm so curious. That's a lot of pills to remember, much less to time perfectly with food. I had no idea. Is that, like, normal? Are they doing anything else to his body?

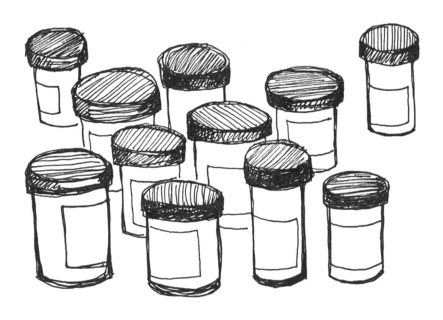

He slides each pill one at a time onto his tongue and then takes a big gulp of water.

Cocktails were something glamorous when 1940s movie stars drank them. Manhattans swirled by Bette Davis. Scotch and sodas slung back by Joan Crawford. Martinis bottomed up by Rosalind Russell. And now it's a bunch of medicine. Little white, blue, and yellow shapes he puts on his tongue and swallows with water. Do they call it a cocktail to make it more glamorous?

Robert arrives with bagels, as if we need more food. He's come to help clean up. After a million plates and half a million serving dishes are washed and dried and put away, we sit down in the sunny living room. Dad goes to his room to lie down. Maybe the pills make him tired?

Robert and I talk about food and friends and school, and then I say, "Can I ask you something?"

"Yes, of course," he says, sitting up.

"Is my dad better or worse than most people who are HIV positive?"

"Well, he's better, I think. I mean, he seems slower than his normal self today, and he is an absolute ass about not sharing when he feels sick, but compared to many of the people I've known, he's doing well. He's taking it all much better than I did, I'll tell you that."

I look at him, confused.

"Oh, geez, I guess I let that cat out of her bag." He looks at me. "Yes, Danielle, I too am HIV positive. T cells: 543. And counting." He makes a soldier's salute.

"Oh, wow, I didn't— I mean, I don't, um . . ." I struggle to figure out the right thing to say.

"Oh, honey, it's OK. It's been so long. It's no secret." He looks out the window for a moment. "But I certainly didn't mean to spring that on you like that. I assume everyone knows at this point."

"I didn't know. I'm sorry."

"You have nothing to apologize for!" He touches my arm sweetly.

"And I guess you're OK? I mean, you look OK. Is that dumb to say?" I feel like everything coming out of my mouth today is wrong.

"Yes, I'm fine, and it is not dumb to say. Thank you for asking."

"I wanted to ask you about Dad, but are *you* doing all the right things? I mean are there things you can do to not get sick?"

"Yes! And we're doing them: eating well, not smoking, getting enough sleep, exercising, and staying away from anyone who's super sick. You know all about the immune system, I presume? How having this virus means we're compromised, or more vulnerable to illnesses?"

I nod. *Compromised*, sounds like a spy movie. Someone got in and is finding all the weaknesses.

Robert adds, "Danielle, a lot of people care deeply about your dad. We're going to hope for the best, do all we can to support him, and manage it, OK?"

"OK," I say, not entirely comforted.

"You aren't alone, is what I'm trying to say." He looks at me with a warmth like Arthur and I exhale.

"Now, I know that leftover turkey isn't gone yet." He gets up and heads to the kitchen.

I glance at Robert's notebook on the table. There's an ACT UP bumper sticker on the cover. It's the same pink triangle symbol Dad drew at yesterday's Pictionary game.

"That's an ACT UP sticker, right?" I ask.

"Sure is." Robert roots around the fridge.

I follow him into the kitchen. "Yeah, I mean, I know they do protests but, like, what is it?"

"It's a way to respond, I guess. Some of us need to act. Try to help, however we can. You know how your dad volunteers by giving free legal advice at ActionAIDS, right?" He rummages through the fridge and finds the stuffing and quietly mutters, "Yes!" As he makes himself a plate, he tells me about the ACT UP group he attends every week and their events and protests.

"I want to help," I say, before thinking about it. Just then, Dad returns to the living room, turns on some opera, and brings his newspaper to the couch.

Robert thinks for a moment and then raises an eyebrow. "What's your schedule tomorrow? Are you still in town?"

I smile. "Um, yes. I'm around. I don't go back 'til Sunday." I look past the kitchen to where Dad is sitting in the living room, coughing more than before.

Robert takes a deep breath. "OK, young lady. I'm picking you up tomorrow morning at ten a.m. sharp. You're coming with me."

"Where?"

"Oh, it's a surprise! Dress warm, though. It's going to be cold as a witch's tit tomorrow."

21
"Five Years"

I once had a teacher who said that as you're drawing from life, your eye has to move as slowly as an ant and then your hand follows the same line, at the same pace. Crawling along each line. Getting to know it. Only this slowly can we really know the shape of something.

I sketch Dad this morning while he sits and reads the paper and drinks his coffee. His face is long and lean. His nose, skinny and pointy. His eyebrows, dark and smooth. His lips, thin and wide. His eyes, big and dark brown, were always warm and sometimes sad.

They look just a little droopier than I remembered them to be. He looks tired.

Reading the very beginning of my sketchbook, I remember when it was warm out and we sat on the beach. His face has changed. It hasn't really been that long.

After more coffee and a shower, I kiss Dad goodbye and head toward the door.

"Have fun, and don't get arrested!" he says, cheerfully.

Get arrested? What's he talking about?

At ten I meet Robert on the street outside Dad's building. The wind is slapping my face like I insulted it. So glad I got this peacoat.

"So . . . where are we going?"

"Darling, I want you to see part of my world." Robert tells me we are going to a meeting of the Philadelphia chapter of ACT UP and then to take part in an action.

"Like a protest march?" I ask, imagining people holding signs, demanding justice.

"Sort of. We do it a little differently, but I guess you could say it's in the same vein. What we do are called *actions*, not *protests* because we're all about assertive disruption, as opposed to reaction to dominant modes of power in society."

I look at him shaking my head. "What are you talking about?" I say. He sounded like he was reading from a textbook all of a sudden.

Robert laughs. "Sorry, honey. That's how we talk." He takes a deep breath. "Basically, we make a fuss, get attention in the media as a way to get our message out. We play offense, instead of defense, I guess is another way to put it. Like today, we're doing this action, which won't really change the world entirely, but it might get on the news and give us a chance to talk about policy without having to pay for our own ads. That, in turn, makes government officials look like a bunch of bozos— or worse—and hopefully leads them to pay more attention to AIDS. We're squeaky wheels. Extremely organized, well-oiled squeaky wheels." He laughs at his own joke.

"What does the name ACT UP mean?" I ask.

"It has a double meaning, really. It's an acronym that stands for AIDS Coalition To Unleash Power. But also 'acting up.'"

"Like acting out, you mean, like a toddler?"

"No, 'acting up' means to not function properly, like, *This toaster is acting up* or *My arthritis is acting up*. But it's also like a call to get involved to make the world better through action," he explains. "Society isn't a given, Dani. It's made by people who stand up and shape it."

We turn off Broad Street onto Pine, the wind whistling through my ears. "Hey, is that jewelry place near here?" I ask, remembering going with Arthur to Halloween, a magical, wonderful jewelry store, full of sparkling treasures. I think he knew the owner.

"Of course, right there." He points across the street to a door with no sign on it. "God, those parties I went to with Arthur, such glorious, ridiculous nights . . ." He sighs.

"What parties? At the store? Tell me."

He loops his arm through mine, "Oh no, honey. The Halloween ball hosted by the man who owns the store. Since 1968 those parties have been a fixture for the gay community here. A spectacular costume party where you could be anyone and kiss everyone. So many things I can't remember happened there. Arthur tried to get Benjamin to come, but you know your dad." He laughs.

"It sounds fun."

"It was more than fun. It was home when a lot of us didn't have that. Those parties welcomed us with open arms for years when the rest of the world wanted nothing to do with us. That man made that happen." He points to the store. "He makes gorgeous jewelry and brings people together. He shapes the world into a beautiful place."

A grateful joy spreads across Robert's face. After a few more moments, he returns to laying out the day's plans to me. "So, first we'll go to this prep meeting for about an hour, and then the action is planned for noon, sound good?"

"Sure, I'm game!" I say, a little scared but mostly excited to see it all.

We walk into a building called "Penguin Place" on Pine Street, its double doors lumpy from repeated paint jobs. The carpeting is old and worn. The floors creak as we walk up the stairs into a large open space on the second floor. It's only slightly warmer in here than outside, and almost everyone has kept their hats and coats on. There are already about twenty-five people gathered, eating doughnuts and drinking coffee out of little white Styrofoam cups. Robert brings me around and introduces me to his friends:

Janice, a weaver and special-education teacher, who has two long braids and wears a lot of patterns. Harry, a historian who runs their library, with a bushy mustache and wire-rimmed glasses. Don, a tall superhero-looking man with blond hair, who works in PR and has a firm handshake. As we walk away from Don, Robert whispers, "He's the cute one, and he gets us meetings with lobbyists." And finally, Randy, an ex–Wall Street broker who goes to health policy hearings in DC. When I look puzzled by this, Randy grins and says, "Yeah, it's wonky but important. Laws need to make sense for a majority, not just rich, straight white people. The government is dragging their heels to fund research about AIDS. We're pushing to make them go faster."

I wonder if it's working. I remember the articles Ms. Franklin helped me find, about how the government is taking too long to respond. This is exactly what Randy is saying. The delayed response by the government means people aren't getting the help they need, and maybe people are dying who could be cured.

Robert and I sit down in the third row. "You know, Dani, there are also a lot of artists who make art about AIDS to fight or get involved in protests. You know that pink triangle shirt I have? Well, the triangle was originally a symbol that the Nazis made gay people wear."

"Like the yellow star for the Jews?"

"Yup. A group of artists wanted to make something direct and gripping, so they took that triangle, turned it upside down, and put it above the phrase Silence=Death."

It makes so much sense: just turning it upside down and claiming it as their own changes everything. I tell Robert about the image I saw of David Wojnarowicz, and how I'm writing a paper about him. He shakes his head and just says, "You, my dear, are amazing. I'm so glad you're here." He squeezes my hand as the meeting starts. I take out my sketchbook. Something in me tells me to take notes.

Someone with big red glasses and a baggy shirt with palm trees on it gets up and calls the meeting to order. Robert leans over and whispers, "That's Chris. He's our ringleader. Also, he was good friends with Bill Way, the man who helped us secure this building. Bill died from AIDS a couple years ago."

"OK, first things first," Chris says, sounding a little like a teacher who needs a vacation. "Thank you to everyone who came last weekend to help make the coffins. We have all eight of them ready to go by the back door."

Coffins? I quickly check Robert's face. He gets my inquisitive grimace and whispers, "Not real coffins. It's part of the action. You'll see . . ." Chris continues, "Happy Thanksgiving, all. Please remember the family you have here. If you or anyone you know needs assistance or food delivered, please let us know. We can connect you to the folks down the street for help." My eyes go from person to person around the room. Maybe some don't have families. Or even homes. Suddenly I feel lucky to have both.

"OK, just a quick roundup of announcements from committee chairs before we head out. We won't meet after today for another week."

A series of people get up, one by one, and report in very fine detail their committee's work: Policy, Action, Media, Finance, Treatment & Data, Graphics, and Housing. I'm picking up pieces like I walked into a class midsemester: messaging around drug trial policies, death on parade actions. This is a tightly run ship, and everyone is buzzing, busy, but still laughing and listening to each other. It reminds me of the frenzy of a theater production mixed with the seriousness of a student-council meeting.

Robert gets up and says, "I want to introduce you all to someone special who is visiting today. This is Danielle Silver. She's my friend Benjamin's daughter . . . Some of you know Benjamin, he does legal work with ActionAIDS. He's home nursing a Thanksgiving hangover." They all laugh. "But Danielle, who is graduating high school in the spring, heard me yammering on about the work I do here, so I brought her to see how we make the ACT UP sausage!"

Everyone laughs again. Someone asks me to stand up and tell them about myself.

Robert flashes a smile. I get up, feeling nervous. But everyone is smiling. "Hi. I'm Danielle. I guess I'm here because, well, I want to know more about what you're doing. I've been learning about AIDS, but I want to know how you stand up and fight. I want to help too. I don't know what I can do, exactly, and I'm still in high school, but I want to be useful. I don't want more people to die if they don't have to." I'm not sure if I've made any sense, but I sit back down. Then I look around the room and half the people there have tears in their eyes.

"Welcome, Danielle," says one woman.

"Yes. We're so glad you're here. Thank you, Robert, for introducing us to this terrific young woman. We're glad you're here today!" says Chris, his eyebrows earnestly raised with excitement.

"OK, big day today, people." Chris claps his hands, getting to the big event. "Remember your training and stay close to the group. It's cold, so let us know if you need gloves or a break. OK? So go pee, grab some coffee or a smoke, and let's meet out back in five minutes. We've called for folks to join us at eleven thirty to start heading down to the hotel."

At the beverage table, Robert and I make some tea and he explains what's happening.

"So, today's main event is to protest George Bush."

"The president?" I ask.

"The very same. He's giving a speech at the Bellevue Hotel later today, so we're going to pay a little visit. You know, welcome him, with open arms and coffins." He smiles in a sly devilish way as we put on our coats and head out the back door.

Suddenly, we are in the middle of a growing crowd, people holding signs that say White House=Death House and Read George's Lips And Die. Some are in the shape of a gravestone saying Never Had A Chance and Killed By The System. More and more people are coming and there's a frenzy in the cold midday air.

A few minutes after noon, I see Chris get up on a folding chair with a bullhorn and address the crowd. There are probably a hundred people or more by now.

"OK, folks. We've been here before, but are we going to just shut up?"

"NO!" yells the crowd around me.

"Are we going to sit on our asses while our friends, our lovers, our brothers, sisters, cousins, neighbors die?"

"NO!"

"Are we going to sit on our hands and let the United States government pick and choose who lives and who dies?"

"NO!" I hear Robert shout loudest next to me, throwing his fist in the air.

"OK then. I want each of you to know how much you mean in this fight. This is America. We tell our elected leaders what we think, and we fight for justice and health and transparency. We're prepared, and we're right, and they know it. Let's go join our brothers and sisters up Broad Street and scream our fucking heads off. If we keep screaming, eventually they'll hear us."

The crowd cheers and movement begins. Robert stays by me.

"All right?" he asks.

I nod.

"You want to do this or head back to your dad's?"

"I'll come. I mean, are people really going to get arrested?"

Robert laughs, then sees my face, which must have notes of terror on it. "Oh, honey, not us. No. ACT UP has trained some people to get arrested. They'll be in the thick of it, deliberately breaking the law by blocking the sidewalk or preventing people from entering the hotel. The goal is to have journalists write articles about the cause. The articles might say that the protesters were prevented from getting a message to President Bush about increasing federal AIDS funding. That media attention is crucial to pressure the government. We can watch the local news tonight to see how they tell the story . . . We'll hang back and not get sucked too far into things. This is a legal, peaceful protest."

"These people don't seem that peaceful," I say. "They seem pissed as hell."

"Well, yes, that's true. We are angry, but we're not violent. That's what I mean. We're simply making our voices heard. We have to be loud sometimes."

"Silence equals death, right?" I say.

The crowd moves, chanting up front.

"You got it. We're going to gather by the Bellevue Hotel on Broad

Street. It's going to get crowded, and maybe a little chaotic," he says loudly into my ear.

I look around and think it's already crowded and chaotic. Robert smiles, reading my mind, "Yeah, no, way more crowded than this. We have women's groups and local unions coming to this one. A lot of folks are mad at Bush and local Republicans."

People have started chanting: "ACT UP, FIGHT BACK, FIGHT AIDS!"

"BLACK, WHITE, GAY, STRAIGHT, AIDS DOES NOT DISCRIMINATE."

We walk down Broad Street's wide sidewalk and eventually onto the large four-lane street. I guess the traffic stopped somewhere. Just people, not cars, fill the space.

I ask Robert how long he's been involved. "Since 1986. So, five years. I worked for a big company doing marketing, and one day I just thought, Nope. I can't anymore. I'm HIV positive. Most of my friends are positive. If I'm going to die, I'm going to use my time doing something worthwhile. So, I consult on the side to make money, but mostly, I focus on this."

"So, does this feel . . . well, does it help?"

He thinks about this. "Yes, and no. It isn't magic. But activists are making people pay attention. They're getting attention from people at the Department of Health and Human Services in DC who've finally started listening."

As we approach the block where the Bellevue is, I hear more yelling, more chanting, and see more signs. Then I see the coffins. Six large painted boxes. And more people with gravestone-shaped signs lining up close to the hotel.

"What are they doing?" I ask Robert.

"It's just your run-of-the-mill die-in. We like theatrics at ACT UP. It's like a sort of street theater that's actually trying to save the world. These brave people are going to lie on that cold, hard ground and pretend to be dead. It's become a staple part of our actions. It drives home the number of human beings dying every day. Makes it real and hard to forget. Also the photos get into newspapers and on TV."

As the afternoon goes on, more and more people join. The police

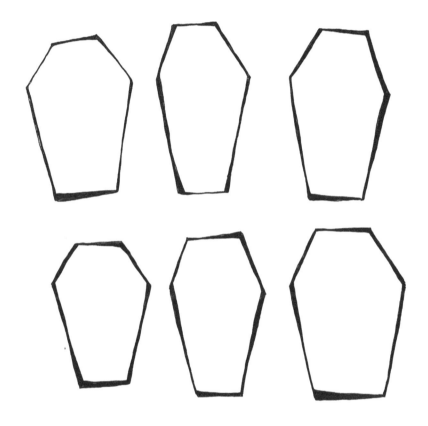

killed by the system
Never had a chance
Act up, fight back, fight AIDS

also increase, as vans come and officers with clubs and helmets station themselves along the sidewalk to form a barricade in front of the hotel. I guess President Bush is still on his way.

Soon we hear sirens and see flashing lights. It's the presidential motorcade. The crowd starts yelling more chants, raising their signs, and booing as a series of limos line the front of the building.

Robert tugs on my coat and motions me to walk back to the other side of the street. "This is starting to get a little much, and your father will rip my head off if anything happens to you. Let's just hang back here and see how this goes, all right?"

"Sure," I say. The people near the front are screaming, and I see police start to push them aside. The yelling increases and soon there's just chaos. Fighting. More screaming—different screaming. From protest chants to screams of terror and outrage—not at some abstract thing, but at this, here, now. I feel both helpless and so glad to be one of the many people here showing up. I mean, I'm not really doing anything, but I feel I should be here anyway.

As the crowd continues to convulse, Robert puts his arm around me. "You know what? I changed my mind about waiting and seeing how this goes. I'm going to get you home." By this time, the screaming and shoving are so loud I can barely hear him, but as he leads me farther away from the hotel I feel relieved.

As we walk I see plenty of people with shopping bags, tourists who came for the Black Friday deals, only mildly curious about what all these people in black T-shirts with pink triangles are. I wonder if ACT UP meant to disrupt their shopping too.

We walk up Locust Street. "So, what happens now?" I ask Robert.

"Well, this will probably go on for a few hours, and most of these good folks will stay as long as they can. The police will arrest some people, they'll get released soon enough, it'll all be filmed and shown on tonight's news, and we'll plan the next one."

"But it's not like you're sitting down with the president and he's actually listening, is it?"

"That's not how we work. We disrupt. We get attention. Then on the news they'll talk about it. And then they'll want to interview one of us, and we have plenty of smart, gorgeous people who the press loves to get on camera. Then that will get attention when we make them look bad. Politicians hate that. It's a long game, but it does work."

I think of the commitment it must take to be willing to get arrested as a part of this long series of events. To be willing to be screamed at, pushed or beaten by police, just to get on the news. But it makes sense now. What's the alternative?

"Robert, thanks for taking me today," I say as we near Dad's apartment building.

"Oh, my pleasure, honey. I'm glad you liked it. Wasn't too scary?"

"Maybe just eye-opening." I didn't want to admit fear to Robert.

"Excellent. Keep those eyes open, Danielle. I have to run, but I'll see you soon."

"Sure, well, you know where to find me!"

"Yes, I do." Robert gives me a cheek kiss and with a loud *Brrrr!* scampers off.

I walk into Dad's place and no one is there. On the coatrack, I see his coat is gone. He must have gone out.

I take off my shoes and am about to make some tea when I see a note on the dining room table. Dad doesn't usually leave me notes. I pick it up. It's not his writing. I know immediately that something is wrong.

Danielle,
    Your dad was having some very bad stomach pains. I took him to the ER at Graduate Hospital. Come over if you can. Maybe bring some of his things in case.
                                                            —Susie

I've only been gone for three hours. The plates from our bagels are still on the counter.

Everything moves in slow motion. What is supposed to happen next? How am I supposed to know what happens next?

I reread the letter and get to the last words: *in case*. In case what?

Pack what things? Like a will, or, like, socks? I wander around the apartment wondering what I need to gather. It is very unfortunate that I am the one who has to think about packing, considering my abysmal abilities in this area. Instead, I think: What would Dad do?

I find a duffel bag in his closet and pretend I am him. Order. Remain calm. Underwear, socks, two long-sleeved shirts, one pair of pants, and a set of pajamas. Sensible. Toothpaste. Toothbrush. Floss. Deodorant. A razor and shaving cream. I leave it at that. "Less is more," I hear Dad saying inside my head. I am not panicking. I am not.

I call Robert. He's just walking into his apartment a few blocks away. He's slightly out of breath as he picks up the phone.

I tell him what the note said and that I'm packing a bag.

"Good, right, yes." I can practically hear him getting into formation, a soldier who's seen this battle before. "Smart . . . I'm heading to the pharmacy for another friend, but I can meet you there in a couple hours."

"Sure," I barely utter, trying not to let him know I've got tears dripping from my face.

"Danielle, I know this is scary, but listen to me . . . take a deep breath, OK?" I gasp for air. Finally realizing it's fine to cry. There's no one here to see it. I finally take one long deep breath. It helps.

"When Dad told me he was positive, he said he would tell me when to worry, and he didn't," I finally say.

"Danielle, your father is never going to tell you such a thing. It's not in his DNA to tell his own child to worry about him."

"But I do. I am. I will."

"Of course, you will. Don't be upset with him. You can be pissed at the HIV, and listen, if you want permission to worry, I'll give you permission to worry, OK? But don't aim your anger or your fear at him. That will not be useful to anyone, all right?"

"All right," I whisper.

The layers keeping me safe are disappearing, and all that's left is the bubbling core of despair that's been inside since Dad told me he was HIV positive. It's like after the snow melts and the rotted leaves and forgotten garbage buried beneath reclaim their domain. My stomach falls deeper still and my hands tingle.

"He's trying to do the impossible: be your dad and cope with this motherfucker of a disease. It's not a winning situation for him, honey." Robert is saying all the right things, I know, but my heart is still pounding too hard.

"OK, I'll see you later? I don't even know what room yet," I say as the enormity of what I do not know continues to swell.

"Don't worry, I know that hospital far too well. You'll find him and I'll find you both."

22

"Just Like U Said It Would B"

The wind is picking up, and I forgot my hat. The hospital is only a few blocks away. It feels like every step I take is one step further away from life as I've known it. That life that revolved around me that I took for granted. I am walking toward Dad, his pain, his disease, his life. I bury my hands in the pockets of my new peacoat, grateful for the warmth.

I've never been super preoccupied with death, but this is not the scene I dreamed up when pondering my parents' mortality. I admit I've imagined them sick and dying in the hospital when they were old. Like, really old. Like ninety. And, I would be way older, like fifty. Or sixty. By that time, I would definitely know how to be a grown-up. And there would be a group of people, somehow, gathered around who share the tasks, hug each other, and feel sad or scared, together. Not just me, alone, worrying about whether I packed enough socks.

When my grandparents got old, sick, and eventually died, there were cousins, aunts, and uncles. Cold cuts and coleslaw magically appeared on dining room tables. I didn't have to make decisions or talk to doctors. I was just a kid. My biggest decisions involved which shoes to wear or whether or not to braid my hair. Aside from missing my grandma, I was mainly focused on getting a turn to play the Atari in my cousin's basement.

So, now, am I supposed to be a grown-up? I guess in some part of the world or other points in history I'd be one by now. In the US we stay children as long as humanly possible. Shaving my legs and getting my period didn't make me feel grown-up. Not in the least. Not like this.

I close my eyes and listen to my Discman as the afternoon sun settles. Sinéad O'Connor sings to me, but the music can't drown out my pounding heart. This is just like I thought it would be. Terrifying.

It's two fifteen. Dad was fine this morning. Tired, but fine. Coughing, yes. And he did have to lie down, yes. Did I ignore something? Should I have taken him to the hospital? Is that my job?

The hospital driveway is quiet. Like it's closed today, but I know better. Hospitals never close. Even in the middle of a city the day after Thanksgiving. I approach the revolving door on the Lombard Street entrance to Graduate Hospital. Outside, I stand still.

I could just go back and find a place to get hot chocolate. I could get on the bus and go back to school. Back to modern art history and the Marshall Plan and physics; and homophobic, overprivileged, hair-flipping nimrods. Back to my studio to finish my application.

But I don't.

I could go to the Diner-on-the-Square and have a piece of the greatest lemon meringue pie ever made.

But I don't.

Because this, honestly, is my only option. I can't bail on Dad. Even though this whole situation is surely well beyond me, there's no one else to do it.

I step into the revolving door and push it halfway around the circle. Then halfway again to go back out. Slowly, so no one notices me. I push it around three more times. Because once I am in, I know that will be, like, it. Done. I know then I will not be a kid anymore. Once I go in, I grow up somehow, suddenly, without fanfare or an audience of any kind.

Just go already.

I walk in, and the warm air feels good, welcoming my cold head.

Even in the entrance, there's that smell, biting my nose like bleach and needles. I approach the receptionist.

"Hi. I'm looking for my dad. He came into the ER earlier, but I don't know where he is now."

She doesn't look up from her newspaper. She just flatly says, "Sign in with your name," as she points to a big book on the tall counter in front of her. She is what Arthur would have called "the opposite of delightful."

I write my name. It is official. It's been recorded. It's real.

"Through those doors, there's an information desk past the lobby on the right." She must say this all day.

I pass a waiting area where the TVs are showing a news report of people protesting. I see a flash of the same pink triangle on Robert's T-shirt. I see signs that say Heal The Sick and Dying From AZT. And at the bottom of the screen, the words *Gay protests in Philadelphia* on the channel six news. I was just there. I guess it all went according to plan.

They don't have special passes for young visitors like me. I am not special. Nobody seems to notice that I'm not even voting age. I'm just a visitor like everyone else.

I go up to a desk where another woman holds a phone to her ear. She stares at me with raised eyebrows, and I'm not sure if I should speak.

"I am here to see my father, Benjamin Silver. He just came in this morning."

She clicks on a computer and looks in a big binder. She doesn't look at me, but acknowledges I'm there with a quiet, "Mmhmm, room 323. Elevator to three. Walk left when you get off, down the hall take another left. And here, wear this." Then she hands me something blue.

A mask. We used one like this once in ninth-grade woodshop. Also doing chemistry experiments. He must be really sick if they think he might infect me. I thought you couldn't get it through the air. I thought it was through body fluids. I'm trying to remember what the pamphlets said. I flash to our Thanksgiving dinner. Are we all going to be infected now? No, it doesn't work like that.

I put on the mask. It covers up the hospital smell with something that isn't foul but isn't fresh. I get into the elevator and push three. It is slow and empty. As I step out to the dingy third floor, the dread swells higher. This is where my dad is? He should be at home, listening to Sondheim and making pasta sauce. I can practically hear him groaning at the color combinations of muddy reds, mustard yellows, and graying greens. I find room 323. I knock, hearing faint voices. No one responds to my knock. I slowly open the door.

Dad is sitting up on the bed with his back to me, his slightly opened hospital gown showing me his bony spine, and a man stands beside him wearing scrubs, his hand on Dad's shoulder. He wears a mask like mine. He holds up his hand like a crossing guard to make me stop, then he quietly says, "My dear, would you mind terribly waiting out in the hall for just a moment?"

His voice is kind. His face seems so young. Is he the doctor?

Dad has his feet on the floor and is sitting on the edge of the bed. There are wires running from his arms to some poles, machines, and hanging bags. He is leaning over, looking down at something on the floor, a green puddle. Vomit. Dad has not noticed me.

On the sheets are drops of red splatter, coming from his arm. I reconstruct what happened just before I opened the door: He'd thrown up and pulled out his IV, and now he's just sitting there, staring at the aftermath. The silent mayhem. Humpty Dumpty is all broken. And a guy in scrubs is trying to put it all back together again.

Blood with HIV. Infected blood. Right there on the bed and the floor. This is what all the fuss is about. It is all over the place. I've never seen a doctor clean up after a patient. Not even on a TV show. I feel like doctors wear those white coats and this guy is just in blue scrubs with pockets on the shirt. Is he a nurse?

Dad coughs again.

More vomit.

It is deep and awful and scary. Strange sounds from his body. Liquid hitting the floor. Nothing to make it stop. Just stop. I freeze. I want to help but can't think of anything to actually do.

Then the scrubs guy looks at me and asks again, "Would you mind terribly giving us a minute?" I can't move. My face is hot under the mask. It smells like chalk and window cleaner. What am I doing here? Where the hell are the grown-ups? Where is Susie?

Dad is muttering something and gesturing toward the table. The scrubs guy leans toward him to hear better and then nods.

"Oh, of course!" He goes over to the bedside table and picks up a piece of paper and hands it to me. "I believe this is for you. If you could please just wait a moment in the hall, I'll come get you in a jiffy." He asks a third time but with the same patient tone, like Eddie Murphy's impression of Mr. Rogers. Sweet and salty at once.

I somehow lift my leaden feet and leave. I close the door behind me, but out in the hall isn't really a place to hang out. A hospital hallway is a strange composition of an airport gate and after-school dismissal—simultaneously still and frantic. The people working there all seem unhappy, bored, and tired. They look like they could use some fresh air.

I open the paper and it's another note from Susie. This has become an unpleasant scavenger hunt.

> Danielle,
>
> I'm sorry I wasn't here when you arrived. I need to go speak at a friend's memorial today. They're doing tests to sort out what the trouble is with your dad, and results might take a day or so. They want him to stay in the hospital overnight. I know he will be thrilled to see you. I'll be back later, hopefully by 7. Visiting hours are until 8 p.m. See you soon.
>
> —Susie

It seems that I'm the person here. Just me. The silence in this realization is awful and enormous.

Robert said he'd be here in a couple hours. Susie will be back. It's OK. I wait in the hallway, wondering if I should use the bathroom, wondering if it's safe. I consider calling Jake but I cannot face looking for a pay phone, or him not answering, or—really, worse than that—the possibility that he simply won't offer to be here with me through this.

Eventually, the scrubs guy opens the door and beckons me into the room. Everything is cleaned up, and Dad is tucked back into bed.

"Hi, Dad."

He slowly looks up at me, like an old turtle. Slow. Dry. Confused. He suddenly resembles my grandpa toward the end of his life. Then something flashes across his face like anger mixed with confusion.

"Danielle! What are you doing here?" His voice is dry and thin. I don't understand where he thinks we are. Then he looks around the room, realizing everything all at once, like waking up suddenly. "Oh God, I'm so sorry," he says, embarrassed. More like a child than I've ever seen him.

An old man turtle child. Lost and worried. Scared and embarrassed.

I kiss his cheek through my mask. Everyone is wearing masks here except him. I look into his eyes and try to smile enough for him to see.

"It's OK, Dad. I came to see you." I speak quietly, like you do to a child with a fever. "Plus, how could I resist this lovely décor?" I attempt a joke.

This makes him smile and he immediately starts to cry. The guy in the scrubs brings him a tissue and stands next to me. He turns and looks at me, somehow validating the entire mess of feelings I am having. This guy knows where we all are, even if Dad and I are both utterly lost.

"Now, who's this, Benjamin?" he asks with the air of someone who wants to be introduced to a new guest at a family picnic. Familiar and sweet.

Dad drinks some water from a paper cup by his bed. He whispers in between sips, "That's my little Bunny, Danielle. Isn't she gorgeous?"

I want to ask why Dad isn't wearing a mask but decide to keep quiet.

"It's a pleasure, gorgeous Bunny Danielle," says the scrubs guy, his eyes smiling above his mask. We don't shake hands, and I know why immediately. Blood.

"Benjamin, do you want to close your eyes for a minute while I take this gorgeous daughter of yours to find you some more ice chips?"

"Oh yes. I'd absolutely love to," Dad says, already lying back into the bed.

The scrubs guy motions for me to come stand near the door. He removes his latex gloves and tosses them into a red bin. He washes his hands, and we walk out into the hall.

He removes his mask, the rest of his face finishing the half portrait my mind was working to complete. Arthur would have said he looks like a Caravaggio boy. Round dark eyes. Full wide mouth. He immediately seems honest, which is a relief. His face is pained, trying to prepare me gently for what is about to happen.

He motions for me to follow him to the room with the ice. "I'm going to guess you need an update, huh?"

"Yes! Thank you!" I sigh, relieved I don't have to ask.

"Sure thing. When he arrived at the hospital earlier, he was having pains in his stomach, trouble breathing, and very high blood pressure." We are walking slowly down a corridor; we pass a few open doors with people in beds. It's awfully sad in a hospital. He continues talking, as I try to focus, "Basically, he was having a panic attack, so they gave him sedation downstairs. His doctor ordered tests to see what might be going on. Could have been anything, but he's tested positive for pneumonia. That's an infection in the lungs, so now they're giving him antibiotics. They'll likely do more tests to figure out the stomach pains. It could be a reaction to the AZT, which we're seeing a lot these days. Could be something else."

He fills a tiny plastic pitcher with crushed ice from a machine.

I stare at him. There is a lot here to process.

"Oh, you can take off your mask now." He puts the top on the pitcher and grabs two paper towels to wrap around the bottom.

I pull off my mask, letting it hang from my neck like a horrible necklace, feeling better but weirdly exposed.

He takes a deep breath, which prompts me to breathe too.

"So, any questions?"

"Why all the vomiting?" I ask as we walk back to Dad's room.

"AZT and all these other meds he's on can be very hard on the system, and together with the antianxiety meds he got when he came in, they can be a hurricane for the stomach."

"And the IV in his arm?"

"He was dehydrated from vomiting. The IV is for fluids to hydrate him, which helps the body cope with all this stress."

"Is he confused? He seems confused."

"That's the sedative. It can make you loopy. But also, there may be early signs of dementia starting. We'll have to wait and see. One day at a time."

Dementia? What? Is Dad going to forget me? Is he going to go crazy? I knew AIDS was bad, but more like the way you imagine the monster under the bed to be bad: you never actually have to see it. So dumb of me to think that maybe I'd never have to see it. So much for keeping it on the shelf. The monster is here, enormous and terrifying.

The scrubs guy sees my face, which must be a big mess of confusion, and suddenly he shakes his head. "Oh, dear. Too much, maybe?" A concerned smile on his face.

"Oh no, I'm just, you know, taking it all in. But I do have one more question for now, if that's OK?"

"Sure. Ask away," he whispers as we approach the room.

"Doesn't he need a mask? I mean, isn't he the sick one?" I ask.

"Yes, you're right, he is sick, but also, the HIV makes his immune system weak, like tissue paper instead of a steel wall. So, we need to make sure we don't give him any additional germs. His body is like a magnifying glass: what might not be a big deal for you and me could be enormously risky for him. He's got enough going on right now, right?"

I nod. Wow, OK, I get it now. Our masks are so that he doesn't get sick from us. It must be lonely and confusing for him to just see half of a face, eyes, and then masks.

"Are you ready to go back in?" he asks, placing his mask back over his nose and mouth.

I nod, doing the same, not at all sure I really am ready.

Dad is asleep, his mouth open. Breathing up and down.

"One day at a time, Danielle. Yes?" the scrubs guy says sweetly like someone's grandmother, as we stand there watching him sleep.

I nod and breathe in deep.

"All right, while I'd love nothing more than to spend all afternoon with you and your dear father, I've got to go make my rounds. I'll check back a little later. Press that red button over there if you need anything."

"Wait," I say before he leaves. "What's your name?"

"Oh Lord, my manners. I'm Nurse Justin," he replies. I could tell by how the mask on his face moved he was smiling. Big.

Thank God for Nurse Justin.

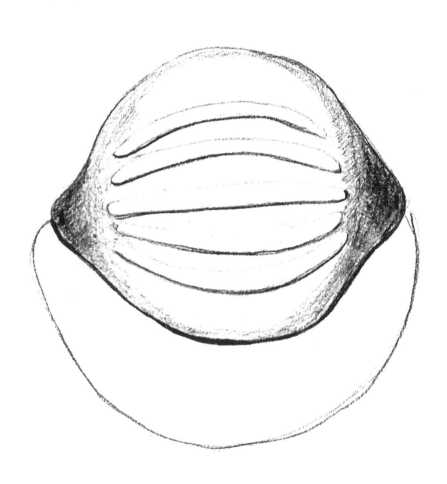

I sit by Dad's bed and take out my sketchbook and my English reading. "The Dead," by James Joyce. Seems like perfectly morbid reading for a hospital.

———

Dad wakes up around four p.m. The cold sky is getting dark already. He looks at me. First a smile. Then scrunched up and perplexed. He doesn't remember. He looks around the room and gradually puts it together. The pain, the hospital, the vomit, the mask, Nurse Justin.

"Hey there, sleepy. How are you feeling?" I ask.

"Oh, you know. Just peachy. What's happening?" He reaches for his glasses and looks at his bare wrist where he usually wears his watch.

I fill him in on the ACT UP meeting. His smile looks painful, he's trying so hard. I run out of things I can tell him. It's quiet. Just the humming of machines. On the wall is a picture in a pink frame of a vase of daisies on a table. It looks like a giant greeting card.

"Bunny . . ." He looks at me.

"Yes?"

"Please don't worry. It's pneumonia. I'll be OK."

I tilt my head, wanting so much to believe him. I realize how much he wants to believe it too, so I say, "All right, Dad."

"Have you eaten lunch?" he asks.

"I'm OK. It's going to be dinnertime soon anyway. Susie said she'll try to come back, and I'll stay until visiting hours end and go back to your place tonight." I take his hand.

He looks out the window. I know he's trying to gain control somehow. To find something to do to make it better, because that's what he does. He lifts his hand, twists his arm, and looks at his bare wrist again.

"Your watch is in the drawer, Dad." I turn my head to look at the clock, "It's 4:12." My stomach twists tightly. He nods. Are we both lying or is this what comforting looks like? He can't see me smiling. How can you tell anything when you can't see anyone's face? "TV?" I ask, finding the remote. The fluorescent buzz is too depressing.

"Sure, Bunny. Find me a movie," he says, now with a gentle smile.

I turn on the TV and surf until I find the old movie station. I hear Dad gasp, "*All About Eve*. Oh, Bunny, remember this?"

"Of course, Dad."

"'Fasten your seat belts. It's going to be a bumpy night,'" Dad says weakly from his bed, winking at me. I'd much prefer to be at a drama-ridden party thrown by Bette Davis than sitting in this hospital room, but at least he's making jokes.

"'Remind me to tell you about the time I looked into the heart of an artichoke,'" I say, doing my best to raise one eyebrow and squint my eyes like Bette Davis.

"'I'd like to hear it,'" he replies with a wink.

We watch a few scenes and then I hear him snoring.

Around five p.m., a doctor comes in. Dad is asleep. The doctor doesn't seem to care though, barely noticing him. He is very short, and his white jacket is a little too big on him, making him look like a clown. A clown doctor who forgot to put on his big red nose and forgot to be funny, or even faintly lighthearted. He doesn't seem to notice me either. I wait for him to see me, but he doesn't. He looks at the chart, writes a few things down, and heads toward the door.

"Excuse me," I say.

"Yes?" he says, like I am keeping him from something more important. But also, not alarmed I'd been there. He knew. He was just ignoring me.

"Can you give me, like, an update?"

"Who are you?" he asks, looking at the chart instead of my face.

"I'm his daughter, Danielle Silver," I say, looking at Dad sleeping.

He looks me up and down, and I can't tell if he's checking me out or trying to see if I'm too young to be here all alone. "Oh. And is your mom . . ." He glances around the room, like maybe she's hiding in the closet.

"She's not here, and they're not married. I'm his . . . um, well, I'm his daughter and just need to know what's happening," I repeat, hoping that's sufficient to continue the conversation. "Please," I add. I can smell

his aftershave, even with my mask on. It's sour and strong. I already hate this guy.

He starts to give me a report, but he doesn't have much more to add than what Nurse Justin has already told me. He says all this with the bedside manner of a piece of sandpaper. Dad will be released tomorrow, probably. If it were serious, they wouldn't let him leave, I guess? Dad told me he really likes his doctor, but I can't imagine anyone liking this guy. "So, are you his regular doctor?" Why is it that every time I ask a doctor a question I feel like an idiot? Like they hold the keys to a chamber of knowledge not permitted to dummies like me, but they're constantly disappointed that we don't know more.

"No, that's Dr. Holland. We work together, but I don't usually see patients in the office. I mostly see them here." I look at the name badge pinned to his white coat: "Dr. Ratner, MD, Infectious Diseases.

I add it up. *Here* is the AIDS ward of a hospital. *Here* is where the patients who do not respond well to their treatments end up. And *here* is apparently not where Dr. Holland likes to see his beloved patients, because maybe once they cross this threshold, they're less likely to be success stories. Dr. Holland must only like seeing healthy HIV-positive people. People who are well enough to gamble their health on drug studies. Dr. Ratner doesn't seem to like sick people though, so I'm wondering how this whole operation really works. From where I sit, I think you'd want the nice doc to be the one here, where things are scary as shit.

"OK, well, thanks for the update," I say. It's all I can do not to scream in his face.

He barely nods and then leaves the room. So now what? More waiting? What happens when he goes home? Will I need to stay there with him? Is he going to get better or worse? This is when I begin to realize that asking questions is not always a helpful process. What happens when the answers all suck? And even if I had them all, who am I supposed to tell?

There's a concert on TV now; Leonard Bernstein conducting an orchestra. It's totally dark outside, and I faintly remember some other people are supposed to be here but they're not. Do I call Jake or Mom now?

But Dad wakes up and smiles at me, suddenly more lucid than earlier, and he suggests we play Where Is Worse?— a trick he and Mom would play on us as kids whenever we were complaining about where we were. List places or situations that would be worse. It's a harrowing game, but I can't say it doesn't do its job. We take turns:

"Inside the bathroom at a Phillies game," I start.

"Under the basement carpet in Grandma's old house," he says.

"At the supermarket in a blackout."

"Ooh good one, Bunny. How about in a snowstorm wearing a bathing suit and flip-flops."

"On a plane next to a stinky, screaming baby," I say.

"At the end of a long movie line just as they sell out."

Not knowing what happens next, I guess that's worse than this.

23

"Two Doors Down"

At six forty-five a tidal wave of noise and energy rushes into Dad's room. Robert, Susie, and Dad's other friends—Peter, Scott, and George—all take off their heavy coats. They all wear the same masks as me, but theirs are all drawn on, personalized. Some of them have red lips, smiles, mustaches, and words like *kiss* and *relax* written on them. This is clearly not their first rodeo.

Dad smiles as they all settle in and greet him. They each blow kisses from their masked faces. They seemed to know their way around this particular section of the hospital—the AIDS ward—finding chairs from the hallway to bring in and knowing exactly how to hang four coats layered on one coat hanger. I feel something in me unclench, the tightness of being alone releasing.

Dad shakes his head as Peter, Scott, and George share tales of the funeral they just attended for their friend Jerome. It strikes me as a little weird that they're talking about a funeral in Dad's hospital room, until I notice Dad's giant grin. He loves it. "Those suburban snots are too much, with their awful loafers and green sweaters," says Peter, before he launches into detail about the food and who was there. "They had cheese balls, Benjamin. Neon orange cheese with some weird crunch all over it."

"Those were delicious," says Scott, smiling fondly. "Reminded me of my aunt Gillian."

"It was horrifying," says George. "They served eggnog. Thanksgiving was the day before yesterday! I mean, how am I supposed to suddenly adjust to eggnog?"

"But the music! Oh, Benjamin, you'll love this," Peter says, walking to sit beside my dad. "Dolly Parton. They played Dolly Parton at the reception, just as background music!"

Scott and George start singing "Two Doors Down" and dancing.

Dad smiles, turning to look at me, holding his hand out for me to take. I'm glad to see him smile. "Jerome did have a thing for Dolly, didn't he?"

Robert comes over and pulls me aside. "Sorry I couldn't be here sooner, honey. Let's just say the drama was intense across town," he says before planting a masked kiss on my cheek. In a flash I see this chaos infecting every single person who has this virus. "How are you? How's he? He's cracking jokes, so that's got to be a good sign."

"I guess . . ." I say, trying to keep myself together.

Robert takes a deep breath, silently opens his arms, and hugs me. He smells like a fireplace, and I breathe him in deeply, relaxing, even if it's just for a moment.

"Thanks," I whisper and do my best to keep from crying.

"OK, well, what's your schedule? Are you going back to school to-morrow? The nurse down the hall said your dad will be able to go home this week, and we've got this covered. I can drive you to the bus station in the morning if you need."

"Yeah, sure. I was going to get the eleven a.m. bus."

Soon, the other friends empty out, blowing kisses to my dad and fussing over his gown. Susie comes over and whispers in my ear, "I know your dad is so happy you're here. Thank you. Anything new from the doctor?"

"Not really. Just met him. Dr. Ratner."

At the sound of his name, she takes a long inhale, stifling something deep, and I sense her eyes rolling as she shuts her eyelids for a brief moment. I can see the mask contract and expand like a paper balloon. She looks down at Dad's chart. It appears she understands medical language in a way I do not. "What did he have to say?" she asks coldly as she reads.

"At first, he seemed annoyed by my existence . . . then said it was pneumonia, which I already knew from the nurse, so . . . nothing really." I can feel something in my face crack open a little, tears starting to form in my eyes.

"Hey . . ." She looks up at me and puts down the chart. "Hey, Dani, my darling, pneumonia is treatable." She puts her hand on my shoulder.

I'm starting to tear up so I stare at the floor.

"Danielle, look at me."

I do. Her face is soft, concerned and kind.

"It's treatable. He's taking medicine. He will be OK. Honestly, darling. I have seen this many, many times before. The drugs are better now; he'll come through this one. I promise, love." Her British accent becomes more a granny, less a headmistress.

I nod and look at her through my wet eyes. I think she's smiling under her mask.

But she said, *This one*, which makes it sound like the first of a series. This one. There will be more.

"Dani, honey, let's go find ourselves some candy and leave these boring grown-ups," says Robert. Susie grimaces but smiles, says she just wants herbal tea, and settles into the chair beside Dad's bed.

As he deftly navigates the hospital halls toward the cafeteria, I ask Robert how the friend he was visiting was doing.

"Jimmy Prescott. Former party boy and male model. Just a smart, funky, sexy man." Robert told me they'd gone to Hunter College in New York together in the seventies. Then he went on to get a job at IBM, selling computer systems to businesses in the eighties.

"He still partied though, like part of him wouldn't grow the hell up, you know? And in 1986 he contracted HIV. He's lucky as hell to still be alive. And when I asked, 'Who did this to you?' you know what he said?"

I shake my head, "No, what?"

"He said, 'I did this. I take responsibility for my disease.'"

Would Dad say the same thing? Maybe he blames someone? Or himself? I've never even thought to ask Dad who did this to him. Maybe he blames himself and that's why he doesn't want to make it a burden for me.

"But you can't give this disease to yourself. I mean, someone has to infect another person, right?"

Robert shrugs and looks at me as we walk past the snacks. "Well, Danielle, I just think we have to be careful when we tell stories to ourselves. It's easy to want to place blame when something bad happens. I mean, maybe the question itself assumes an answer that is, in and of itself, unreasonable. I mean, whose fault is it that you're a human being, susceptible to disease, altogether mortal? We don't blame our parents for being human, do we?"

"But if someone knows they're positive, isn't it, like, wrong to spread it? Why isn't it that person's fault?"

"Well, of course, we have to make choices that will minimize risk for ourselves and other people, right? Sadly, the world is full of people who don't even know they're positive, and many who don't really think ahead." Robert unwraps a tea bag and pours water in the cup. I grab a Snickers bar.

"I guess so, but wouldn't anyone having sex be putting themselves at risk?" I remember having sex last spring with Brian, the broken condom, my worry about pregnancy eclipsing any worry about AIDS. Was it my own fault for saying yes to sleeping with him, then? Or was that just a random accident? Who would I blame if that had given me HIV? I feel pretty sure I'd have blamed him, and I wonder if I'm one of those people who doesn't want to be responsible.

"It's a scary time, and we all just need to be careful," Robert says, stirring the tea he's made for Susie. "And don't forget, people can have HIV and not even know it. Many people don't have any symptoms, and they pass it around. So how can you blame them for something they're not even aware of?"

"I guess." I hadn't thought of that.

"This virus is tricky. There are several different ways to get it, and some people just take more risks with their bodies. Or think they're immune or immortal. Or they're careless, or suicidal, or just ignorant." He quickly scans the candy selection and grabs some Junior Mints before we pay.

Back in the hallway, I ask, "But if you get AIDS, aren't you, like, a victim, kind of?" I hope I don't offend him, but I really am curious.

"It's all how you choose to see it. Perhaps, yes, but I've never thought of myself as a victim. Unlucky, yes. But that's different. I don't blame myself as much as the world seems to want me to." We carry our snacks and cups back toward Dad's room.

"God, it's all so complicated and messed up," I say as we pass a lounge full of people in hospital gowns, watching TV. "Blaming the people who are dying from a disease that modern medicine cannot seem to treat and the government is ignoring."

He nods enthusiastically as we enter Dad's room, "Right! The very premise of blame is all wrong. It's an excuse to further ignore and disparage homosexuals. Why do people need someone to blame? I mean, if we're playing that game, we all should blame President Reagan."

I laugh, as Dad chimes in. "Good Lord, Robert, can we NOT invoke another Ronald Reagan vitriolic diatribe just now?"

Robert looks at me and winks. "Your father knows me too well. OK, OK, I relent!" He hands Susie her tea and places the candy we bought on the table by Dad's bed. "Let's talk about this god-awful room, dammit." I see Robert shifting gears for Dad's sake. The others start to look around at the decor. "Whose job is it to select art for hospitals? It's absolutely atrocious what they do in this place." He laughs, and Dad is smiling.

Before we know it, visiting hours are ending. I kiss Dad before leaving, suddenly feeling a pull. As my masked face touches his cheeks, I wonder how many more times we'll be able to do this. To touch our faces, to say goodbye. Life is so finite and fragile. We all have only so many times to touch each other's faces. It's nearly too much and he can see it in my eyes.

"Dani. Please, don't worry," he pleads with me, his eyes fleeting with his own worry.

I nod and my eyes fill with juicy, salty tears.

"I'll see you tomorrow. Sleep tight," I say.

"Don't let the bedbugs bite," Dad says back.

"They better not . . . I'm sleeping at your place, Dad."

He laughs. "I love you, Bunny."

"I love you too." I squeeze his hand.

Robert, Susie, and I walk toward the exit. As I look around to other visitors zipping their coats and heading to the exit, I imagine they've been visiting someone they love, and I wonder if they feel how I do. Terrified and grateful and very tired. I find myself wanting everyone in that hospital to have someone who loves them, who can handle it and show up.

When you're a little kid, being an adult seems like endless freedom. The idea of no one telling you when to go to bed, or what to eat, or when to be home sounds so dreamy. Like a permanent vacation. But I'm beginning to think that being a grown-up is really just carrying a bigger bag of rocks.

Back at Dad's I put on my pj's and call Marco. I recall the day to him, the ACT UP meeting, the protest, the hospital. Marco listens patiently. With all that space, I can finally hear myself. The worry, the fear. I'm not frantic; I'm actually peaceful. Almost like I'm floating, calmly watching what is happening below.

"Is what I'm doing enough?" I ask.

Marco just hums a little into the phone and finally says, "You'll never feel like it's enough, but trust me, it is. You do what you can, and other people are there for him too, Dani. You're not alone."

I smell him before I open my eyes.

It's morning. I am on Dad's bed, still wearing yesterday's clothes. The dream lingering in my brain. I try to get it all into my sketchbook, fast.

He sat on a throne. I was drawing him.

He wore a velvet cape and a crown. Like King Henry VIII.

I sat a few feet away with a pencil and paper and I

examined the shape of his eyes.

The line of his nose.

And his lips, wide and thin and moving.

He was talking and talking and talking.

Telling me stories of history,

Of fables,

And monarchies,

And music,

And how to chop onions.

All his lessons

Coming right out of his mouth.

Like gifts I could hardly keep up with.

But I needed him to stop talking so I could see the line of

where his lips met.

So I could see how the light hit his upper lip when it was

resting.

So I could know every inch of his face.

I asked him to stop talking, and he just laughed and began

explaining the plot to another opera where someone dies.

I make the bed and put yesterday's dishes away. I hear Dad in my head telling me what and how to clean up. *Stack them by size. Don't leave crumbs on the counter. Do you think I want to walk into a pigsty?*

I leave the food in the fridge because Dad will be home soon.

I walk back to the hospital, through the revolving door, sign in, and take the elevator to the third floor, mask in hand. The air, stale as yesterday, lingers. There is no motion in a hospital room. Instead, there's a suspension of progress. You know that feeling where you're making something or going somewhere? It's momentum, I think, feeling your blood pumping? A hospital is the total opposite of that. Nothing moves at any kind of useful-seeming pace. It's like a bunch of people standing at a bus stop, waiting for the motion to arrive. Healing is slower than the eye can see.

I guess that's why hospitals have so many TVs. They remind you there's life outside; they indicate another plane of reality where life is lived in bursts, edited with music and brightly colored commercials. TV makes a still room feel lively. But here there is just a lot of slow recovery or worse—slower endings. Here it's vinyl upholstery and posters of still life in pink plastic frames. Still life. Still, stuck, stopped.

Susie and Robert are sitting by Dad's bed. I bring him a sticky bun I picked up at DiBruno's on the way here, but he doesn't even open it. He doesn't eat much. Robert finds a humor piece in the newspaper and reads it out loud.

Susie looks over Dad's chart with a scrunched-up face, like she's trying to read handwriting that's illegible. I wish I knew what to look for on his chart. I wish I had more time to stay and ask questions, even if it meant having to see that Ratner doctor from yesterday. But if I plan on getting back to school, I have to get moving. The clock on the wall reads ten fifteen, and my bus is at eleven a.m. Maybe I should just stay. I'm hoping Dad hasn't read my mind or caught me checking the time every few minutes while telling myself I can wait a few more.

"It's getting late," Dad says a split second after my eyes return from the clock to that spot on his bed that I stare at when I don't want to look at his IV. "I don't want you to miss your bus. I'll be out of here soon, and winter break will be here before you know it. I'll be OK, Bunny. I've got these two."

I say goodbye, holding his big warm hand and trying my best to smile extra big so it translates through my mask.

"Goodbye. I'll call you when I'm back home, OK?"

I raise one eyebrow, like he does, and say, "You better!"

He takes my hand and kisses it.

At the bus station, Robert hugs me and, before he lets go, he says quietly, "Take care, sweet Danielle. I'll let you know when you need to come back." I shudder. He said *when*, not *if.*

The bus is packed. I sit next to an old lady with a cat in a carrier. The cat whines the entire ride. Luckily my headphones work their magic, and I submerge myself listening to Joni Mitchell singing about afternoon parties in a canyon. I wish Marco was here to distract me with his silly jokes.

Left to my own devices
I search for wisdom inside.
All this trying out, experimentation,
rough drafts at best
barely legible faint renderings of instructions.
Invisible ink where the wetness once hit the page,
leaving secret codes.
Meanwhile, you sit in a plain cotton gown,
Neither elegant nor sparkly,
not even yours.
While you endure the bad lighting
and terrible art,
I'll carry these rocks around and try to look in another direction.
Forward, maybe.
Wherever that is.
Because fear shouldn't win me over. Not yet anyway.
It turns out the answers aren't in the back of the book
So I am inventing a way to carry my rocks,
to carry all this stuff, inherited stuff,
Stuff I didn't ask for.
I spin a web of connections like a clock mechanism
To whoever seems kind and willing and close.
We just want to feel like we are a part of something that
works, just a little bit.
It is such a letdown when the latch doesn't catch, when
the lid won't close—
but still, what choice do we have?
We make our own devices.
It's all we have.

24
"Mad World"

Things feel out of scale back at school. Like Alice in Wonderland, I ate the growing cake, and now I have to squeeze myself back into this tiny world. I thought the staircase up to the science building was bigger. And the doorway into the hall where I go to art history class seems narrower than when I left. Crossing the big lawn, all these kids frolic in Baxter's perfect, manicured world, and now—right now—all over the place, people are dying in hospitals. People are vomiting on the floor and being treated terribly by doctors who are exhausted and mean. People. My dad. And the politicians who were voted into office are ignoring the problem. It is unlikely that these precious spoiled kids in their beautiful sweaters and boots have ever seen their parent vomit in a hospital gown.

You build the thin, fragile parts, leaning on one another,
Defying weather or the occasional shudder of footsteps.
They stand, proving your instincts for three dimensions,
for structure, for reason.
Until one day, a breeze passes, shifting one piece.
Then another,

and then the raindrops pour and the giants stomp,
and in no time
it's gone.
Time slows down.
A test failed.
A paper lost.
A class missed.
A drawing torn.
A future interrupted.
You're left with a messy pile of slivers.
Remnants of your foolish plans.
You wait for the wind to die down.
You wait for a good moment to whisper,
"Try again."

It's December first. The leaves are gone. The grass is frosty, and there are snowflake decorations everywhere. I have forty-five days before RISD's regular application deadline. After art class in our new compressed space, I sneak over to the gym to get twenty minutes of studio time. On the floor is a letter. It's short, but not sweet.

Dear Student,

Due to an accelerated construction schedule, this room must be vacant by December 11. Whatever remains here will be disposed of thereafter.

Thank you for your cooperation,
The Baxter Facilities Department

Standing in the middle of my studio, I wonder ten thousand things simultaneously: Where will I find boxes? Can I fit all these paintings in my dorm room? Will Amy mind? Should I ask for help from Mrs. Funk or Ms. Davis? Why is the construction happening now, during the school year? Does it have to do with showing off like Daria said? Am I about to pack up my whole life here just so the pretty kids can

play their stupid games? Are they kidding me? Can I finish my portfolio and application essay in a month? What day will Dad be discharged?
What is happening to my life? Everything was so planned out and now
it's in pieces on the floor.

I never should have gotten used to this in the first place. I was pretending that I was a grown-up artist with a studio. It was all make-believe.
What a ridiculous bunch of crap. It's all make-believe here anyway. I walk
to art history class in a stupor, wishing I was back in Philadelphia. At
least there I could be useful. Should I even be at school? I'm distracted,
wondering how I might salvage old drawings to make some semblance
of a portfolio. Maybe I shouldn't even apply to college. I mean, won't
Dad need someone to take care of him? Should I really be so far away
now and even farther next year? My chest is tight; the atmosphere is
compressing me into a tiny little ball.

And do I just lie down and take this studio thing? I could fight and
complain and piss people off, but do I want to? I mean, *really* want
to. As my breath gets thinner, I imagine not having art. Not having
paint under my nails and the smell of turpentine on my shirt. Not
ever feeling that I can go anywhere in my mind and make whatever
I want with paint. That freedom to spill and shred and make perfect lines or blobs of color. I imagine having free time at night. For
what? To flirt with boys? Read books? Knit sweaters? What would I
do? Did Picasso ever wonder if it was worth it? I bet he just knew.
Or everybody told him how great he was so he never doubted himself. Fucking Picasso.

"Oh, Danielle, come now," I hear Arthur's voice, buttery smooth.
"You aren't going to let a little bump in the road get in your way now,
are you?"

Maybe it's a sign? Losing my studio, losing our art classroom,
losing Dad.

"He's not dead yet, dammit," Arthur says. "And we both know his
protests are a front. He loves that you love to make art. He's baffled by
it but enthralled by you. Don't give up," Arthur says gently. "Not after
all you've done."

I'm supposed to fight this alone? This place is for jocks. Nobody cares about me here.

"What a load of horseshit," Arthur says, sitting next to me, pulling out a nail file and starting with his left index finger. "Open your eyes, my dear."

"Open your eyes, Danielle," I hear again, a higher voice. Not Arthur anymore.

Ms. Davis. Standing over me. My head is on the desk, there's a little drool seeping across my lower cheek. I sit up. The classroom is empty.

"Rough weekend?" she asks, smiling. She thinks I was partying the weekend after Thanksgiving.

I wipe my hand across my face and try to smile.

"Sorry. Wow, I'm sorry." I rub my eyes and try to remember what's going on.

"You all right?" She sits next to me slowly.

I stare at her. How I wish I could tell her everything. About the hospital, Nurse Justin, and the ACT UP meeting. Pneumonia. The vomit.

"Yeah, it was intense," I finally say.

"Oh, really? Good, intense or bad?" She sits next to me. I'm not entirely sure why she isn't mad. I slept through her class. I would be mad.

"Well, it started good, but then, well . . . my dad had to go to the hospital."

"Oh no. Is he OK?"

"He has pneumonia." I wonder if she knows that pneumonia is a common ailment associated with AIDS. Shit, did I just spill the beans? When I told Ms. Davis that Arthur died from AIDS, she was understanding and then suggested I research Wojnarowicz. She nods and sits back in her chair and waits for me to continue. "But I think he'll be OK. He's on antibiotics." I am nodding, like I'm trying to convince myself I'm telling the truth.

She looks at me, long and hard.

"Well, I hope for his speedy recovery. That's bound to be hard. And is your mom around?"

"Um, no, she lives in California, actually. She's coming back over Christmas. They're not married, though."

"Well, if there's anything I can do for you, please let me know."

"Yeah, thanks," I say, leaving the room.

Thirty minutes later I'm in English class. As they discuss Joyce's "The Dead," which I remember starting, I begin writing in my sketchbook. I realize I probably look incredibly studious, but instead, I'm writing a letter to the headmaster. I'm trying to explain myself, trying to ask for what I think is fair. Luckily, the teacher doesn't call on me.

Later, I walk back to Ms. Davis's office during my lunch period. She usually eats her own lunch in her classroom, sometimes reading magazines. I knock quietly, and she looks up, surprised.

"Danielle, hi!" She touches a napkin to her mouth. "What's happening?"

"Can I talk to you for a minute?"

"Sure." She wraps up her sandwich.

"You said if I ever needed anything . . ." I start.

"Yes, how can I help?" She sits upright, readying herself.

"So, I got this earlier." I hand her the note. "It's about my studio space."

Her eyebrows raise as she reads it. "Gosh, that's tough. I'm not sure I can do much about this, to be honest. Faculty usually don't get involved in facilities issues."

"Oh, I don't need you to. But I wrote something to Headmaster Turner. Would you look at it, and be totally honest?"

Her eyes get wide as she grins. "Ooh, of course."

I hand her my sketchbook.

Dear Headmaster Turner,

    I write to you today to formally object to the decision to remove me from my basement art studio to make way for gym renovations without offering an alternative workspace. I do not believe it is fair or right for Baxter to prioritize sports over art.

Allow me to explain.

Art enables us to see the world and to understand each
other. It can be pleasing or upsetting, but either way, it's
essential. I've been lucky enough to attend Baxter for four
years and my time here will surely serve me throughout my
life. Much of that is due to teachers like Mrs. Funkelberg
and Ms. Davis, who teach us the importance of art as a way
of understanding the world. But, regardless of this, the
school does not invest in the arts like it does with sports.

I know many things are considered when buildings
are built, removed, or renovated. This studio has kept
me growing as an artist and as a student. By having a
space of my own, to use after hours and on weekends, I
was able to make more and do more than I would have in
the classroom. But it's not only this studio space that is
being taken. It is the classroom too. Moving our art class
into a small room in Clark has lessened what we can do.
By reducing our space, you've reduced our potential for
learning.

Your brochures say Baxter is a place that welcomes
everyone, but I want to ask you: Is that really true?
Is art as important as sports, science, or history? I think
it should be.

I know I can't stop the construction, but I'm hoping
we can find another space, somewhere on campus, we
could use during our free time to make art. The world,
and even Baxter, needs artists. Surely, the founders of
Baxter knew this when they built the grand architecture
we call home.

I hope you can reconsider these choices and think about
finding another space for myself and my friends to create,
explore, and continue our learning.

Sincerely,

Danielle Silver, Class of 1992

I look over and Ms. Davis has a funny smile on her face. "Nice," she says.

I excitedly say, "Yes!" under my breath. "You don't think it's too much?"

"We can work on it, but yeah, Danielle, it is a really good argument."

"I just want to do something, you know? And not just for me. I'm only here for a few more months. I mean, for all the other kids who come here and want to make art?" Going to that ACT UP protest in Philly made me realize how much can happen when people invest their time, their energy, and their emotions to shape the world into one they want.

"I'm really pleased you're so fired up, Danielle. This is good. But I also want to caution that with any fight, the outcome is unknown. The result might look different from what you want, or you might only move the needle a little bit for yourself but pave the way for others in the future."

"I know," I say. "It just feels good to take part." I guess this is acting up.

"It's just that these decisions about building renovations aren't just made off-the-cuff. But I like that you're flexible, and maybe you can work something out somewhere else. That will make things easier."

"But I can't think about losing before I even start, right?" I say, actually smiling.

"Yes, you're right . . . Let's work on your argument in this letter later this week, but aim to get this into his hands before winter break. Can I make a quick photocopy of the letter and give you some notes?"

"Sure!" I say, excited to have her on my side.

"Great. Check in with me later this week, all right?"

It's six ten p.m. Peak dinner time in the dining hall. But we got here early to get first dibs on meatballs. You get more if you come early. I think they're always worried they'll have leftovers. I'm telling Marco and Amy about the whole studio thing and the letter.

"Wow, Danielle, bold move," says Marco, twirling his spaghetti into a spoon.

Amy, flipping over the leaves of a salad, says, "I don't know, I just don't want you to be super bummed out if this goes nowhere."

"You never know until you try, right? I mean, maybe no one's really shown Baxter another side of the story, you know? I feel like I can make a really good point. Anyway, I have nothing to lose."

Just then Derek walks by, dripping with sweat and hormones, accompanied by his side puppy Donald, and under his breath, but loud enough so we are sure to hear, he says, "Hey, lookit! It's faggot boy and his girlfriends." He laughs and glances for agreement from Donald, who snickers.

In no time flat, my head has burst into flames. That word. *Faggot.* It's sharp and ugly and nasty. It burns because it's meant to destroy the dignity of a gay person. It is a word used by lazy, stupid assholes who feel entitled to be cruel. Every time I hear it, I want to throw things. But usually, when I hear it at Baxter, I take a breath and ignore it.

Today is different. Maybe because I've seen so much the past week. I cannot accept this. My patience has run out on this moronic jerk. He cannot be allowed to do this. I stand up and yell to his back, "Hey!"

I hear Amy say, "Just let it go, Dani."

Derek turns and looks at me: angry, mocking, gross.

"Do not talk to us like that," I say. Plain, simple. I'm remaining calm but my mind is spinning with memories of Dad and the ACT UP protest.

He stares at me, then at Amy, and then gives Marco a creepy smile, making me shiver.

"What the fuck did you say?" He turns back to me. He has ugly whiskers trying to grow out of his upper lip. He's at least six foot three and probably weighs two hundred and fifty pounds. He looks exactly like an ogre from a fairy tale.

He walks close to our table and picks up Marco's plate of half-eaten spaghetti. He drops it on the floor, splattering sauce on my Doc Martens and all over Marco's pants. I continue to stare into his eyes as a meatball rolls across to the next table.

"Oops," he says in a drippy voice. "Faggot dropped his little balls." He laughs at his own joke. Like a moron.

Marco is silent. Eyes red. Lips shut tight. He is staring at the table, shrinking down, getting smaller. Amy puts her arm around him and glares at Derek.

I step right up close to him.

He smells like bad deodorant and sheer stupidity.

"Derek," I say calmly and quietly into his face. "Don't use that word."

"What word? *Faggot?*"

"Don't. Use. That. Word." I repeat slowly, staring into his beady eyes.

"Get out of my face, you fag-hag. What are you anyway, his body-guard? Does he need a girl's protection?" As he says this, he lifts his hand in that limpy way people imitate gay men, which I've never understood. Why do people think gay men have floppy wrists?

The room has gone quiet, but I don't care because the flames are now shooting out of the top of my head.

"I don't like that word. In fact, a lot of people don't like it. It's demeaning and cruel," I say louder, in case anyone in the back of the cafeteria hadn't heard me.

He smiles and opens his mouth again. "It's a free country, in case you forgot. Fag . . . got."

"Stop."

"God, can't you take a joke? You're so uptight!"

My fingers are tingling, and my eyes start to sting.

"Derek, I know you maybe don't have a large enough brain to understand this, but when you say that word, it doesn't only insult him. It insults all gay people."

"So what?" he says, rolling his eyes.

The room has gone quieter. More people are listening to us.

"Would you like it if I insulted football-watching, straight, overweight men? 'Cause I'm guessing that's a fairly accurate picture of your dad. Or maybe I insult your mom for how pitiful she is for having to look every day at his ugly face?" I say, before thinking twice. "'Cause I'm guessing that might make you a teeny bit upset."

"Don't talk about my mom and dad," he says, his nostrils flaring.

"Then don't use that word, 'cause you're talking about my dad. My dad is gay, and I'd like you to stop using that word."

I said it. Out loud, at Baxter.

"Ugh, gross. How does that even happen? Oh my God." He is laughing in a confused way and looks at stupid Donald for reassurance.

"What precisely is the problem, Derek? Why do you even care? Are you so obsessed with dicks and butts that you can't stop thinking about them? Are you threatened by Marco, or like, ALL gay people? And what exactly is he doing that's so threatening, anyway? Is it because he's so much better looking than you? Or cause he's on two varsity teams while your plentiful butt keeps the bench warm and toasty at football games? Or maybe the fact that he doesn't need to cheat to pass math."

I say that last part particularly loudly.

"Stop," I barely hear Marco whisper. But my eyes are set on Derek, whose face is red as he breathes loudly. But he doesn't say anything, so I keep talking. "You insulted my dad with that word, and yes, you insulted my friend. I mean, what do you even care if he's gay? He's a super nice person who doesn't do anything to hurt anyone else. How could his sexuality possibly affect you?"

"Dani!" Marco whispers again, trying to shush me.

Derek stands with his mouth open.

"Wait, this kid, for real? He's seriously gay?"

"Derek, so what?"

"Ugh, God!" He's shaking his head, trying to laugh but he's visibly confused. "Dude, that's just so gross."

"No. You're the one who's gross. You insult people. You make a mess, you smell really ripe—like, all the time—and you're now taking up a lot of people's precious free time with your bullying Marco about being gay. And for what? For a laugh? So you can feel big? It doesn't make you cool, Derek. It's just sad." I look around the room at all the people still listening. I finally smile. Burn.

Amy is staring at me, eyes wide. I think she's impressed with my Derek-slamming. I'm standing up for my friend. I feel so powerful.

"What the hell?" Derek pretends to laugh, but I can see he is nervous that maybe some of the teachers could hear me.

"You need to stop with this f-word garbage. It's 1991. Get it together. And go get a mop and deal with this mess you made. No one wants to clean up after you." I twirl my finger like a fairy godmother doing magic on the spilled meatballs.

He stares at me, speechless, as people all start going back to their dinners. Headmaster Turner is walking toward us, as Derek puts up his middle finger at me.

"Derek," he says, "that's enough. Let's go talk. You too, Donald." Headmaster Turner looks at me, Amy, and Marco as if to say, *I'll deal with you later*, and walks off with them.

I sit down, grab a paper napkin to clean off my boots, smile, and say, "Marco, did you eat my pudding?"

They stare at me.

"Holy shit, Danielle," Amy whispers.

"I know. I'm amazing." I'm reeling from that. It feels so good to stand up to that gigantic dipshit. Wow!

Marco is staring at me, eyes thin. I don't understand what's happening. I just stood up to that jerk-off for him.

"Don't worry about Derek. He's just a big asshole," I say, scanning the table for another napkin to clean off my boot.

He keeps staring.

"No, you . . ." Marco whispers with tears in his eyes. "You were supposed to keep it to yourself." Keeping his head down, he takes his tray to the trash and walks out. It's only then that I realize everyone is staring at him. I look back at Amy.

"Wait, is he mad at me? What did I do?"

"Dani," she leans in to whisper to me, "you just told everyone that Marco is gay."

Oh my God. Did I or did Derek? I guess I did. Oh my God. I suddenly sink down into the moment and realize. Oh. My. God.

25

"In Between Days"

I knock again.

"What?" Marco says through the door.

"It's me. Can we talk, please?" I say, gently.

I stand there waiting.

"Marco . . . I just— I didn't mean to . . . it just came out," I say without thinking.

"Very funny," he mutters through the door.

"Oh God. Bad word choice. I'm sorry."

He opens the door and says very calmly, "Are you sorry for that stupid joke or are you sorry for outing me in front of the entire goddamned school?"

"Both? Maybe it's not that bad . . . maybe no one heard?"

"Danielle . . . you have a very loud voice, which gets louder when you're mad."

"Could it maybe be for the best? Like ripping off a Band-Aid?" I suggest, grasping at straws.

He breathes in hard through his nose and shakes his head. "Are you for real?" he says. His eyes are red, and he's wearing his bathrobe. I hear the Cure coming out of his boom box inside.

He breathes in again and says, "I know you think of yourself as all, like, in the know, or whatever, about gayness and all, but seriously? Do you honestly think coming out is like ripping off a Band-Aid? Like it's just a little blip and then everything is a big sparkly musical number?"

"No," I say, dropping my head. Maybe I am insane. Maybe the word *faggot* blew my brain out of my head and I shouldn't be allowed out in public because I'm just a stupid straight girl who clearly has no idea what she's talking about and thinks she can go around telling other people's secrets. Shame invades my whole body, and my stomach is full of dry cement. Saying *I'm sorry* feels so minuscule. So easy. Instead, I just stand there, staring at him. Waiting for more, because it's clear I deserve it.

He continues. "Danielle, you were the first person I told for a reason. You think it's going to be easy now? You think because you stood up to that asshole that ALL of his friends aren't going to come after me now? You don't have to live with the bullying and the names and the looks. When they call you a lezzo, you just think it's funny. I've noticed. You and Amy joke right back. It doesn't hurt you. Because it's not true, and it can't actually hurt you."

"Right," I say. Still looking at his feet because if I look at his eyes, I will cry and I don't deserve to be the one crying.

"There are five hundred and forty students at Baxter, and how many of them are out of the closet? None. None." He pauses, to let that sink in. "There's a reason for that . . . And now my wrestling teammates— They're not going to want to even touch me. I told you that. I told you it would jeopardize my even being here, Danielle. And what about my dad? Fuck. It wasn't yours to tell. Just because your dad is gay doesn't give you some kind of pass to tell all the gay secrets in the world. They're not yours."

The cement inside me hardens and I can't move.

Because I can think of nothing else, say, "I know. I'm so sorry, Marco."

He says nothing and closes the door.

I walk out into the cold and dig out my sketchbook.

My mind is so small.
How do I make it bigger?
I mean well and still do harm.
The world swells beyond me and I can't keep up.
I forgot how much I could harm you;
I thought I was being brave
and then,
I said your truth really loudly. Your secret. Your story.
I thought I was protecting you, but I was hurting you more.
I wanted to stand up. Make a difference.
All I did was make a mess.

I wake up to a knock on my door. The clock says 7:17 a.m. Even half-asleep, I remember how I fell asleep, and my guilt covers me like a sack.

I opened the door and it's the house mistress. She is wearing pajamas and her hair is all ratty. "Urgent call," she sighs.

Urgent? Life or death? Is it Marco?

I stumble out into the hall barefoot. I pick up the receiver dangling from the wall phone.

"Hello?"

"Danielle, it's me." Jake. He sounds hoarse.

"Hi." I rub the sleep out of my face. "Where are you? It's so early."

"I'm in Philly. I got in yesterday." I remember now, Jake's semester ended earlier than mine, and he headed down for Christmas break. "Dad's worse, Dan."

"What? Why?"

"He had a fall last night."

"What?" I'm still waking up and rubbing my eyes to be sure this is all actually real.

"He got up to go to the bathroom in the middle of the night. Susie said he's unsteady because of the neuropathy. It makes his feet numb and he stumbles. But, Danielle . . ."

"Yeah?"

"He broke his hip."

Oh God. My grandpa broke his hip when he was eighty-three. He never recovered and died a few weeks later.

"And there's more," he goes on.

"More?" I alternately warm my bare feet on my calves. A slow, tired dance.

"They've also found something in his stomach."

"When? What is it?" I imagine a LEGO piece showing up on an X-ray.

"Cancer. They were concerned about the tests they did last time, so they tested him again last night to confirm. It's stomach cancer. Stage four."

I understand the words but I'm having trouble getting it all. I'm imagining four stages, like a music festival.

"Stage four . . . is bad, right?" I say this, hoping I'm wrong.

"Yeah, it is. Susie said it's aggressive, and it's probably spreading to other organs. They'll do more tests today."

"So, what do they do for that? Is there medicine?"

"Well, the problem is the treatment is more than he can withstand now."

"So, what does that mean?" I'm holding the phone under my chin and wrapping my arms around my chest to stay warm.

"It means his body can't . . . he's too weak and . . ." Is Jake crying, distracted, or unsure of what to say? Finally, he says, almost whispering, "I think you ought to come home . . . Now."

"But winter break doesn't start until . . ." I stop. Did he just say *now*?

"Dad will want you here." He's talking about the worst thing.

"But a week ago he said he was OK. Robert told me he'd tell me . . . And he said Dad was going to get better."

There's a silence that lasts far too long. It's the enormous space between hope and fear, shrinking instantly.

"He's not going to get better," Jake says flatly. "Robert told me to tell you, it's time to come home."

Robert told him to tell me. That's what I was waiting for. All week.

Running from this. Seeing a path forward that doesn't include this awful, urgent news.

"All right. I'll start packing," I finally say.

I hear him take a deep inhale and exhale. "We'll talk more when you get here. Yeah, you should pack for . . ." He doesn't know how to finish this sentence.

The pain in my stomach from yesterday takes a turn for the worse. Now, it's like a heavy rock inside me. "I got it. I'll let you know my timing," is all I can say before hanging up the phone gently. And then dread slows everything down.

I walk back into my room, my feet nearly numb. I wonder if that's how Dad's feet felt when he fell. What time did it happen? How did he get help? Was Jake there already?

I walk into our room, and Amy is sitting up in bed, waiting.

I just stare at her and say, "It's Dad. I need to go home. Now." I rub my eyes and shake my head to wake up.

Amy puts her hair in a ponytail, pulls my suitcase from the top shelf in the closet, and just starts packing for me. I look at my desk, where I'd left my English notebook, my physics textbook, and my history notes, all open. Last night's attempt to distract from the other terrible thing. I suddenly wonder: How do I tell my teachers that my dad is dying from AIDS?

As Amy pulls shirts from my dresser, I start placing books into my backpack. I start listing off all the things I need to do. "Will you tell Ms. Davis that I'll work on that art history project? And can you get my physics homework? Oh shit, there's an English test next Monday. Could you ask Mrs. Fox if I can make it up later? And this book needs to go back to the library. And can you let Funk know I'm gone?"

Amy takes notes.

I want to tell her to let Marco know. I want to ask her to beg Marco to forgive me, but it's my mess. I can't make it her problem.

But she looks at me, as I am trying to sort all this out, and she says, "I'll tell Marco. Don't worry."

An hour later I'm on the bus. It's empty and smells like cinnamon potpourri. This bus ride feels like that revolving door at the hospital. This will change me, and I cannot make it stop.

These interruptions slash you right
in half.
Heartbreaks, injustices, violence.
You rip apart but
days keep coming,
leaving no time to recover and mend.
Leaving no room for sorrow or screaming.
Let alone breathing in and understanding what in God's
name is going on.
This bus drives straight down the highway. There is a
straight line between us.
An arrow, sharp, piercing through the heart.

26

"The Man That Got Away"

I know my way around this hospital now. Same front desk lady, new hairdo. I politely tell her my dad's name, hoping she won't grimace like she did before. She types and chirps, "Benjamin Silver! Oh, Ortho. Seventh floor." She sounds almost chipper. "Here you go." She hands me a pass. "Room 760. Have a good day, dear." Someone's in a good mood.

I get off the elevator. Somehow it's brighter on the seventh floor. Are the flowers up here real? It isn't the windows because it's gray outside. The nurses look happier. Do they wear a different color uniform? Do they just have more lightbulbs? On his door is a sign that asks visitors to wear a mask. There is a box of them outside the room.

I walk into his room.

Dad is reading a newspaper and looking better than I expected.

"Hi, Dad," I say, putting down my backpack and duffel bag and pulling up a chair.

"Hi, Bunny." He smiles and puts down his paper. He looks super cheerful for a guy with a broken hip and cancer.

"How are you?" I ask.

"Well, I've made it to the seventh floor, so that's good news."

"Yeah, what's up with the seventh floor? It's so . . . nice here." Even the cheesy framed posters here are better.

"Ortho ward."

"What?"

"Orthopedic ward. Broken bones."

"That's why it's so nice? Does good lighting heal bones faster?"

"No, Bunny-bun, that's why it's nicer than the third floor."

"Why?"

"The third floor is the AIDS ward. I'm not here because I have AIDS. Not this time. I'm here because I broke my hip." He says all this in a weird singsong way. He sounds drunk.

I sit down next to his bed, looking at a variety of machines and clear bags hanging off poles, like deflated water balloons.

"So, what exactly happened, Dad?"

"I got up to go to the bathroom like I always do in the middle of the night. I couldn't feel my feet, and I fell. I couldn't get up. I laid there for what felt like forever, thinking, 'This cannot be it. I cannot breathe my final breath upon the bathroom floor on a Thursday.' I managed to pull myself to the phone and call Susie, who came to my rescue. They brought me back here in an ambulance! Can you imagine? The doctor men carried me out on a stretcher. Paramedics! They were so adorable." His smile looks like he was telling a joke that I didn't quite get.

I ask if it hurts.

"It did. But now it doesn't." He looks at the collection of bags and tubes connected to his arm.

"Oh, is that your painkiller?"

"Yes, it's wonderful," he says, smiling. I smile back at him. He is being so silly. "Jake was here before but maybe now he's visiting the pizza?"

"Visiting the pizza? Is he getting lunch?" I want to laugh but stop myself.

"Of course. Lunch! So, how are you, my sweet Bunny? I'm so happy to see you. You look pretty. I love that color on you." He points to my shirt.

I look down at my old red sweatshirt.

It's clear to me now that my dad is high. He seems so cheerful and mellow, like the stoner kids at school.

"What's wrong?" he notices me trying to smile.

"Oh, nothing." I try a bigger smile.

"Bunny . . . what happened? You have a look." He makes a slow circle with his finger like he's tracing my face.

I'm not going to tell him how terrified I feel that he has cancer, AIDS, and a broken hip; that his body is on a downward spiral, swirling and swirling; and that the despair and helplessness are bafflingly overwhelming to me. No, I cannot say that to him, not at this moment when he seems to be genuinely enjoying himself. Instead, I tell him about things I never mentioned last weekend: the dance, the kiss, Marco being gay, and then I tell him about yesterday's disaster.

"Oh, wow. This is indeed a juicy episode of your life, sweet Bunny," he says in a wistful singsong way. "But yes, it sounds like a terrible mistake with the meatballs and the bully. You made a huge decision for him without his consent."

"I didn't mean to."

"Oh, sweet Bunny, of course you didn't, but that's a big deal." He's shaking his head over and over.

"I know. And now he won't speak to me, and I don't know what to do."

"Just wait a bit. Let it air out. Life is long. He will come back to you, I think. Marco seems like a sane, reasonable boy. And he clearly cares about you. He'll talk to you eventually. And when he does, just listen. Coming out is scary, honey." He touches my hand and continues: "Hatred seethes like a snake in the grass, everywhere. Like a stupid, mean monster that lives in all kinds of people, and sometimes even inside you as well. When I came out, I couldn't sleep for months. I got so paranoid, I felt like the secret straight police were going to scoop me up and throw me in jail. I told one person at a time and it took years."

"Who was the first person you told?" I ask him. I'd never felt like I could ask him this before, but then again, I'd never seen him high before.

"It was about fifteen years ago, now. I was struggling. Things with your mom were fine, but the problem was growing inside me. Keeping a secret is exhausting. I was on a business trip, and I met Andrew. He had freckles and strawberry blond hair. He looked like a tall cupcake." Dad is smiling, thinking about freckles. Stoned Dad is really quite delightful.

"Sounds cute," I say. Not sure what else to say.

"Yeah. Major cute." He sighs and continues, "I found myself feeling sunlight inside my head." I stay quiet so he can continue. "It felt confusing, but also, at the same time, totally true. I was attracted to him. And he was so sweet, I guess I felt OK telling him. Also, since he was a complete stranger, it wouldn't get back to anyone I knew."

I can't believe we're having this conversation, but it's like I opened a secret trap door to find a whole world inside him. Also, he's all gooey, so if I don't ask now, when? "Did you always know?"

"I knew that the person I was trying to be wasn't who I really was. I hid it. For a long time. And the longer I hid it, the more I knew the truth. But people weren't out in the open then. I mean, let's face it, they still aren't."

I flash to Baxter and suddenly imagine others, aside from Marco, who must be hiding it still.

"What happened when you told the cupcake? How'd it go?"

"Well, I didn't know if he'd try to hit me or hit on me. But he simply nodded. He understood. He told me he was gay too. It felt good to finally be honest. We didn't fall in love and live happily ever after, but it was a step for me. I thought of him a lot after that. The man that got away . . ." Dad smiles, looking toward the window. I wait for him to continue, to let the memory linger in his cloudy brain.

"I knew my coming out would eventually change everything for us— your mom, you, and Jake. And then, eventually, everything changed, and I felt terrible."

"What made you feel terrible?" I just want to keep him talking.

"I wanted to be accepted, and suddenly I wasn't. I'd been afraid. A lot of us were. Robert's family still won't speak to him. Other friends of mine lost jobs, their homes, their friends, their religious communities."

"Do you think it's any different now? Any easier in the nineties than the seventies?" I ask him, wondering what's changed in fifteen years.

He thinks about it for a while.

"Perhaps a little. I mean, the more people know, the more they grow, right?" He laughs. "Oh, Danielle, my love . . . your generation will make progress. More understanding will lead to more acceptance. I believe that. But now there is this." He motions to the hospital room, the tubes, himself.

"AIDS," I say softly.

He nods. "I cannot imagine how scary it must feel to come out now." Dad continues, "I mean, between the hatred and this virus just waiting to kill you. Good God, sweet Marco. The poor boy must be terrified."

Oh, Marco. My gut flips with another round of guilt.

Dad keeps talking, "There are more people who accept it, but there are still so many people who truly, deeply believe that being gay is wrong, like, morally wrong."

"But why? I mean, what do they care?" I ask.

"Maybe it's fear of the unknown. Or fear of difference." He trails off and gazes out the window. "It feels threatening to them, I think. It's all these scary *queers*, like zombies coming to force Donna Summer and quiche Lorraine down their throats and threaten their whole way of life, I guess . . . It's so silly when you really think about it." He laughs.

"It is silly. And terrible."

"Danielle, I'm sorry," he finally says, looking at me, his face changing suddenly.

"What for?"

"This. Me. Here. Now. The world. I'm sorry we couldn't fix it for you kids."

"Fix what?"

"All of it. All the anger and bitterness, the racism and homophobia, the need for control. I'm sorry you're going to have to keep on fixing the world, my smart little Bunny. We couldn't get it all done." He is exhausted. Fixing the world is exhausting.

He closes his eyes and falls asleep. I still hold his hand.

Dear Marco,

    I thought I was being helpful and fighting for justice, but I was just being ignorant and really selfish.

    I was trying to prove I was some sort of badass, but I used you in the process.

    I talked to my dad today about coming out and how painful it is to be gay in this world. I cannot pretend to know how you feel, but I understand that what I did will make that hurt worse, and I feel absolutely awful about that truth.

    Marco, I hope one day you can forgive me. I hope I can make this up to you, so you feel safe talking to me, because I want to be your friend.

                  In hopes of someday,
                  Danielle

I rewrite the letter again in my sketchbook. I tear it out and fold it up into an envelope I get from a nurse. I find a stamp in my wallet and mail it outside the hospital.

I want to slow things down. I feel like I'm on that spinning thing at the playground and someone has pushed too hard. I wonder if it's time to call Mom yet. I'll talk to Jake. I guess we should both decide and call her together.

In the afternoon, Susie and Robert come to see Dad. Jake returns around two thirty. Doctor Ratner comes in with another doctor who specializes in cancer treatment, an oncologist. Stage four stomach cancer, metastatic, which means it's spread to other organs. They barely mention his broken hip.

"Aren't you just the Good Ship Lollipop?" Dad jokes.

"Benjamin, behave!" says Robert, smiling at him. Dad's not even trying to make sense now.

"The course of treatment for this type of cancer is aggressive chemotherapy, and that's tough on people who don't have an already compromised immune system," says the oncologist.

"Ouch. Talk about adding insult to injury," Dad jokes. He and Robert both laugh. Susie rolls her eyes like a mom with two teenage stoners in her kitchen.

Susie chimes in, "We'll need to discuss this, but I know Benjamin's medical directive tends toward less intrusive treatments."

The oncologist ignores this human interaction altogether and says, "Well, this is up to you, and I should also let you know that if you refuse treatment, you'll need to go to hospice."

Hospice. What a funny word. It sounds like a cold house. "No, thank you very much. I am not doing chemo, and I am not going to a hospice," Dad says nonchalantly, like he's refusing half-and-half in his coffee. "I'll just take a check, thank you." He laughs at his joke. I want to laugh, but I read the room and keep stoic. But how funny is my dad?

I look at Robert for interpretation as Susie continues talking to Dr. Ratner about options. Robert leans over and whispers in my ear, "Doctors don't like it when their patients don't take their advice. Your dad cannot withstand chemo. Not anymore. But this guy doesn't want to hear that. But also, your dad doesn't want to go to hospice, which is where many people go to die."

I whisper back, "He's going to die?"

Robert tilts his head, purses his lips, flares his nostrils, and stifles tears.

"But wait," I ask everyone, "who's going to help him if he's in pain? Don't we need people who know what they're doing? Who's going to help him if he's at home?" Eyes rolling, Jake glares at me like I just asked him to take out the garbage.

Writing something on a clipboard, Dr. Ratner just says, with no feeling, "You will."

So that's that? Case closed? He's our problem now? Susie's face shows no sign of alternative routes, no secret measures that might change the course of all of this. Are we supposed to fight this? Or shout at the doctors? Susie and Robert are both so calm. Is this normal? Does this happen to people with AIDS, like, all the time?

Dad's eyes are glazed over like doughnuts. Is he getting any of this? Does he truly understand what's going on? I mean, I barely do, and I'm not hopped up on painkillers.

Finally, Dr. Ratner puts the chart down on the end of the bed and shakes Dad's hand. Like, *Pleasure doing business with you, so long buddy. Better luck next time.* He and the oncologist silently walk out without turning back.

I feel like I just got hit by a truck. But the room is still and quiet. Bad news doesn't come accompanied by loud cymbals crashing. It is awful and silent.

I hear a sniffing sound and turn to see Dad has started to cry. He gets it. Of course, he does. He looks at me as tears roll down his cheek. Robert goes to sit with him while Susie gets out her address book and starts making calls. She calls a nursing agency for an at-home aide. Jake gets up and comes over to me. He puts his hand on my shoulder. He's trying to comfort me, but it feels like trying to clean up a tsunami with a sponge.

I turn to him and just say, "We have to call Mom."

"Yeah. We do."

Across the room, Susie makes another call to order a hospital bed for Dad. "Yes, 210 West Rittenhouse Square. There's a loading dock on Twentieth Street. Apartment 1902." Then she listens and turns to Dad with a horrified look on her face. "Let's start with," her voice cracks and her eyes start to glisten, "let's say a month?" She says this as she and Dad stare at each other. Dad smiles with tight lips, nodding his head so slightly.

Susie finishes the call, and Robert puts his arm around her. "Tea, darling?" he asks.

"God, yes," Susie exhales. "Benjamin, cuppa tea?"

"No, thanks, my dears. I have sweet Dani and Jake here." He squeezes my hand.

We sit together. Dad cuts through our stunned silence, saying, "Sometimes the thing you fear the most actually does happen," and then he closes his eyes to rest.

The room is full of defeat.

Like a dead end.

Like we've already lost.

Like this room held no more solutions.

Downhill.

Sometimes the thing you fear the most actually does happen. And then what? Do you face it or run away? Do you build a fortress to keep it out, or let it invade and take over? How can you fight what is unstoppable?

27
"Cloudbusting"

After a stream of visits from nurses, social workers, and hospital administrators; signing papers, packing his bags, and rolling Dad down long hallways; waiting for elevators, then finally a quick ride in a transport van, we are back in his apartment. Wincing in pain, still buzzing from the drugs, Dad knows this trip home is something final. Perhaps there's relief underneath all this pain. Perhaps.

We no longer wear masks.

His double bed has been replaced with a single one with guardrails that does his sitting up for him. Dad winces as he folds into an upright position to greet his new home-hospice nurse.

"Hello, Mr. Silver. My name is Izzy." She extends a long, graceful hand to my dad and smiles a big smile. She speaks with a voice like dark, warm honey. Her hair is held behind her head with a yellow ribbon, and she wears scrubs with clouds and rainbows. She smells like soap and cinnamon.

"Call me Benjamin," says Dad. He raises his hand slightly to try to shake her hand. She gently meets his hand with hers. "Hello."

"What is Izzy short for?" he asks, resting his head back on a pillow, clearly tired.

"Isadora," she says.

"Beautiful," he says, closing his eyes.

Robert runs out to get groceries, and Susie is on the phone with a pharmacy.

"Hi, I'm Danielle," I say as Izzy begins to settle in, arranging her book and notepad on the table near the armchair she is making into her workspace.

"Hello, Danielle, nice to meet you." She is tilting her head, looking at my face like she's reading a book. "You have his eyes."

A kind stranger in my dad's bedroom. This robotic bed. Bit by bit, this familiar home changes. Quietly and immediately, pointing to a dead end. I stand in one place and barely notice that I've started to cry.

"Oh yes. I know. Here." She produces a tissue from what seemed like midair. She hands it to me. I blow my nose and dab my eyes. She nods. This is what happens. Beds fold, people cry, and nurses have hidden pockets filled with tissues. I get myself together and go sit next to Dad.

"Danielle," he says in a hoarse whisper. His eyes struggle to open for me.

"Hey, Dad. Want anything?"

"Oh, my sweet Danielle," is all he says.

Izzy sits down in the comfy chair in the corner, unpacking a bag with books and knitting supplies. She seems to know how to be in a room without taking up space.

Some music comes from the living room stereo. Robert is back. I think he put on Kate Bush, quietly passionate melodies. I hold Dad's hand, big and warm. His eyes are closed and he has a vague smile on his lips. Robert stands in the doorway and waves a silent hello, tilting his head.

"I like this song," I say, smiling and trying not to cry.

An hour later Jake returns from a walk. For a moment when he comes in from the cold evening, I see his face like he's twelve and I'm eight. He'd give me his gloves when it was cold out. I'd wear them layered around mine. For a time, he wanted to protect me. For a time, he smiled when he saw me. He used to put his arm around me when I got scared or hurt myself. He hasn't done that for a long time. But when he comes in, the layers of concern and comfort are clear on his cold red face.

I suddenly know he's not my big brother anymore. He's just my brother. And he's as scared about all this as I am, and he cannot protect me.

Dad calls the two of us to sit by his bed. He reaches over to the nightstand drawer, and I help him find what he needs. "The black book, there." He points to a small black planning journal. I give it to him. He opens it, putting on his reading glasses.

"Listen, kids, I just wanted to talk to you about some of my decisions." He is holding a list he'd made.

"What kinds of decisions?" Jake asks.

"What comes next."

I take a deep breath. I wonder if I need to take notes. I look around for a pen and paper, but Dad starts talking. "First off, I already have a will. Robert is the executor; Susie has medical power of attorney. Everything I own goes to you two. So, I trust you will work it out, together."

Jake and I glance at each other awkwardly, then we say in unison, "Sure." I don't know what else to say. How is anyone supposed to know what to do here?

"Second," Dad continues, "I don't want a religious funeral. I haven't been to a synagogue for years, and just, well, that's it really. No rabbis, no religion, no need."

"Sure," I repeat. My mind feels numb. Is Jake taking this all in? I look over and he's clearly listening intently, but I can't imagine he's not freaking out.

"Third, I want to be cremated. I wrote this in my will. Susie knows. I do not want to be buried in a casket. Got it?"

Cremated? We're talking about what to do with his body. It's like we hit a fork in the road and are bombarding down Death Avenue. To the dead end—not even figuratively. He is going to die and then we are going to burn up his body and be left with a box of ashes.

"Got it," Jake says, the words a strained whisper. It's rare to hear him show any weakness, but then again, I can't even muster a word, my voice lodged in my throat, like a cork in a bottle. Jake sits up straighter and clears his throat. "Do you want us to scatter the ashes somewhere specific?"

"You know, it's funny, I haven't even thought about that. I just know

I don't want to be buried in the ground." He smiles at me, then adds, "I'm too claustrophobic."

I can't help but hiccup a laugh and the tension eases in my throat. I get it, being buried freaks me out too, but so does the thought of an urn full of my father sitting on a mantel somewhere. If Amy were here, we'd grab each other's hands and shiver at the thought. She'd also have some good ideas about scenic places to spread a loved one's ashes, having traveled so much with her family. But then again, people in movies talk about their final resting place, and it's always a place they love.

"How about the beach?" I manage to utter. If ever there was a resting place, it's there. Especially for Dad. It's his favorite.

"Well . . ." He looks out the window, considering this, thinking hard for a long time, then finally saying, "I don't know, that might be a tough trip for me to make."

Is he joking or is it dementia talking? This is, like, super surreal, and my hiccup turns into a giggle. Jake is trying to hold back a smile too, and it's maybe the first time in a long time that we're thinking the same thing and wanting to laugh. We both instinctively stop looking at each other; cracking up right now would be way too inappropriate. It's not that I'm laughing at Dad, I am simply out of ways to respond.

I shove the laugh inside. "Don't worry about that, Dad," I say. "We can figure it out." We can wait to have this conversation.

Nodding, he lowers his head. Is he sad or did he forget what we were talking about?

"Do you want to rest? We can talk more later." The weight of this conversation is wearing all three of us down. Really, everything is in order. Of course, it is. My dad is the most organized person I know. He's even going to die neatly.

"Hey, why don't we order Chinese takeout from Mandarin?" I ask both Jake and Dad.

"Yeah, great idea, Dani. Dad, do you want anything?"

"Oh, Jakey, thanks. Maybe just the oranges." Dad says to Jake, who is smiling a little now. They always serve fresh sliced oranges after the meal there. Our weekly Sundays with Dad usually included a matinee movie then

dinner at Mandarin. All the waiters loved my dad there. And they always brought us extra orange slices because he'd eat a whole plate by himself.

"You got it," says Jake, who goes to the kitchen to call in our order.

"I can walk there with you if you want," I tell him.

"Bunny," Dad says, as he watches Jake walk out. "One more thing," he whispers.

"Sure, Dad, what is it?" I ask.

"Look out for Jakey. He's not as tough as you, and he'll never ask for help. But he's going to need you, just like you'll need him. Just do me a favor and be there for each other, OK?"

I want to cry and laugh simultaneously. "Sure. Of course."

Dad winks at me.

Jake and I get our coats on and walk out of the apartment. Neither of us speaks as the last few hours sink in. This isn't a dream. This isn't a nightmare. It's just life, and I guess death. And somehow, I finally feel like Jake and I are on the same side and it feels warm. Like his gloves.

In the elevator, I ask, "So, Mom?"

"Yeah, I've been thinking about that," he says.

"Maybe she'll be . . ." I start.

"Calm?" he asks.

I laugh. We both know she usually comes around, calms down, and thinks things through clearly, eventually. But at first, it can be messy.

"We should have told her before, Jake."

"Yeah, I know." He sighs.

I take a deep breath. "OK, maybe tomorrow?"

"Yeah, sure." Jake is staring at his feet, dazed.

I thread my arm into his. "Dad told me to take care of you," I say quietly.

"He said the same thing to me about you." He turns to me with a small smile.

I squeeze his arm tighter until the elevator door opens, and then I let him go.

28
"Landslide"

The next morning, I dial the dorm hall phone and ask for Amy.

"Hey," I say after she breathlessly picks up the receiver.

"Is everything, um, is, um . . . What's happening?"

"Everything is OK, sort of," I say without thinking.

"Really?" she says brightly, forcing me to realize the load of horse-shit I just uttered.

"I'm sorry . . . um, no. Not really, actually. He's back home." I fill her in with the past day's updates. "It's Friday, right? I think I will be here for the next while. I just don't know what I need to do to tell the school."

"I can talk to Ms. Davis later today if you want. And Mrs. Funk. Who else?"

We go through my list of teachers.

"What else?"

I pause. Take a deep breath in, "Has he said anything to you?"

She knows exactly who I mean, "No, he's not ready, Dan. I'm sorry. Want me to tell him anything?"

"No, I guess not. I mean, I don't want him to forgive me just because my dad's dying. That's too much."

"He'll forgive you, babe. If it makes you feel any better, I heard Derek got in big trouble. Headmaster Turner heard about the whole thing, apparently. Daria told me."

"Of course, she did; she should work for the CIA. Well, I guess we can be grateful for karma," I say flatly.

The whole scene with Derek and Marco flashes in my mind as we talk, and I feel a wave of shame pass through me once more. So many moments you long to rewind and play differently. Say better words, do better things. Be a better you.

"Well, if you talk to him, tell him I'm still sorry." I don't know how to make it better.

"If he asks about your dad, what do you want me to say?"

"The truth, I guess."

"The whole truth?" she asks.

"Yeah, why not? Oh, hey, what's up with Noah?"

"Oh yeah, we talked. He's a wreck. Like, he's all clingy, telling me he loves me and now he doesn't want to break up."

"And? Do you believe him?"

"I want to but no, I don't . . . Honestly, I think he just doesn't want to spend the rest of senior year being single. But I mean, come on . . . I'm better than that, right?"

I feel so relieved. I wasn't sure how I would manage to sound cheerful if she told me they got back together. "Yes. Hell yes. Good for you, babe."

"Thanks. You know, it's fine. I have so much more time to get things done now." Honestly, if anyone could replace romance with productivity, it's Amy.

"Stay strong, lady. And if you can't, call me." I say.

"Thanks. You too."

We say goodbye. I promise to call her.

Everywhere, right now, people are making mistakes.
Big ones or tiny ones. Known or not.
We mess up. Someone drops a dollar bill from their pocket,
or a glass shatters on the floor. Spilled juice, or a car wreck.

We misconstrue, misunderstand, misremember, or just miss
the mark, miss the turn, miss a call, miss a name, miss the
deadline, miss the show.
We sometimes miss, and we sometimes lose.
Mistakes cost us. Our friends, our health, our families. Ourselves.
If we listen to what each mistake can teach us, maybe we
grow a little.
Before anything makes sense, you have to bleed and feel
the searing interruption inside and out.

After lunch, Jake goes into the kitchen, and I go into the study. We each pick up a phone in different rooms to call Mom in California. It's almost ten in the morning there. We stay quiet as we hear ringing tones all the way across the country.

"Hello?" Mom says in her fast, impatient voice. I know instantly she's tired. Great start.

"Hi, Mom," I say.

"Dani? Is that you? I was just about to leave for a meeting. But what time is it there? Are you having breakfast? I haven't heard from you in so long. How's school?" She fires off each question without taking a breath or letting me answer.

"Oh, yeah, school is fine."

"Oh? What's wrong?" Crap. She's not really buying my vagueness. I take a deep breath. This is definitely going to suck.

"Mom, I'm here with Jake."

"Hey, Mom," Jake says.

"Jakey? Is that you? Are you visiting Danielle at Baxter?"

"We're at Dad's," Jake and I say at the same time.

"Oh?" She slows down a touch.

"Mom," Jake says, "we need to tell you something."

"Oh my God, what is it? Who's hurt? What happened?" She's gearing back up for the catastrophe. I hear her blood pressure rising.

Jake continues, "It's Dad. He was in the hospital. But now he is home."

"What? Why didn't he, or you . . . What is it? Is he OK?"

"Well, so, Mom, there are a few things we need to share with you. Are you— Can you sit down?" Jake says.

"What? Why should I sit down?" She's getting frantic. She should sit down.

"I think it would be a good idea," Jake says.

"OK, Jake, for God's sake, I'm sitting down! Now, what is going on?" Mom demands.

There's silence. He can't say it. I can't wait one more second.

"Dad is HIV positive, and he wasn't sick but now he is, and now, well, now he's pretty much in AIDS-land," I blurt out in one breath.

"AIDS-land?" She shrieks. I can almost hear her skull cracking. "Are you joking? Is this a joke?" She's starting to use her shrieky voice.

"No!" we both say.

"Sorry, Mom. We only found out recently," I say calmly, trying to make it sound less awful. As if that's possible.

"How could—? When did—? What?" Her panic sounds like anger.

"He told us about a month ago that he's HIV positive, but he wasn't sick. And in the past month, he's begun to have some trouble." Jake takes over for me, thankfully. "Just after Thanksgiving, he went to the hospital after having stomach pain, and it turned out he had pneumonia." I can't see Jake, but I wonder if, like me, he's realizing how much sooner we should have made this phone call.

"So, he went home to recover from the pneumonia, but then the other night, he fell and broke his hip. And this time in the hospital, they found that he has advanced stomach cancer," I continued.

"I see." Then there is a long pause, as wide as an ocean. "And why hasn't anyone told me about this?" Here comes the actual anger.

"Well, Mom," I say, "it unraveled really fast, and we didn't know what was going to happen."

"I guess too fast to call your mother, clearly." That sharpness in her voice starts to make my heart race.

"Mom," I say, "we just didn't know day-to-day how things would go. It's been up and down, and we didn't want you to"—I pause, then I say—"worry." She's right. We left her out. I felt just as pissed at Dad when he first told me that he was positive, and when I learned about Arthur.

"Well, I am sorry I'm just so much trouble that you couldn't even tell me about your father's illness."

"Oh my God, Mom, do you hear yourself?" Jake bursts out.

"Jake, don't," I try to intercept.

He ignores me. "Dad left it to us to decide whether to tell you. We didn't think there was anything to tell, but it snowballed quickly and now here we are, in Dad's apartment, and he's on morphine and has a broken hip and stage four cancer, so maybe, please, God, could you cut us some slack and stop with the blaming and finger-pointing."

"Jacob Michael Silver, stop talking to me like I'm a child," she snaps.

"Oh my God, Mom, we called to tell you Dad is dying. How did this conversation become about you?" Jake goes on.

"I don't know, Jake, you're the one who knows everything. Why don't you tell me?"

"Why bother?" He hangs up. I hear him clomp into the hallway and then the apartment door slams shut. Great. I hold the phone, terrified of the next bit. Somehow, I am the one left holding the phone, still in the room, trying to catch all the parts of her after they both explode. I never leave like he does. I always stay. I always clean up.

I put my ear back against the receiver. My mother's breath is coming in fast and shallow from across the country. She might be crying. I can't tell. After about thirty seconds, she speaks again. I'm hoping this is the part where she pivots to another emotion, hopefully one less angry.

"Danielle? Are you still on the line?" she asks quietly.

"Yes, Mom."

"Are you all right?" Her voice has changed. I feel my chest relax. I remember her generosity. It feels so confusing after her outbursts. But her voice is soft now, comforting.

"Yeah, I guess," I say.

"How is he?" She is still cold, but less angry. I realize this is eggshell-walking time, and I'm careful how I speak.

"We are trying to keep him comfortable. He's on a lot of pain medication," I say, quietly, honestly.

"Did he get high? He was always a lightweight with painkillers," she says, reminding me of the years they spent together, and Dad's silly stoned state.

"Yes! He was pretty spaced-out and funny," I say, relieved we are agreeing about something. Anything. I hear her chuckle.

"And is anyone else there with you? Helping you through this? It must be scary, honey."

"Susie and Robert are here. And a nurse. Her name is Izzy. She's very nice. She's a knitter."

She asks for a list of the doctors he's seen and any other medical info. She asks for Susie's phone number. She is calm, collecting and asking all the questions an adult is supposed to ask.

"OK, what do you need from me?" She sounds like the mom I know who can seriously take care of business.

"Um, I don't think anything at the moment."

"Right, well . . . I have this conference to run here next week, but I could fly back after that. Do you think I should come back?"

I pause.

Why is she making me decide? Say yes. It's OK to need your mom. Stop being mad at her and let her be your mom.

And now I begin to cry. Just the thought of saying yes to this question fills me with something vast and heavy I can't define. If I say no, then I won't have her here and I really actually do want her here, and if I say yes, then the bag of rocks is real, more real somehow than before. And she can help us hold them.

"Yeah, Mom," I finally say, relieved to just choose a path. "I just don't know what's going to happen. He's sick, and we're giving him medicine, and he may go into a coma and . . . I don't know." The words start getting swallowed into my throat.

"OK, sweetie. OK." She hears me. She hears my sniffles and my cracked voice. "I'm so sorry. OK. I'll look at flights and let you know my plans, OK? Are you both staying there?"

"Yeah," I whisper.

"Please send your dad my love and give Jake a hug. Just don't tell him it's from me."

I laugh and say, "OK."

"Do you need anything else? How about I call Baxter? They should know."

"Sure," I say. I guess it makes more sense for my mom to do that than Amy. I exhale, finally. "I love you, Mom."

"I love you too, sweetie. Take care and call me anytime. I'll look at my calendar and flights and get there soon." I guess it's worth some anguish to get your mom when you need her. Grown-ups can be full of surprises.

29
"Old Friends"

I think it's Wednesday. The weather isn't helping. It's three thirty p.m. and the sky is cold and white. Susie's gone out to run errands, and Robert is cooking lentil soup, making the apartment smell sweet and spicy. Dad's been asleep since I tried to give him lunch, which he didn't eat.

When he wakes up, he asks me to put on the CD of Bach's *Goldberg Variations*, and soft piano notes float through the apartment.

"Poor Arthur . . ." he says quietly, looking out the window.

I go over and sit with him. "Why do you say that, Dad?"

"If only he'd told me . . ."

"Told you what?"

"About this. I could have helped him. He was so alone, and that was just wrong. It wasn't fair to us, but it was so unfair to him. He thought he didn't need us around him, and he was stubborn." He starts to cry. I hand him a tissue.

"It's OK, Dad." I try to soothe him.

"No, Bunny, it really isn't." He screws up his face in frustration. "We all need each other. It wasn't right. Arthur should have had us by his side. We should have been there. We shouldn't have let his depression control things."

I put my hand on his boney hand.

"Wow, Dad, I didn't know Arthur was depressed. I always thought he was happy."

Dad grasps my hand firmly. "He was to a degree, but there was always a part of him that was out of sorts. Lost. He'd always had trouble letting people in."

"But what about you? He let you in, right?" I ask.

"Well, we had a long friendship, but there were a number of years, before you were born, that we didn't even speak to each other; we had such a big fight."

"Really? What about?"

"Well . . . he was mad at me for not coming out." He looks up to the ceiling, like a confession.

"He knew you were gay that long ago?"

"Yeah, he did." Dad smiles, remembering their connection.

"But why did Arthur care so much?" I ask.

"Well, he was frustrated with me. I mean, he'd already done it. He'd been out and paid the price for it most of his life: being called names, not getting hired for jobs he wanted, enduring the world's nonsense. He said I was living a lie. I had 'no balls,' I think is how he put it. And honestly, I thought he just wanted to make that decision for me . . ."

"He wanted to pull you out of the closet?"

"Yeah. For a bit. And we fought until we just stopped talking for a while. But then we made up."

"How did you make up?" I ask, hoping he might shine a light on how I could make up with Marco.

"He called to tell me he'd made a lemon meringue pie and asked if I wanted to come over." Dad smiles at me sideways. "I said yes, of course . . . You know I'm a sucker for lemon meringue."

"But what made him call you after all that time? Just pie?"

Dad laughs softly. "No, it wasn't the pie. We'd received some news . . . your mom and me."

"Bad news?"

"No, Bunny. The best news: a second baby. We found out about you." He looks at me with a sweet smile.

"Wait, me being born brought you and Arthur back together?" How did I never know this?

"Yup," he says smiling. "Your mom always loved Arthur and had no idea we were even fighting, much less why, so she told Arthur she was pregnant again. Arthur called me right up and as we ate pie together, he said, 'Think of the children, Benjamin, they need me. Who the hell is going to teach them how to swear properly or who Piet Mondrian was?'"

"So that was it? You just became friends again?"

"We never weren't friends, Bunny. We just paused. Like an intermission. It happens. Old friends are just, as Sondheim said, like a habit." Dad sighs, grinning at me. "And then, of course, he was madly in love with you from the very second you were born. He couldn't get enough of those cheeks. I never saw anyone else make him shine like the sun. You two were a sight to see."

I take this in. Dad looks at me and finally says, "People will surprise you, Danielle. They are imperfect and unpredictable and beautiful."

We sit in the quiet room. His words cover my tired, sore heart. When he closes his eyes, I find my journal.

We sit and watch. We walk; we drink tea and we wait.

For you to wake up.

Or to go back to sleep.

Or for more smiles.

We sit and wait, and we never know when it's almost about to end.

Arthur, you'd know what to do.

Dad in bed.

Won't eat. Eyes keep closing. Pain is immense.

You'd know how to soothe us, like you always did.

His arm is still connected to the tube. The medicine eases his pain.

Erasing his wholeness.

You would help us navigate, having gone through it yourself.

You would know how to make us all smile and be some semblance of grateful.

Dad keeps checking his watch to see the time.

Something in his control. Something familiar.

Eyes open, wrist twists, check the time, eyes close.

Downhill.

He is going downhill.

All we can do is feel gravity in slow motion.

Winding down.

The days are melting into one another. Dad wakes and sleeps and wakes and sleeps. Not much eating, and less and less talking. I've flipped through all the *Architectural Digests* and *Food & Wine* magazines here, and even opened my winter reading assignments. Jake has been focused on writing an essay for his junior seminar. Maybe Izzy can teach me to knit.

The phone rings and startles everyone. We're growing used to long blocks of silence. Is it Friday or Saturday? I think I've been here for five days now. Or six?

Jake picks up the kitchen phone and then comes to get me. "It's for you. It's Nicole Davis?" I barely compute what just came out of Jake's mouth. It's one thing to see your teacher at a grocery store buying bananas, but this is something else altogether. Ms. Davis is calling me? Here? How does she even know this phone number?

"Hello? Ms. Davis?" I say, not sure if I'm in trouble.

"Hi, Danielle. I hope I'm not interrupting anything."

"Uh, no. Is something wrong?"

"This is unusual, I know, but I happen to be in Philly at the moment. I'm heading down to Virginia to my aunt's house for the holiday, and I stopped here to meet some friends for lunch today. I hope you don't mind me calling."

Holiday? Vacation? Wait, did winter break already start? I struggle to remember what day it is. I settle on Saturday, so maybe the break just began.

"It's fine," I say, still unsure why she's calling.

"So, I wanted to see if I might drop off some things for you and say hello?" Teachers don't visit students off campus, do they? Was she bringing me work I'd missed, or reading, maybe?

"Oh. Thanks. Do you want me to meet you? I'm at my dad's apartment on Rittenhouse Square."

"That works," she says. "I'm about ten minutes away. Is now a good time?"

In a million years I would not call sitting around my dad's apartment while he slowly slips into a coma a "good time," but I say, "Sure," because I can't say all that. I tell her I'll meet her at the edge of the Square. I explain where the goat sculpture is near the corner.

Fifteen minutes later Ms. Davis walks up to the rounded stone bench, surrounding the bronze goat where Philadelphia kids always play. She's carrying a canvas tote bag from Baxter.

"Hi. How are you?" She sounds genuinely interested in my answer, but not cheerful. I don't choose to get into it all, so I just nod and say, "OK," still not sure why she is here.

She studies my face, looking for clues to what's really going on.

"What is today?" I ask her. We sit on a bench in the sun. It's warm for a December afternoon.

"You mean the date?"

"Yeah. I mean, is it Saturday? Did winter break already start? I think I left on a Thursday. Sorry . . ."

She takes a deep breath and looks a little bit sad. Is she feeling sorry for me because I am clearly a ding-dong? Eventually, she smiles and looks at me.

"It's Saturday, December nineteenth, the first full day of winter break. You left last Thursday, I believe. I spoke to your friend Amy a couple times. I'm headed to see my family for the holiday, so I was just passing through."

"Ms. Davis, do you know why I've been here? About my dad?"

"Yes, Danielle, your mom called the school. It's all right. I know."

She understands I've been keeping this a secret, and she wants to take a few rocks out of my bag.

"Is this normal for you? Like, a house call?" I sort of joke, and she sort of laughs. "I mean, you don't do this for every student, do you?" I don't know why she'd go out of her way to be so helpful. Am I going to have to repeat twelfth grade? God forbid.

"Not everyone, but I thought it might be helpful for you. I know having a sick parent is tough. And this disease is . . . Let's just say, I know what you're going through. I just wanted to be helpful."

"Well, um, thank you." She knows it's AIDS. My worry melts away instantly when I realize I'm actually talking to the coolest teacher in the school and she completely gets it. I don't quite know how, but I feel weird asking.

She takes out a folder from the bag and starts going through it with me: math assignments, English reading, physics labs. She tells me I can do makeup tests and have extended deadlines for term papers, so I won't be in jeopardy of not graduating. We even talk about my RISD application.

"Also, I know you'd planned to apply early to RISD, but if you're even thinking about other schools, I'd be happy to discuss it with you."

I have no energy to tell lies, so I spill out the truth. "I never sent in the early application. I haven't finished the artwork. I have a bunch of drawings in my studio at Baxter I was going to photograph when I get back . . ." My words tumble out like every suitcase I've ever packed, messy and chaotic. My eyes fill up and I can't hold this together anymore.

"OK," she says, politely disregarding the tears all over my face. "You might consider widening your search now though. Open up some more doors, give yourself more choices. Also, it's typical to have a safety school. Just in case."

Safety. What a thought. Just in case. She pulls out *The Insider's Guide* to *Colleges* and shows me that she's marked eight schools with good art programs. For the first time, a safety school sounds like a good idea. Safety sounds appealing.

"Danielle, can I ask you a serious question?"

I nod and say, "Sure."

"I know you want to be an artist, but I'm curious to hear what that means to you?"

I sit quietly for a bit before answering. "I think it's partly about creating a language with images that other people can understand even if they never meet you in person. Like how you can hear a piece of music and know instantly that it makes you feel happy, or sad, or angry, or whatever."

She smiles and nods. "I love that," she says. "It sounds like you want to connect with people. Use your art to communicate?"

"Yeah, I think so . . . Why do you ask?" Is this some weird pop quiz for kids who've missed school? Or does she think maybe I shouldn't study art?

"I guess I'm encouraging you to keep a bigger picture in mind for yourself. You can be an artist whether you go to RISD or somewhere else. I just wanted to say that to you. In person. And applying to college isn't something you want to do year after year, so why not widen your avenues of opportunity? Especially now?"

"Now?" I'm not following her.

She raises her eyebrows. "Danielle, you're going through something profound. This experience is likely to shape who you become. But I know you're smart, and I've seen how you observe and respond to what is around you. I'm just saying maybe don't limit your options. You can decide how this will shape you. You write the story." I smile and want to hug her.

"There's something else," she continues, "I showed Headmaster Turner your letter."

"Oh no! Wait, didn't you think I should work on it more?" Oh God, what happened to my studio? I haven't thought about it once. I never moved my stuff.

"You know what? I reread it and decided it was perfect as it was. All you. All your passion and determination, and I thought he should see it." She looks proud.

"Wow, thanks, so what did he say?" I ask, wanting to hear that he changed his mind.

"He said that when you get back, you should go speak to him. He's got some alternative spaces he's considering. It might require climbing stairs or smelling cooking fumes near the cafeteria, but he's open to finding a space for an art studio. Your argument got to him." She's grinning, pleased to be delivering me something positive.

I can't believe it. "So, that's good news." I smile back, my tears nearly dry.

"Yeah. It is." She smiles.

"I left everything in there," I admit, feeling like I've abandoned all my work, my brushes, my paints. "I guess they threw it all away."

"Oh no, don't worry about that. It's been safely stored."

I suddenly feel a wash of gratitude run through my veins. I think back to when Dad visited me at Baxter a few months ago. So much has happened since.

"Ms. Davis, did you know my dad was HIV positive when he came for Parents' Day?"

"I wasn't entirely sure. He seemed different from when I'd met him before, but I could see something in his face."

"You could? I mean, you know how people with AIDS look?"

She paused and nodded. "Yes. Danielle, we haven't talked about this, but my older sister passed away three years ago from AIDS. She'd been sick on and off for two years. In and out of the hospital. I know this roller coaster all too well."

"Oh . . . How did she . . . ?" I suddenly regret beginning that question, even though I still want to know how her sister got the virus. "Never mind, I'm sorry," I say quickly.

"No, it's OK. She had a blood transfusion in 1984. She was a hemophiliac and got infected before hospitals started testing donations from blood banks."

I imagine Ms. Davis in the hospital, getting ice chips, talking to doctors, and feeling as scared as me. "Wow, I'm so sorry."

"Thank you, Danielle."

"Is that why you're here? Because my dad is dying from AIDS?"

She smiles, raising her eyebrows in surprise. "Well, I don't like to admit to any preferential treatment, Danielle, but the truth is, I know this disease. And I know it can be a particularly lonely experience to witness someone you love disappear. So yeah, I wanted to offer you something . . . Support, guidance, warmth, I guess."

Her words ring in my mind with so much truth and wisdom.

She continues, "AIDS is unpredictable, and it's also so stigmatized, so I know you can't really talk about it. Especially at Baxter . . . I thought maybe having someone from your school community to even just acknowledge it could be . . . well, valuable to you."

She pauses until I look up at her. I honestly cannot form words in the face of this kindness.

"I haven't talked about my sister's death with anyone at Baxter, just so you know. I also haven't told anyone at Baxter what I predicted about your dad." She confides in me, sharing this secret, trusting me.

"I understand," I say, looking her in the eye. "Thank you for all of this, Ms. Davis. I know you didn't have to come here, and I just want you to know it means a lot. I don't take it for granted."

I look at the college book again, seeing the little Post-its sticking out, and then I wonder if Ms. Davis and her sister looked alike.

In my mind I multiply her story times my story times all the thousands, maybe millions of stories of people AIDS leaves behind. Broken. Devastated. Sad. Ashamed. Terrified. And I'm overwhelmed at the loss. Enormous and awful.

As she gets up to go, Ms. Davis puts her hand on my shoulder. "Take care of yourself, Danielle. Stay in touch. See you in January." Then she gives me a brief hug. She smells like lilies.

30
"In Your Eyes"

Dad opens his eyes. I say, "Hi."

His face slowly morphs from confusion to surprise to a soft, gentle recognition and relief, trying to communicate without the luxury of words.

Like a baby.

He reaches his big bony hands out to me, and I hold them to my cheek. They are warm and soft and wrinkly and his.

"Danielle, I'm so sorry," he says, tears starting to form in his eyes.

"Dad, it's OK. You don't need to be sorry. You didn't do anything wrong," I say, holding his hand in two of mine.

"But you don't deserve this. You should be out there, enjoying your life. Not stuck in here, watching me sleep. So boring."

"It's OK, Dad. I'm fine," I say.

"And your art? How's your art? Did you get into RISD? Did I give you the letter? Arthur's letter? You got it, right?"

I don't know what he's talking about. I know he's foggy, but I try to answer him anyway.

"I haven't heard yet, Dad. It's the end of December. I won't hear for another couple months."

"You'll get in. You have such talent."

"Thanks, Dad. I appreciate that."

"You always did. So joyful and so creative. I don't know where it all came from, but it just pours out of you and it's been . . ." He stops talking and takes a long deep breath before he continues, "It's been my greatest joy to witness you grow into this beautiful, kind, gracious young woman. Please know that. No matter what, please remember how much I love you . . . More than love you."

"I will, Dad. I know. I know," I say, holding his hand tight.

He closes his eyes.

Doors take you from here to there,
but sometimes the next door will simply disappear after you
walk through it
leaving no way to return
When the future seems sadder than anything you can
possibly imagine.
Because you will be forever changed, and it seems far worse
than it does better.

It's been days. I think it's Monday. Or maybe Tuesday? Every day seems to pass slowly then the sky is suddenly dark. The stillness is remarkable, soft, terrible. Music selections throughout the day help the time pass. We rotate through Sondheim musicals to Verdi operas to pop music that isn't for parties, music for watching someone go away. Izzy knits. I draw. Robert cooks, Jake reads, Susie writes.

Dad wakes up and softly groans. Izzy's sitting by the bed, gently holding his hands, as she and Susie speak quietly to each other. Susie checks her watch and then nods to Izzy.

Susie gets up from her chair and turns to see me watching them.

She takes a deep breath and walks over to me, "Come on, let's go into the kitchen and make some tea. Where's your brother?"

"He's in the bathroom."

"All right. Come with me," she says calmly.

We walk into the small kitchen, and her silence fills the room. Susie is not one to shy away from a difficult conversation, so her hesitation is obvious. She takes out the electric kettle she bought my dad last year and fills it up with water. She turns over the teapot from the drying rack and slips in two teabags. The bathroom door opens, and Susie is nodding to herself; she's been waiting for Jake to come out. She needs to speak with both of us. Jake comes into the kitchen quickly, not realizing we are both there.

"Oh, hey. Is there still coffee?" he asks, unaware of the waiting that's been done these past few minutes.

"Yes, darling. Here." She gets a mug from the shelf and fills his cup. As she hands it to him, she says, "Could you both have a seat? We need to talk." She pours the hot water into the teapot, then brings honey and spoons and two cups to the table. Why do I feel like we've been called into the headmaster's office?

"So, I think it's time to discuss next steps for your dad." She is looking at me. I wait and then glance over to Jake, who is also looking at me.

"What does that mean?" I ask them, as it feels more and more like they're teamed up and I'm being ambushed.

"Well, darling, your father isn't getting better." Susie says this like I haven't been paying any attention all this time.

"Yes, I know that. I mean, of course I know that," I say, irritated by this condescending conversation. Again, looking at Jake, who is looking at the floor. He is not surprised by this conversation. They've already discussed it before this, I can just tell.

"Right," she responds to my tone with some slight annoyance and pauses before continuing. "In these situations, the only option is to make someone as comfortable as we can. There will be no more doctors. No more visits to the hospital. No more treatments. Do you understand what I'm saying?"

"Right, he's not getting better. You JUST said that." My head is a little dizzy. What is she talking about?

"Dan, he's going to die really soon," says Jake, like a blunt young man swooping in with his giant stick. Subtle.

Susie takes a deep breath. "Now, darling, we need to give him more medication, morphine, which will keep him from feeling pain. But it will also, well, slow him down, bit by bit, until it's over."

"Until he dies?" I ask.

She nods, looks into her teacup, and a tear falls down her face.

"We're giving him something that will make him die? Is that allowed?"

"Yes. It's in his living will and it's what he wanted," Susie explains. I knew my dad didn't want a prolonged death. He used to tell us, "As soon as I start getting old, just push me off the top of a building." I always thought he was just being dramatic.

"How long is this supposed to take, this slowing down?" I ask. How many more times can I talk to him, hold his hand, see his eyes open? My mind races through a list.

"A day or two, maybe. It's hard to say."

"This is it? This is all we can do?"

"Yes, darling. I wish it were otherwise." She purses her lips.

I look at Jake. "Did you know this?" I ask him.

He stares into his coffee. "We talked about it yesterday."

"And so, this isn't a discussion so much as an announcement," I say, feeling rage pulsing through my neck and into my temples.

Susie speaks before Jake can say anything, "Danielle, your father left me in charge of his medical decisions. He and I spoke at length about this during his last hospital stay. I wasn't asking Jake's permission yesterday, so much as discussing how best to tell you. But you are correct: we are not discussing or debating this. It's already been decided. By your dad." She says all this calmly, but with authority. She is not going to let me get away with being an ass right now.

I still sit in rage, not drinking her fucking tea and not looking at my fucking brother.

"I know this is terrible and painful, and you've every right to be angry and sad. Just know that your father loves you, Jake loves you, and I love you. All your feelings are OK, and nothing is going to make this better. But if you need to scream, then scream. If you need to go throw rocks into the river, then do. If you need to cry, we are here. Your dad put me in charge so you and Jake wouldn't have to make this awful decision. And it is awful. Your dad is my best friend. Second to yours, my loss is immense here, but I am trying to follow what he wants. And he wants to end this pain and be at peace."

I nod. And nod. And nod. If I open my mouth, it won't be pretty. I just say, "Fine," and go put on my shoes and coat, grab my headphones and Discman, and walk out the door.

I press play when I get in the elevator. Dammit. Jake borrowed this yesterday and left his Peter Gabriel CD in here. I listen anyway. I advance a couple songs and "In Your Eyes" starts to play. I guess Jake's taste in music isn't a total catastrophe.

The cold air bites my cheeks as I walk fast up Walnut Street. Before I know it I'm on the bridge looking over the Schuylkill River. The cars on the expressway have their headlights on. It's foggy and wet and cold and sad outside. I wish Amy was here. I try to imagine what she'd say and realize nothing she could possibly say will change what is happening. And that's all I want. To change what is happening. But I can't. No one can.

This rage, this pain, is what must be fueling the people at those ACT UP meetings. It didn't have to be this way. It shouldn't be this way.

But here, today, there is no one to scream at. Only the river, which accepts my sobs and my grunts with its wide, cold rush.

How do I do this?

How do I do this?

How do I do this?

How do I do this?

Crossing the street back to Dad's building, I see, through the lobby window, a familiar green scarf wrapped around a familiar neck.

Marco.

I walk in and stand in front of him. His nose is in a book, so I wait for him to look up and notice me. I'm still scared that he might be angry; my heart races. Next to him on the couch are a big bag and a file box.

His head tilts up, seeing my black-and-white boots, then his eyes raise to meet mine.

I do a quick search of his face. Is he here to yell at me or give me a hug? At this point, I am both ready and completely unprepared for anything.

"Hi, Marco," I say. "What's, um . . . Hi. What are you doing here?" I say, unsure if I am supposed to talk or wait for him. Is he waiting for me to apologize? "I'm sorry, Marco. I really am." I'm biting my lip so hard I might draw blood.

Please, please, just look me in the eyes and understand I wish I could take everything back.

He's looking down at the box. I notice how his nose curves so perfectly. He's so beautiful.

Finally, he looks at me. "I'm sorry too, for not talking to you," he says. "That was immature. I guess I needed to process. But it wasn't fair."

"You don't have to apologize. I know I messed everything up, and I would understand if you could never trust me again." I've waited to say these things to his face ever since that day in the cafeteria. "I just hope you can forgive me someday for what I did."

"Yeah, it was bad. But on the other hand, I never had anyone stand up for me before. Not even the cool guys on the wrestling team stand up to Derek. They're scared of him. But you stood in his face and pushed back. It was problematic, to be sure, but also, you were kind of a badass."

"I was?"

"Um, yeah! I mean, outing me to the school was horrible, and for sure, you're going to have to help me with that until graduation, but I know you were trying to stand up to that guy. And by the way, a bunch of other people have now given him a piece of their minds. He got a shitload of Saturday detentions."

This feels like a dream. I nearly pinch myself, but then all of a sudden, he throws his arms around me. We hug for a long time, and it's like a warm bath.

He finally pulls away and looks me in the eyes. "I'm so sorry about your dad, Dani. How's he doing? Amy told me what's been going on. I should have called or come sooner."

"No, Marco, really . . . you had school. And I was an asshole . . ."

"Oh, I have this for you." He looks down at the box.

I'm confused.

"Did you bring me a puppy?" I ask, trying out smiling. Is it too soon to smile?

"No," he laughs. "So, last week was our final practice before break, and as I was leaving, I saw this pile of stuff by the dumpster at the end of the hallway and some of it looked familiar."

Why is he telling me about a pile of trash he saw?

"And, well . . ." He pauses to look at my face, like he's silently bracing me for bad news. "It was yours. From your studio."

As he opens the box, I see my pencil case, my watercolor paper, tubes of paint and brushes. My rainbow coffee mug, Arthur's laminated quotations, my copy of Rilke's *Letters to a Young Poet*, and some CDs.

He packed my studio for me. Ms. Davis said it was safe but she didn't tell me that Marco made it safe.

"You saved my stuff?" I say, shaking my head.

"I did," he admits.

"After what I did, you saved my stuff?"

"Yes." Now he smiles. It cracks my heart open.

"Thank you, Marco," I say, slowly taking his hand.

"You're welcome." He holds my hand back.

"Not to sound ungrateful, but I guess everything else was trashed, huh?"

Marco looks at me with confused horror. "Oh my God, no way! I got some help from the guys on the team, and we put everything else in a storage room down the hall. It's safe. I just brought this stuff for you to have while you're here. I mean, I wasn't sure what you'd want, but I just put things in here that looked special. And I told Ms. Davis I stored your stuff, since Amy told me you'd talked to her about the eviction letter."

"I can't believe you did all that for me," I say quietly, still in shock.

"I couldn't let them throw your studio in the garbage, lady. I'm not a monster!"

I throw my arms around him and hold him tight. A warm swirl of gratitude and sorrow stirs inside me; I find it hard to breathe suddenly. He hugs me back and puts his perfect hands through my hair to try to calm me down. I want to stay like this for a week or two.

"I'm so sorry. I'm so sorry," I mutter over and over into his chest.

"OK, lady, listen." He pulls back from the hug and stares me in the face. "I officially open my heart to you once again, but you and I need to stop saying sorry to each other. It's enough already."

"Deal," I say, still not wanting to let go.

He takes my hand and says, "Instead, we'll just fight when we need to and figure it out. But Danielle, believe me when I say this: I always want to be on your team."

I nod. It's not a demand. It's a vow. Fewer rocks in my bag.

I guess we never weren't friends.

31

"Addio del passato"

I hold his hand while he sleeps.

Veiny. Bony.

His fingers are the same shape as mine. Just bigger and older.

I assure him, "It's OK." Again, and again.

I whisper, "It's OK."

I think it's not really OK, but I have to tell him this. Am I lying? Should I lie?

"It's OK. It's OK." Again and again.

This is a one-way street I know. No U-turns, no second lane.

But I'd rather hold his hand than not. I'd prefer that.

It's OK, I think. Lying to myself to try to make it better.

You can let go, Dad.

It's OK.

I'll be OK.

The breathing slows down but it doesn't stop so easy.

We take shifts sitting beside him.

I want it over and I want it to never ever stop.

The chest
up
And down
up
And down.
He looks at me and smiles.
He starts to try to say, "Bunny."
But he doesn't make any sound.
I whisper, "I love you, Dad." Right up close to his ear.
His eyes close and his mouth curls up at the ends.
I say it over
And over
And over.

It's been two days since he started on morphine. Christmas is maybe today, or yesterday, or tomorrow. In here we aren't celebrating anything. I know Susie mentioned doing something. And Robert maybe was going to a party, but we're just here.

I set up Dad's desk with my watercolor set, and I've been on a steady rotation of drawing and painting, walking in the cold, and sitting by his bedside. Four visits to the grocery store, two to the pharmacy, six pots of tea, and three pots of coffee. We ordered too much lo mein and orange chicken, so Jake and I are living on the leftovers.

We take turns alone with him. Whispering in his ear, letting him hear our voices. While he goes away in the slowest motion there is.

I whisper, "Marco came by and we made up."

I whisper, "I don't want anything to hurt you anymore."

I whisper, "I will miss you every day, but I'll be fine. I'll be fine."

He keeps turning his wrist like he's checking the time. The ghost of that gesture, the shadow of an intention, now empty. And that's all this physical semblance is now, a shell of something former, someone healthier.

When it is Susie's turn, I hear her say, out loud and matter-of-factly, "It's OK, Benjamin. It's OK to let go. We're fine. Jake's fine, Danielle's fine. I know you want to hold on, but you can let go. We all love you and we're all OK."

I don't know how anything is going to be OK. I don't know how fine I will really be.

He hasn't opened his eyes for about twenty minutes. The bones in his face have gotten more defined, his skin, thin like tissue paper, drooping down, thinner, giving in. A balloon that's lost most of its air.

But his hands are still warm and soft.

I whisper in his ear, "Dad. It's OK."

Stillness. Did he hear me? Does he know I'm here? I just sit and hold his big warm hands. Waiting.

It is my turn to comfort him, let him curl up in my lap, so to speak. His chest rises and falls slowly.

Up and down.

Jake comes in and pulls up a chair on the other side. We both hold his soft warm hands.

Up

And

Down

"Remember when Dad wore his tuxedo for your friend's seventh birthday party?"

"Or how he told us to watch for bears when he went to the super-market?"

"That time when he stepped on that horseshoe crab in Cape Cod and screamed?"

"Remember how he told us he was gay but that he wouldn't go dancing down Spruce Street in a red dress?"

Remember.

Yes

Yes

Up

Yes

Down

Yes

Up

Down

And then, suddenly, there is no up.

I wait. I look over at Jake and he is staring at the floor. He hasn't noticed, so I say, "Jake, look. I think it . . . I think he . . . stopped."

We sit and stare and wait.

Then, Dad inhales a massive heave, an inward gasp. Like he's trying to revive himself. Trying to hang on. It is loud and impossible. Then, it goes out, slowly.

All I can hear is my heart pounding in my head.

And another gasp.

Four, five more times.

Another minute.

Another ten minutes.

By this time Robert and Susie are in the room with us. Watching this extravagant, excruciating finale.

Heave.

Silence.

Heave.

Silence.

And then more silence.

And he is done.

Done.

Go.

Gone.

The room is still full of our breathing bodies. And his still, motionless form. It just stopped moving up and down. He's just stopped.

I get up and walk to the bathroom, my legs suddenly rubbery. They fold down on the bathroom floor under me like a floppy doll's. And the tiles hold me, cold and hard while tears splash one by one.

32

"They Can't Take That Away From Me"

Susie and Jake call the funeral home to arrange for them to pick up his body. The four of us wait in the dark, quiet apartment. Susie makes lists. Robert straightens up the living room, saying, "God, I hate this part." I look at him and wonder how many times he's been through this.

I sit, staring out the window into the city, lights twinkling as most of its inhabitants sleep. "What are we supposed to do now?" I ask no one in particular.

"Well, sleep first, and then we'll need to plan. You and Jake discussed what he wanted, yes?" Susie asks. I am struck that she doesn't know this, but maybe her role was the hospitals, the medicines, the morphine. Not the aftermath.

"Yes. Well, kind of. No religion. And cremation. That's really all I remember," I say.

Jake says, "We never quite figured out where to spread his ashes. I mean, specifically."

"Yeah, I thought we did. The beach we used to go to in Cape Cod." I wonder why he can't remember.

Jake nods.

Sitting on the couch, Robert puts his arm around me and says, "Right, well, we'll get the planning committee together tomorrow after we've all gotten some sleep, OK?"

I look at the clock and do the math. It's almost ten p.m. in California. "Jake, let's call Mom." He nods and gets up to join me in the bedroom.

It rings only once before she picks up.

"Hi, Mom."

"Dani, honey? Is that you?"

"Yeah. Mom . . . it's . . ." My voice starts to crack, and Jake takes the phone gently out of my hand.

"Hey, Mom," he says quietly.

I sit there as he explains the last few hours. I hear strange sounds that aren't quite words. I'm glad Jake has the phone. I would try to comfort her, but I have nothing left. Jake is quiet as I hear Mom cry far away.

They're both so far away now, but at least I can hear her.

Jake stays patiently talking to her, all his usual irritation depleted. "No, Mom, it's OK. There's people here. We're OK . . . Yeah, tomorrow we will plan a memorial . . . Maybe on Sunday? Or Monday? Not sure yet, but sure, invite anyone you think should come. That would be good." Something softens in me when he's kind to her. It's a relief.

I hear more sounds from Mom, and Jake sighs from the exhaustion. "No, he's not being buried, Mom . . . No . . . Cremated . . . Yeah . . . Yes, we did talk about it. Yes . . . I don't know, Mom, we haven't gotten that far . . . Listen, I need to go, someone's at the door." There's no one at the door, but I put my hand on the receiver to take over and he lets go of it. Mom is still talking.

". . . And you know that there is a prayer shawl your grandfather gave him in a box somewhere and . . ."

"Mom, it's me. Listen, we're fine, just really tired. Let's talk when you're back. Have a safe trip, all right?"

"OK, sweetie. I love you so much."

"I love you too." I hang up the phone. On the bed where he once was, is now a collection of skin and bone and muscle with nothing inside. His face is a different color. All blue tones. Like a Picasso. His mouth is still open, frozen midheave. Frozen in that expression—surprised, or accepting.

In the movies, people die and then immediately they're in a coffin, or being buried, or scattered from an urn. In real life, a body remains, still. Until it is taken elsewhere. It just lies there.

But he is gone. Disappeared. Far, far away.

I'll keep the other parts safe. Deep down. With me.

Then there really is a knock at the door, and it's two men coming to take Dad away. Because it's a special hospital bed, they simply cover him up with a sheet, unlock the wheels, and roll the whole thing out of the apartment, down the hall, and into the freight elevator.

Eventually, everyone says goodbye, and Jake and I are left here. Alone in Dad's apartment. Neither of us can speak. We brush our teeth side by side in the bathroom. As it turns out, even after someone you love dies right in front of you, you still brush your teeth.

I lie down on the sofa under the afghan Dad always meticulously folded. Jake puts a pillow on the floor next to me and makes a bed there. Neither of us wants to go into his room. Not yet.

We leave the lights on. When I close my eyes, I see Dad's face.

Breathing up.

And down.

I wake up and my eyes are swollen shut. When I finally get them open, it all comes rushing back like a movie montage. Some mornings, you have to relive everything that's ever happened until you crash headfirst into now.

Jake gets up and takes a shower. I make a full pot of coffee because I could drink a gallon of coffee right now. Outside, the sky is ferociously blue. A cold sliver of wind comes through the window panes sending shivers up my neck. All that sun still can't make it warm. Jake comes into the kitchen, smelling like shampoo. He looks at the coffee brewing. "Right," he says, nodding small little nods.

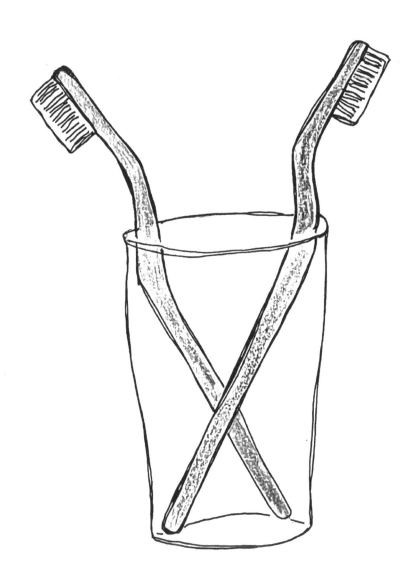

I call Amy at her parents' house. "Hey, it's me," I say quietly.

"Hi. How's he doing?" As she waits for a response, I suddenly realize I have no idea how to answer her. I take a sharp inhale to keep myself from falling apart, and she hears it. "Oh, babe. Are you OK? I can drive down tonight or tomorrow."

"Come tomorrow. We have to do all this stuff today. I think we're planning the funeral for Monday or Tuesday."

"OK, should I call Marco for you?"

"Nah, I'll call him now."

"Love you," she says.

"Love you."

I call Marco. "Dani? What's going on?"

"It's um . . . He . . . It's . . . He's gone," I utter, realizing I need to figure out a better way to say this.

I'm breathing in and out to try to stay calm, and it isn't working. I can't get another word to come out of my mouth.

"Are you . . . What can I do?" he asks.

I don't say anything. He waits a few seconds then says, "Want me to come over?"

"Yes," is all I can muster.

After lunch, a stream of phone calls from Dad's friends: offers of help and condolences.

Robert and Susie have been calling people this morning from Dad's address book. Now, Jake has gone to the funeral home to sign papers with Robert, and the apartment is humming with the sound of Peter, Evan, George, and Michael: four opinionated men. Kate arrives soon after and is clearly someone used to getting things done in a short amount of time. She reminds me of the stage manager at school. Very little bullshit and very much in charge. Marco and I sit on the sofa with them. We are all a team. Marco takes notes. Dad would appreciate this.

"Music, music, music . . . And coffee," says Evan, flipping through

Dad's records. "Dear Lord, is everything here classical music and Stephen Sondheim musicals?"

"Pretty much," I say, as I get up to go make another pot of coffee.

"Aha. Perfect!" Evan exclaims, pulling out an Ella Fitzgerald and Louis Armstrong record. "They Can't Take That Away From Me" plays. Dad loved that song. We pour coffee and George lays out some doughnuts. Planning requires calories and rhythm. Peter puts his arm around me and kisses the top of my head. He's not too talkative, but sweet as can be.

"OK, first things first," says Michael, spooning sugar into his coffee. "Venue?"

"Susie told me she talked to the Ethical Society, and booked it for Monday," Evan says.

Kate jumps in, "I know Dana there; we used to bowl together. I'll call and see if she's working that day. She knows stuff like where all the extra chairs are." She pulls out an address book and goes to the phone.

Wow, these people don't mess around.

Michael continues, "Next: flowers. Calla lilies, roses, or white tulips?" I love how he says this as though they are the only flowers that exist. Dad did love calla lilies, but Peter explains that they're not in season yet. "You can't rush the calla lilies, dammit." Regardless, Evan and George will find some in New Jersey. "You can find anything in New Jersey. Don't worry, we have a car," says George.

"Printed programs?" asks Michael. "I can do the layout on my Macintosh and bring a floppy disk to Kinkos, but can one of you pick them up?" I let them know that Jake and Robert already wrote an obituary, so we can use that.

"I'll pick up the programs from Kinkos," George offers.

My head spins, and I look at Marco, who seems enrapt with delight and wonder.

"OK now, the reception is here?" Michael asks as he looks around, and I can tell he's already rearranging furniture. "Tablecloths, napkins, plates. Gray, white, black, or blue?" he asks the group. "Show respect and celebrate, simultaneously, dammit." Gray and white, they decide.

"Good colors for winter," says Kate. The group nods in agreement. Peter is doing the weekend crossword and keeping up with this conversation thread, which is impressive. Michael moves on, checking through what occurs to me is a tried-and-true funeral checklist. "OK, drinks, prosecco or Bloody Marys. It's an essential decision. The drink sets a tone, dammit." All agree that prosecco is far too New Year's Eve-ish. Peter wants it more *All About Eve*–ish. They decide on Bloody Marys and vodka martinis.

I ask, "So, actual cocktails?"

They all turn to me smiling and simultaneously say, "Yes."

"What about music at the service? Dani, anything your dad loved? Aside from Sondheim? We are not playing 'Send in the Clowns' at this memorial!" Michael has strong feelings about this.

"Well, opera, I guess," I say.

"Which one?" Michael asks.

"He loved so many," I say.

"A requiem! That's what we need," says Evan, thrilled.

"Wagner. He loved Wagner," says Peter, not looking up from his crossword. I love how Peter can multitask this whole thing.

"Wagner was an anti-Semite!" Michael says emphatically.

"Michael, please, let's honor Benjamin's thing for Wagner, regardless of the hateful undertones," Evan replies.

"You can't deny the dead, dammit," George says, ending the conversation there.

It seems *dammit* is the decision gauntlet, the ender of arguments.

"OK, do we want food at the service, keep up blood sugar and whatnot?" asks Michael, to which they all pause, but I know the answer this time.

"No," I say without thinking. "People can eat at the reception afterward. It's not dinner theater, dammit." They all look at me, then at each other with raised eyebrows, slowly nodding in approval at my certainty.

I look over at Marco, who is enjoying this more than he wants to let on. I whisper, "Thank you, dammit!" He winks at me.

After we've made plans and set assignments, people start peeling off to get things done.

"OK, you go take care of yourself, Danielle. Go buy a dress, or a suit, or some combat boots . . . whatever you need. We're here. We are on the case." Michael hugs me.

"From the bottom of my heart, thank you!" I say as they file out.

Marco and I take a walk to get hot chocolate and window-shop in a daze. Christmas decorations still hanging up everywhere. I'd probably be feeling something different if I weren't a Jew who just watched her father die. It's all so bizarre that the world just moves on while my entire body is falling inward, folding and shrinking and wringing itself out.

Marco and I wander through the Wanamaker's shoe department.

"Michael asked if I want to speak at the service," I say, walking to the boot section.

"Right. A eulogy." Marco nods.

"*Eulogy* sounds religious. It's not supposed to be religious." I'm holding a pair of white patent-leather boots, half wondering if I could wear these to the funeral. Are they funeral fancy? Suddenly, I see my father's face, a mixture of disgust and outrage. "Absolutely not." I even picture him closing his eyes and slowly shaking his head.

"I think *eulogy* is still the right word. It's about remembering someone; it doesn't have to be about God. It actually means *good words* from the Greek," Marco says, touching a pair of furry pink slippers.

"How do you know these things?" I ask, looking at him in wonder.

"Oh, you know, you hang around, you learn. What can I say? Steel trap," he says, tapping his finger to his temple.

"OK, smarty pants, then how do I begin these 'good words'?"

"I think you just say what you feel. Say what you want everyone to know about him. Or tell him how you feel and why you loved him."

"*Tell* him? I'm pretty sure he's the one person who can't hear me."

Marco puts down the boot and glares at me.

"What? What's that face for?" I ask.

"Danielle Florence Silver, he can hear you." He's saying this like it's an obvious truth everyone knows except me.

"Dead people can hear us all talking about them?"

He takes a deep breath. "Listen, you can keep talking to him. You can decide to believe he hears you, and saying things to the people we love is, I don't know . . . I think it's important. You can keep parts of him inside you even if other parts are gone." I nod my head long and slowly.

"Like how I hear Arthur sometimes," I mutter.

"What's that?" Marco asks while taking a very close look at some blue suede oxfords.

"Nothing. I need to go write this thing."

"I know the perfect place." He leads me up an escalator to the furniture department, where we find a bright yellow couch.

I pull out my sketchbook and Marco reads brochures about mattresses.

After twenty-five minutes of silent writing, I pass it to Marco, who reads it slowly and looks at me with a serene smile.

"Dammit, Danielita. Don't change a thing."

"Really?"

"Yeah, but I think we need to leave this place. That saleswoman is looking at us like we're going to swipe a dresser."

"Oh, wait, Marco! I need a dress."

"A dress?"

"Or a suit? For tomorrow? Something black or gray or . . . I don't know?"

"What, from here? From Wanamakers?"

"Oh God no. Let's go to Zipperhead." I suggest Philly's motherload of punk clothing on South Street.

"Ooh, yes, then can we get cheesesteaks at Jim's?" He clasps his hands together, as though he has to convince me.

"Um, duh."

One black dress, a pair of white leather combat boots, and two cheesesteaks later, we get back to Dad's place. Jake is reading but looks up when we arrive.

"Dani, Mom's back tonight, late. I told her we'd have breakfast tomorrow."

"Breakfast? Don't we have to set up for the memorial?"

"The service isn't until eleven thirty. I told Mom we'd meet her at the diner at nine thirty. Plenty of time," says Jake.

"Yeah, well, Robert and those guys are all planning to arrive at eight a.m. to set everything up, and Marco and I told them we'd be there," I say. Doesn't Jake understand how long it takes to arrange flowers, dammit?

Marco says goodbye, and I make up the sofa like a bed again. We still aren't going into Dad's room.

I didn't think you'd be gone before I got to college
Or graduated high school
Or figured out what to do with my life
Or fell in love
Or got my own place where I could cook you dinner
Or maybe got married
Or had a kid
Or grew up some more.
I am definitely not in the least bit ready for you to be gone.
Not at all ready to carry this bag of rocks.
I thought you'd be around for more.
A bit longer, anyway.

33

"Dim All The Lights"

I shower early and put on my dress and boots. On top I look like a lady in a 1950s murder mystery and on the bottom, like Siouxsie Sioux. I think about how excited Dad would be to see me all dressed up, and it makes me smile, which feels super weird. In the bathroom, his toothbrush is still here. I throw it in the trash before I let myself think too long about it.

"Hurry up, Bunny. You needed to leave five minutes ago," I hear Dad saying. "Don't forget your lipstick, and throw away those tissues on the floor." He nags me, but then I hear, "You look fabulous by the way." Obviously, Marco is right. I can choose to hear Dad.

I put on earrings then grab Dad's big gold ring from the box on his dresser and put it on my middle finger. I need something of his to hold.

I tell Jake I'll meet up with him and Mom at the diner later on, and head out. Out in the cold, I turn the corner, and another moment passes, then another, that Dad is still gone. Each moment stings. Loss is like a snowball. More and more each moment builds on the last one. How does anyone move past all this growing grief? If this is permanent, how does this feeling ever end?

I walk into the Ethical Society, an old building a block away we rented for the funeral. The Ethical Society sounds like a fancy name, but it is not a fancy place. Dad liked the Society, which he called an all-purpose place for communities to explore humanity. My only memories of it include a dance class I took in kindergarten and a craft market my mom's friend organized to raise money to end apartheid in South Africa.

Evan greets me, "Well, hello, gorgeous. You dress up nice." I smile and give him a little bow. "You all right? Need anything?"

"I'm good. Thanks."

He hugs me. "It's a big, bad, hairy day; let us do what we can to support you, m'kay?"

I nod back. I take off my coat and hear a voice from behind say, "Well, hello, Liza, welcome to the Oscars!" It's Robert, standing over a table full of vases, waiting for flowers. We hug. "How are you holding up?" he asks, his face scrunched up in concern.

"Steady," I say.

"Danielle, he is so proud of you." Robert says this in the present tense, tears already starting to well up in his eyes.

"Thanks. He is proud of you too, Robert. I know he is," I say, throwing my arms around him.

"Stop it right now," he says as he holds me tight. "I cannot start sobbing at eight fifteen in the morning." The others set up chairs and move tables around while Donna Summer belts out of a boom box. It's never too early for poignant seventies dance music, I guess. Kate's in the corner talking to someone I don't recognize, and George is bringing in coffee.

Michael walks in and belts out in a Katharine Hepburn accent, "The calla lilies are in bloom again!"

"Finding calla lilies in December in New Jersey is some sort of torture. One place we went to had only three. Three calla lilies, can you imagine?" he says as we carry in buckets of them. Inside, Kate and her friend are pulling extra chairs out of a closet, and Evan is arranging some side tables.

Kate introduces me to Dana, who shakes my hand warmly and says "My condolences, Danielle. Your father and I served on a committee

together for people giving legal advice at ActionAIDS. He was such a good man, and I'm sorry for your loss."

"Thank you," I say, suddenly struck by all the life Dad lived that I wasn't even aware of. Her face tells me he's been a positive force in her life, and it makes me proud and terribly sad at the same time.

"You let me know if there's anything here you need, OK? You've got a good team here," she says looking over at Michael, who's started arranging flowers while dancing to the music.

Peter comes in with a notebook, updates me about the food for the reception, and George unpacks a set of programs. After most of the chairs are set up, I tell Robert I'll be back in an hour, and I go around the corner to the diner.

Jake is in a booth, reading a gigantic novel. Mom is late. I order coffee and French toast.

"So, are you going to say anything?" Jake asks me.

"Um, to who?" I ask as the waitress places a steaming cup of coffee in front of me and I pop open a creamer.

"At the service? You don't have to. I mean, if it's too hard."

"Oh, no. I have something I wrote," I reply, stirring my coffee. "Did you send off the obituary? The guys are already setting up flowers and chairs, and George dropped off the programs. Also, Peter called Schlesinger's and they're all set with our menu for the reception at Dad's place after."

Jake looks at me.

"What?" I ask. "Did I forget something?"

"Um, when did you turn into a grown-up?" he says to me, with a curious grin.

I smile, about to thank him, then I hear Mom. "Jakey! Dani! Hello!"

She is wearing a long plaid coat and a big black hat and holding bags like she's been shopping. How does she look like she's already been shopping and it's first thing in the morning? She hugs us and gives three side kisses, like in Paris.

Jake and I are mostly quiet while Mom adjusts herself and starts handing out gifts from her bags. A sweater for Jake, a pair of giant vintage

Audrey Hepburn sunglasses for me. Mom is never empty-handed, that's for sure.

"So! I got in two hours late and Charlotte picked me up and brought me to her place. The flight was awful. A screaming baby a few rows back from me, and the food was horrific. Luckily, I brought my crackers and salami." Mom's always been proud of her travel snacks. Used to drive Dad crazy. "A purse full of nosh," he'd call her handbag.

All this aside, it feels like she's acting like this isn't a weird, sad day. Could she be trying to avoid the obvious or just wanting to brighten us up? She asks Jake about college and me about Baxter. I eat my French toast slowly. We don't have a lot to say, so she fills the space with stories about San Francisco traffic, dinner parties, local politics, and her work. Eventually, she pivots to today's expected guests. So now I know she is entirely aware that today is Dad's funeral, but for whatever reason, she is not sliding into place with us on this. She is holding her own and doing, I guess, what she needs to do, which, right now, is talking. She lists all the people she notified about the funeral. Old friends and neighbors, distant cousins, Dad's old law partners. I guess anyone can come; it's not like there's formal invites or applications.

Application. Oh, crap. It's December 27. OK, there's still time. Focus on this. Focus on now.

"So . . . I need to get going soon, Mom," I say. I know who I need to be with right now and they're not in this booth.

"OK, honey. You go. Let me know if you need anything at all." I put my coat on and lean in as she gives me a kiss.

I step outside, put on my new sunglasses, and talk to Dad in my head. "I know she's trying. You just always organized things. It must be tough for her, all of this."

"Don't worry, Bunny. Just remain calm," he says inside my head.

Back at the Ethical Society, everything is set. There are calla lilies all over the place. Robert and the guys are all busy and sweet and keep stopping to see if I'm OK. The more they ask, the harder it is to lie.

People start arriving at ten forty-five. Robert tells me to go stand at my chair in the front row next to Jake.

"What's going on?" I ask as we sit.

"The line," he says.

"What line?" I turn to see that a line of people waiting to talk to us has already formed.

A person leaves behind so many living, breathing echoes. Life's footprints.

I meet men in suits who used to work with Dad at his law firm, men in leather jackets, academic lesbians, and drag queens in black. I greet some of the activists I saw at the ACT UP meeting, some old family friends, and some Jewish relatives I haven't seen since my Bat Mitzvah four years ago. One by one, they shake our hands or offer gentle hugs.

I remember Arthur explaining that when you're having an art opening, you have the same conversation over and over, and all anyone really needs to hear from you is "Thank you for coming." He said to make each person feel like your special favorite. It's not that I don't appreciate them being here, I just go into autopilot.

Then, suddenly, Waverly is standing before me, all splendor and sparkle, wearing a pillbox hat with a veil. My father would have adored her ensemble. She opens her enormous arms like she did last summer at Arthur's unveiling, embracing me. "Honey, honey, honey. Dear, sweet Danielle. I'm so sorry. Your father was a treasure. A delightful, wise, tidy, and honest-to-God mensch. May his memory be a blessing, my dear." My head lays on her big muscular chest. I breathe in all that love and perfume.

"Thank you, Waverly," I sigh. "You are a treasure too. And may I just say, your hat is divine." Why not say it now?

She holds my hands and says, "Ugh, my God, honey. You're his girl, all right. OK, don't let me hold up this line. I'll see you later. Remember, he's always here." She places both her giant hands on her heart.

Once the room is full, Robert asks everyone to find a seat. Jake speaks first. He tells a story about Dad bringing us to the opera when we were little kids. I'd forgotten most of that day except that my shoes were too tight. But Jake told a story of a parent opening his kids' minds and introducing them to history, mythology, justice, and beauty. As he finishes and comes down to sit next to me, he gently elbows me, "Ready?" I bite the inside of my cheek to remember this is real. This is happening. I clutch my sketchbook and walk up to the microphone at the front of the room.

"Hi. I'm Danielle. I'm Benjamin's daughter. Thank you all for being here."

I glance over at the big urn placed on the table beside his photograph.

I take a deep breath until my chest opens up. Here goes. I read aloud from my sketchbook:

I've never known life without my dad. Without his hands and his brain and his love. My dad always rooted for me—when I was a kid playing kickball, or later, when I started making art. He always wanted me to be happy, to be curious, and to be kind.

In art class, I learned to approach everything in steps. Pull it apart and deal with it, piece by piece. See big shapes, then smaller shapes within them, and make sense of how to put the picture together. So, now I'm pulling apart my dad's death. I'm figuring out what I have to let go of and what I get to keep.

What is a person? A person is a body. The flesh, bones, blood, hair, those hands, and that face, his voice. Only his. The space he occupies. His bald head and loud sneezes. His pointy nose and tall upper lip. His dark eyes. His hands. The way his long arms wrapped me up, made me feel safe. All this has vanished right before my eyes. Before all our eyes. The body cannot be recovered—the withered, sick, frail, and failing physical body. We all lost this part of him.

A person is also a mind. Thoughts, ideas, opinions. I know the lessons he taught me: How to maintain order in a kitchen; how to listen to music, voices, and even silence; how to remain calm; how to take in beauty when you're lucky enough to be near it. How to see your options, even when

things feel hopeless. How to find a path, even if it's murky.
And how history shapes us and helps us to see the big picture
and organize it as needed. I will bring these lessons with
me every day. It's my job now to keep them safe.
And finally, a person is a heart. Dad taught me how to
forgive, how to be good to others, how to be respectful.
And he taught me how to be brave about who you are and
what you want. How to apologize—not with humiliation,
but with love and generosity. How to be honest with
yourself and the people you love. How even if you mess up,
you can clean up. I get to keep these lessons inside.
I'm learning how we remember a person. We keep what
we love with us, and when we need it, we bring to the
surface—we keep on living with them, some part of them,
always.

My eyes lift to the people in the silent room. There is no applause
at a funeral. But I don't want applause. Seeing all these faces reflecting
on my words, sharing this moment of sorrow, that feels like what ought
to happen now. There is something unusual in this room, a beauty he
would have relished, I think. Dad fills this space; these people make
him less absent, less gone.

I sit down, and Jake puts his arm around me. I can't remember the
last time he did that. It helps. It reminds me of Dad.

After a few others speak, Susie invites everyone to the reception at
Dad's apartment. People come up to us, shake our hands or hug us, and
tell us how they'd known our dad. I want to know everyone, and I also
want to go take a nap.

Amy stands beside me and, when no one else is around, looks deep
into my eyes and says, "Good job, Dan. Your dad has always been so
proud of you. Also, this is all so well organized." This was high praise
from her.

"It was a team effort," I say. "Ask Marco."

Marco nods and says, "These people are Olympic-level event

planners. I mean, they know what they're doing . . . And the calla lilies are perfect, dammit."

He throws his arm around me and holds tight.

"How did I do? Good words?" I ask him.

"Great words."

Behind us, Robert and the guys sweep through picking up programs and folding chairs. Susie gives a vase to my mom, who smiles. I watch them embrace.

I wish you were here, Dad. You would have loved it all.

"So, this is the food part?" Amy asks in the elevator.

"Yeah. Death makes Jews hungry," I say, sort of half serious, looking around Dad's apartment, crowded and solemn.

"Death makes everyone hungry," Marco corrects me.

"True. I'm starving," says Amy.

"So, are we celebrating? Or mourning?" I ask them quietly because I'm not really sure what's supposed to happen here. "Should we be quiet and crying? Or should we be sitting in a circle talking about him?"

"No, Dani, you're fine," Marco reassures me. "No circle. I think we just gather, and people talk and meet. All the remembering doesn't need to happen in the next two hours."

"Right." I nod, as it hits me again that Dad will still be dead tomorrow.

We walk into Dad's apartment, and it's already full of people. I wander around the room. Everyone touches my arm or gives me slight hugs to offer words of comfort.

A thousand conversations go something like this: "Oh, Danielle, hello. I'm (fill in the blank). I knew your dad from (fill in the blank), and he was such a wonderful person. So (kind/thoughtful/helpful/smart/such a good cook) and I'll always remember him. You look so much like him."

I just can't digest most of it. Not all at once. After two hours, I finally sit down in a corner. Mom comes over and sits next to me. She smiles and says nothing. I close my eyes and take a deep breath. Acting like a grown-up is exhausting.

"You need anything, sweetie?" She gently rubs my shoulder.

"I'm tired," I say, wishing I could lay my head in her lap. Wishing I was a kid again and she could make everything better by baking blueberry muffins.

"He'd have been proud of you," Mom says. "He always was, and he always will be. You can say a lot about Benjamin, but there was never any question how much he loved you." Her words are almost as good as a lap. I'm glad she's here. "You want to come stay with me at Linda's tonight? There's an extra bed," she says, sweetly. It occurs to me how my parents complemented each other. Like blue and orange. Her optimism, his skepticism. But tonight, I just need to sleep, wrapped up in one of Dad's polos.

"I'll stay here. Amy's going to sleep over. I'll call you tomorrow though."

She gets herself together and tours the room saying goodbyes.

By four p.m., most people have left. Robert and Susie and a few others stay for an "after party." I take off my boots and sit on the couch with Amy, listening to the conversations swirling around me. I don't have energy to do much more. I feel like I'm on a merry-go-round but stuck in the middle: all the horses painted gold and silver and red are rising and falling around me, and I'm just staying in one place.

Finally, after everyone is gone, Jake, Amy, and I put the last dishes in the dishwasher. We wipe off the table and throw the cloth napkins in the laundry. We set up the coffee maker in total silence. Dad always taught us that doing chores now makes later so much more pleasant. None of us have any words left. Jake flops down on the sofa in the den; I pull several photo albums from the shelf and sit between him and Amy.

Each page has half a dozen color photos from Cape Cod vacations. Jake and me in matching bathing suits, running down the dunes. A sunset over the bay. All of us on the porch eating lobster and clams. I open another album: Dad's parents on their wedding day. Dad's grandmother, taken by a studio photographer, soft lighting, looking like a silent-film actress. I pull a few photos out of the book to bring to Baxter with me. To hold them close.

Moments flowing backward in time.
All these lives I cannot see made me possible.
We come from people we will never know.
You're with the rest of them now.
Each day you'll fade
as my memory forms and reforms
and merges with these photographs to become what was,
once, you.

34
"You'll Never Get Away from Me"

Your veiny hands,
the mechanical bed,
the face masks,
the blood.
What do I do with all this stuff in my mind?
Remnants of moments, painful and true.
Where do these thoughts go now?
New Year's Eve 1991
Saying goodbye to this palindromic year.
The whole city is still.
Another step away from this year,
another step away from you.
Another moment you are gone, still, and I am here, still
Wondering where you went.
How long will I wonder?
How long until your being gone makes sense?
I actually hope that day never comes.
I want your life to make more sense than your death.

After coffee and a shower, Amy tells me, "It's New Year's Eve, and yesterday was heavy, so we're taking you out. Marco's on his way."

I look out the window hearing wind wheezing, but the sun is bright. They won't tell me where we're going.

"Just come on!" Marco and Amy chirp in unison.

Outside in the bright cold morning, we walk north, toward the Benjamin Franklin Parkway, the big avenue that looks like the Champs-Élysées in Paris. We talk about the future, each of them locked arm in arm on either side of me. Right by my side.

Amy tells us she got in early to Berkeley and wants to maybe go into public health, government, or law. Marco is still applying to Philly schools, but he is also applying to NYU for film school, which he hasn't told his dad yet.

"And you, Dani?" asks Amy, always the pusher.

I sigh, hard. "I obviously want to make art, but I also want to, I don't know . . ." I take a moment to think about what I'm trying to say. "The world is such a mess, and I want to help make it better. And to work with other people who want to do that too." We keep walking, breath puffing out of our faces. "I can't walk away from all this awful stuff and make art in a dark lonely basement. It'd be like sticking my head in the sand. I can't just sit in the negative space."

"Negative space?" Amy asks. "That's an art thing, right?"

"Yeah. It's the space around the main subject in a picture. Usually, it's the background, I guess."

We stop at a café to get warm coffee, as much for our hands as for our bellies. Amy and I find a table by the door where it's still cold but a little less windy. The line wraps around our table as people pack in to warm up. Marco waits in line, orders our coffees, and returns to the table.

"OK, the negative space is the background?" asks Marco, handing us our coffees. "So, what's positive space in art?"

"Well, what's positive is the main thing in the picture, like the main character of the story. It's the object you're focused on. Like a person or a tree. The subject. The main character. The negative is all around, behind that main thing." I sprinkle sugar into my cup and place the lid back on, swirling it around.

"So, what, you feel like you're in the negative space?" asks Amy.

"I mean, in a way . . . I guess we each consider ourselves the main character of our own lives, but when I think about myself, it's like I've always sort of been hiding. Maybe that's why I've always wanted to just sit in a studio, alone. No one to notice or judge me for having a gay dad, or anything else," I say louder than I would back at Baxter.

"You just wanted to be in the background? Maybe it's easier?" Marco asks.

"Right," I say, noticing a girl staring at me from the next table. She wears a yellow knit cap with a pom-pom and mittens that look like ladybugs. She's probably eight years old. Two pigtails. Wide eyes. Staring.

"You want to step into the front and take up some space," says Marco. "That would make Benjamin proud. But more importantly, maybe it would make you happy?" He notices I'm not paying attention anymore. I am still looking at the girl.

I finally smile and say, "Hey."

"Hi," she says and gives a small smile back.

"Do I know you?" I ask. Maybe I babysat for her once?

She shakes her head, still staring.

I take a sip of my coffee, wondering why she's staring.

When I look up, she's standing right next to me. Marco smiles, checking out her hat. Amy starts looking around, wondering why an eight-year-old girl is all alone in a café.

"Did you say your dad is gay?" she asks me with no hesitation.

"Um, he was, but yeah. My dad was gay. Yes, I did say that." I swallow after saying this, wondering when I'll get used to Dad being in the past tense.

"My dads are gay too," she whispers and then quickly tilts her head toward two men standing in line.

I laugh, quickly putting it together. "Oh, wow, that's awesome. I'm Danielle!" I say and put out my hand to shake.

"I'm Chloe." We shake hands. She smiles. Major props from a third grader.

"Do they make you listen to their music?" I say quietly, like we're telling secrets.

"Oh my God, yes! Papa likes disco dancing music, but Daddy only listens to boring classical music and show tunes from a million years ago." She sits down in our extra seat and takes her hat off, twirling her finger through her curly pigtails.

"Yeah, well, that sure doesn't change, but you know what?"

"What?" she asks eagerly, leaning in closer to me.

"One day you might just be weirdly glad they made you listen to their music. I know way more music than my friends do." Amy nods and smiles.

Suddenly, her dads are standing next to our table. They look like a nice couple, one with wavy grayish hair and a big smile, the other with wire-rimmed glasses and tight dark curls. "Hey, Chloe, someone took our seats!" says the dad with glasses.

"Sorry," Chloe says not sounding sorry at all.

"Hi," says the dad with gray hair, "did you make some new friends?"

Chloe rolls her eyes. This kid is a pro.

"Hi!" I say, "We were just bonding over having gay dads," I say as loud as I can. "I'm Danielle."

"Oh, terrific. I'm Glenn," says the one with gray hair and a giant smile.

"Peter," says the other shyly. I bet he's the one who likes classical music.

I stand up and shake their hands. Chloe seems like one lucky little kid. "Hey, we're all warmed up, why don't you take our table?" I say.

"Yes!" Marco and Amy jump up to give them our seats.

"Well, if you insist," says Glenn. "That's very kind of you."

Before we leave, I lean over and whisper to Chloe, "Having a gay dad is like a superpower. Trust me."

As we walk toward the door, I hear Peter ask Chloe, "What were you talking about?"

Tonight we are at a New Year's Eve farewell dinner Mom planned before she flies back to San Francisco. Mom's friend Ruth is cooking risotto, and I spend most of the night in the kitchen with her. She's this cool woman who works for the Federal Reserve and who's telling me all about how she's going into politics.

"I just got tired of listening to one dim-witted, white-collar idiot after another," she says, sipping a giant glass of wine, as she stirs a risotto.

"But did you feel that you needed to, like, have more of a political background?" I ask.

"At first, sure. I thought I needed to be a lawyer or, I don't know, a political science major at least, but then it occurred to me, you know what? I just want to make the world a little goddamned better than it is." She chops fresh oregano vigorously and hurls it into the pot while taking another gulp of wine. "I can put a sentence together, I know how to talk to a stranger, but more importantly I know how to listen." That's funny because she's doing all the talking, but I'm hanging on her every word. Without asking, she hands me a block of Parmesan and a grater and points to an empty bowl.

"Those assholes in Congress aren't sent from God, and most of them aren't even that smart. And listen, I think there's going to be a whole new generation of leadership, starting with us, and then we'll have girls like you, turning into smart women who can get into positions of power and undo some of the crap these fuckers have gotten us into." She stirs the pot like she wants to murder it. I grate the cheese.

"I totally get it," I say. "I mean, I don't know if I want to go into politics, but this year has been . . . well, eye-opening."

"Oh shit, of course, babe," Ruth says. Dropping the wooden spoon into the pot to give me a hug with both arms.

"Yeah, I mean you never think when you're a kid that your own government wouldn't want to help people dying from a disease." She listens to me, holding both my hands.

"Yeah well, the US government holds on tight to some really old stinking bullshit," she says, squeezing my hands. Ruth is nothing if not vivid.

Mom comes in and rushes over to the risotto. "Oh my, Ruth, let me help you," she says, rescuing the spoon and the risotto simultaneously.

"Laura, you've got a great kid here, you know that?"

Mom smiles at me, "I know, Ruth. I sure do."

The apartment is still how he left it, mostly. Our bags exploding all over the den are the only evidence that Dad is no longer here. He'd never stand this level of mess for any sustained period of time. Jake and I plan to come back during spring break, take stock of everything, and start selling, donating, or storing it all.

In his very neatly organized closet, I find a framed photo of Dad with me and Jake on his lap when we were babies. I put it in my bag, wrapped in one of his polo shirts. In the kitchen, the fridge was emptied by someone wiser than me. It's almost like he's on vacation.

Dad's cassette tape collection is slowly collecting dust on the media console, so I grab some things I recognize, including *Bach: The Goldberg Variations* by Glenn Gould, Miles Davis's *Kind of Blue*, and *Gypsy*, the original Broadway cast recording with Ethel Merman. Some familiar tunes for my travels back to the other side of the river.

I look through Dad's desk for an envelope to put all the photos I pulled last night. I find a small stack of envelopes and underneath it, a sealed envelope with a Post-it written in Arthur's handwriting:

BEN— TELL HER TO KEEP EXPLORING. —ART

What is this?

The buzzer rings. It's Mom. She's come to say goodbye on her way to the airport.

I put the envelope into my sketchbook to look at later.

Jake and I meet her in the lobby. Mom hugs us both at the same time, smushing our faces. Jake's unshaven cheek scratches me, but it's actually nice to be so close to him again, even for a moment.

"I love you both so much," Mom says in a singsong way. I look at my mom and my brother. "I love you, Mom," I say. "I'm sorry if you felt left out of all this stuff with Dad. We just didn't know the right thing to do, and then everything happened so fast. And Dad didn't know what to do either. He wanted to leave it up to us, and well, we didn't know what we were doing." I spill all of this out, finally. It's been in there for so long, under so many other layers of fear and worry and uncertainty.

"Oh, my lovely girl." Mom hugs me again, then looks at us both and does that thing parents sometimes do so magically when they stroke our cheeks, petting us like kittens. "Thank you, and I understand. For the record, you don't need to take care of me." Jake is looking at Mom, with a small, unexpected smile on his face. "Not yet, anyway!" she cracks, smiling. "Check back in on me when I'm ninety!"

Jake walks me to my bus. We haven't got too much left to say to each other, so it's a quiet walk through a cold rainy afternoon. At the station, he hugs me.

"Stay in touch, OK?" he says into my ear.

"Will do," I say. We look at each other a little longer than usual. It feels good. He has Dad's eyes too.

We'll look after each other. We promised, after all.

On the bus I open my sketchbook and the letter falls into my lap.

BEN— TELL HER TO KEEP EXPLORING. —Art

I open the envelope to find a letter I've never seen.

Arthur Dreyfus
1013 Clinton Street
Philadelphia, PA 19107
December 1989

Dear Sir or Madam,

I am writing to offer my recommendation of Danielle Silver, applying to attend your college. Due to personal circumstances, I am writing far in advance of her deadline, so forgive me if this letter does not completely answer all your required questions. There is no doubt, however, that I have the greatest regard and belief in Danielle as a student, an artist, and a young woman.

I have known Danielle since she was a child. As a close friend of the family, I know Danielle to be a kind person, a passionate student, and an artist of the highest caliber. I believe she will excel in your school, as well as become a committed, compassionate, and constructive member of your school community.

She has always been an explorer—interested in form, color, and all matter of materials. From quilting with her mother to cooking with her father, Danielle brings an artistry to everything she does. As a professional artist myself, I have always offered her my guidance, support, criticism, and advice. I would tell her stories of artists and how they unfolded their careers, how they developed their work. I encouraged her to look and absorb. I believe she has taken this advice to the deepest part of her own heart, and this is how she walks through the world.

Whether she too chooses art or another path, I can say with true conviction that this young woman is a truly remarkable person who will make the world a better place.

This letter does not have a specific recipient because I am writing it far too early in her process. I may not be able to write another version due to health complications, but I made a promise to her to write a recommendation, so I sincerely hope you can accept this. Please know that if it is included in her application, then your school would be extremely fortunate to have her. I trust her and know she will find her place.

Sincerely,

Arthur Dreyfus

35

"Brass in Pocket"

Winter makes the campus nearly black and white.
Every time I sit down for a class, your death comes back.
Your hands, your eyes, your breath.
I'm trying, but most of the time, I am weary.
I keep looking for a note to tell me you've called.
I keep forgetting, then remembering, over and over.

After class, I meet Marco at the gym entrance. He's holding a big jangly set of keys. He smiles and raises his eyebrows, "Come on." We walk through the gym, past screeches of basketball sneakers, and into some back room I never even knew existed.

Down another small hallway, Marco searches the keys he borrowed from his assistant coach. Unlocking the door, he says, "Here are your babies. We literally rescued them from a dumpster and kept them safe for you." I follow him into the room, as he pulls a string from the ceiling to turn on a single bulb—and there they are, stacked along the wall.

"Wait, Marco, you did all this when you were mad at me?"

"First of all . . . you're welcome." He smirks at me with his sparkly eyes. "And yes, I was mad, but I guess I figured sooner or later I might not be. I also figured if we never made up, I'd just leave it all here forever."

I gently punch his arm.

"Thank you."

I pick up a portfolio and smell something funny.

I flip through a stack of paintings one by one and then I see it.

Water. All over the floor and seeping into everything.

I lift up one of the paintings and realize they are wet and have gotten moldy in the two weeks they've been here. Behind the canvases are black portfolios where I kept my drawings, and they're soaking wet. I start groaning, "Oh no."

"What's wrong?"

"Water. There's water everywhere." I pull out a portfolio, the one with the remaining drawings I'd been hoping to use for my application, and open it up. Half of every drawing is fine, and the other, less fortunate half is a lasagna noodle, colors running, staining the entire side of the paper.

"Oh, Dani," gasps Marco, looking over my shoulder at this. "What happened?"

"The universe is making it clear to me that I might not be meant to apply to RISD," I say with resignation.

"I'm so sorry, Dani. It was bone-dry when I put them here . . . Come on, there's got to be something that's not entirely ruined? Look at all this stuff."

I breathe in a deep, wide breath. "Marco, it was so generous of you to try to help me. Maybe I can save some of it." I sit on a radiator that's ice cold. "Do you think anyone will care if I leave this here for a little while? I need to figure out where I can take it," I ask.

"Oh yeah, Coach Kelly said barely anyone even comes back here. Now we know why." He looks around the room, taking in its grossness more clearly.

We walk out together. I try to take my mind off everything by asking Marco how his own applications are going.

"Well, I finished a third draft of my essays and sent the applications off well before the January 15 deadline. Now I just need to bug my coaches to finish their recommendations."

"You're remarkable, King Marco. Your mom would be proud."

He smiles and puts his arm through mine, "Thanks, m'lady."

Every now and then I think of Chloe. I remember how she looked at me as I walked out of the café, like I possessed magic. Like I could teach her something.

In art history, we each present an oral report on our chosen artist. Jonah chose Andy Warhol, and he manages to bring advertising and corporate America into it. Colin chose Robert Rauschenberg and talks about his own multifaceted interests. Maybe one day I'll find it in my heart to appreciate Colin. I mean, he sure does try hard. And Joanne, randomly, chose her own grandmother's needlepoint, which turns out to be awfully moving.

Once everyone goes, Ms. Davis glances at me. She knows what happened during break, so she's trying to be gentle on me.

"Danielle, want to share anything?"

I stand up and walk to the front before I think too much about it.

I take a piece of chalk and write Silence=Death on the blackboard.

Then I write David Wojnarowicz.

I turn and look at each of my classmates. I'd spent so much time this year being annoyed, I never really looked at them. Joanne's curly hair, Nigel's bright blue eyes. Even Colin—freaking Colin—has a kind smile.

"David Wojnarowicz is a poet, artist, and activist. His work is autobiographical. He was a gay kid who came from a messed-up family in New Jersey and ended up in New York City, homeless at seventeen. He worked as a prostitute and did a lot of drugs. And he also became a writer and an artist."

I pause and look around the room. No one is laughing. I continue.

"Wojnarowicz writes poems; plays music; makes drawings, collages, paintings, photographs; and shoots films. He speaks up about injustices in the world. He exhibits and performs in important art galleries." I take a deep breath. "He was diagnosed with AIDS in 1987 after his boyfriend died. He wants people to understand what AIDS is, and to see the person who has it. He isn't really making art to be famous. He just wants to form his voice and make it heard." I take a deep breath, and then keep talking.

"*Silence=Death* is the title of one of Wojnarowicz's most famous photographs. But he didn't make up the phrase. It came from an AIDS activist group called ACT UP. Wojnarowicz actually sewed his lips together with a needle and thread, and then took a photograph of himself." Someone in the back of the room says, "Yikes," but I keep going. "That photo shows the excruciating pain of remaining silent. That phrase, Silence Equals Death, refers to staying quiet about a deadly, awful disease. Not speaking of it only causes more harm, more death."

I pause, not yet finished. But grateful no one has interrupted me.

"My dad died two weeks ago. From AIDS. My dad was also gay . . . And that's partly why I picked Wojnarowicz. I also like that his artwork tries different things. He doesn't want to be silent. And neither do I."

I stop and look at Ms. Davis who has a look I've never seen on her face before. It's either sad or elated, or both on top of each other. Only she truly understands what it is I just did. I feel lucky to be witnessed by her. I go back to my desk and sit down.

For the rest of the period, I focus hard on not crying. These days it can require all of my energy to keep my face together. When class is finally over, I begin to pack up my bag, and Ms. Davis walks over and sits next to me.

"Nice work today, Danielle. Really brave and well-spoken."

"Thanks. I didn't finish the paper. I'll try to get it to you next week. Is that OK?"

"Sure, that's fine. Listen, Danielle, if you're free now, I want you to come with me to talk to Headmaster Turner. He has something he wants you to see."

"I'm not in trouble, am I?"

"No, Danielle. Not at all. Just wait." As we head upstairs to his office, I wonder if he got me a special cake. Is that a thing? Do people get a cake when their parent dies? Oh God, Danielle, a death cake? You're out of your mind. Just don't say that out loud, whatever happens. Morbid humor is usually best kept to oneself.

We walk into his office, and he motions us to sit down. "Danielle, how are you doing?" Looking around, I confirm that indeed there's no cake. Not even a biscotti. I think I missed breakfast. I realize he's waiting for me to reply.

"I'm doing all right, thanks," I say quickly, trying to stop thinking about food.

"I'm very sorry to hear about your father. This must be a very tough time for you." He says this with the warmth of a cold cup of coffee.

"Thank you," I reply, wondering if anyone told him it was AIDS.

"So, Ms. Davis gave me your letter." He picks up my letter sitting on his desk. "I understand you had your own art studio?"

"Yes . . . I did, in the gym building. But I don't anymore. In fact, no one really has a good place to make art, because the art room was relocated to a tiny dark space in another building. And then the gym renovation made me have to move out, and my paintings got . . ."

"Danielle," Ms. Davis interrupts me, "let's hear what Headmaster Turner has to say."

I sit back, close my mouth, and wait.

"Well, I know this has been a tough time for you, and I know art has certain, um, healing, qualities."

I have no idea where this is going, but I stay patient.

"There's a room upstairs I want to show you. I think it might solve your little problem here." He stands up and goes to his secretary's desk and asks for the keys to the fourth floor.

I look at Ms. Davis. She's smiling. Why is she smiling?

We all get up, walk down the hall, and start up the stairs. As we reach the second flight, it occurs to me that I've never been to the top floor of Old Main. It's dusty and forgotten. Someone decided a long time ago to give up on the top floor.

"So, there's not enough heat up here and it needs some repairs, as you can see. The floors are uneven, and the walls are cracking. But there's one space I think you'll like." Turner seems genuinely excited now. Where is he taking me?

At the end of the hall, we pass a big open room. Oh, wow! Giant arched windows and huge empty walls. This must be it. But he passes this room and continues to the end of the hallway where he unlocks a door.

It's actually a closet about one-quarter the size of my dorm room. The walls are empty, yes, but it's tiny and has only fluorescent lights. There's one small window and it's covered with dust. This is it? This is what he's all excited to show me? This is my dead-parent cake? A scuzzy, dark closet?

"Pretty great, huh?" he says, waiting for me to jump for joy. "Danielle, we know you only have a few months left at Baxter, but we wanted you to have a space to make your art. You shouldn't have to lose that."

"Can I ask a question?" I say, backing up into the hallway.

"Of course," he says, brushing the shoulders of his blazer.

"What is that room used for?" I point back to the bright open space we passed. "With the windows and the light?"

"Oh, that. Um, well, once upon a time it was where students learned dance," he says laughing, to think such a thing was taught in school. "But there are no doors, and well, it's rather enormous, isn't it?"

We walk back to the big room. It's open, with big windows and enough space for easels or a little exhibition. It's perfect.

"Can we have this room instead?"

"We? I thought you wanted a studio for yourself?" Headmaster Turner says.

"Well, I did. But this is, well, it's a magnificent room. This could be a place for my whole art class to work during free periods or on the weekends." I wander around the room, imagining it full of people drawing, looking, making. "We could set up a model platform here, or have a still life on a table over by the window—this light is so good. Our art class had to move into a dark little room recently, so it's kind of hard to think big there. But this is perfect. It's already dirty. And it's big and open and bright. Our art class needs a space to be together. Much more than I need a space to be alone."

Headmaster Turner looks at Ms. Davis.

"There's no door," says Ms. Davis.

"Don't need one. Anyone can come in. We can bring our supplies and take them with us when we're done. And no one is up here anyway, right?"

"These walls . . ." he says, looking at the cracking plaster and splintered molding.

"We'll fix it or learn to love it. Listen, you raised a lot of money for the gym, right? Don't you think it's time to give something for the arts too? It doesn't even need to cost anything. We can create here; we can learn here. We'll be productive."

Finally, he walks through the room, one lap around, thinking.

"I can probably talk the Facilities department into it." He smiles a little.

As we walk back downstairs behind Headmaster Turner, I silently turn to Ms. Davis with my mouth wide open. Ms. Davis winks at me and whispers, "Well done, Squeaky."

36
"I'll Take You There"

"This Terrible True Thing"
Application Essay, Danielle Silver
January 1992

Crises show us how we face the unknown. Epidemics show us who and what matters. Illnesses show us how we love one another. Losses show us the value of what we had—and what, if anything, we wish to keep.

My story is one among all the stories of the millions who have died in the AIDS crisis.

AIDS develops when someone gets human immunodeficiency virus, HIV, which attacks their immune system. So, the virus itself does not kill the body. It just removes your protection so other things can kill you more easily.

Today we see a lot of fear about AIDS. And

as kids, we don't hear much useful information like how to avoid it, how to get tested, how to talk about it, or how it spreads. It just feels like a terrifying monster we need to run from, but how can we know which way to run if we don't even understand the disease itself? Newspapers sometimes write about it, but few people want to talk about it.

My father died from AIDS, and I have a lot to say now. I have a lot to share now, and I don't want to keep quiet about it. I think people ought to know how it works and how to help those who are sick.

The real threats, I believe, are ignorance and isolation.

Ignorance keeps us from seeing what is right in front of us. It lets us push what should matter into the background, to make it go away. To hide it because it's scary. But to many people, AIDS is their everyday reality. Thousands and someday millions will have lost their best friends, their partners, their children, their cousins, aunts, uncles, or parents.

Isolation starves us. We sink in loneliness. We forget that we are the subject. We forget that we are our own beautiful thing and that we need light and color and air to thrive. But most importantly, we need to feel seen. All of us do. We need relationships to comfort and excite us and to keep us moving forward.

In the world of AIDS activism, there is a slogan used often: "Silence Equals Death." I share my story to make some noise, to bring life into the world, and to help other people. My father died from AIDS. He didn't have to, and so I am angry. I choose to speak out and speak up and tell this true story.

Art gives some of us a way to shout, to scream, to wake other people up. It also allows us to get closer to ourselves and others, maybe closer than we want. But I believe art gives us new ways to understand ourselves and others. It tells our stories.

I am not scared of AIDS anymore.

I am scared of ignorance and isolation.

I am scared that people will one day forget this ever happened. Because if we forget, then ignorance will destroy us eventually. This will happen again in another form. It will seem like a new problem, but it will be the same. People fearing difference, and people using power over others in some terrible effort to make them disappear. People dying as a result. Over and over.

We have to scream. And keep screaming.

We have to remember. And keep remembering.

We have to fight. And keep fighting.

Using whatever we can.

I want to learn to express ideas more fully, absorb history more deeply.

I want to find new ways of communicating, new ways to scream or whisper.

I want to find my tools and find my voice.

So here it is.

My story. This year. The reflections of what happened.

From September to January, I made these
pages. This story—from this angle.

A portrait of a time frame when unthinkable
things became real.

These pages.

Filled with secrets and possibilities.

This terrible true thing.

I spend the morning in the library, holding the copy machine
hostage. Ms. Franklin clearly thinks I'm out of my mind, but I
don't care.

For the next three hours, I drain the wheezing machine of its
dusty toner, and when I'm done, I'm left with small stacks of paper
that have the potential to determine my future: four copies of my
essay, four sets of slides of my paintings (sophomore year's self-
portrait in oil, junior year's landscapes and still life, senior year's ab-
stracts), four sets of completed application forms, four different
checks for application fees. And four copies of my sketchbook, every
single page, from the beach to this moment, from September to
January.

I slip each into a different color envelope, ready to be postmarked
by the January 15 deadline.

The blue one to Wisconsin.

The purple one to NYU.

The orange one to Wesleyan.

The yellow one to RISD.

All the possibilities.

"Oh my God, Danielle, what's in here, rocks?" Amy asks me, grunting
as she heaves a box up the stairs.

I've managed to enlist her and Marco to help me move supplies into
the new art studio. As we reach the top, I can smell it, but I stay quiet.

"Come see the space." We leave the boxes and walk down the hall. The room feels larger than I remember.

"This is awesome," Amy says, and then she sees the source of the good smell.

"Oh my God. Pizza!" she screams.

"You didn't?!!" Marco hoots.

"Fancy Magic for you both," I say. This is what Baxter students call the rare moments when Domino's Pizza comes to campus. Birthdays, parties, the end of finals, or just a boring Tuesday when someone finds twenty dollars in their coat pocket. It's really fancy, and I arranged for it to be delivered with three bottles of Sprite all the way upstairs.

Once they're both sitting down and eating, I stand in front of them, holding my soda like I'm making a toast.

"OK, listen. I've been a serious head case these last few months." Marco and Amy are chewing quietly, with concern and sweetness. "And I know that I've made some mistakes and said things because I was so wrapped up on my own stuff."

Marco has a mouth full of pizza but nods in agreement.

"But what is astounding to me is how you've both been here for me: you helped me study, made lists, pack my stuff, and showed up when I needed you most. I thought I could just sort of float through senior year, holed up in my little basement cave with my art to keep me company." I take a deep breath. "But you're my company. You're my people. Art is something to do, sure, and I hope I get to make it for the rest of my life, but you two have kept me going. Art lets me ooze all the hard stuff out. But you hold it for me . . . You help me feel part of the world. So, thank you."

By this point, we're all crying. It's kind of beautiful. I give them both a big hug, smashing their faces together.

The beach wind blows into my ear. Tiny grains of sand
whip my face,
telling me I got here too early.
But you always wanted to be early.
This day is not warm enough yet. The seagulls don't stop
circling.
The sun cannot get through the hazy clouds.
The air is not ready for summer, for this next part.
But I am.
Ready to let you be.
To move through the world.
Floating through chaos and silence.
I untie the bag inside the box.
The chalky white dust of your ashes. Heavy and waiting to go.
I tell you I love you in all the ways I know how.
Poems, songs, and silence.
Until I know,
at last, you can hear me.
And I let you go.

ACKNOWLEDGMENTS

I owe foremost thanks to my friend, literary agent, and master of existential despair, Kevin O'Connor, who tossed me headfirst into the realm of intrigue by suggesting I write this book. Thanks for your persistent belief in me and what I could accomplish. All the olives for you, friend.

Thanks to the entire Blackstone team, including my editor Daniel Ehrenhaft, who championed this book from day one. Thank you Kathryn Zentgraf for your close reading and Sarah Riedlinger for persisting with me to arrive at a truly perfect cover design and interior layout.

Heartfelt thanks to all those who read drafts, shared wisdom, and offered support over the years: Rachel Abrams, Diane Bartoli, Alexis Danzig, Justin Evans, Ramzi Fawaz, Julie Grahame, Terry Guerin, Caroline Guindon, Suli Holum, Katie King, Kelsey Klosterman, Gigi Lamm, Rebecca Layton, Mike Milley, Leni Isabel Schenkel, Joanne Sciulli, Eve Simon, and Dito van Reigersberg. You're all fancy magic to me.

Extra special thanks to Joel Dankoff for the endless conversations about every little thing that confounded me along the way. Your tireless readings, close edits, and deep questions made this book better. You make everything better. Especially me.

To Amy Sananman, thank you for always rooting for me, supporting my choices and being the best friend I could ask for, and letting me name Amy after you.

Danielle Silber, thank you for always finding depth, meaning, and joy in every single moment of life, for having more gay parents than anyone, and letting me honor your rainbow sparkle by using your name.

Alysia Abbott, thank you for sharing your own beautiful story, helping those of us who lost a parent to AIDS feel less alone. To all the COLAGEr's and Recollectors, thank you for showing yourselves to one another and welcoming me into a place I finally felt belonging.

Thanks to John Andreis and Christopher Bartlett at the William Way LGBT Community Center for allowing me access to numerous boxes of AIDS education pamphlets.

To my mother, Caroline Simon, who continues to show boundless optimism for life and endless love for me and my child, and to my big brother, Tony Laden, who holds enormous insights and can crack me up with the right look.

To Isadora Laden, thank you for allowing your mama the time and space needed to make this book. Thank you for making me a mother and teaching me how big my heart can grow. You make my heart shine so bright.

To my father, Richard B. Laden, born October 3, 1940, died February 15, 1996. I will always be grateful that you saw my notions of an artist's life not with trepidation but with endless wonder and whole-hearted encouragement. You are in the air I breathe each day, in my daughter's eyes, and in the deep Atlantic Ocean. I'm forever grateful I got you.

Finally, my infinite thanks to all the people who fought and fight to provide affordable and accessible medical care, sensible public health policy, and dignity and humanity around stigmatized disease. And to all who lost their loves, thank you for holding their hand and looking into their eyes. The fabric of our society is made stronger by what you've done.